# The Pledge of Allegiance

I pledge allegiance to the Flag

of the United States of America,

and to the Republic

for which it stands,

one Nation under God, indivisible,

with liberty and justice for all.

# HARCOURT HORIZONS

# South Carolina

## Harcourt
SCHOOL PUBLISHERS

Orlando   Austin   New York   San Diego   Toronto   London

Visit *The Learning Site!*
www.harcourtschool.com

# HARCOURT HORIZONS
## SOUTH CAROLINA

### General Editor

**Dr. Michael J. Berson**
Associate Professor
Social Science Education
University of South Florida
Tampa, Florida

### Contributing Authors

**Dr. Sherry Field**
Associate Professor
The University of Texas at Austin
Austin, Texas

**Dr. Tyrone Howard**
Assistant Professor
UCLA Graduate School of
   Education & Information
   Studies
University of California at
   Los Angeles
Los Angeles, California

**Dr. Bruce E. Larson**
Associate Professor of Teacher
   Education and Social Studies
Western Washington University
Bellingham, Washington

### Series Consultants

**Dr. Robert Bednarz**
Professor
Department of Geography
Texas A&M University
College Station, Texas

**Dr. Asa Grant Hilliard III**
Fuller E. Callaway Professor
   of Urban Education
Georgia State University
Atlanta, Georgia

**Dr. Thomas M. McGowan**
Chairperson and Professor
Center for Curriculum and
   Instruction
University of Nebraska
Lincoln, Nebraska

**Dr. John J. Patrick**
Professor of Education
Indiana University
Bloomington, Indiana

**Dr. Philip VanFossen**
Associate Professor,
   Social Studies Education,
   and Associate Director,
   Purdue Center for
   Economic Education
Purdue University
West Lafayette, Indiana

**Dr. Hallie Kay Yopp**
Professor
Department of Elementary,
   Bilingual, and Reading
   Education
California State University,
   Fullerton
Fullerton, California

### Content Reviewers

**Monti Caughman**
Resident Teacher Consultant
South Carolina Geographic Alliance
Columbia, South Carolina

**Dr. Marcus Cox**
Department of History
The Citadel
Charleston, South Carolina

**Dr. Robert P. Green, Jr.**
Professor
School of Education
Clemson University
Clemson, South Carolina

**Dr. Wanda A. Hendricks**
Department of History and
   Women's Studies Program
University of South Carolina
Columbia, South Carolina

**Dr. William C. Hine**
Department of History
South Carolina State University
Orangeburg, South Carolina

**Kevin Lynch**
Director of Education and Interpretation
Historic Brattonsville
McConnells, South Carolina

**Dr. Eldred E. Prince, Jr.**
Professor and Chair
Department of History
Coastal Carolina University
Conway, South Carolina

**Sherman E. Pyatt**
Archivist
College of Charleston
Charleston, South Carolina

**Dr. Jason H. Silverman**
Department of History
Winthrop University
Rock Hill, South Carolina

### Classroom Reviewers

**Maryanne Baggett**
Teacher
Briggs Elementary School
Florence, South Carolina

**Dr. Debra P. Cox**
Curriculum Coordinator
Northside Elementary School
Seneca, South Carolina

**Dawn LaRosa**
Teacher
Ballentine Elementary School
Irmo, South Carolina

**Marian McFadden**
Teacher ESE
Greenwood Elementary School
Florence, South Carolina

**Sarah Lauren Simmons**
Teacher
Fairforest Elementary School
Fairforest, South Carolina

**Angela Slagle**
Teacher
North Myrtle Beach Elementary School
Little River, South Carolina

**Carol Swan**
Teacher
Hanahan Elementary School
Hanahan, South Carolina

**Maps**
researched and prepared by

**Readers**
written and designed by

Copyright © 2005 by Harcourt, Inc.

All rights reserved. No part of this publication may be reproduced or transmitted in any form or by any means, electronic or mechanical, including photocopy, recording, or any information storage and retrieval system, without permission in writing from the publisher.

Requests for permission to make copies of any part of the work should be mailed to:

School Permissions and Copyrights
Harcourt, Inc.
6277 Sea Harbor Drive
Orlando, Florida 32887-6777
Fax: 407-345-2418

HARCOURT and the Harcourt Logo are trademarks of Harcourt, Inc., registered in the United States of America and/or other jurisdictions. TIME FOR KIDS and the red border are registered trademarks of Time Inc. Used under license. Copyright © by Time Inc. All rights reserved.

Acknowledgments appear in the back of this book.

Printed in the United States of America

ISBN 0-15-339722-5

1 2 3 4 5 6 7 8 9 10   032   14 13 12 11 10 09 08 07 06 05

# Contents

- xii    Reading Your Textbook
- A1    **Atlas**
- A16    Geography Terms

## UNIT 1    All About Places and People

- 1    **Unit 1 Introduction**
- 2    **Unit 1 Preview**
- 4    **Start with a Song**
  **South Carolina on My Mind**
  by Hank Martin and Buzz Arledge
  illustrated by Billie Harmon

### 7    Chapter 1   A Place Called South Carolina

 **Main Idea and Details**

- 8    Lesson 1   Learning About Our State
- 16    **Map and Globe Skills**   Read a Map
- 18    Lesson 2   Where Is South Carolina?
- 24    **Chart and Graph Skills**   Read Graphs
- 26    Lesson 3   South Carolina's Land and Water
- 32    **Map and Globe Skills**   Read a Landform Map
- 34    **Chapter 1 Review and Test Preparation**

### 37    Chapter 2   People and Government

 **Categorize**

- 38    Lesson 1   One State, Many People
- 42    **Examine Primary Sources**   A Heritage Museum

iv

| | |
|---|---|
| 44 | **Lesson 2** Local Governments |
| 48 | **Citizenship Skills**<br>Solve a Problem |
| 50 | **Lesson 3** State Government |
| 56 | **Chart and Graph Skills**<br>Read a Table |
| 58 | **Chapter 2 Review and Test Preparation** |
| 60 | **Visit**<br>The South Carolina State House |
| 62 | **Unit 1 Review and Test Preparation** |
| 64 | **Unit Activities** |

# · UNIT · 2  South Carolina Long Ago

| | |
|---|---|
| 65 | **Unit 2 Introduction** |
| 66 | **Unit 2 Preview** |
| 68 | **Start with a Story**<br>**The Great Ball Game: A Muskogee Story**<br>by Joseph Bruchac<br>illustrated by Susan L. Roth |

## 73  Chapter 3 Early Peoples

**Focus Skill** Compare and Contrast

| | |
|---|---|
| 74 | **Lesson 1** People of the River |
| 80 | **Map and Globe Skills**<br>Find Intermediate Directions |
| 82 | **Lesson 2** People of the Mountains |
| 88 | **Map and Globe Skills**<br>Use a Cultural Map |
| 90 | **Lesson 3** People of the Lowcountry |
| 94 | **Map and Globe Skills**<br>Use a Distance Scale |
| 96 | **Examine Primary Sources**<br>First Carolinians |
| 98 | **Chapter 3 Review and Test Preparation** |

v

**101 Chapter 4 Newcomers Arrive**
 **Generalize**

102 Lesson 1 Cultures Meet
108 **Map and Globe Skills**
Follow Routes on a History Map
110 Lesson 2 The French and the Spanish
116 **Chart and Graph Skills**
Read a Time Line
118 Lesson 3 An English Colony
124 **Citizenship Skills**
Resolve Conflict
126 Lesson 4 Early Plantations
132 Lesson 5 Settlers and Settlements
138 **Chapter 4 Review and Test Preparation**
140 **Visit**
Historic Brattonsville

142 **Unit 2 Review and Test Preparation**
144 **Unit Activities**

· UNIT ·
3

# An Independent Spirit

145 Unit 3 Introduction
146 Unit 3 Preview
148 Start with a Legend
**The Swamp Fox**
by Pleasant DeSpain
illustrated by Rick Farrell

**155 Chapter 5 From Colony to State**
 **Sequence**

156 Lesson 1 The Colonies Grow
160 **Reading Skills**
Identify Cause and Effect
162 Lesson 2 Colonies Unite
168 Lesson 3 The American Revolution
174 **Map and Globe Skills**
Compare History Maps
176 Lesson 4 South Carolina Statehood

182 **Map and Globe Skills**
Use a Map Grid

184 **Chapter 5 Review and Test Preparation**

## 187 Chapter 6 Civil War and Reconstruction

**Cause and Effect**

188 Lesson 1 Southern Life
196 **Reading Skills**
Determine Point of View in Pictures
198 Lesson 2 Differences Divide the Nation
202 **Chart and Graph Skills**
Compare Bar Graphs
204 Lesson 3 The Civil War
210 Lesson 4 After the Civil War
215 **Citizenship Skills**
Make a Thoughtful Decision
216 **Examine Primary Sources**
Charleston's Children
218 **Chapter 6 Review and Test Preparation**
220 **Visit**
The Old Exchange and Provost Dungeon

222 **Unit 3 Review and Test Preparation**
224 **Unit Activities**

## UNIT 4

# Into Modern Times

225 Unit 4 Introduction
226 Unit 4 Preview
228 Start with a Story
**Circle Unbroken**
by Margot Theis Raven
illustrated by E. B. Lewis

## 235 Chapter 7 A Changing World

**Draw Conclusions**

236 Lesson 1 Old Ways and New
242 Lesson 2 A New Century Brings Change

| | | |
|---|---|---|
| 248 | | **Chart and Graph Skills**<br>Use a Line Graph |
| 250 | | Lesson 3 South Carolina and the World |
| 256 | | Lesson 4 Changing Times |
| 262 | | **Reading Skills**<br>Tell Fact from Opinion |
| 264 | | Lesson 5 South Carolina in World War II |
| 268 | | **Map and Globe Skills**<br>Read a Product Map |
| 270 | | Lesson 6 The Struggle for Equal Rights |
| 278 | | Chapter 7 Review and Test Preparation |

## 281 Chapter 8 Today and Tomorrow

**Focus Skill** Summarize

| | |
|---|---|
| 282 | Lesson 1 A Modern Economy |
| 286 | **Citizenship Skills** Make an Economic Choice |
| 288 | Lesson 2 South Carolina Today |
| 294 | **Map and Globe Skills** Use Latitude and Longitude |
| 296 | Examine Primary Sources Communication Artifacts |
| 298 | Chapter 8 Review and Test Preparation |
| 300 | Visit Congaree National Park |

## 302 Unit 4 Review and Test Preparation
304 Unit Activities

# Reference

- **R2 Almanac**
  - R2 Facts About South Carolina's Counties
  - R4 Facts About South Carolina's Governors
- **R7 Biographical Dictionary**
- **R10 Gazetteer**
- **R15 Glossary**
- **R20 Index**

# Features You Can Use

## Skills

### CHART AND GRAPH SKILLS
- 24 Read Graphs
- 56 Read a Table
- 116 Read a Time Line
- 202 Compare Bar Graphs
- 248 Use a Line Graph

### CITIZENSHIP SKILLS
- 48 Solve a Problem
- 124 Resolve Conflict
- 215 Make a Thoughtful Decision
- 286 Make an Economic Choice

### MAP AND GLOBE SKILLS
- 16 Read a Map
- 32 Read a Landform Map
- 80 Find Intermediate Directions
- 88 Use a Cultural Map
- 94 Use a Distance Scale
- 108 Follow Routes on a History Map
- 174 Compare History Maps
- 182 Use a Map Grid
- 268 Read a Product Map
- 294 Use Latitude and Longitude

### READING SKILLS
- 7 Main Idea and Details
- 37 Categorize
- 73 Compare and Contrast
- 101 Generalize
- 155 Sequence
- 160 Identify Cause and Effect
- 187 Cause and Effect
- 196 Determine Point of View in Pictures
- 235 Draw Conclusions
- 262 Tell Fact from Opinion
- 281 Summarize

## Citizenship

### DEMOCRATIC VALUES
- 78 Government

### POINTS OF VIEW
- 165 Loyalist vs. Patriot

## Music and Literature

- 4 "South Carolina on My Mind" by Hank Martin and Buzz Arledge illustrated by Billie Harmon
- 68 The Great Ball Game: A Muskogee Story by Joseph Bruchac illustrated by Susan L. Roth
- 148 The Swamp Fox by Pleasant DeSpain illustrated by Rick Farrell
- 228 Circle Unbroken by Margot Theis Raven illustrated by E. B. Lewis

## Primary Sources

### EXAMINE PRIMARY SOURCES
- 42 A Heritage Museum
- 96 First Carolinians
- 216 Charleston's Children
- 296 Communication Artifacts

### ANALYZE PRIMARY SOURCES
- 112 Getting Food Supplies
- 181 The Cotton Gin
- 195 A Dave Jar

## Biography
- 106 Hernando de Soto
- 113 Juan Pardo
- 120 Anthony Ashley Cooper
- 131 Eliza Lucas Pinckney
- 166 Andrew Pickens
- 171 General Thomas Sumter
- 193 Denmark Vesey
- 199 John C. Calhoun
- 239 Robert Smalls
- 251 Woodrow Wilson
- 255 Mary McLeod Bethune
- 258 Susan Pringle Frost
- 273 Reverend Joseph Armstrong DeLaine
- 275 James Strom Thurmond

## Geography
- 30 Table Rock Mountain
- 111 Port Royal Sound
- 205 Charleston Harbor
- 289 Myrtle Beach

## Heritage
- 40 Gullah Festival
- 91 Native American Place-Names
- 252 Fort Jackson

## Science and Technology
- 19 Mapping from Space
- 92 Weirs
- 208 CSS *Hunley*
- 246 Anderson Automobiles

## Charts, Graphs, and Diagrams
- 3 State Symbols
- 25 Picture Graph of South Carolina's Biggest Cities
- 25 Bar Graph of South Carolina's Biggest Cities
- 28 Landforms and Bodies of Water
- 51 The Branches of South Carolina Government
- 56 Model Table
- 57 Offices in the South Carolina State Government
- 67 Native Americans of South Carolina
- 67 Native American Language Groups in South Carolina
- 75 Two Language Groups
- 77 Making Pottery
- 80 Compass Rose
- 85 A Cherokee Village
- 86 Cherokee Chiefs
- 103 Early European Ships
- 107 Explorers in South Carolina
- 119 English Products Made from Colonial Materials
- 121 Lords Proprietors
- 129 A Plantation
- 137 Free and Enslaved People in Carolina in 1708
- 147 Population of South Carolina in 1760–1880
- 147 The Thirteen Colonies
- 158 Conestoga Wagon
- 160 Cause and Effect
- 161 Growth of South Carolina
- 182 Grid Pattern
- 203 Cotton Production in 1800–1860
- 203 Slavery in 1800–1860
- 215 Choices and Consequences
- 227 South Carolina Population in 1900–2000
- 227 Age Groups in South Carolina

243 Steam Locomotive
248 How to Read a Line Graph
249 Cotton Production in 1910–1922
276 African American Voter Registration in the United States
283 Employment in South Carolina

## Maps

A2 World: Political
A4 World: Physical
A6 Western Hemisphere: Political
A7 Western Hemisphere: Physical
A8 United States: Overview
A10 United States: Political
A12 United States: Physical
A14 South Carolina: Political
A15 South Carolina: Physical
2 South Carolina
17 Charleston, South Carolina
20 Dividing the World into Northern and Southern Hemispheres
21 Dividing the World into Eastern and Western Hemispheres
22 South Carolina in North America
27 Physical Regions of South Carolina
30 Table Rock State Park
33 Landform Map of the United States
63 Landform Map of the South
66 Carolina in 1670
76 Catawba of South Carolina
81 South Carolina and Intermediate Directions
83 Cherokee of South Carolina
87 Native American Trading Paths
89 Native American Cultural Regions
91 Native American Places
93 Cusabo of South Carolina
95 South Carolina
109 Early European Explorers in South Carolina
111 Port Royal Sound
114 The Columbian Exchange
123 Charles Town in 1680
135 Early Map of English Colonies in North America
136 South Carolina Townships in 1735
143 Colonies in the South
146 South Carolina in 1790
157 South Carolina Settlements and Roads in 1770
170 The American Revolution in South Carolina
175 The Thirteen Colonies in 1775
175 United States in 1800
183 Downtown Columbia, South Carolina
205 Historic Charleston
223 Eastern South Carolina
226 South Carolina
243 Railroads and Factory Towns
257 Women's Suffrage Map
269 South Carolina Products
289 Myrtle Beach
290 Museums and More
294 Latitude and Longitude
295 South Carolina Latitude and Longitude
303 Latitude and Longitude of the Southeast

## Time Lines

116 Time Line of South Carolina Exploration
138 Chapter 4 Summary Time Line
146 Unit 3 Preview Time Line
184 Chapter 5 Summary Time Line
218 Chapter 6 Summary Time Line
226 Unit 4 Preview Time Line
278 Chapter 7 Summary Time Line

# Reading Your Textbook

## Getting Started

Your book has four units.

Look at the first pages of a unit to learn what the unit will be about.

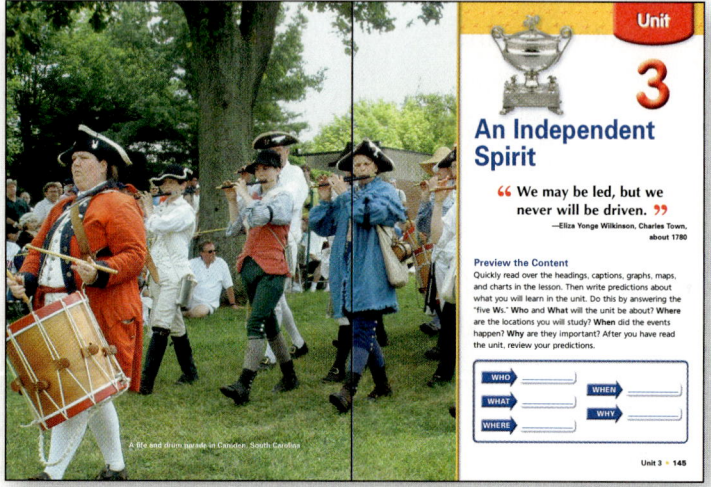

You will see some of the most important facts and events in the Unit Preview.

You can read a story or song about the main topic of the unit.

# The Parts of a Lesson

**Read the Big Idea section to know what to look for as you read the lesson.**

**Learn the new vocabulary.**

**Read the introduction and each short section of the lesson.**

**Answer the 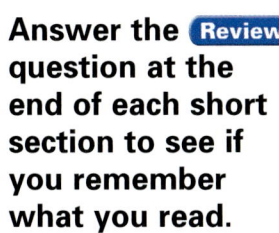 question at the end of each short section to see if you remember what you read.**

**At the end of the lesson, answer the questions and do the activity.**

xiii

# Skills

You will practice all these kinds of skills as you read this book.

**Map and Globe Skills**

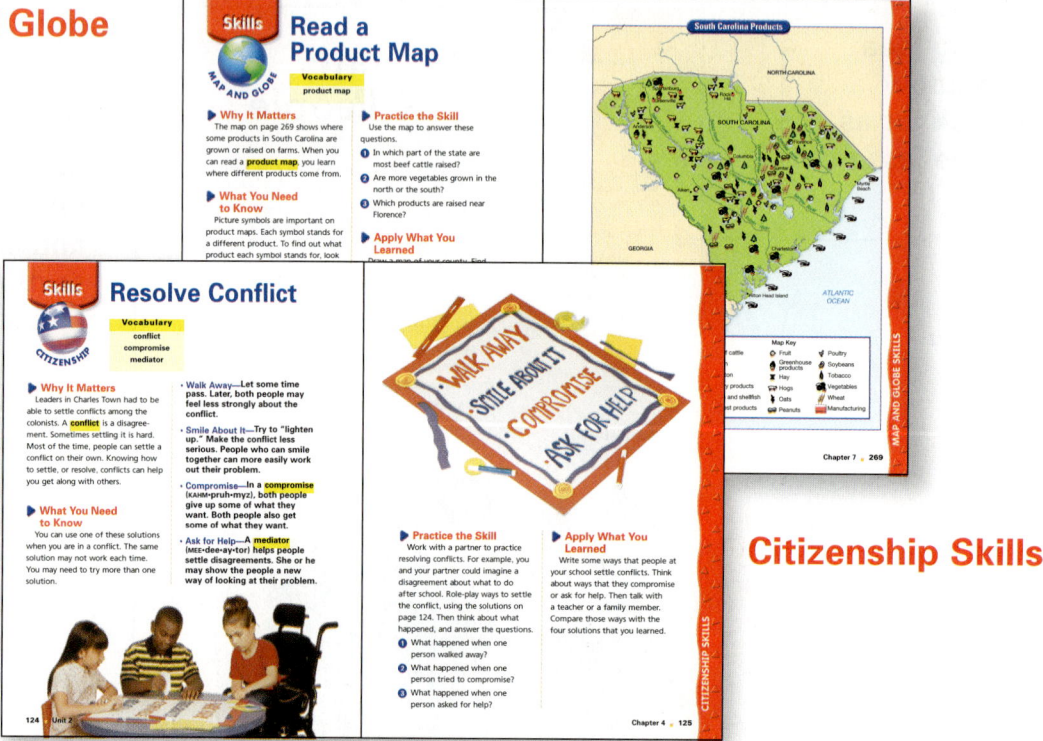

**Citizenship Skills**

**Chart and Graph Skills**

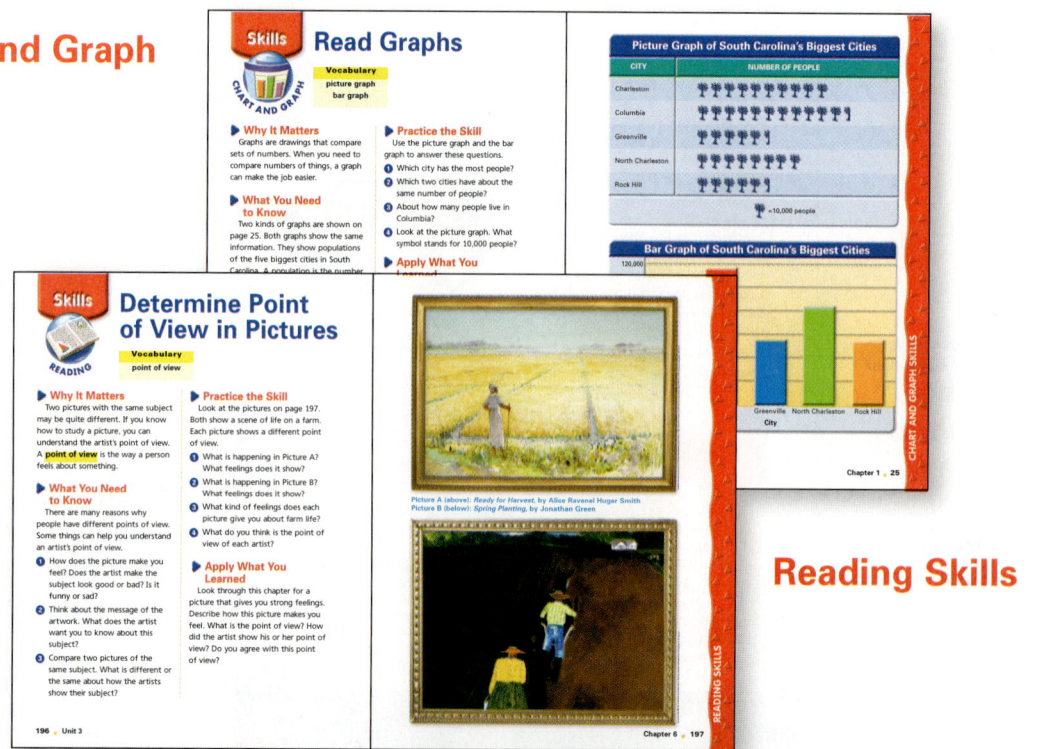

**Reading Skills**

# Special Features

## Examine Primary Sources

Learn about documents and objects from the past that are important to the present.

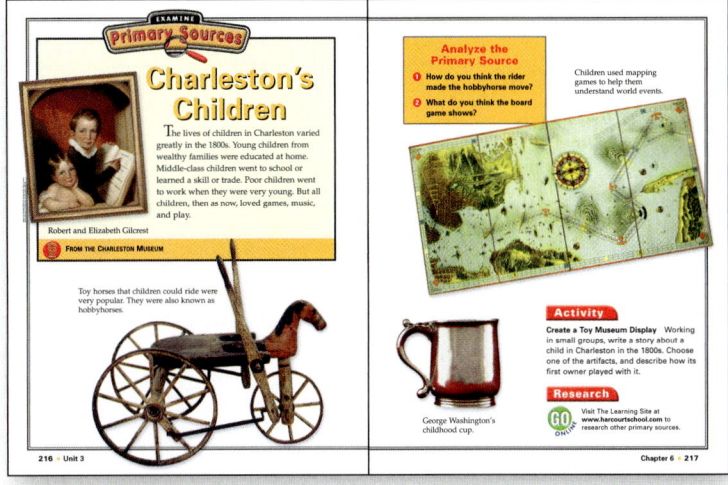

## Visit . . .

See and read about places in South Carolina.

## Atlas

Study maps and learn about kinds of land and bodies of water.

# For Your Reference

## Almanac
Learn facts about South Carolina.

## Biographical Dictionary
Read about the people in your book.

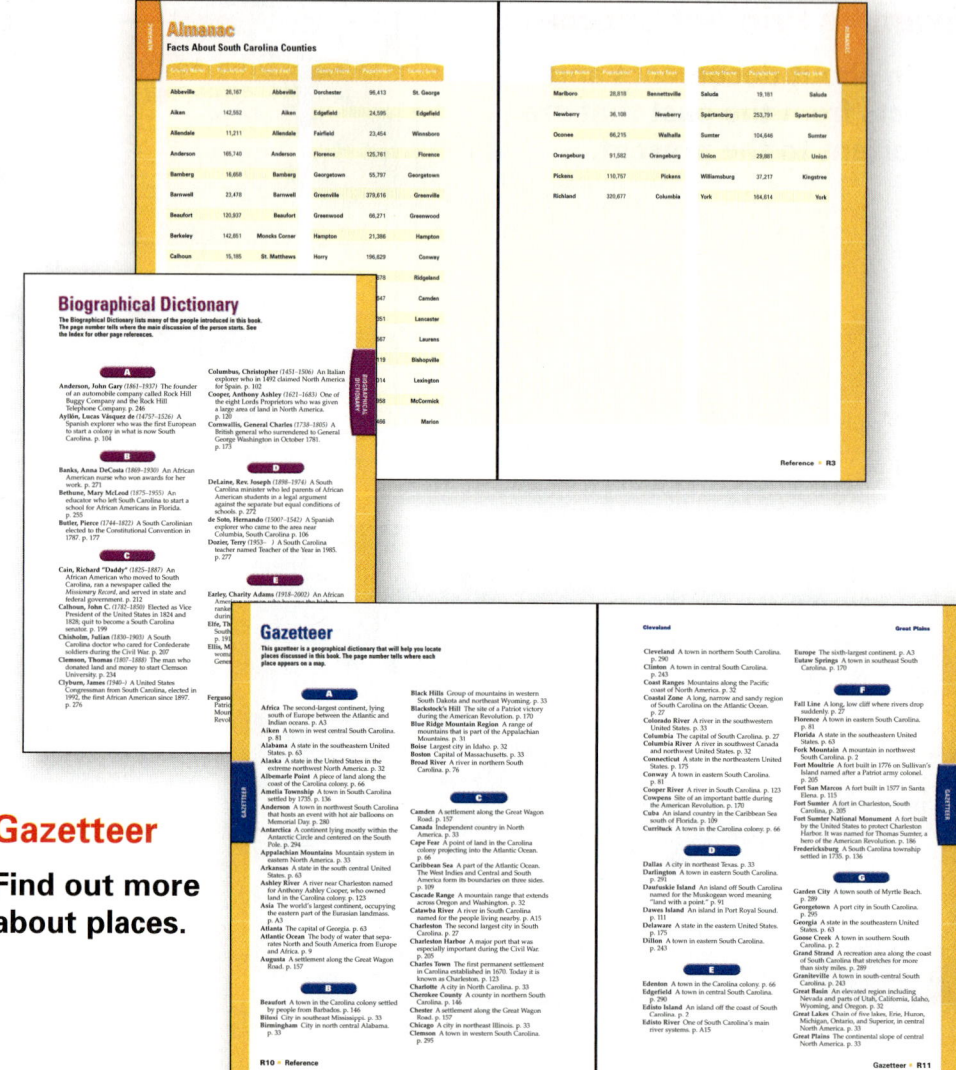

## Gazetteer
Find out more about places.

## Glossary
Look up definitions, or meanings, of vocabulary words.

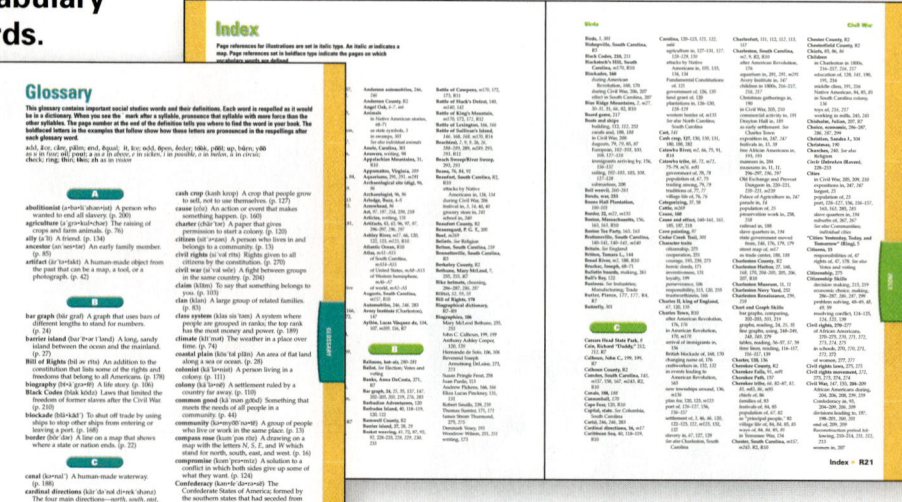

## Index
Look up topics you want to read about. The page numbers with the topic names tell you where to find the information in your book.

# Atlas

## 🌎 The World
**A2** WORLD: POLITICAL
**A4** WORLD: PHYSICAL
**A6** WESTERN HEMISPHERE: POLITICAL
**A7** WESTERN HEMISPHERE: PHYSICAL

## United States
**A8** OVERVIEW
**A10** POLITICAL
**A12** PHYSICAL

## South Carolina
**A14** POLITICAL
**A15** PHYSICAL

## Geography Terms
**A16**

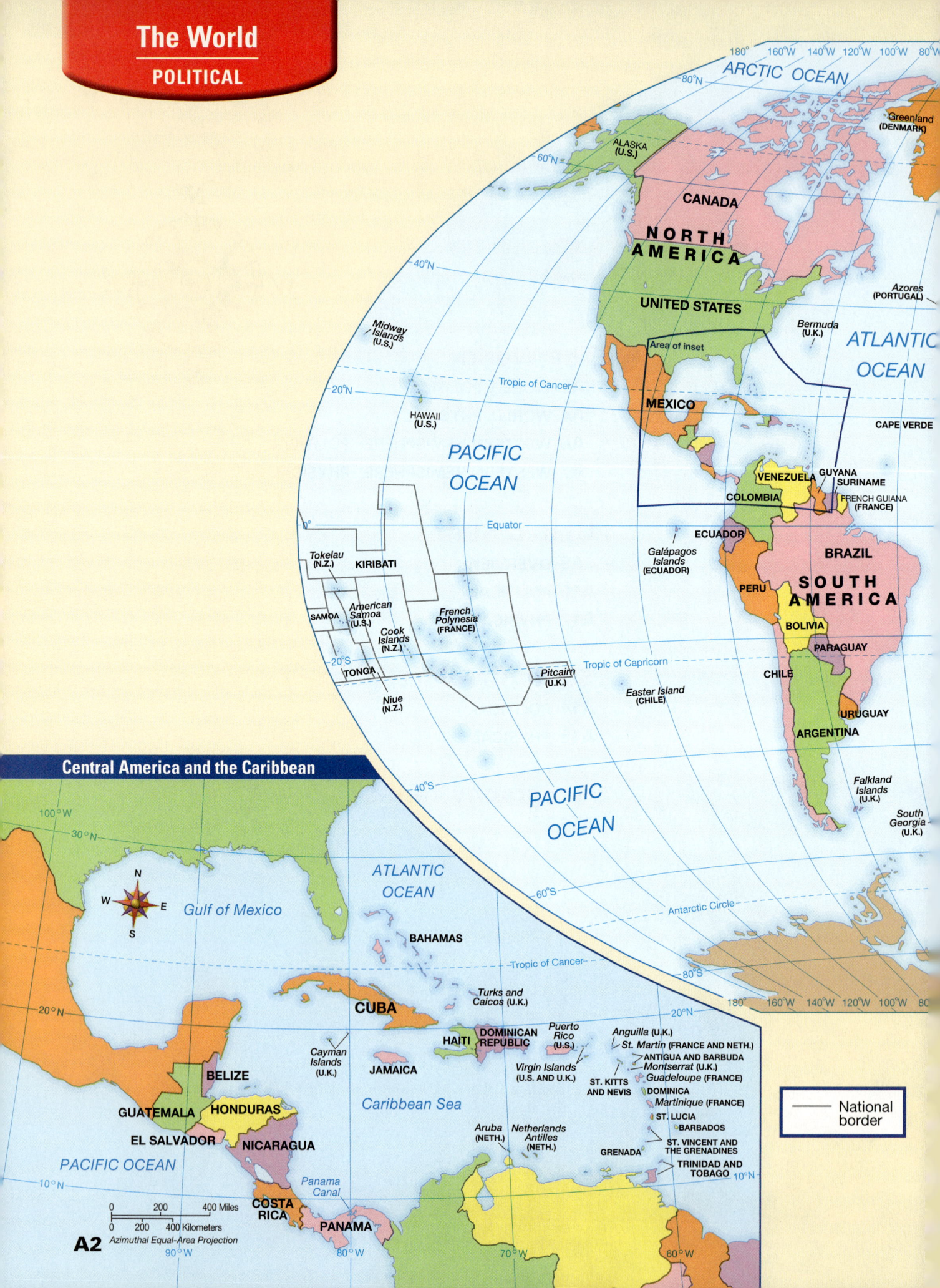

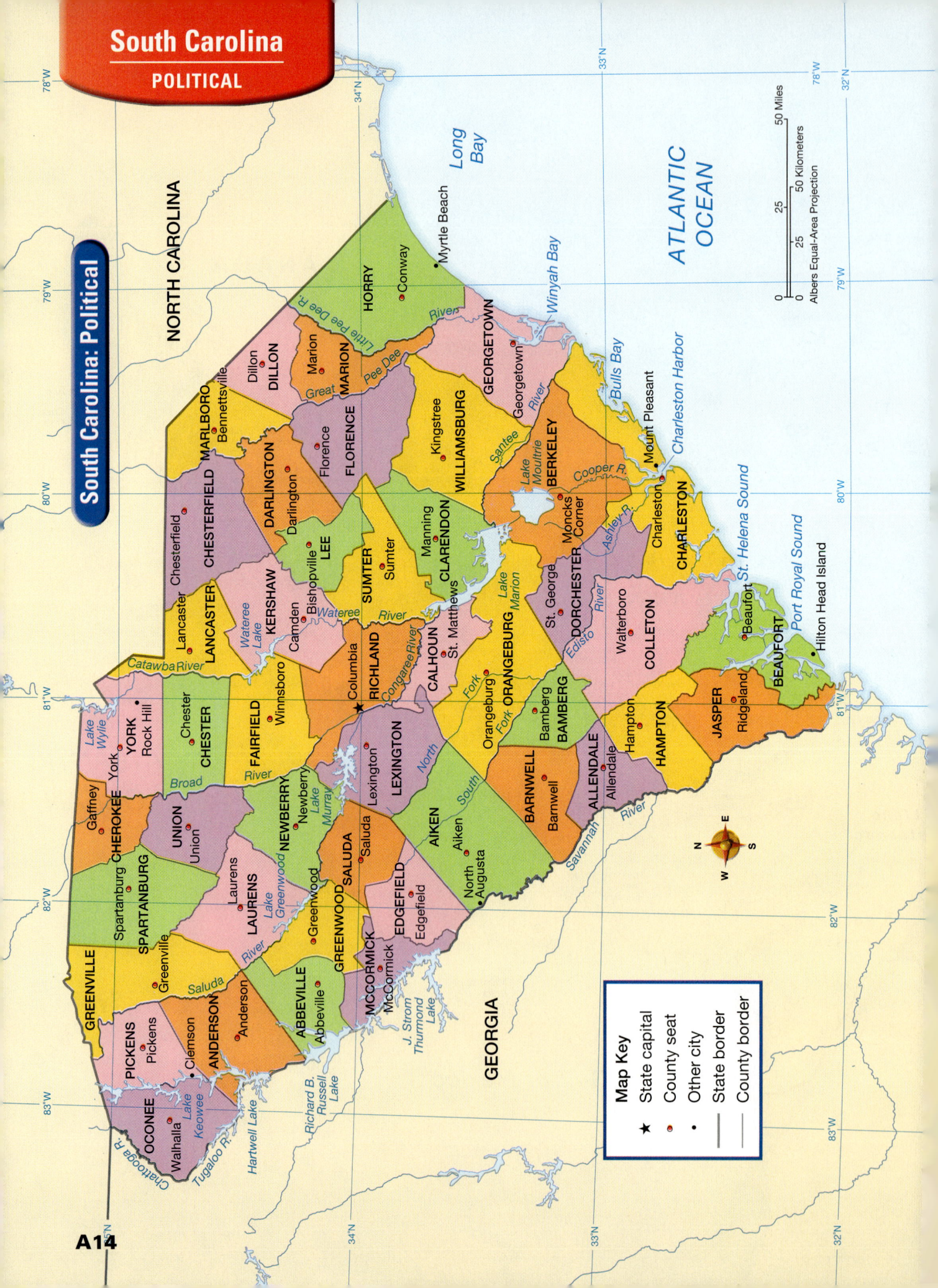

# Geography Terms

1. **bay** an inlet of the sea or some other body of water, usually smaller than a gulf
2. **canyon** deep, narrow valley with steep sides
3. **channel** deepest part of a body of water
4. **coast** land along a sea or ocean
5. **coastal plain** area of flat land along a sea or ocean
6. **desert** dry land with few plants
7. **gulf** part of a sea or ocean extending into the land, usually larger than a bay
8. **hill** land that rises above the land around it
9. **island** land that has water on all sides
10. **lake** body of water with land on all sides
11. **mountain** highest kind of land
12. **mountain range** row of mountains
13. **ocean** body of salt water larger than a sea
14. **peak** top of a mountain
15. **peninsula** land that is almost completely surrounded by water
16. **plain** area of flat or gently rolling low land
17. **plateau** area of high, mostly flat land
18. **river** large stream of water that flows across the land
19. **riverbank** land along a river
20. **source of river** place where a river begins
21. **valley** low land between hills or mountains
22. **volcano** opening in the earth, often raised, through which lava, rock, ashes, and gases are forced out

# All About Places and People

Flag

**Brookgreen Gardens, Pawleys Island, South Carolina**

# Unit 1

# All About Places and People

> **❝** I salute the flag of South Carolina and pledge to the Palmetto State love, loyalty and faith. **❞**
>
> —Pledge to the South Carolina flag

## Preview the Content
Before you study the unit, write a few sentences telling what you already know about places and people. Then organize your sentences in a two-column chart with the headings **Places** and **People**.

| Places | People |
|--------|--------|
|        |        |

# Unit 1 Preview

## South Carolina

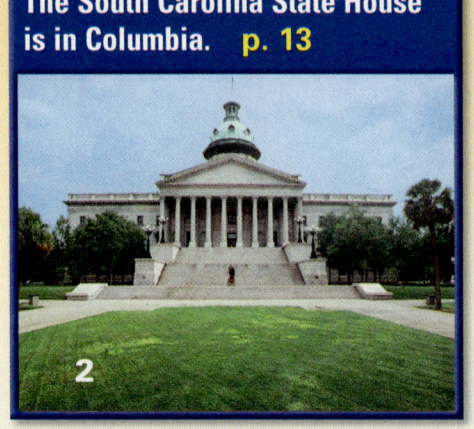

**The South Carolina State House is in Columbia.** p. 13

**Many people visit South Carolina's beaches every year.** p. 26

**Part of our state is in the Blue Ridge Mountains.** p. 31

## State Symbols

Flower: Carolina Jessamine

Tree: Palmetto

Gemstone: Amethyst

Animal: Whitetail Deer

Fruit: Peach

Bird: Carolina Wren

**Map Key**
- ★ State capital
- • Other city
- ▲ Mountain peak

**The Gullah Festival takes place in Beaufort each May.** p. 40

**Charleston began as an English settlement in 1670.** p. 46

**The House of Representatives meets in the State House.** p. 52

**START with a SONG**

# South Carolina on My Mind

By Hank Martin and Buzz Arledge

Illustrated by Billie Harmon

South Carolina is a beautiful state. People here are proud of their home. Being proud of where you live is called patriotism. Each year we celebrate our great state on South Carolina Day.

Hank Martin and Buzz Arledge wanted to share their patriotism with others. They wrote the song "South Carolina on My Mind." Many people think this song is special. South Carolina's leaders agreed. In 1984 the song was named as an official state song.

At the foothills of the Appalachian chain,
Down through the rivers, to the coastal plain,
There's a place that I call home,
And I'll never be alone,
Singin' this Carolina love song.

Chorus:
I've got South Carolina on my mind
Remembering all those sunshine Summertimes,
And the Autumns in the Smokies when the leaves turn to gold
Touches my heart and thrills my soul to have South Carolina on my mind,
With those clean snow-covered mountain Wintertimes
And the white sand of the beaches and those Carolina peaches,
I've got South Carolina on my mind.

## Think About It

1. What does the song tell you about South Carolina?
2. Think about the land around your community. What part of the song describes the place where you live?

## Read a Book

## Start the Unit Project

**Make a Class Magazine** With your classmates, make a magazine about South Carolina. As you read this unit, take notes about the people, places, and events in our state. Your notes will help you decide what to include in your magazine.

## Use Technology

Visit the Learning Site at **www.harcourtschool.com** for additional activities, primary sources, and other resources to use in this unit.

Unit 1 • 5

### Angel Oak, Johns Island

Angel Oak is one of the largest living oak trees in the world. It is more than 1,400 years old! Some limbs are the length of three school buses lined up end to end.

**LOCATE IT**

SOUTH CAROLINA

Johns Island

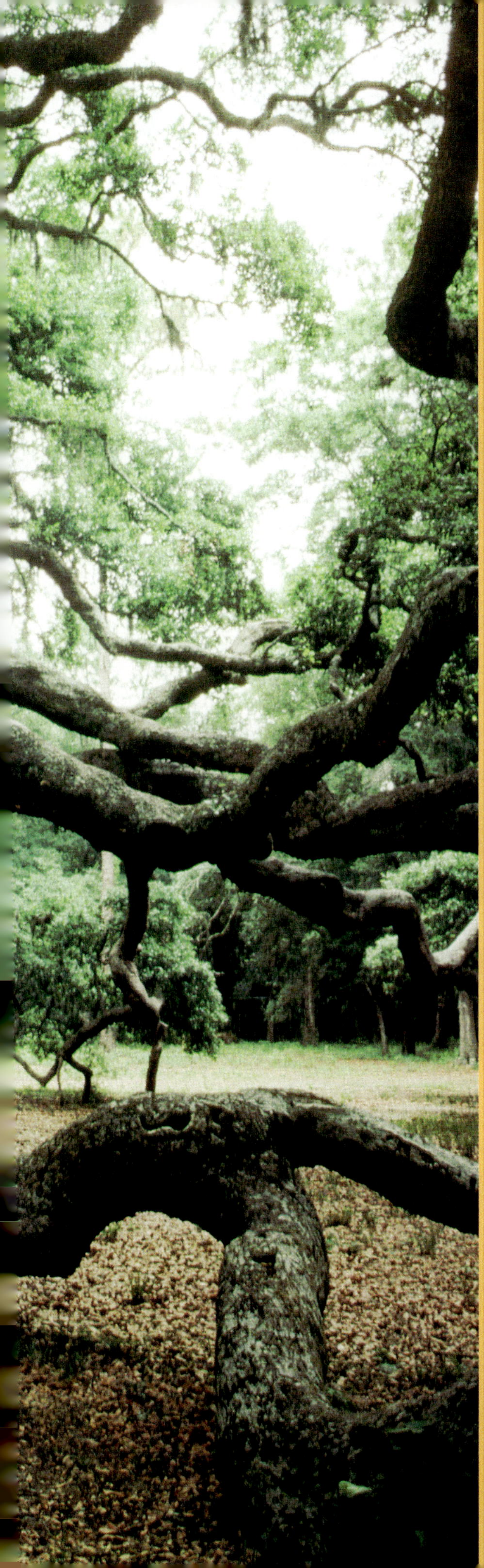

# Chapter 1

# A Place Called South Carolina

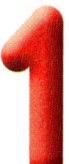

“Knowledge is the prime need of the hour.”

—Mary McLeod Bethune, 1955

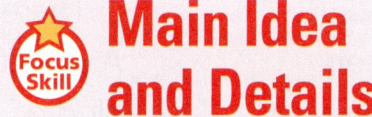

## Focus Skill: Main Idea and Details

The **main idea** is what the selection you are reading is about. The **details** are the things that show the main idea is true.

**As you read this chapter, be sure to do the following.**

- **List the main ideas.**
- **Under each main idea, list the supporting details.**

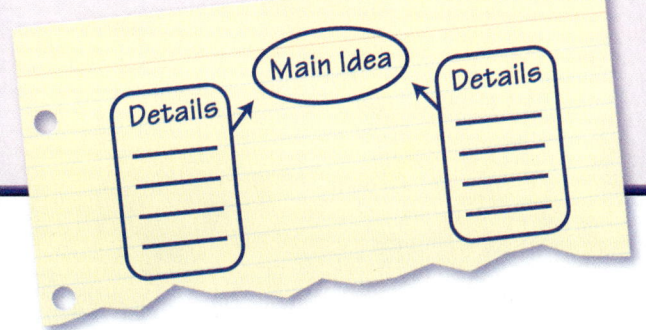

## Lesson 1

# Learning About Our State

**Big Idea**
You can use social studies to learn about places and people.

### Vocabulary

geography
history
museum
economics
government
law
community
citizen
culture
society

It is important to learn about the world around you. Social studies can help you. You can find out how people live today or how they lived long ago. You can also learn about the features of Earth.

## Geography

Geography is the study of Earth's features. A person who studies Earth and its people is called a geographer. When geographers want to learn about a place, they study its features.

There are two kinds of features in geography. A physical feature is something found in nature. This kind of feature includes the mountains, forests, and rivers. The Pee Dee River is a physical feature of South Carolina.

Other features of Earth were made by people. Human features are things people have built. People build cities and roads. The city of Columbia is a human feature. Interstate Highway 26 is one, too.

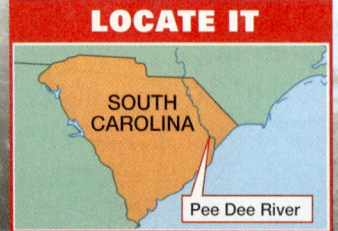
LOCATE IT — SOUTH CAROLINA — Pee Dee River

The Pee Dee River is over 400 miles long. It flows south from North Carolina, through South Carolina, to the Atlantic Ocean.

**People who enjoy the mountains live near Caesars Head State Park.**

Some people choose to live in a place because of its physical features. For example, many people like to live near water. Some people like to watch the ocean. Other people enjoy swimming in the water. Myrtle Beach and Charleston are near the Atlantic Ocean.

**Review** What are two kinds of features?
MAIN IDEA AND DETAILS

**People come to Myrtle Beach to enjoy the sand and to swim in the ocean.**

# History

**History** is the story of what has happened in a place. South Carolina has its own history. Historians are people who study history.

Historians are like detectives looking for clues to the story. They read newspapers and other written records. They also look at photographs, clothing, and tools. Historians study all parts of the story. Then they use what they have learned to tell the story.

This photograph was taken in 1862. It shows a group of enslaved African Americans on a plantation on Edisto Island.

Historians study written documents to learn about the past.

The South Carolina State Museum is in Columbia. The building used to be a textile mill. It was the first mill anywhere to use electric power.

Some historians work in museums. A **museum** is a place where objects from other times and places can be seen. Many communities in South Carolina have a museum. The South Carolina State Museum is in Columbia. Museums help to tell the history of South Carolina.

**Review** What is history?
**MAIN IDEA AND DETAILS**

This telescope was built in 1849. At the time, it was one of the largest telescopes in the United States. You can see it at the State Museum.

Chapter 1 ■ 11

# Economics

All people have needs. These are things we must have to live, such as food, clothing, and a place to live. People have wants, too. These are things people would like to have. The way people use resources to meet their needs and wants is called **economics**.

Most people work to meet their needs and wants. Some people make goods. In South Carolina, some people make cloth or paper. Others work in service jobs. Service jobs are work that someone does for someone else. Banking, health care, and teaching are all important service jobs.

Workers use their pay to buy what they need or want. Economics can help you spend money wisely.

**Review** What is economics?

MAIN IDEA AND DETAILS

Doctors provide a service. They help people stay healthy.

People can buy the food they need at a grocery store.

The South Carolina State House is in Columbia.

# Government

A **government** is a group of leaders who solve problems and make laws. **Laws** are rules for living together.

Countries, states, and communities all have governments. A **community** is a group of people who live or work in the same place.

To work well, governments need good citizens. A **citizen** is a person who lives in and belongs to a community. Good citizens share their ideas for making things better. They help other people in the community. They help to solve problems.

When you are grown up, you can vote for government leaders. Learning about government can help you be a good citizen.

The Great Seal of South Carolina shows a palmetto tree and a woman who stands for hope.

**Review** What are some things good citizens do?
MAIN IDEA AND DETAILS

Chapter 1 • 13

The Gullah Festival in Beaufort celebrates culture.

Charleston has a St. Patrick's Day Parade every year.

# Culture and Society

As you read this book, you will learn about different groups of people. Many groups helped to make South Carolina what it is today. You will learn where South Carolina's early people came from, how they dressed, and what they believed. You will also learn about the languages they spoke and the foods they ate. All these things make up a **culture**, or a way of life.

Each human group, or **society**, has a culture. Many societies have shaped the culture of South Carolina. People from many parts of the world have lived in South Carolina. All of these people have shared parts of their culture.

**Review** What is culture?

MAIN IDEA AND DETAILS

People build sand sculptures during the Sun Fun Festival in Myrtle Beach.

Artists perform during the Spoleto Festival in Charleston. This couple is dancing the flamenco.

## LESSON 1
### Review

 **Main Idea and Details** What are two details that show that South Carolina's culture was shaped by many societies?

**1 Big Idea** How can you use social studies to learn about South Carolina?

**2 Vocabulary** Write a sentence using the words **history** and **community**.

**3 Economics** What are three needs that all people share?

 **Performance—Draw Pictures** Draw pictures of one human feature and one physical feature in your community. Label your pictures. Then write sentences telling why you chose these features. Share your pictures and sentences with the class.

Chapter 1 ■ 15

## Skills: Read a Map

### Vocabulary

| | |
|---|---|
| map title | distance scale |
| map symbol | compass rose |
| map key | cardinal directions |

### ▶ Why It Matters

Maps are helpful tools. They can tell you about a place. They can also help you find a place.

### ▶ What You Need to Know

Most maps have the same parts. If you know how to use each part, you can read a map more easily.

**Map Title**—The **map title** tells you what the map is about.

**Map Key**—Nearly all maps use **map symbols**. The **map key** tells what the symbols mean. The map key can also be called the map legend.

**Distance Scale**—Most maps have a **distance scale**, or map scale. You can use it to find the distance, or how far it is, between two places. Find the distance scale on the map on page 17. Use a ruler to measure it. How many feet does 1 inch equal?

**Compass Rose**—The **compass rose** is a drawing with the letters *N, S, E,* and *W*. These letters stand for the directions *north, south, east,* and *west*. Directions tell you which way you need to go to get to a place. These four main directions are the **cardinal directions**.

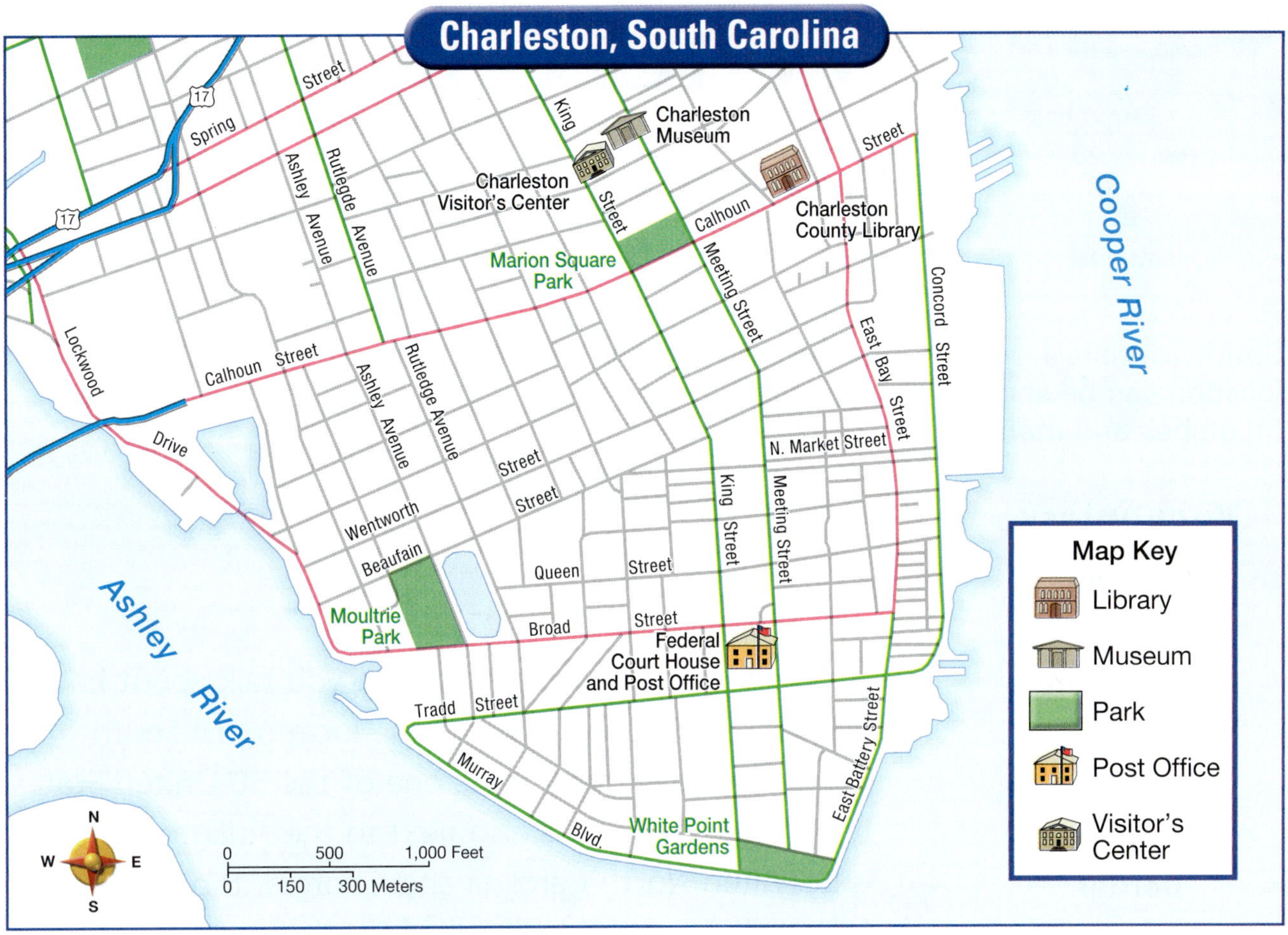

# Charleston, South Carolina

**Map Key**
- Library
- Museum
- Park
- Post Office
- Visitor's Center

## Practice the Skill

Use the map to answer these questions.

1. What is the title of the map?
2. In the map key, what is the symbol for a museum?
3. In which direction would you go if you walked from the Charleston Museum to Marion Square Park?

## Apply What You Learned

Draw a map of your community that includes a title, a compass rose with cardinal directions, a map key, and a distance scale. Share your map with a family member. Ask that person to point to a place such as a park, a school, a library, or a post office.

Practice your map and globe skills with the **GeoSkills CD-ROM**.

Chapter 1 • 17

MAP AND GLOBE SKILLS

## Lesson 2

# Where Is South Carolina?

**Big Idea**
South Carolina's location can be shown on globes and maps.

**Vocabulary**
location
globe
hemisphere
equator
continent
region
border

How would you tell someone where you live? You could name your community. You might say that you live in South Carolina. However, there are other ways to describe where you live.

## Location

When you tell where a place is, you talk about its **location**. You can tell about the location of South Carolina in many ways. It is one of the 50 United States. It is in the South. It is also next to the Atlantic Ocean. It is between North Carolina and Georgia, too. All these facts tell about the location of South Carolina.

There are many ways to describe the location of your community. You could say that you live near the coast. You could say that you live near the mountains. You could say that you live in a big city or a small town.

**Review** What is location?
MAIN IDEA AND DETAILS

Daufuskie Light is located on Daufuskie Island. In the past, the light in the tower helped sailors to sail safely at night and during storms. African Americans farmed and fished on the island for many years. Today, visitors come to the island, too.

## SCIENCE AND TECHNOLOGY

### Mapping from Space

Satellites help people make maps of Earth's surface. A satellite is a spacecraft without a crew that orbits Earth. It uses cameras and computers to take pictures of the landforms on Earth. These photographs are used in many ways. Maps made from satellite photographs help scientists study climate change. City planners also use maps made from satellite photographs.

# South Carolina on a Globe

To show someone South Carolina's location, you could use a globe. A **globe** is a model of Earth. Because it is round like Earth, a globe shows the true shapes of land and water.

A globe can be divided in half to find locations. Another way to say "half the globe" is **hemisphere** (HEH•muh•sfeer). *Hemi* means "half." *Sphere* means "ball."

There are two ways to divide the globe in half. One way is to cut it in the middle along the equator. The **equator** is a made-up line. It runs around the globe, halfway between the North Pole and the South Pole. If you cut a globe along the equator, you get a northern hemisphere. You also get a southern hemisphere. South Carolina is in the northern hemisphere.

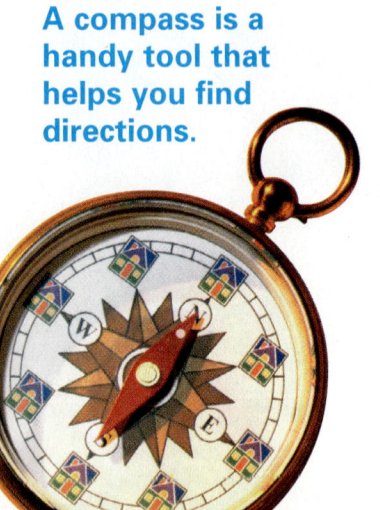

A compass is a handy tool that helps you find directions.

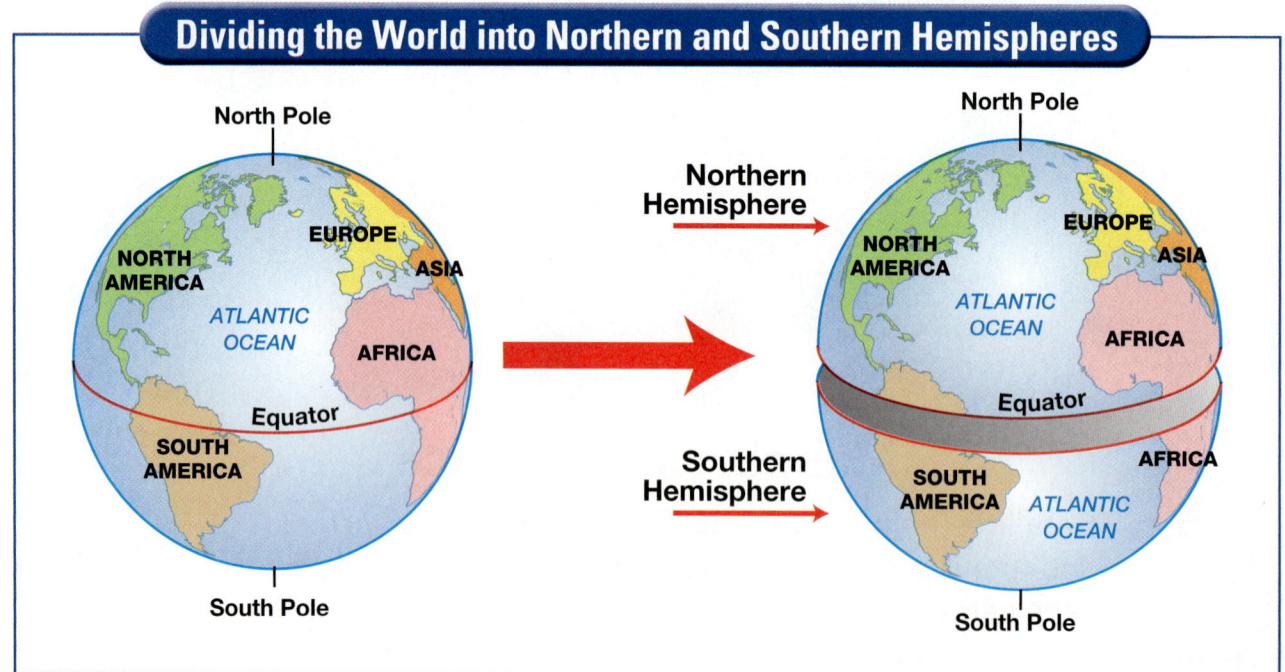

**Dividing the World into Northern and Southern Hemispheres**

**Location** This map shows how a globe can be divided along the equator.

❖ In which hemisphere is North America?

Geographers also divide the globe another way. A made-up line runs from the North Pole to the South Pole. If you cut the globe along this made-up line, you get a western hemisphere. You also get an eastern hemisphere. South Carolina is in the western hemisphere.

Every place on Earth is in two hemispheres. Can you name the two hemispheres where South Carolina is located?

**Review** What does a globe show?
MAIN IDEA AND DETAILS

These students are using a globe to find the location of their community.

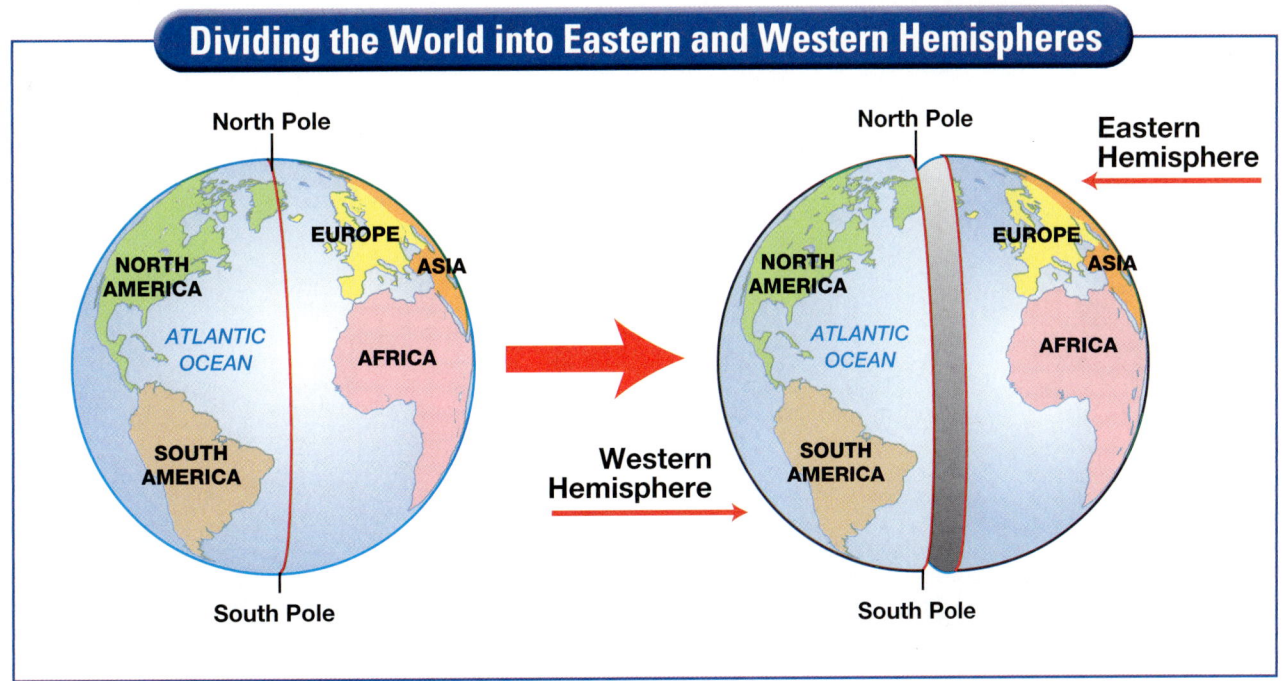

 **Location** This map shows how a globe can be divided from the North Pole to the South Pole.

◆ In which hemisphere is South America?

Chapter 1 ■ 21

# South Carolina on a Map

A map is also a model of Earth. A map is flat. It is much easier to carry than a globe. A map can also show the whole world or just parts of it. For example, a map may show North America. North America is a **continent** (KAHN•tih•nehnt), or one of the seven largest land areas on Earth.

On this map, you might see our country, the United States. A map of the United States might show the location of a region. A **region** is an area that has at least one feature that makes it different from other areas. So South Carolina is in the South, in the United States, in North America.

A map can also show South Carolina's neighbors. We share a border with both North Carolina and Georgia. A **border** (BOHR•duhr) is a line on a map that shows where a state or nation ends.

**Review** In which region of the United States is South Carolina?

**MAIN IDEA AND DETAILS**

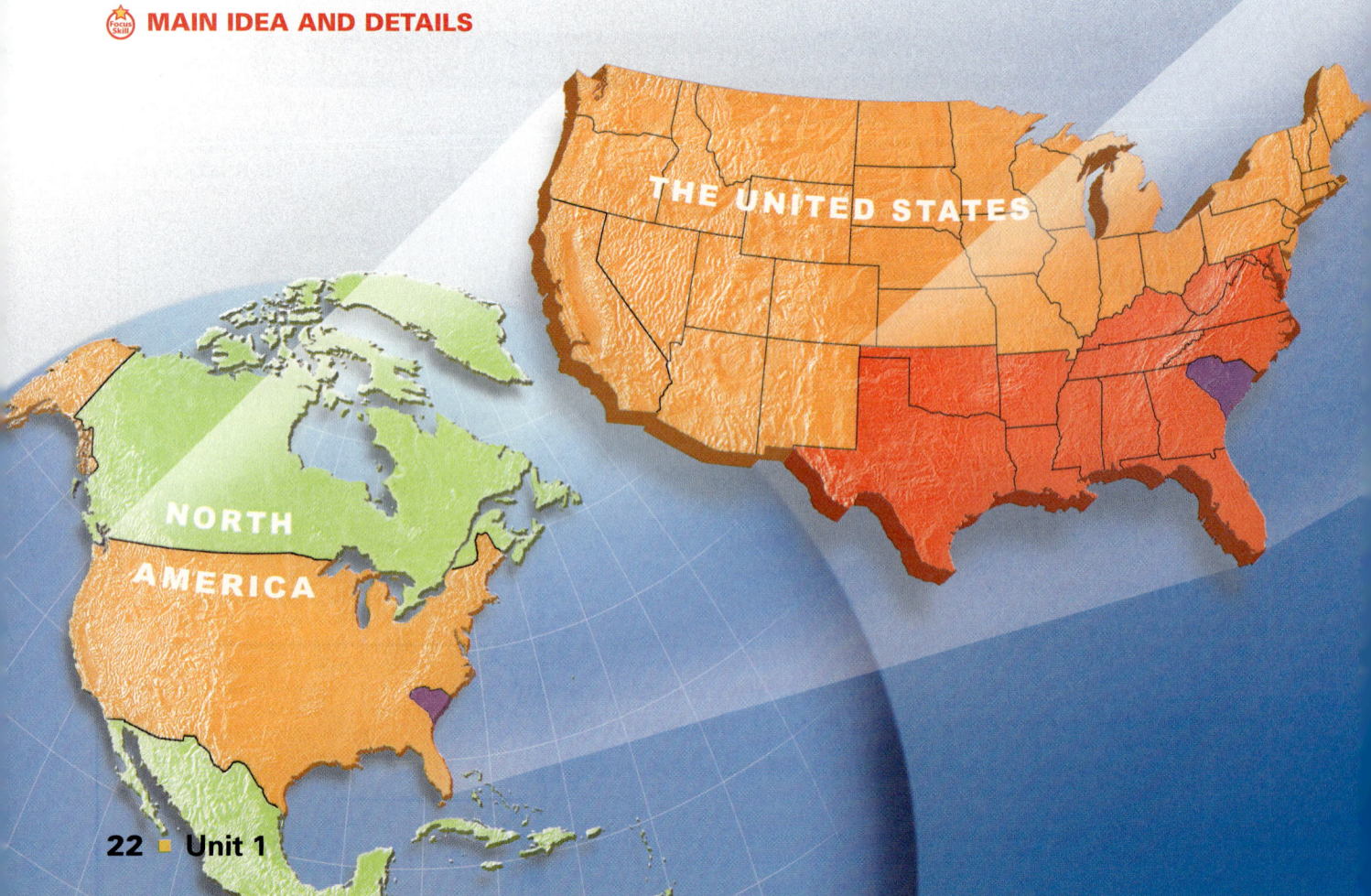

22 ■ Unit 1

**Analyze Diagrams** South Carolina is one of 50 states in the United States.

❓ How would you describe South Carolina's location in the South?

## LESSON 2 Review

 **Main Idea and Details** What are Earth's four hemispheres?

**1 Big Idea** Which continent is South Carolina on?

**2 Vocabulary** Use the words **region** and **border** in a sentence about South Carolina's location.

**3 Geography** What two states border South Carolina?

 **Performance—Draw a Map** Make an outline map of South Carolina. Label and show the state's borders. Label the Atlantic Ocean. Color South Carolina green. Make a key for your map. Then share the map with a classmate.

Chapter 1 ■ 23

# Skills: Read Graphs

**Vocabulary**
picture graph
bar graph

## ▶ Why It Matters

Graphs are drawings that compare sets of numbers. When you need to compare numbers of things, a graph can make the job easier.

## ▶ What You Need to Know

Two kinds of graphs are shown on page 25. Both graphs show the same information. They show populations of the five biggest cities in South Carolina. A population is the number of people living in a place.

The first graph is a picture graph. A **picture graph** uses small pictures or symbols to stand for numbers. This picture graph has a title and a key that tell what the pictures show.

The second graph is a bar graph. A **bar graph** uses bars of different lengths to stand for numbers. This bar graph has a title and labels that tell what the bars show.

## ▶ Practice the Skill

Use the picture graph and the bar graph to answer these questions.

1. Which city has the most people?
2. Which two cities have about the same number of people?
3. About how many people live in Columbia?
4. Look at the picture graph. What symbol stands for 10,000 people?

## ▶ Apply What You Learned

Find out the population of your community. Find the same information for two nearby communities. Use the information to make both a picture graph and a bar graph. Explain your graphs to a family member.

24 ▪ Unit 1

# Picture Graph of South Carolina's Biggest Cities

| CITY | NUMBER OF PEOPLE |
|---|---|
| Charleston | 🌴🌴🌴🌴🌴🌴🌴🌴🌴🌴 |
| Columbia | 🌴🌴🌴🌴🌴🌴🌴🌴🌴🌴🌴½ |
| Greenville | 🌴🌴🌴🌴🌴½ |
| North Charleston | 🌴🌴🌴🌴🌴🌴🌴🌴 |
| Rock Hill | 🌴🌴🌴🌴🌴½ |

🌴 =10,000 people

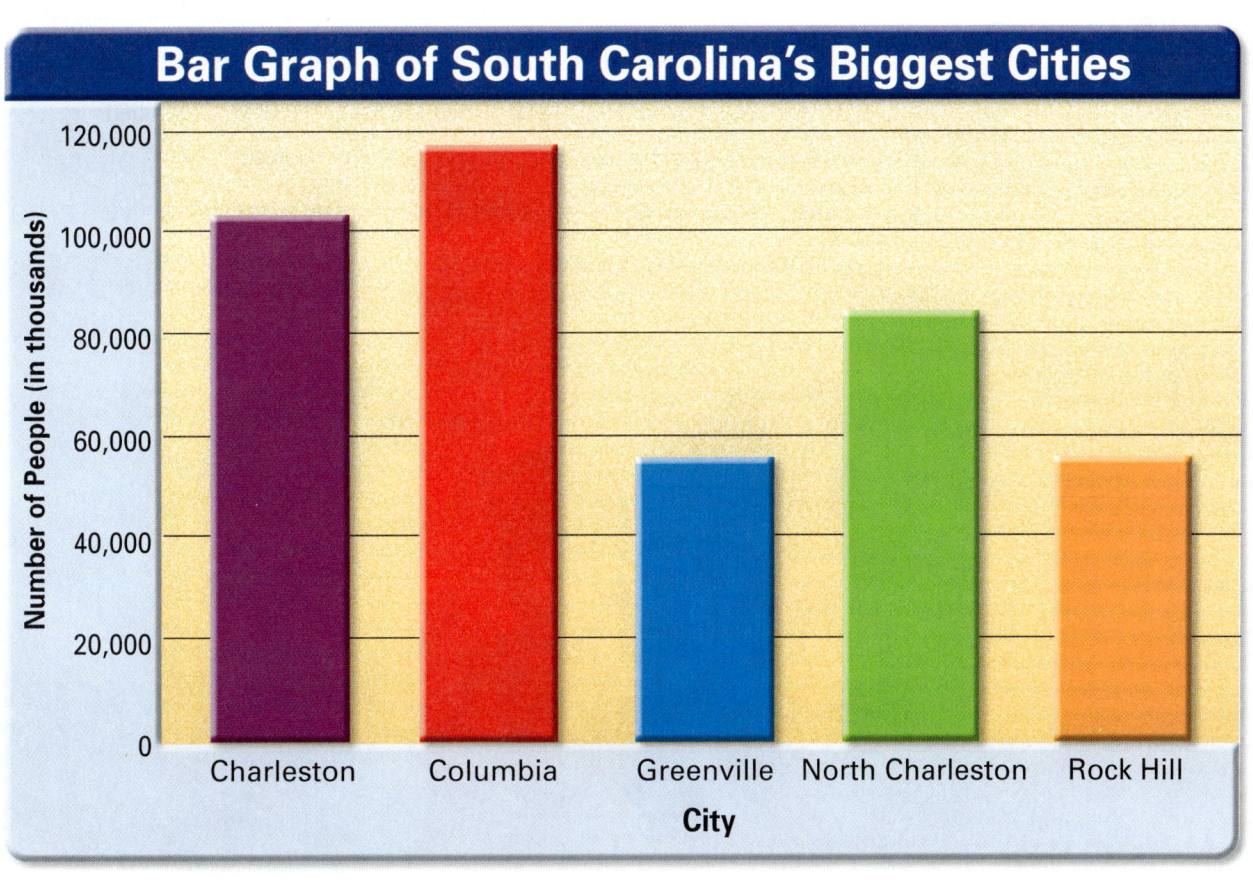

Bar Graph of South Carolina's Biggest Cities

## Lesson 3

# South Carolina's Land and Water

**Big Idea**
South Carolina has six physical regions.

### Vocabulary

physical region
landform
swamp
barrier island
harbor
coastal plain
fall line
natural resource
river basin

South Carolina can be divided into physical regions. A **physical region** is a region that has the same kinds of physical features. **Landforms** are shapes on the land, such as mountains and rivers. South Carolina has six physical regions. They are the Coastal Zone, Outer Coastal Plain, Inner Coastal Plain, Sandhills, Piedmont, and Blue Ridge regions.

## Coastal Zone

Ships come to South Carolina from the Atlantic Ocean. They land on the first of three coastal regions. This is the Coastal Zone. It is a long, narrow, and often sandy area. The beaches here are popular vacation spots. Along with sandy areas, the Coastal Zone may also have swamps. A **swamp** is a wet area where woody plants grow.

FAST FACT
Nearly 15 million people visit South Carolina beaches every year.

26 • Unit 1

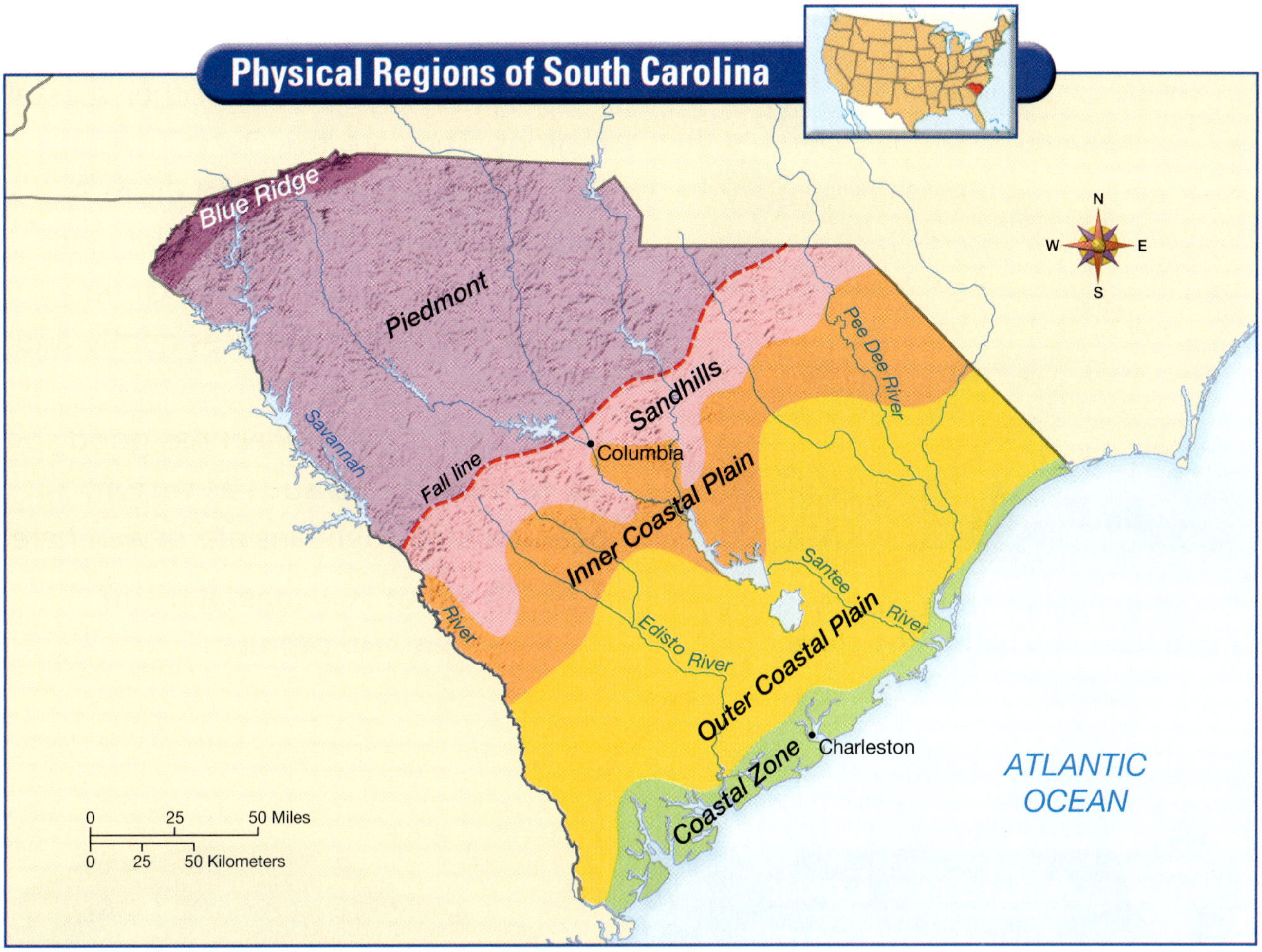

### Physical Regions of South Carolina

**Regions** This map shows the six physical regions of South Carolina.

❖ Which two regions are divided by the fall line?

The Coastal Zone includes a group of islands called the Sea Islands. Some of the Sea Islands are barrier islands. A **barrier island** (BA•ree•er EYE•luhnd) is a long, sandy island between the ocean and the mainland.

Charleston, the state's second-largest city, is in the Coastal Zone. Charleston's harbor makes it an important place for business. A **harbor** (HAHR•ber) is a protected place with deep water where large ships can come close to shore.

**Review** What are some features of the Coastal Zone?
MAIN IDEA AND DETAILS

Chapter 1 ■ 27

# The Coastal Plains

South Carolina has two other coastal regions. They are the Outer Coastal Plain and the Inner Coastal Plain. A **coastal plain** is an area of flat land along a sea or ocean. In the Outer Coastal Plain, the land rises gently and steadily.

The Inner Coastal Plain has good soil for farming. Crops such as cotton, peanuts, and soybeans are grown here.

**Review** What is a coastal plain?
MAIN IDEA AND DETAILS

South Carolina's coastal plains cover more than one-half of the state.

## A Closer Look
### Landforms and Bodies of Water

There are many different kinds of landforms and bodies of water. In this drawing you can compare them.

1. A swamp is a wet area where woody plants grow.
2. A barrier island is a long, sandy island between the ocean and the mainland.
3. A coastal plain is an area of flat land along a sea or ocean.
4. A harbor is a protected place with deep water where ships can come close to shore.
5. A river basin is land drained by a river.
6. A fall line is a long, low cliff where rivers drop suddenly.

Which of these landforms or bodies of water are near your community?

## The Sandhills

In the center of the state, called the Midlands, are the Sandhills. They are rolling hills of rough, sandy soil that begin at the fall line. A **fall line** is a long, low cliff. At the fall line, rivers drop suddenly.

Because a fall line is a stopping point, it makes a natural border. The fall line in South Carolina forms the border between the Sandhills and the Piedmont.

**Review** What is a fall line?

**MAIN IDEA AND DETAILS**

The Sandhills region gets its name from the landform and the sandy soil.

# The Piedmont

The word *piedmont* (PEED•mahnt) means "foot of the mountain." True to its name, the Piedmont is at the edge of the Blue Ridge Mountains.

In South Carolina, the Piedmont covers about one-third of the state. It is rich in natural resources. **Natural resources** are materials from nature, such as wood, stone, and water.

Both the Pee Dee and Savannah Rivers and river basins start in the Piedmont. A **river basin** is land drained by a river.

**Review** What does *piedmont* mean?
MAIN IDEA AND DETAILS

The Piedmont region is full of low, rolling hills. Some rocks in these hills are more than 300 million years old.

## • GEOGRAPHY •

### Table Rock Mountain

#### Understanding Physical Systems

Table Rock Mountain is part of the Blue Ridge Mountains. It is in Pickens County, near the border with North Carolina. This huge, flat, rocky landform rises 3,124 feet above the ocean.

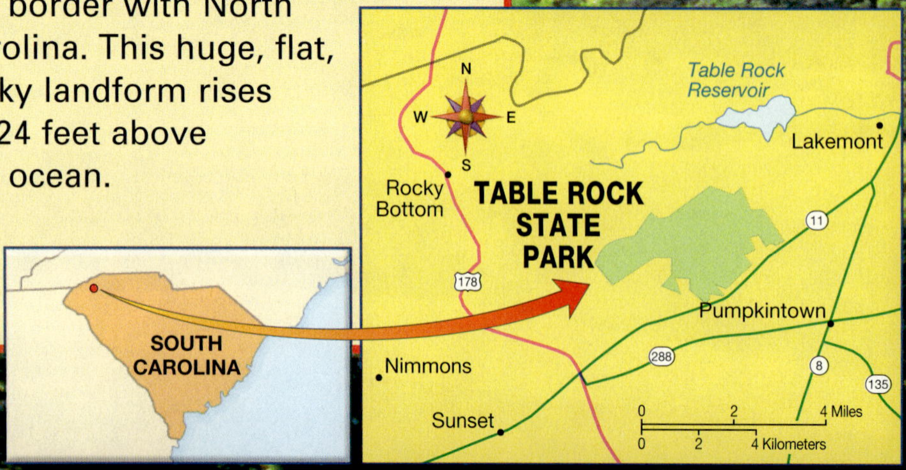

## The Blue Ridge

The Blue Ridge Mountain Region is a small part of South Carolina. Sassafras Mountain, the tallest mountain in South Carolina, is located in the Blue Ridge. It rises 3,554 feet above the ocean.

The Blue Ridge Mountains belong to a bigger mountain range or group of mountains. They are the Appalachian (a•puh•LAY•chuhn) Mountains.

**Review** What is Sassafras Mountain?

MAIN IDEA AND DETAILS

### LESSON 3 Review

**Main Idea and Details**
What are South Carolina's six physical regions?

1. **Big Idea** What are one physical feature and one human feature of the Coastal Plains?

2. **Vocabulary** Use the terms **physical region** and **barrier islands** to tell about the Coastal Zone. Write two or three sentences.

3. **Geography** Which feature divides the Piedmont and the Sandhills?

**Performance—Make a Postcard** Make a postcard showing one of South Carolina's physical regions. Draw a picture of the region on a notecard. On the other side, write a note to a friend. Tell what you might see and do in this region. Share your postcard with the class.

Chapter 1 • 31

# Skills: Read a Landform Map

**Vocabulary**
landform map

## ▶ Why It Matters

There are many kinds of maps. Each kind has a special use. For example, to find where a friend lives, you can use a street map. If you want to know about the geography of a place, you can use a landform map. A **landform map** shows you the physical features of a place. It can show mountains, plains, hills, lakes, rivers, and oceans.

## ▶ What You Need to Know

On a landform map, different physical features are shown by different colors or patterns. The map key tells you what color stands for each kind of physical feature.

**32** ▪ Unit 1

▶ **Practice the Skill**

Use the map and the map key to answer these questions.

1. Which city is on higher ground, Columbia, South Carolina, or Boise, Idaho?
2. Are the Coast Ranges in the eastern or western part of the United States?
3. Which major body of water is close to New Orleans?

▶ **Apply What You Learned**

Look at the landforms shown on South Carolina and its border states. In a paragraph, describe landforms in your state. In a second paragraph, compare South Carolina's landforms to those of the border states.

 Practice your map and globe skills with the **GeoSkills CD-ROM**.

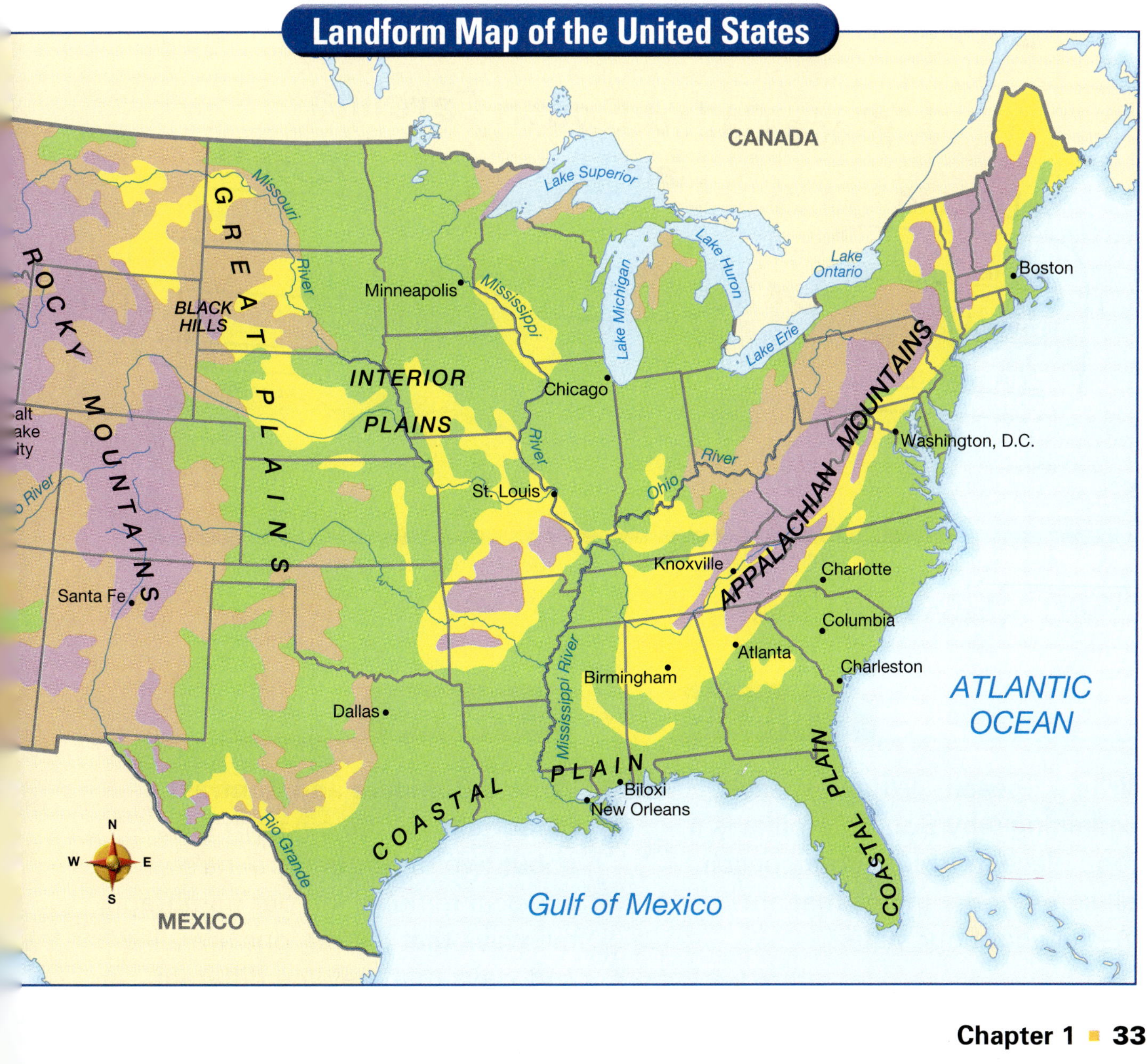

**Landform Map of the United States**

Chapter 1 ■ 33

# Chapter 1

# Review and Test Preparation

## Focus Skill: Main Ideas and Details

Copy the following graphic organizer onto a separate sheet of paper. Use the information you have learned to tell details about the location of South Carolina.

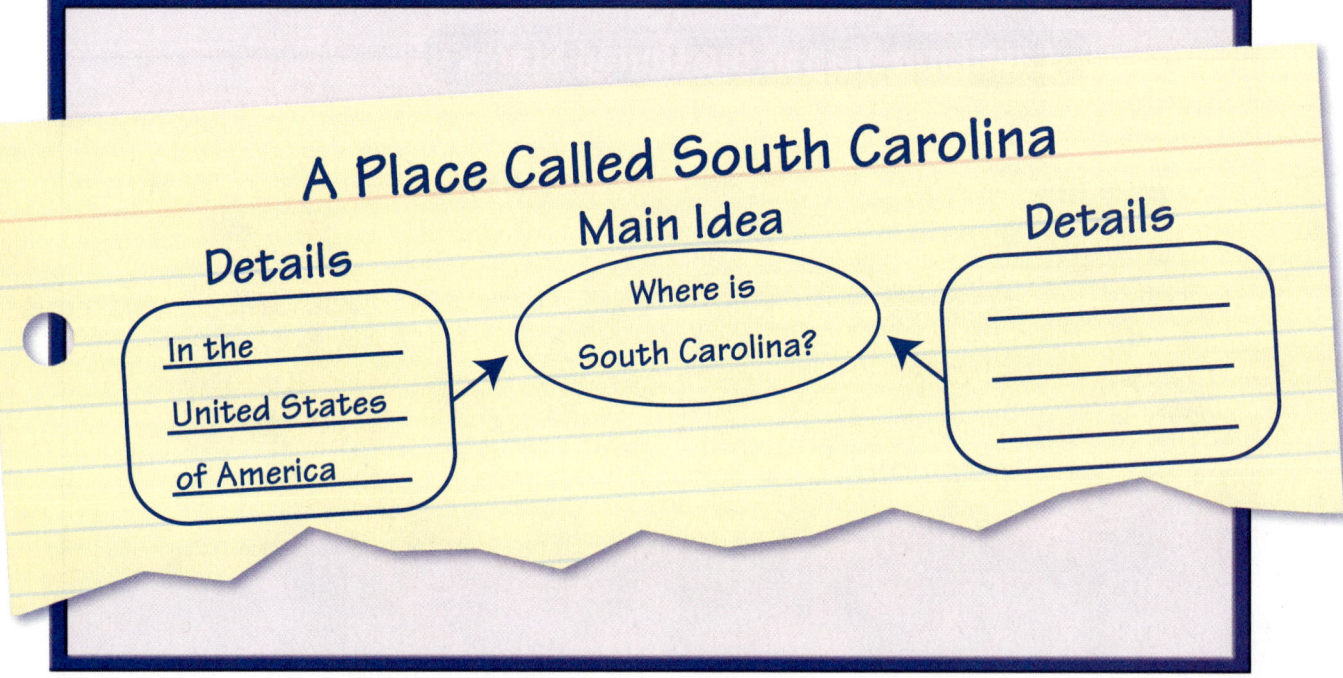

## THINK & WRITE

**Write a Speech** Write a speech explaining why South Carolina is a good place to live. In your speech, tell some of the things that are special about our state.

**Write a Compare and Contrast Paragraph** Write a paragraph about two of South Carolina's physical regions. In your paragraph, tell ways that the regions are alike and ways that they are different.

## Use Vocabulary

Choose the term that correctly matches each definition.

economics (p. 12)   society (p. 14)
continents (p. 22)   swamp (p. 26)
coastal plain (p. 28)

1. the way people use resources to meet their needs and wants
2. a wet area where woody plants grow
3. Earth's largest land areas
4. an area of flat land along a sea or ocean
5. a human group

## Recall Facts

Answer these questions.

6. What made-up line goes around Earth, halfway between the North Pole and the South Pole?
7. In what region of the United States is South Carolina?
8. Where is South Carolina's fall line?

Write the letter of the best choice.

9. Studying geography can best help you—
   A learn about the past.
   B choose a good way to earn a living.
   C be a good citizen.
   D describe places and their features.

10. If you wanted to go to the beach, you would visit the—
    F Sandhills.
    G Coastal Zone.
    H Blue Ridge region.
    J Piedmont.

## Think Critically

11. What are some ways that people share their culture in South Carolina?
12. You are planning a car trip to the Coastal Zone. Would you use a map or a globe? Explain.

## Apply Skills

**Read a Map**

13. Look at the map on page 17. If you were at the Charleston County Library, in which direction would you go to reach the post office?

**Read Graphs**

14. The numbers below tell how many cartons of milk were sold. Make a bar graph and a picture graph that show this information.

| Monday | 200 | Tuesday | 185 |
| Wednesday | 195 | Thursday | 175 |

**Read a Landform Map**

15. Look at the landform map on pages 32–33. Look at the landforms near Santa Fe and Charleston. In a paragraph, compare the landforms.

## Fourth of July Fireworks

South Carolina loves fireworks! Throughout the state, cities and towns gather to celebrate July 4th, also known as Independence Day. In the picture, the city of Charleston holds a fireworks display for everyone to enjoy. People also like having fun on July 4th by having parades and barbecues during the day.

**LOCATE IT**

Charleston, SOUTH CAROLINA

# Chapter 2

# People and Government

> **" Nothing could be finer than to be in Carolina. . . . "**
> —from a song by Gus Kahn, 1922

##  Categorize

To **categorize** means to divide information into groups. In this chapter you will learn about the many different people in our state and about different governments.

**As you read this chapter, categorize information about our state.**

- Cultures
- People
- Local governments
- State government

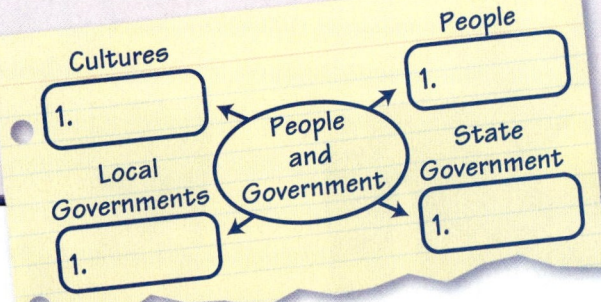

## Lesson 1

# One State, Many People

**Big Idea**
South Carolina has been shaped by many cultures.

**Vocabulary**
immigrant
diversity
custom
ethnic group
heritage

People have come to South Carolina from different places. A person who comes from another country is called an **immigrant**. The many people who live here shape life in South Carolina. They give our state diversity. **Diversity** (duh•VER•suh•tee) means a rich mixture of cultures.

## A Mix of Cultures

People from the same place have certain customs. A **custom** is a way of doing something. For example, people dress in different ways. In India, it is a custom for women to wear a sari (SAR•ee), a brightly colored long dress. In Scotland, men sometimes wear a kilt, a plaid skirt.

People from many different backgrounds live in South Carolina.

**The Scottish Games and Highland Gathering takes place in Charleston every year.**

**FAST FACT** Many people left Scotland and Ireland in the 1700s and 1800s. Many of these Scottish-Irish immigrants came to South Carolina. We honor their traditions at these annual games.

Different ethnic groups have different customs. An **ethnic group** is made up of people with the same culture, or way of life. There are many ethnic groups in South Carolina. Each one has its own culture. The different cultures can be seen in clothing. They can be heard in music. They can be tasted in food.

Different cultures and customs enrich our lives in many ways. One way is with new foods. You can eat Mexican food in South Carolina. You may also try Chinese foods. You can enjoy the music and the arts of different cultures, too. In South Carolina, you can hear songs from West Africa. You can listen to music from England.

**Review** What is an ethnic group?

**Different groups bring different foods to South Carolina.**

Chapter 2 • 39

## A Mix of Peoples

The people of South Carolina came here at different times. Native Americans lived here first.

Next, people came from the continent of Europe. They came from countries such as Spain, France, and England. Some lived in Barbados before they came to South Carolina. Barbados is an island in the Caribbean Sea. Many people came here from West Africa.

**Review** What are three groups of people who lived in South Carolina long ago? **CATEGORIZE**

### • HERITAGE •

### Gullah Festival

The Gullah Festival takes place in Beaufort each May. It celebrates diversity. Storytelling, African dancing, gospel music, and jazz are all performed. People come from other parts of the United States and from other countries to attend this five-day festival.

# South Carolina's Heritage

In Unit 2, you will read more about the people who came to South Carolina long ago. These groups changed South Carolina. The people who came later did, too. They all gave South Carolina a rich heritage. A **heritage** is a set of beliefs and customs handed down from people who lived earlier.

In South Carolina, there are many events that celebrate different cultures. These festivals and holidays help to keep the state's mix of cultures. They show respect for our heritage, too.

**Review** How do celebrations help preserve customs?

**Basket weaving is part of South Carolina's heritage.**

## LESSON 1 Review

 **Categorize** Categorize examples of different customs and cultures in your community.

**1 Big Idea** What are some cultures in South Carolina today?

**2 Vocabulary** Use **immigrants** and **customs** in a sentence about South Carolina.

**3 Culture** What are some ways that different ethnic groups can celebrate their culture?

 **Performance––Make a Poster** Choose a holiday or event that your community celebrates each year. Make a poster that shows the celebration. Then add your poster to a bulletin board titled "Our Community."

Chapter 2 ▪ 41

# Examine Primary Sources

## A Heritage Museum

Have you ever wondered what your community was like long ago? How could you find out? You could visit a heritage museum.

One heritage museum is the Historical Center of York County. This museum holds many artifacts from the past. An **artifact** is a human-made object. It can be a map, tool, or photograph. The museum lets visitors look at the artifacts. This helps people to learn the history of their community.

 **FROM THE HISTORICAL CENTER OF YORK COUNTY**

## Primary Source

When you study the past, you can use primary sources. A **primary source** is a written or printed artifact. It was made by a person who saw or took part in an event. Maybe the person wrote his or her story in a diary or told it in a newspaper. The person may have taken a photograph or drawn a picture.

42 ■ Unit 1

## Secondary Source

Once you have gathered information from a primary source, you can write a report. Your report would be a secondary source. A **secondary source** is written by someone who was not there when an event took place. Your textbook is a secondary source.

### Analyze the Primary Source

1. How do artifacts tell about history?
2. How can primary and secondary sources be put together to tell about the history of a place?

### Activity

**Compare and Contrast** Choose two or more primary sources. Pick things that tell about life in your community today. Write a sentence about each source. Give information that would help a future historian know what life was like today.

### Research

 Visit The Learning Site at **www.harcourtschool.com** to research other primary sources.

Chapter 2 ■ 43

# Lesson 2

## Local Governments

**Big Idea**
Local governments give services and keep people safe.

### Vocabulary

common good
public service
election
county
county seat
rights
responsibilities

When people use the word *community*, they often mean "city" or "town." South Carolina has 270 cities or towns. Your community is one of them. The word *local* means "nearby." There are two kinds of local governments in South Carolina—community and county.

## Community Government

Each South Carolina community has its own leaders. They make up the government for the community. They write laws. They work for the **common good**. This means they try to meet the needs of all people in the community.

Local governments hire police officers.

They do this partly by providing public services. A **public service** is work that helps everyone.

Community governments hire and train firefighters. They hire teachers and police, too. Many community governments provide clean water. They build streets and sidewalks. They put up traffic lights. They care for community parks.

Adult citizens choose their government leaders. They do this in elections. An **election** is a time when citizens vote, or make a choice.

**Review** What are three examples of public service? **CATEGORIZE**

Building and repairing streets is a public service.

Adult citizens choose government leaders by voting in an election.

Chapter 2 • 45

**FAST FACT**

Charleston began as an English settlement in 1670. It was first called Charles Town. Then it was called Charleston. Today, many people come to Charleston to learn about its past.

# County Government

County government is another kind of local government. A **county** is part of a state. It is smaller than the whole state and may hold many communities. There are 46 counties in South Carolina.

One community in each county serves as the **county seat**. This is the center of the county government. Often the county seat is the largest city in the county. It might have the same name. Florence is the county seat of Florence County.

Each county in South Carolina has a council. Its members make up the county's government. The council decides how money can best be spent to serve the whole county.

Voters elect the county council. They also elect other county leaders. The sheriff makes sure that people obey the laws. The county clerk keeps important records.

**Review** How is the county council chosen?

This sheriff's badge tells people that the person wearing it will enforce local laws.

# Rights and Responsibilities

Citizens have rights. **Rights** are freedoms all citizens share. In the United States, people have many rights. One is the right to share ideas freely. Citizens also have **responsibilities**. These are things citizens should do because they are necessary and important. People in the United States have many responsibilities. One is to help care for their communities.

**Review** What is one right that people in the United States have?

Citizens of a community can help each other.

## LESSON 2 Review

 **Categorize** What are two kinds of public services?

1. **Big Idea** What are the two main kinds of local government?
2. **Vocabulary** Use **county** and **election** in a sentence.
3. **Civics and Government** How can citizens take part in government?

 **Performance—Role-play an Interview** Make a list of good citizenship skills. Then think of someone who has these skills. It may be someone in your community or a well-known American leader. Write a list of questions you would like to ask that person. Then, with a partner, role-play an interview with that leader.

# Skills

# Solve a Problem

| Vocabulary | |
|---|---|
| problem | solution |

## ▶ Why It Matters

In a community government, citizens work together to find solutions to problems. A **problem** is something difficult, or hard to understand. A **solution** is an answer to a problem. People need to be able to find solutions to their own problems, too. Knowing how to find a solution to a problem is an important skill that you can use now and in the future.

## ▶ What You Need to Know

There are steps you can follow to solve a problem.

**Step 1** Identify the problem.

**Step 2** Gather information. Think about solutions.

**Step 3** Think about the outcome, or what will happen.

**Step 4** Choose the best solution. Try it.

**Step 5** Think about how well your solution worked.

**Step 6** Make changes if they are needed. Practice the solution that works.

Working together is often an important part of solving problems.

What problem do you see in this picture? What would you do to solve it?

## ▶ Practice the Skill

1. Look at the picture.
2. Identify the problem.
3. Think of some possible solutions. Also think of the outcome.
4. Explain the steps for finding a solution.

## ▶ Apply What You Learned

Read or listen to local news reports. Identify a problem in your community that you could do something about. Talk with a family member about a solution. Share your problem and the solution with your classmates.

# Lesson 3

## State Government

**Big Idea**
The three branches of state government have different jobs.

**Vocabulary**
constitution
nation
legislative
judicial
executive
taxes
jury
governor

A **constitution** is a written plan for government. Our country, the United States, has a constitution. It divides the government into three branches, or parts. It tells how the government of our **nation**, or country, works. South Carolina's constitution tells how our state government works.

### Branches of Government

The South Carolina government has three branches. The **legislative** branch makes laws. The **judicial** branch decides if laws are fair or unfair. It also decides if laws have been carried out fairly. The **executive** branch sees that the laws are obeyed.

**Review** How many branches make up South Carolina's state government?

A palmetto tree and the moon appear on the South Carolina State Flag.

**FAST FACT** The palmetto tree is an important state symbol. It is found on both the state flag and the state seal. It is also the state tree.

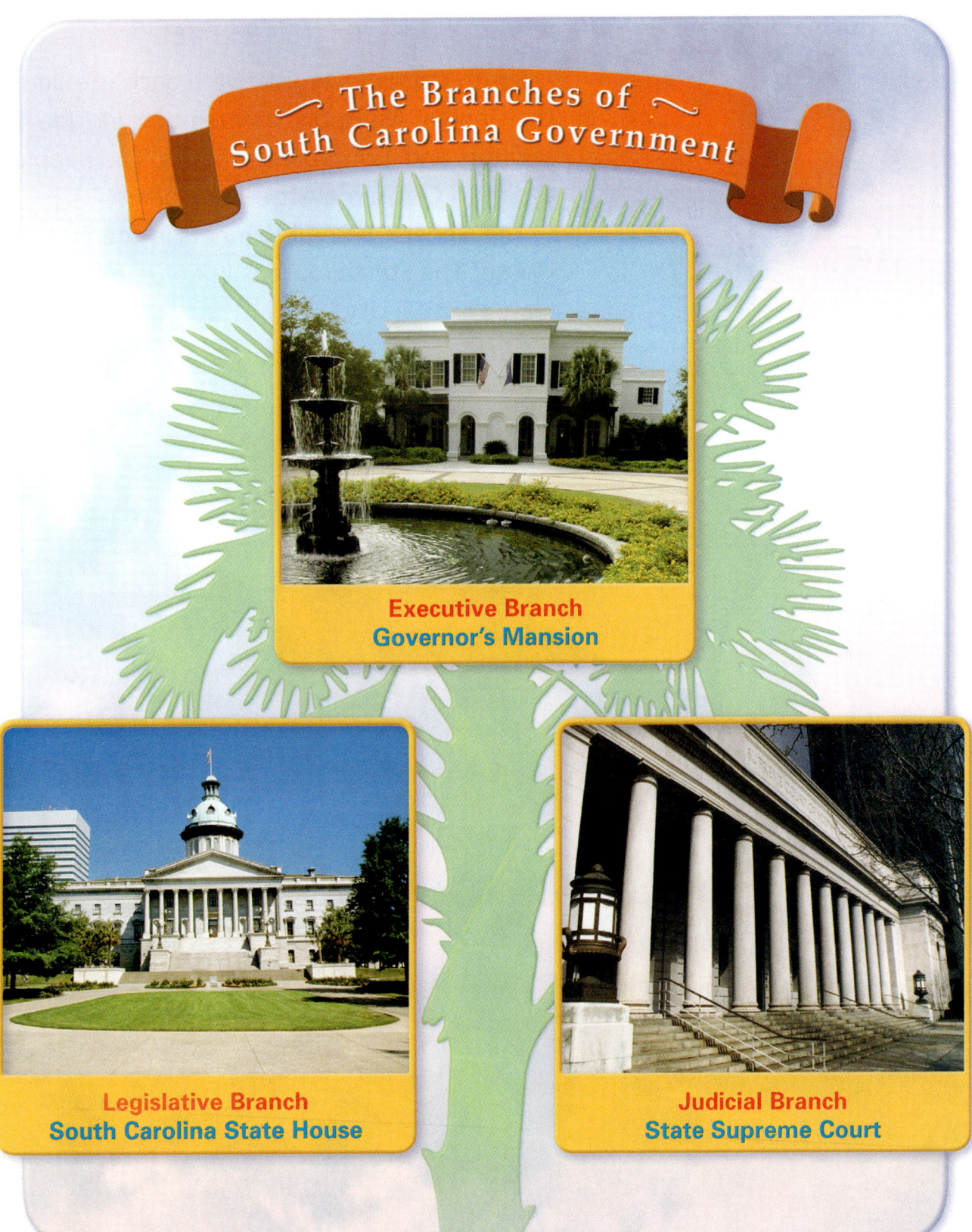

The Branches of South Carolina Government

**Executive Branch**
Governor's Mansion

**Legislative Branch**
South Carolina State House

**Judicial Branch**
State Supreme Court

**Analyze Diagrams** This diagram shows the different branches of government.
◆ What are the branches of state government?

A new law is called a bill until it is signed by the governor.

# Legislative

South Carolina's legislative branch is called the General Assembly. Its members include 46 senators and 124 representatives. The people of South Carolina elect these leaders.

The General Assembly meets in the State House. The State House is in Columbia, our state's capital city.

The South Carolina House of Representatives is one part of the General Assembly.

School buses and books are paid for by taxes.

Money for state government comes from taxes. **Taxes** are money that citizens pay to the government. Taxes pay the government leaders for doing their jobs. Taxes also pay for public services.

The state government provides many public services. It helps to pay for schools and hospitals.

**Review** What are some public services the state government provides?

 CATEGORIZE

Chapter 2 • 53

# Judicial

South Carolina's judicial branch has three main jobs. It makes sure that the state laws agree with the state constitution. This branch decides how a person who breaks the law will be punished. It works to make sure that the laws are fair to everyone.

Members of the judicial branch are called judges. They work in the state courts. Judges hear and decide cases, or arguments about the law. There are different kinds of courts. In some courts, cases have a jury. A **jury** is a group of citizens who listen to the facts of a case.

The State Supreme Court is the highest court in South Carolina. It checks decisions made in all the other courts. Five justices, or judges, work together on this court. Lawmakers in the General Assembly elect the justices.

**Review** What is the highest court in South Carolina?

**There are five justices in the State Supreme Court.**

**A jury listens to arguments about the law.**

# Executive

Voters in South Carolina elect a **governor** to lead the state. The governor is the head of the state's executive branch. South Carolina's governors serve for four years. No governor can serve more than eight years in a row.

The governor directs government departments and works with their leaders. The departments help to run our schools. They protect workers and make sure everyone obeys the law. The governor also signs laws to make them official.

**Review** Who is the head of the executive branch?

The governor must sign any new law.

## LESSON 3 Review

**Categorize** Read the lesson again. Make a table with two headings: *Branches of Government* and *Jobs*. List the branches and tell what they do.

**1 Big Idea** How are the three branches of state government different?

**2 Vocabulary** What does the **legislative** branch of government do?

**3 Economics** Where does South Carolina's government get money for public services?

**Performance—Do Research and Report** Research to learn about one state government department. Take notes about the kinds of public services it provides. Write a paragraph about this department and its jobs. Read your report to your classmates.

Chapter 2 ■ 55

# Skills: Read a Table

**Vocabulary**

table

## ▶ Why It Matters

A **table** is a drawing that is used to organize information. Knowing how to use a table will help you compare numbers and other kinds of information more easily.

## ▶ What You Need to Know

Like charts and graphs, tables have titles that tell what they show. They use columns and rows to show information.

Columns go up and down. Rows go across. On the table below, you can see there are four columns. There are three rows.

The table on the next page gives information about the offices, or jobs, in South Carolina's state government. It lists the name of each office. It lists how often members are elected. It also lists the age a person needs to be and the number of people who serve in that office at one time.

To find information about each office, look for its name in the first column. Then read across that row.

### Title

|       | Column 1 | Column 2 | Column 3 | Column 4 |
|-------|----------|----------|----------|----------|
| Row A |          |          |          |          |
| Row B |          |          |          |          |
| Row C |          |          |          |          |

### Offices in the South Carolina State Government

| STATE OFFICE | HOW OFTEN ELECTED | AGE NEEDED TO SERVE | NUMBER IN OFFICE |
|---|---|---|---|
| Governor | 4 years; can be elected twice | 30 or older | 1 |
| Member of the Senate | 4 years | 25 or older | 46 |
| Member of the House | 2 years | 21 or older | 124 |
| Supreme Court Justice | 10 years | 32 or older | 5 |

### ▶ Practice the Skill

Use the table above to help you answer these questions.

1. How often is a member of the state senate elected?
2. How many times can a governor be elected?
3. How many members of the House serve at a time?
4. How old does a person need to be to become governor?

### ▶ Apply What You Learned

Think of information you could show in a table. Your table might be about sports facts. It could show the ways classmates come to school, their favorite foods, or their pets. Make a table to show the information. Be sure your table has a title, columns, and rows. Write two questions about your table. Work with a partner. Read each other's tables to answer the questions.

# Chapter 2

# Review and Test Preparation

##  Categorize

Copy the following graphic organizer onto a separate sheet of paper. Use the information you have learned to show that you understand how to categorize information about our state's people and government.

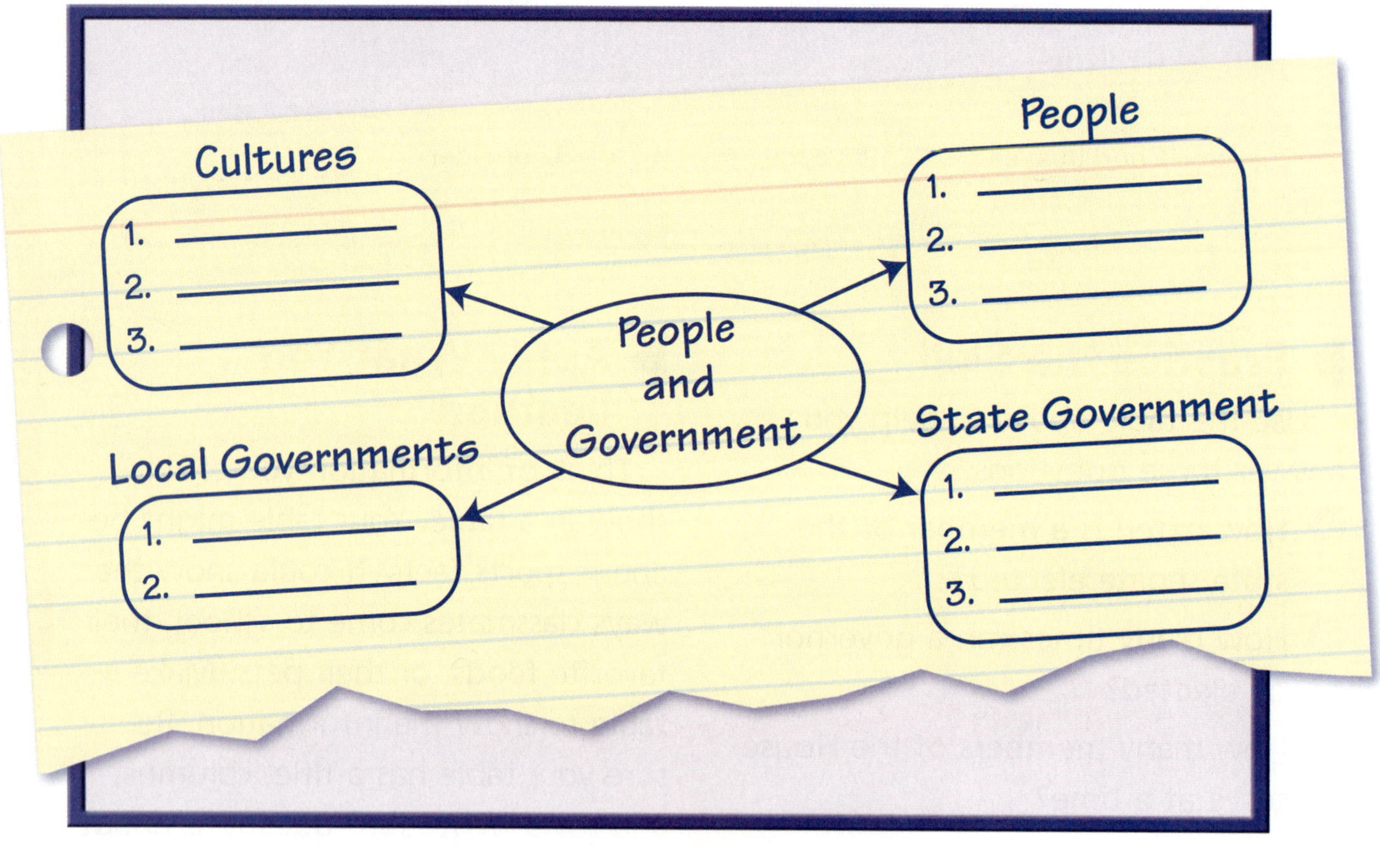

**Cultures**
1. _____
2. _____
3. _____

**People**
1. _____
2. _____
3. _____

**People and Government**

**Local Governments**
1. _____
2. _____

**State Government**
1. _____
2. _____
3. _____

## THINK & WRITE

**Write a Persuasive Letter** Think about the kinds of things that people can do for the common good. Write a letter to a friend. Persuade him or her to help in the community.

**Write a Paragraph That Explains** Imagine that you have been asked to explain state government to a younger student. Write a paragraph that tells about state government.

## Use Vocabulary

Write the term that best completes each sentence.

> heritage (p. 41)     legislative (p. 50)
> public service (p. 45)   jury (p. 54)
> election (p. 45)

1. A time when citizens vote is called an ___.

2. ___ is a set of beliefs and customs handed down by people who lived earlier.

3. A group of citizens who listen to the facts of a case is a ___.

4. The branch of government that makes laws is the ___ branch.

5. Work that helps a community is called ___.

## Recall Facts

Answer these questions.

6. What are three cultures that helped to shape South Carolina?

7. What are the two kinds of local governments?

8. Who is the leader of the state?

Write the letter of the best choice.

9. What is a right?
   A a responsibility
   B a law
   C a freedom that all citizens share
   D something a government does

10. The branch of government that decides if laws are fair is the ___ branch.
    F judicial
    G executive
    H elected
    J legislative

11. The governor is the head of the ___ branch.
    A legislative
    B county
    C judicial
    D executive

## Think Critically

12. Why do you think our government has three branches?

13. What are two ways to be a good citizen in your community?

14. Why is it important to have both local and state governments?

## Apply Skills

**Solve a Problem**

15. Look at the information on page 48. How would you use the six steps to decide how to do three different homework assignments?

**Read a Table**

16. Use the table on page 57. How old must a person be to become a member of the Senate?

# VISIT

# THE SOUTH CAROLINA STATE HOUSE

## Get Ready

Columbia is the second city in South Carolina to serve as the state capital. The capital moved here from Charleston in 1790.

The present-day State House building was started in 1851, but not finished until 1900. It is built out of granite stone found only two miles away. The park around the State House has 25 statues and monuments to our state's history.

### Locate It
South Carolina

Columbia

## What to See

A statue of our country's first president, George Washington, stands outside the north entrance.

At the top of this stained glass window you can see the front of the state seal. The Latin words mean "Prepared in Mind and Resources."

Inside the State House you can look up and see this beautiful dome.

The desk at the front of the Senate Chamber is old and valuable. The state seal is on the front. It was carved by hand.

## Take a Field Trip

**A VIRTUAL TOUR**
Visit The Learning Site at www.harcourtschool.com to take virtual tours of other sites in South Carolina.

Unit 1 • 61

# Unit 1
# Review and Test Preparation

## Use Vocabulary

Read the sentences below. Look at each group of underlined words. Choose a word from the box to replace them.

> history (p. 10)
> citizen (p. 13)
> landforms (p. 26)
> harbor (p. 27)
> fall line (p. 29)
> immigrant (p. 38)
> constitution (p. 50)
> taxes (p. 53)

**1** Greg's aunt is a person who came from another country to live in South Carolina.

**2** Charleston, South Carolina, has a protected place with deep water where large ships can come close to shore.

**3** The story of what has happened in a place is one of the social studies.

**4** A long, low cliff forms a natural boundary between the Sandhills and the Piedmont.

**5** Different physical regions have different shapes on the land.

**6** Our state uses money from citizens to pay for public services.

**7** A person who lives in and belongs to a community is a member of the community.

**8** South Carolina has its own written plan for government.

## Recall Facts

Answer these questions.

**9** On which continent is South Carolina? In which two hemispheres would you find it?

**10** What are the main jobs of each branch of South Carolina's government?

**11** How many justices are on the State Supreme Court?

Write the letter of the best choice.

**12** The study of Earth's features is called—
 A social studies.
 B economics.
 C geography.
 D government.

**13** South Carolina has six physical regions. The region closest to the Atlantic Ocean is the—
 F Piedmont.
 G Coastal Zone.
 H Sandhills.
 J Outer Coastal Plain.

## Landform Map of the South

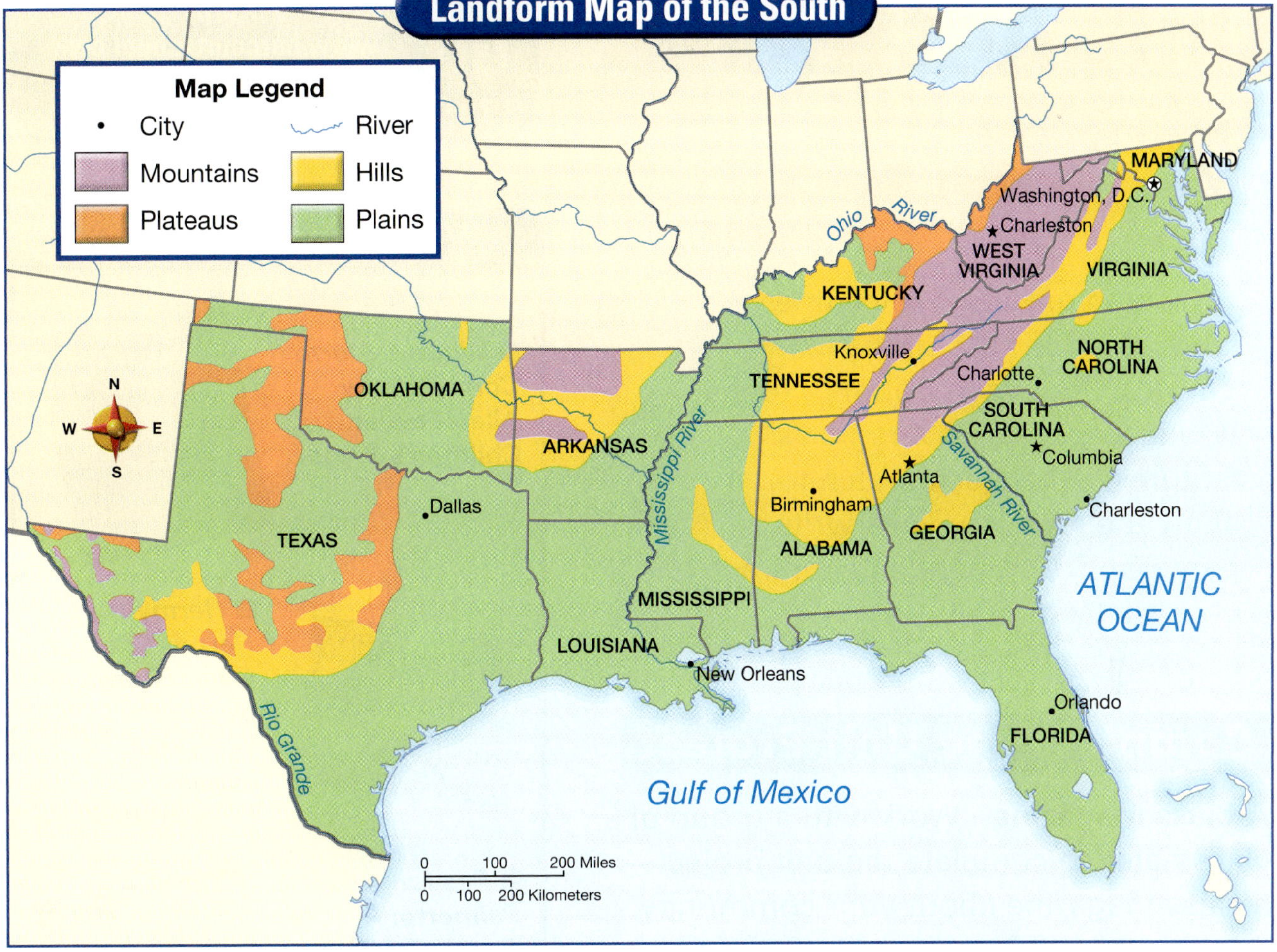

**Map Legend**
- City
- River
- Mountains
- Hills
- Plateaus
- Plains

---

14. The South Carolina government makes laws for all the people in—
    A South Carolina.
    B the South.
    C Washington, D.C.
    D the United States.

## Think Critically

15. What are three places in South Carolina where people go to enjoy themselves?

16. Why is it important for people to be responsible citizens?

## Apply Skills

**Read a Landform Map**
Answer the following questions. Use the landform map on this page to help you.

17. Which city is on higher ground, Charleston, West Virginia, or Charleston, South Carolina?

18. What landforms are found in Georgia?

19. Through which landform does the Mississippi River flow?

20. Which states in the South do not have mountains?

Unit 1 ■ 63

# Unit Activities

 Visit The Learning Site at www.harcourtschool.com for additional activities.

### Sketch South Carolina Landscapes

Work in groups. Sketch one landscape for each of the six physical regions in South Carolina. A landscape shows a region's features. Label each sketch to show the features. Then write a paragraph. Compare and contrast your six landscapes.

## Complete the Unit Project

**A Class Magazine** Work with a group of classmates to complete the unit project— a class magazine about your community. Decide which events and people you want to include in your magazine. Then write short paragraphs about them. Make maps, drawings, and charts for your magazine. You and the members of your group can take turns reading your items aloud to the other groups.

### Visit Your Library

■ *When a Storm Comes Up* by Allan Fowler. Children's Press.

■ *Hermy the Hermit Crab Goes Shopping* by Andrea Weathers. Legacy Publications.

■ *P is for Palmetto: A South Carolina Alphabet* by Carol Crane. Sleeping Bear Press.

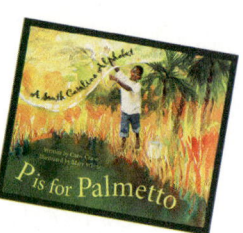

# South Carolina Long Ago

Santa Elena Pottery, 1500s

Falls Creek Falls, South Carolina

# Unit 2

# South Carolina Long Ago

 **One of the most delightful countries in the Universe**

—Jean Pierre Purry, 1720s

## Preview the Content

Think of what you know about life in our state long ago. Then create a K-W-L chart like the one below. In the first column, write what you know about South Carolina long ago. In the second column, write what you want to know. When you have finished reading this unit, write in the last column what you learned.

### K-W-L Chart

| What I Know | What I Want to Know | What I Learned |
|---|---|---|
| | | |

Unit 2 ■ 65

# Unit 2 Preview

## Carolina, 1670

## Preview

The Catawba lived near the Catawba River. p. 75

The Cherokee lived in the Piedmont and Blue Ridge. p. 82

The Cusabo lived by the Ashley and Savannah rivers. p. 90

## Native Americans of South Carolina

| Tribe | Population |
|---|---|
| Catawba | ▪ |
| Cherokee | ▪▪▪▪▪▪▪▪▪▪ |
| Cusabo | ▪ |

▪ = 5,000 people

## Native American Language Groups in South Carolina

| Language Family | Number |
|---|---|
| Iroquian | ⌂ |
| Muskogean | ⌂⌂⌂⌂⌂⌂⌂⌂⌂⌂⌂⌂⌂⌂⌂⌂⌂⌂ |
| Siouan | ⌂⌂⌂⌂⌂⌂⌂⌂⌂⌂⌂⌂⌂ |

⌂ = 1 tribe

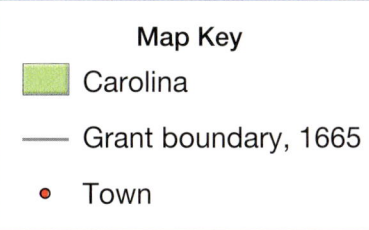

**Map Key**
- Carolina
- Grant boundary, 1665
- Town

**King Charles II signs a charter for the Carolina colony.** p. 120

**African slaves arrive at Charles Town.** p. 122

**Charles Town moves to Oyster Point.** p. 123

**START with a STORY**

# THE GREAT BALL GAME:
## A MUSKOGEE STORY

by Joseph Bruchac – illustrated by Susan L. Roth

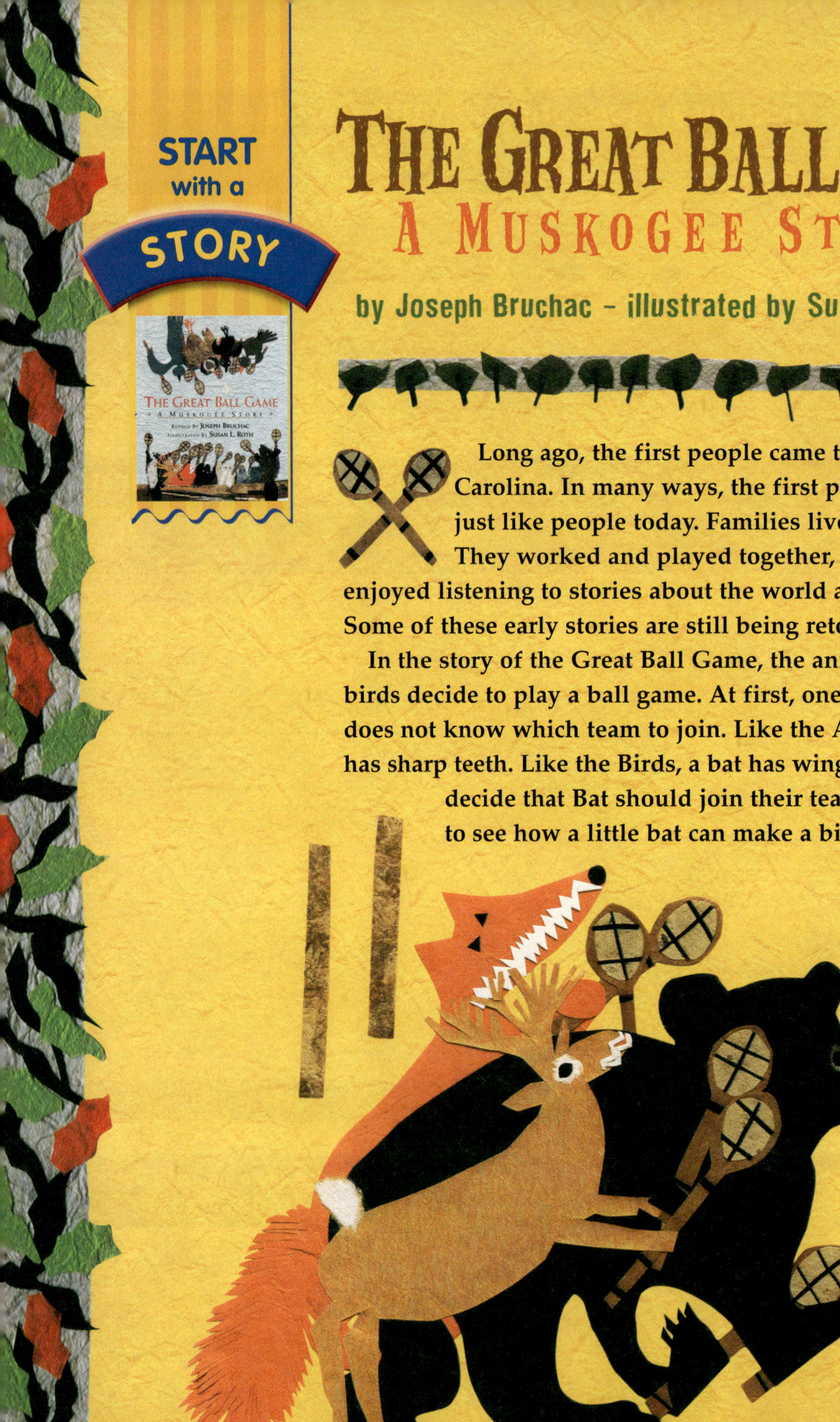

Long ago, the first people came to South Carolina. In many ways, the first people were just like people today. Families lived together. They worked and played together, too. People enjoyed listening to stories about the world around them. Some of these early stories are still being retold today.

In the story of the Great Ball Game, the animals and the birds decide to play a ball game. At first, one tiny player does not know which team to join. Like the Animals, a bat has sharp teeth. Like the Birds, a bat has wings. The Animals decide that Bat should join their team. Read now to see how a little bat can make a big difference.

**T**wo poles were set up as the goalposts at each end of the field. Then the game began.

Each team played hard. On the Animals' side Fox and Deer were swift runners, and Bear cleared the way for them as they played. Crane and Hawk, though, were even swifter, and they stole the ball each time before the Animals could reach their goal.

Soon it became clear that the Birds had the advantage. Whenever they got the ball, they would fly up into the air and the Animals could not reach them. The Animals guarded their goal well, but they grew tired as the sun began to set.

Just as the sun sank below the horizon, Crane took the ball and flew toward the poles. Bear tried to stop him, but stumbled in the dim light and fell. It seemed as if the Birds would surely win.

Suddenly a small dark shape flew onto the field and stole the ball from Crane just as he was about to reach the poles. It was Bat. He darted from side to side across the field, for he did not need light to find his way. None of the Birds could catch him or block him.

Holding the ball, Bat flew right between the poles at the other end! The Animals had won!

This is how Bat came to be accepted as an Animal. He was allowed to set the penalty for the Birds.

"You Birds," Bat said, "must leave this land for half of each year."

So it is that the Birds fly south each winter. . . .

And every day at dusk Bat still comes flying to see if the Animals need him to play ball.

## Think About It

1. What penalty was given to the losing team?

2. Today, many people enjoy playing on a team. Draw a picture of a team game that you have played.

### Read a Book

### Start the Unit Project

**Make a Museum** Make a classroom museum about South Carolina's people long ago. Choose a topic, such as art, technology, or history. As you read the unit, list important people, places, and events related to your topic. Your list will help you create a museum that will be displayed in your classroom.

### Use Technology

Visit The Learning Site at **www.harcourtschool.com** for additional activities, primary sources, and other resources to use in this unit.

Unit 2 • 71

### Yap Ye Iswa (Day of the Catawba)

This annual cultural festival in Rock Hill, South Carolina, celebrates the Catawba culture. The event offers traditional drumming and dances. Artists display Catawba pottery, beadwork, and baskets. Visitors can enjoy special foods.

**LOCATE IT**

Rock Hill, SOUTH CAROLINA

# Chapter 3

# Early Peoples

❝ Our culture and language are still vibrant and living. ❞

—Dr. Wenonah Haire, Catawba Cultural Preservation Project Director

## Compare and Contrast

When you **compare and contrast** people, places, ideas, or events, you think about how they are alike and how they are different. In this chapter, you will read about the first people who lived in South Carolina.

**As you read, do the following.**

- Look for ways in which groups of early people are alike.
- Look for ways in which they are different.

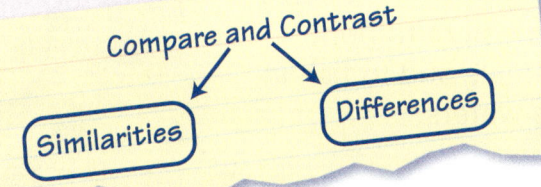

Chapter 3 • 73

# Lesson 1

# People of the River

**Big Idea**
Native Americans were the first people in South Carolina.

### Vocabulary
river system
climate
tribe
language group
agriculture
tradition
council
trade
dugout

Long ago, Native Americans were the only people who lived here. Many rivers in South Carolina are named for Native American words and peoples.

## A Good Place to Live

Early people lived near rivers, where they found food and water. They also traveled on the rivers.

When small rivers and streams flow into larger ones, they make up a **river system**. Early people used river systems much as we use highways today.

South Carolina's main river systems are the Pee Dee, Santee, Savannah, and Edisto. These rivers and the mostly mild climate make South Carolina a good place to live. **Climate** is the weather in a place over time.

**Review** What are South Carolina's main river systems?

**FAST FACT** People have lived in South Carolina for more than 10,000 years. Early people probably came here to hunt animals and to fish in the waters.

74 • Unit 2

## The Catawba

Like other rivers in our state, the Catawba River is named for an early people who lived nearby. They called themselves "the people of the river." Today, they are known as the Catawba tribe. A **tribe** is a group of related people who share a way of life. Members of a tribe speak the same language, too.

The Catawba belonged to the Siouan (SOO•uhn) **language group**. A language group is made up of people who speak similar languages. The Catawba were the largest group of Siouan speakers in South Carolina. The Catawba tribe had about 5,000 people.

**Review** How is a tribe like a family?

**COMPARE AND CONTRAST**

### Two Language Groups

| English Speakers | Siouan Speakers |
|---|---|
| England | Catawba |
| United States | Cheraw |
| Australia | Congaree |
| Canada | Pee Dee |
| Ireland | Sugeree |
| Scotland | Waccamaw |

**Analyze Tables** Many groups of people speak English. Long ago, many Native American tribes spoke Siouan.

◆ Which language did the Catawba speak?

Chapter 3 ■ 75

Catawba of South Carolina

# Village Life

The Catawba lived in small villages enclosed by tall wooden walls for safety. The Catawba leaders met in a meetinghouse big enough to hold all the people. Games or dances took place in an open space in the village.

Both men and women supplied food. Men fished in the rivers and hunted deer and other animals. Women worked in **agriculture**, the raising of crops and farm animals. They grew corn, beans, gourds, and squash.

The Catawba wore clothing made of deerskins. Men wore leggings and shirts. Women wore skirts and shawls.

**Review** Which crops were part of Catawba agriculture?

**Location** The Catawba lived near rivers, which provided them with plenty of fish and water.

❓ Which rivers did the Catawba use?

Villages had 5 to 15 roundhouses made of bent poles covered with bark. Large families lived in each roundhouse.

## Traditions

Like people today, the Catawba had many traditions. A **tradition** is a custom or way of doing something that is passed on by families to their children. One Catawba tradition was pottery making.

Everyone in a Catawba village helped make clay pottery. Men and boys gathered clay from the riverbank. Women and girls shaped it into pots, jars, and other items.

Catawba potters used a special stone to smooth the clay. It was important to use this traditional tool. Sometimes a rubbing stone was passed down in a family for many years.

**Review** What makes Catawba pottery a tradition?

### A Closer Look
### Making Pottery

Catawba people in South Carolina used clay to make bowls, jars, and other items.

1. Mix crushed rock into the clay to make it stronger.
2. Shape the clay into bowls, jugs, or cooking pots.
3. Smooth and decorate the pottery.
4. Place the pottery in a fire to make it hard and ready to use.

Why were the clay shapes put into a fire?

## Democratic Values
### Government

The Catawba chose a few people to represent, or speak and act for, them. The representatives formed a council. The council made laws for the village.

Today, citizens of South Carolina choose people to represent them in government. Voters choose representatives who make laws for our state.

**Analyze the Value**

1. How do representatives help people?
2. Why do large groups need representatives?
3. **Make It Relevant** Use the library or the Internet to find the name of your representative in the General Assembly. Write a letter to your representative, telling your ideas about voting. Share your letter with the class.

## Government

In some ways, Catawba government was like South Carolina's government. Each Catawba village had a leader, or chief, like our governor. Both men and women could serve as chief.

Each Catawba village had a council. A **council** is a group of people who make laws. South Carolina has a General Assembly that also makes laws.

The chief and the council met in the meetinghouse. They decided what was best for the people. All villagers could come to the meetings. However, the chief and council made the final choices.

**Review** How was Catawba government like our state government?

**COMPARE AND CONTRAST**

## Economics

The Catawba traveled and moved goods by water. They used the rivers to **trade**, or exchange one thing for another. Trading helped the Catawba get things they could not make or find nearby.

To make travel by water easier, the Catawba made dugouts. A **dugout** is a boat made from a log hollowed out by burning and scraping the wood. The Catawba shaped the inside of the dugout with sharp stones.

Some places could not be reached by dugouts. Catawba traders used trading paths to reach neighbors over land. Some of those paths are South Carolina's roads today.

The Catawba traded many things such as these beads.

**Review** How were rivers important to Catawba trade?

A dugout is an early kind of canoe.

## LESSON 1 Review

 **Compare and Contrast** How was the Catawba council like today's General Assembly? How was it different?

**1 Big Idea** Who were the first people who lived in South Carolina?

**2 Vocabulary** Write a sentence using the word **agriculture**.

**3 Economics** How did Catawba people get things they could not make or find?

 **Performance—Write a Scene** Work with a partner to write a scene about Catawba culture. You might choose a scene showing farming or making a dugout. Then role-play the scene for your classmates.

Chapter 3 ■ 79

# Skills · Map and Globe

# Find Intermediate Directions

**Vocabulary**

intermediate directions

### ▶ Why It Matters

You can use directions to find where something is. There are four cardinal directions. They are north, south, east, and west. Between the cardinal directions, there are **intermediate directions**. The intermediate directions are northeast, southeast, northwest, and southwest. They tell more exactly where a place is.

### ▶ What You Need to Know

A compass rose can show both kinds of directions. Notice that each intermediate direction is halfway between two cardinal directions. For example, southeast (SE) is halfway between south and east.

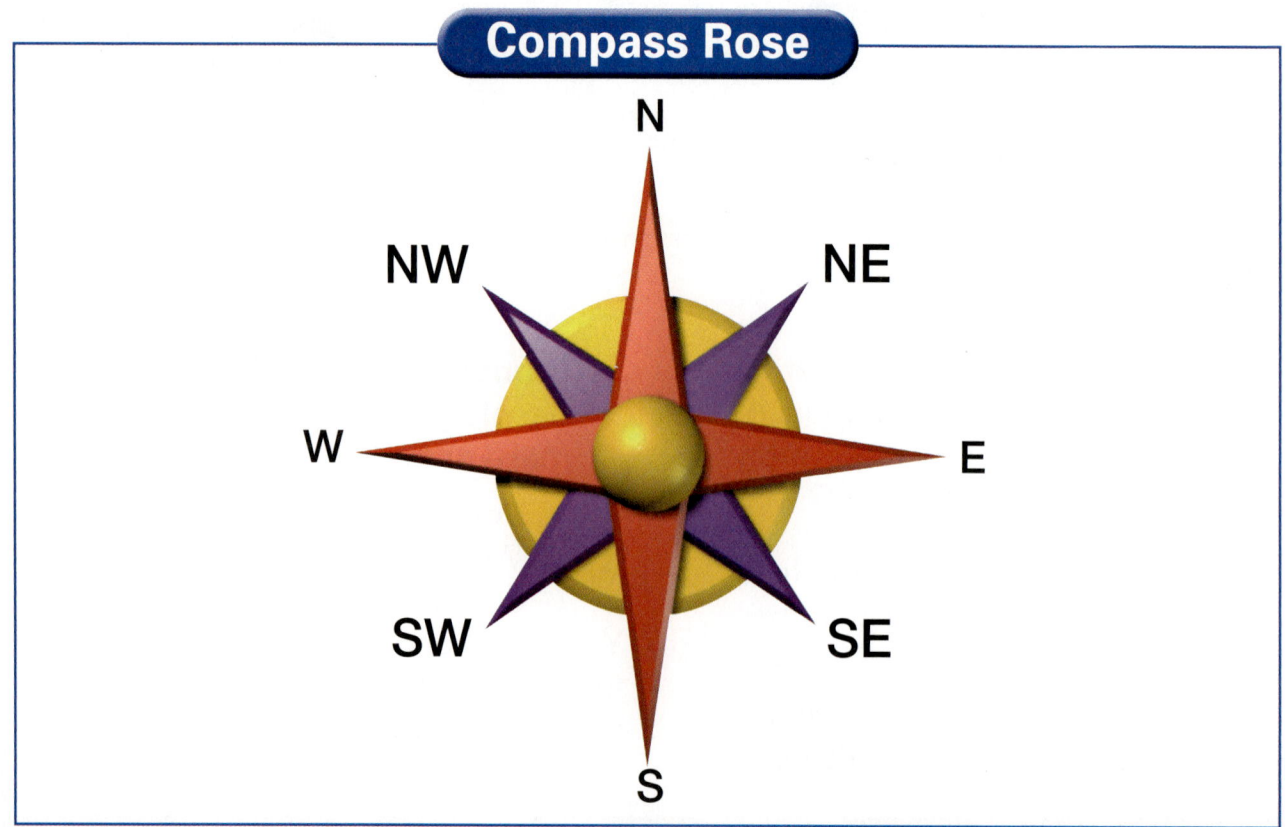

**Compass Rose**

## South Carolina and Intermediate Directions

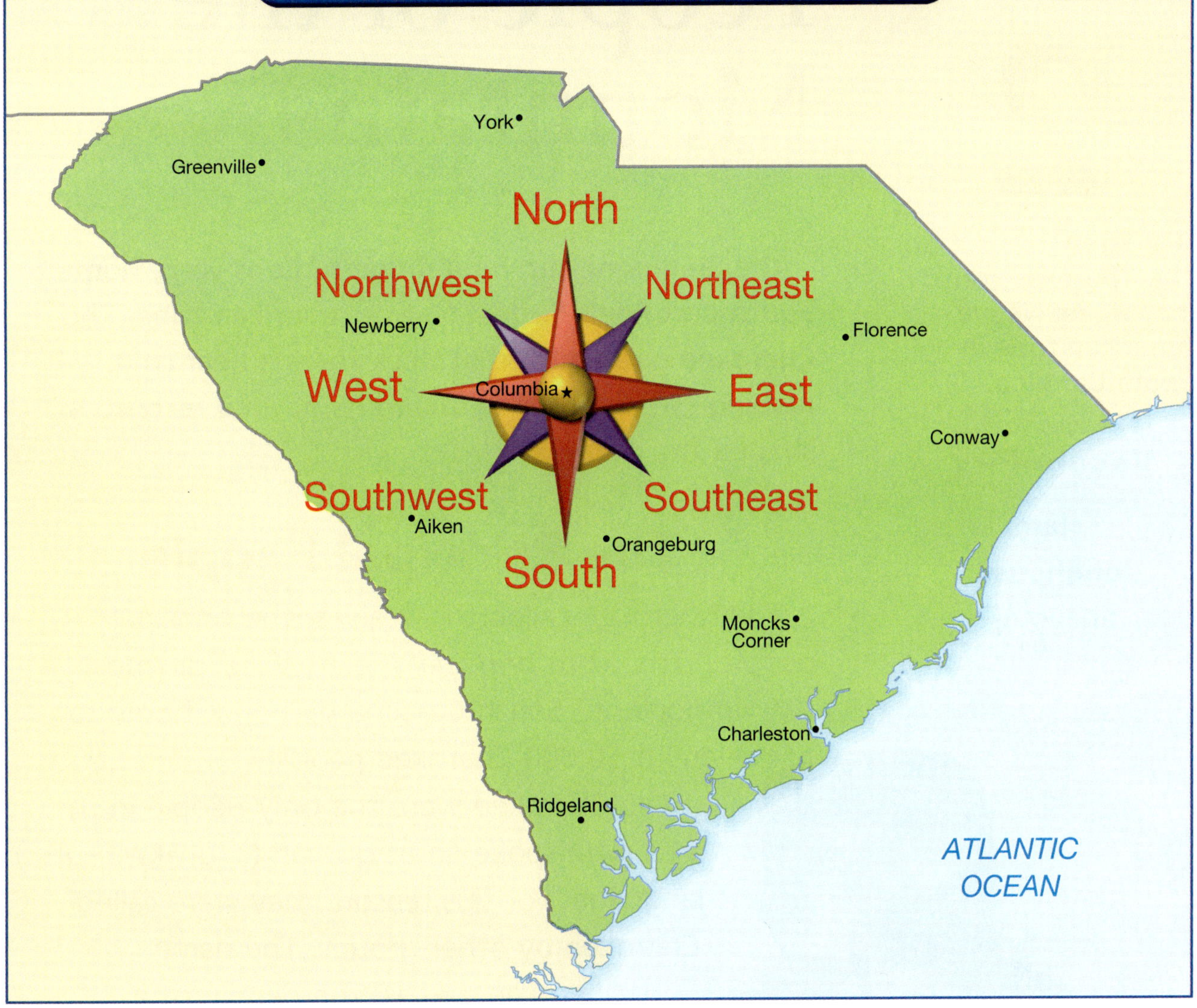

### Practice the Skill

Use the compass rose on the map to help you answer the questions below.

1. Is Greenville northwest or northeast of Aiken?
2. To travel from Orangeburg to Florence, in which direction would you go?
3. To get from Moncks Corner to Newberry, you must travel in which direction?

### Apply What You Learned

Make a chart with four columns. Write one of the intermediate directions at the top of each column. Find objects in your classroom in each direction. Write each object in the correct column.

 Practice your map and globe skills with the **GeoSkills CD-ROM**.

## Lesson 2

# People of the Mountains

**Big Idea**
The Cherokee were the largest Native American tribe in South Carolina.

**Vocabulary**

clan
longhouse
ancestor

The Piedmont and Blue Ridge regions were home to South Carolina's largest Native American tribe. The Cherokee people lived in thick forests near cold, rushing streams. The land and its natural resources shaped their way of life.

### The Principal People

The Cherokee called themselves "the principal people." The word *principal* means "first" or "most important." South Carolina was once home to about 50,000 Cherokee people.

The Cherokee were the only people in the area who spoke an Iroquoian (ir•uh•KWOI•uhn) language. For this reason, they were called Cherokee by other groups. The name *Cherokee* means "the people of a different speech."

**Review** How many Cherokee once lived in South Carolina?

This Cherokee woman today, makes pottery in the same way the early Cherokee people did.

This is a copy of a Cherokee longhouse. Many longhouses were grouped together in a village.

## Cherokee Families

The Cherokee had seven clans. A **clan** is a large group of related families. Clan members lived together in fenced villages of 400 to 500 people.

Cherokee families lived in the 30 to 60 longhouses found in each village. A **longhouse** is a long, narrow building with a curved roof.

The longhouses belonged to women. When a man married, he went to live with his wife's family. There were separate living spaces in each longhouse. The parents lived in one space. Each married daughter had her own living space.

**Review** What is a clan?

**Cherokee of South Carolina**

Map Key
Cherokee lands

 **Location** The map shows that Cherokee lands were only a small part of South Carolina.

❓ In which part of South Carolina did the Cherokee live?

Chapter 3 ■ 83

# Cherokee Ways

Agriculture was more important to the Cherokee people than it was to the Catawba. The Cherokee lived in forests and ate less fish. Their main foods came from farming. They grew beans, corn, and squash.

Children helped their mothers gather wild plants, berries, and nuts. The men hunted deer and bear, and they fished in streams.

The Cherokee celebrated six main festivals. One of the most important was the Green Corn Ceremony. It was celebrated when the first corn ripened each year.

**Review** How was agriculture different for the Cherokee and the Catawba?

**COMPARE AND CONTRAST**

Beans, corn, and squash were called "the three sisters" because they were planted closely together.

## The Village Center

Cherokee **ancestors**, or early family members, probably built the mounds. Many village activities happened around the mounds. The council house, the largest building in the village, was located near the mounds.

In most villages, events took place in the central square, or open area. Here, young people played "chunkey" by throwing spears at a rolling, wheel-shaped stone.

Cherokee people also played stickball, with rules and equipment like the present-day game of lacrosse. The game of stickball was used to settle differences. Games of all kinds were played during festival times.

**Review** What games did the Cherokee play?

Cherokee people today play stickball as they did long ago.

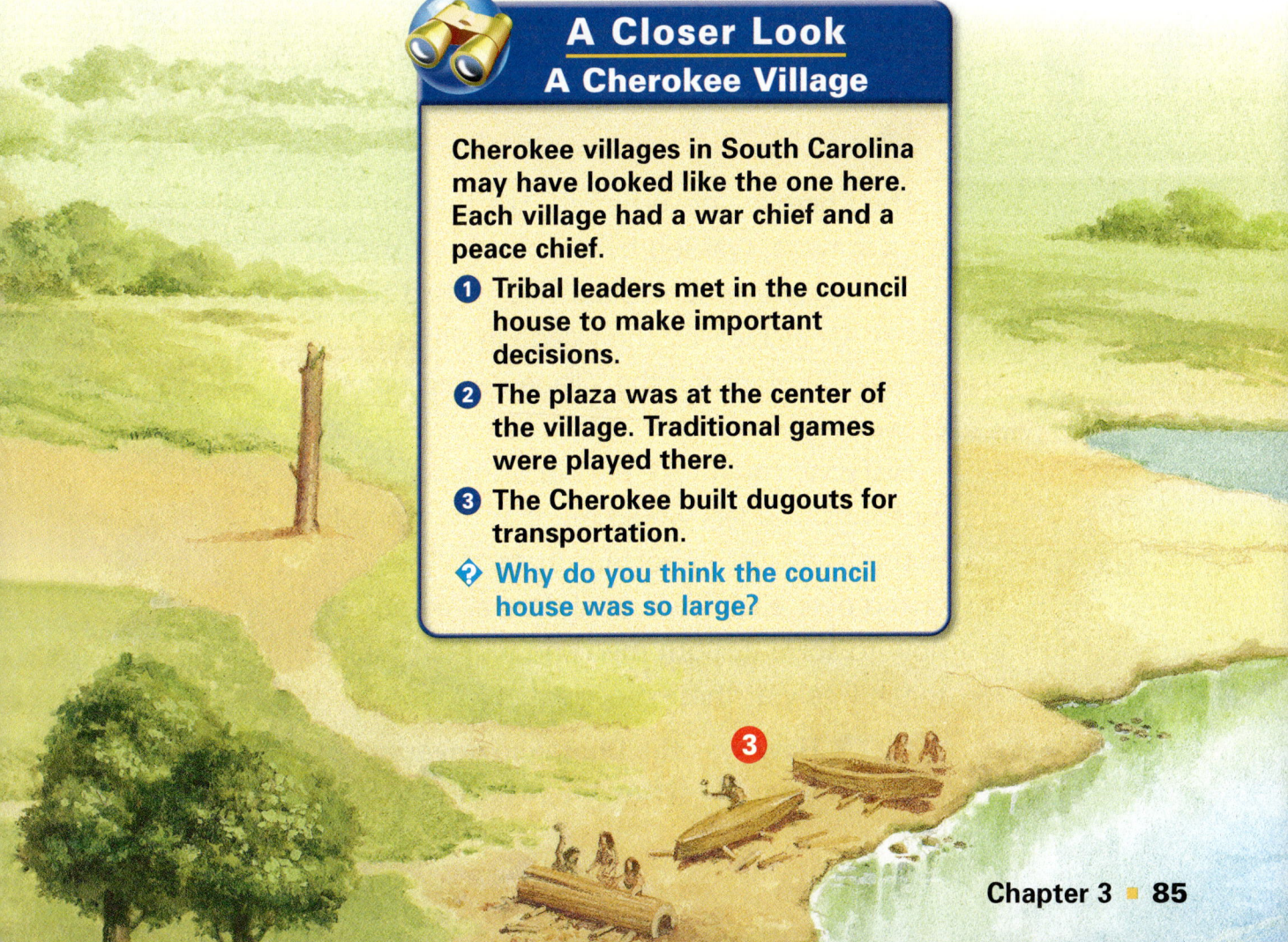

### A Closer Look
### A Cherokee Village

Cherokee villages in South Carolina may have looked like the one here. Each village had a war chief and a peace chief.

1. Tribal leaders met in the council house to make important decisions.
2. The plaza was at the center of the village. Traditional games were played there.
3. The Cherokee built dugouts for transportation.

**Why do you think the council house was so large?**

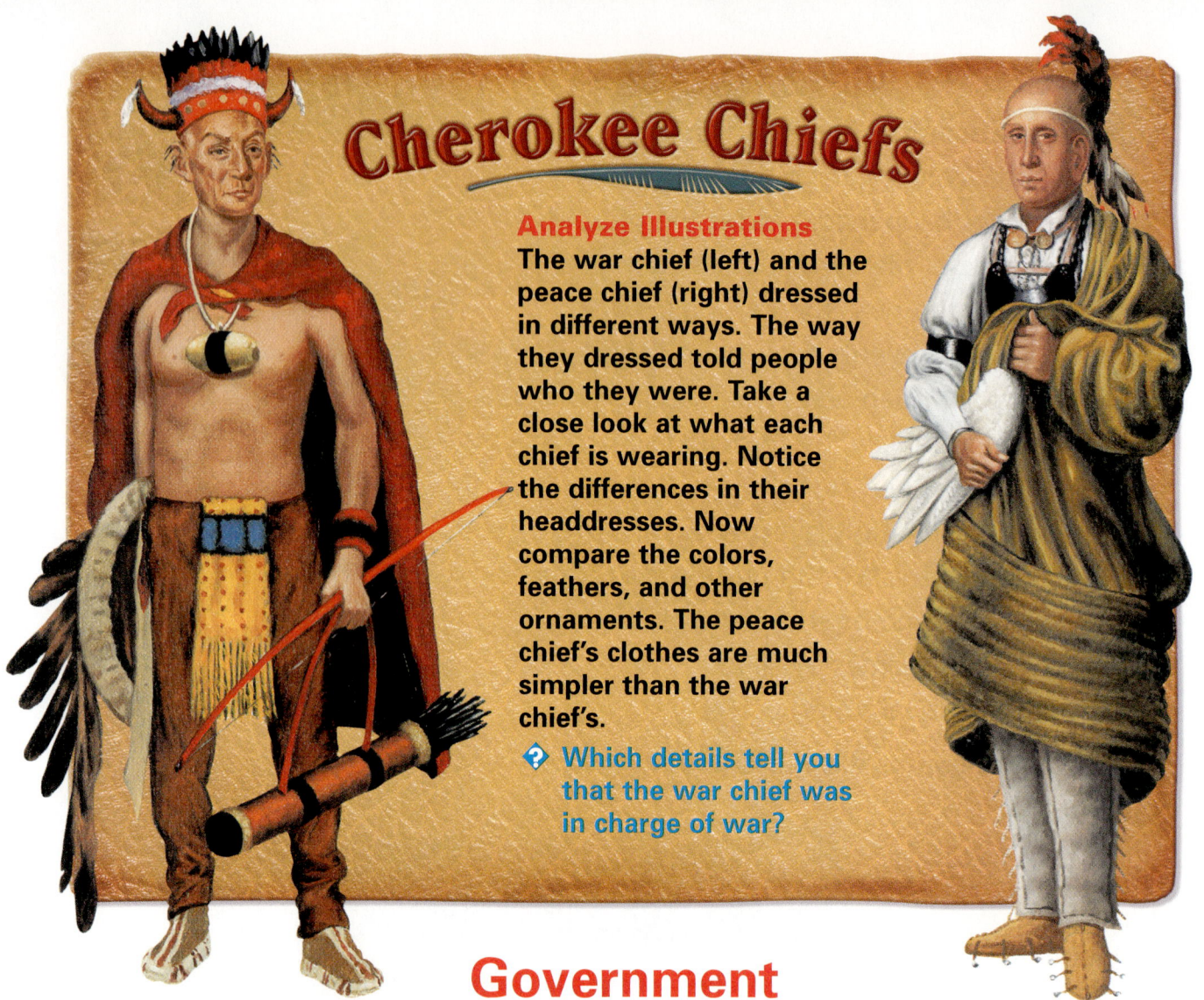

# Cherokee Chiefs

**Analyze Illustrations**
The war chief (left) and the peace chief (right) dressed in different ways. The way they dressed told people who they were. Take a close look at what each chief is wearing. Notice the differences in their headdresses. Now compare the colors, feathers, and other ornaments. The peace chief's clothes are much simpler than the war chief's.

❓ Which details tell you that the war chief was in charge of war?

## Government

The Cherokee government, like that of the Catawba, was led by the chief and the council. However, Cherokee villages had two chiefs. One chief led the village in times of peace, the other led the village during times of war.

Everyone could take part in council meetings. Leaders would meet in the council house to discuss important matters. They talked over each issue until they all agreed on how to solve it. Both men and women could speak freely at these meetings.

**Review** How was the Cherokee government different from the Catawba government?
🍊 **COMPARE AND CONTRAST**

## Economics

Much like the Catawba, the Cherokee people used trade to get the things they needed. Cherokee traders were known to travel great distances. They would trade deerskin leather, foods, and crafts such as baskets and pottery.

The Cherokee traveled both on footpaths and on the rivers. People who lived on higher lands usually walked. Those who lived near rivers made dugouts. Some of the dugouts were very large. They could carry as many as 15 people at one time.

**Review** Why did the Cherokee who lived near rivers make dugouts?

Native American Trading Paths

**Movement** Many Native American footpaths were well traveled.

→ Which direction would a Cherokee travel to reach the area near Charleston?

## LESSON 2
### Review

**Compare and Contrast** How was the war chief different from the peace chief?

**1 Big Idea** Why did the Cherokee call themselves "the principal people"?

**2 Vocabulary** Write a paragraph describing a **longhouse**.

**3 Civics and Government** How did the Cherokee council settle important matters?

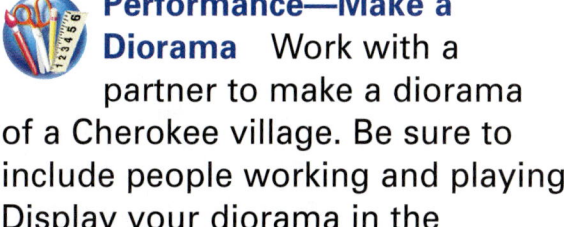

**Performance—Make a Diorama** Work with a partner to make a diorama of a Cherokee village. Be sure to include people working and playing. Display your diorama in the classroom.

Chapter 3 ■ 87

# Skills: Use a Cultural Map

**Vocabulary**
cultural region

## ▶ Why It Matters

You are learning about Native Americans in South Carolina. To know just where they lived, you can use a cultural map. A cultural map shows **cultural regions**. These are areas where people have the same ways of life.

People in a cultural region speak similar languages. They often share beliefs, customs, and traditions, too. Knowing how to read a cultural map can help you understand where different cultural groups lived.

## ▶ What You Need to Know

Look at the map on page 89. It shows where different cultural groups lived in South Carolina.

Each color on the map stands for a different cultural region. Labels show the tribes belonging to each culture. You can look at the map to see where different tribes lived. You can also see which cultural group a tribe belonged to and who its neighbors were.

Native Americans today celebrate their heritage. There are about 25,000 South Carolinians with Native American ancestors.

## Native American Cultural Regions

*Map showing South Carolina with Native American tribes:*

- **Iroquoian** (yellow): CHEROKEE
- **Siouan** (pink): KEYAUWEE, CATAWBA, SUGEREE, WAXHAW, CHERAW, WATEREE, WACCAMAW, PEE DEE
- **Muskogean** (green): CONGAREE, SANTEE, WINYAH, WANDO, SEWEE, KIAWAH, ETIWAN, COOSA, EDISTO, ASHEPOO, STONO, COMBAHEE, WIMBEE, ESCAMACU

ATLANTIC OCEAN

Map Key:
- Iroquoian
- Muskogean
- Siouan

## Practice the Skill

Use the cultural map to answer these questions.

1. What three cultural regions does the map show?
2. What color is used to show Muskogean tribes?
3. Which culture includes the Catawba?
4. Which culture lived in the northwest?

## Apply What You Learned

Make a three-column table of South Carolina's Native American groups. Label the columns *Siouan*, *Iroquoian*, and *Muskogean*. Use the map to find tribes within each group. Then list each tribe in the correct column. Color your table to match the map key. Share your table with a classmate.

Practice your map and globe skills with the **GeoSkills CD-ROM**.

Chapter 3 ■ 89

# Lesson 3

# People of the Lowcountry

**Big Idea**
Smaller tribes worked together for protection and to trade.

**Vocabulary**

permanent
weir
confederation

Early people in South Carolina's lowcountry lived on the islands and coastal lands. They used resources from the beaches, swamps, and bodies of water to live. The Cusabo (koos•AH•boh) people once called this area their home.

## The Cusabo

The Cusabo were a group of tribes that shared a culture. They lived between present-day Charleston and the Savannah River. They spoke a Muskogean (muh•SKOH•gee•uhn) language. There were about ten tribes in the lowcountry. Together, they had only about 3,200 people.

The Cusabo lived in fenced villages of 10 to 100 houses. Cusabo houses were round and built of bent poles covered with bark. Holes in the walls were filled with clay or moss. This helped keep the homes warm in winter and cool in summer.

During the summer, the Cusabo caught a variety of freshwater fish from nearby rivers.

90 ■ Unit 2

Unlike the villages of the Cherokee, Cusabo villages were not **permanent**, or built to be long-lasting. Cusabo tribes lived inland most of the year. Then, in summer, they moved their villages closer to the ocean.

Each village had a council house for meetings. The village also had an open space. This was where the Cusabo played ball games. They held dance ceremonies there, too.

**Review** How was the Cusabo house like that of the Catawba? COMPARE AND CONTRAST

## • HERITAGE •

### Native American Place-Names

South Carolina has many places with Native American names.
- **Cherokee Falls** got its name from the people who lived in that area.
- Many rivers were named for tribes. They include the Edisto, Pee Dee, Santee, Congaree, and Catawba rivers.
- Towns with Native American names include Tamassee, Catawba, Cheraw, Congaree, Santee, and Yemassee.

Native American Places

Chapter 3 ■ 91

# Cusabo Ways

Fish were a main source of Cusabo food. Cusabo men taught boys to catch fish by using a weir (WIR). A **weir** is a fence or net that can be put across a river to trap fish.

The Cusabo tribes also hunted animals and grew crops. Their agriculture included corn, beans, and squash.

The Cusabo were skilled artists. They made fine pottery like that of the Catawba people. They used grasses and palmetto leaves to weave baskets. Some artists painted designs on animal skins.

**Review** What did the Cusabo use to catch fish?

**Basketweavers today use the same materials the Cusabo used long ago.**

## SCIENCE AND TECHNOLOGY

### Weirs

To catch fish, some Native American tribes made traps, called weirs. They stretched a weir across a stream at the point where the stream flowed into the sea. The incoming tide caused water to rise above the top of the weir. Fish would swim over the weir and enter the stream. When the tide went down, the fish were trapped inside the weir. Then the people could spear or net the fish.

92 ■ Unit 2

## Government

The Cusabo tribes sometimes needed protection from other tribes. They formed a confederation (kuhn•FEH•duh•ray•shun). A **confederation** is a group of tribes that agree to help one another. The Cusabo agreed to protect one another. By joining together, the tribes gained strength. They were better able to defend themselves against other tribes.

**Review** Why did the Cusabo form a confederation?

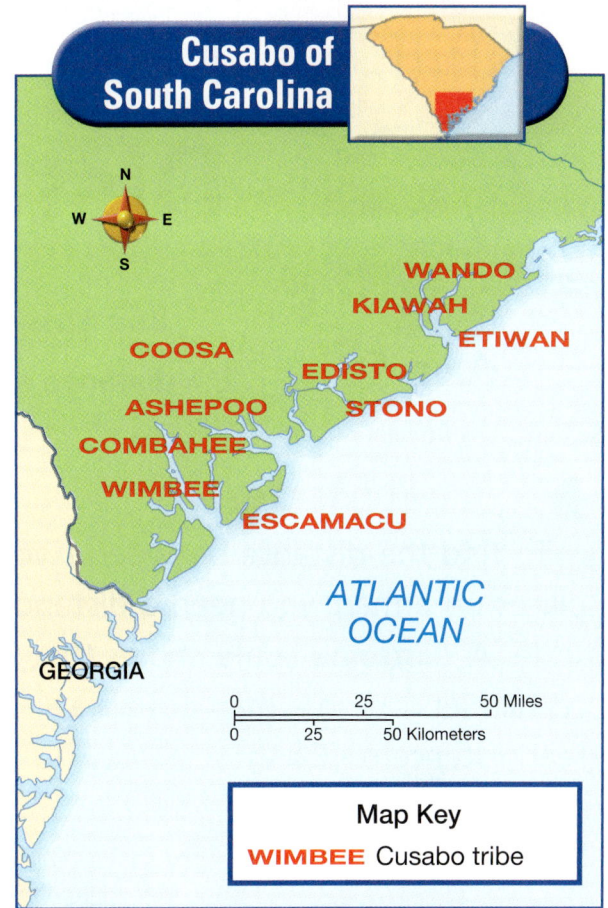

**Location** The Cusabo were a group of tribes that shared a culture.

❖ Which tribe lived farthest from the coast?

# LESSON 3 Review

 **Compare and Contrast** How were Cusabo villages different from those of the Cherokee?

❶ **Big Idea** Why did the Cusabo tribes form a confederation?

❷ **Vocabulary** Use the word **weir** in a sentence about Cusabo culture.

❸ **Civics and Government** How are a confederation and a council different?

 **Performance—Design a Symbol** Imagine that you are an artist in the Cusabo confederation. Think about your ways of life. Design a symbol to show what the confederation means to your people. You may want to use brown paper to represent an animal skin. Color your design, and display it in the classroom.

Chapter 3 ■ 93

# Skills: Use a Distance Scale

**Vocabulary**
distance scale

## ▶ Why It Matters

To find the distance between two places on a map, you need a distance scale. A **distance scale** shows that a certain length on a map equals a real distance on Earth.

## ▶ What You Need to Know

The map on page 95 shows five cities in South Carolina. It also shows the locations of five Native American tribes. People today live in many of the same areas as people long ago.

Look at the distance scale. The top part has the word *Miles*. The bottom part has the word *Kilometers*. Kilometers are another way of measuring distance. You can find distance with either kind of measure.

Use a ruler to measure the distance scale on the map. The scale is one inch long. Now read the number of miles on the distance scale. On this map, one inch stands for 50 miles. Two cities marked one inch apart on this map are really 50 miles apart.

A distance scale can help you understand distances on a map.

## South Carolina

[Map of South Carolina showing Native American tribes in 1670: Cherokee, Catawba, Congaree, Pee Dee, and Edisto, with present-day cities Greenville, Rock Hill, Columbia, Myrtle Beach, and Charleston. Bordered by North Carolina, Georgia, and the Atlantic Ocean.]

**Map Key**
- **PEE DEE** Native American tribe, 1670
- • Present-day city

## ▶ Practice the Skill

Use the map and distance scale to answer the questions.

1. In miles, what is the distance between the Congaree tribe and the Edisto tribe?
2. In miles, what is the distance between Greenville and Myrtle Beach?
3. About how many miles would a Cherokee trader travel to reach an Edisto village?

## ▶ Apply What You Learned

Use the map of South Carolina on page A14. Locate your community. Use the distance scale to find the distance between your community and two other cities. On a sheet of paper, write the cities you chose and the distances in miles.

Practice your map and globe skills with the **GeoSkills CD-ROM**.

Chapter 3 ■ 95

# Examine Primary Sources

## First Carolinians

The first people to live in South Carolina were Native Americans. We don't know much about these first Carolinians, because they did not leave written records. However, archaeologists have found many items that these early people used. Archaeologists are scientists who study artifacts left behind by people. The site where archaeologists work is called a *dig*.

Most of the items you see here are from the Mississippian culture. The people of this culture came to South Carolina by the year 1100.

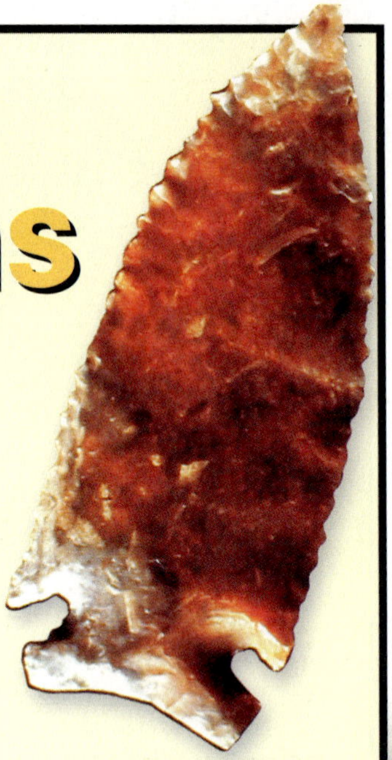

Early Carolinians made sharp points called arrowheads.

FROM THE ARCHAEOLOGICAL SOCIETY OF SOUTH

This piece of broken pottery shows a human face.

This stone tool may have been used for chopping.

Clay pots were used to cook and store food.

The first South Carolinians decorated this wall. Large stones shelter the painting.

## Analyze the Primary Source

1. Why do you think the pottery piece was decorated with a face?
2. What natural resources did early people use to make these artifacts?
3. Which of these artifacts are similar to items in use today? Which items are no longer in use?

### Activity

**Study an Artifact** Imagine you are an archaeologist. Look at the image of the stone tool. Write a paragraph telling your ideas about how it might have been used. Explain why you think there is a deep groove in the middle of the tool.

### Research

 Visit The Learning Site at www.harcourtschool.com to research other primary sources.

Chapter 3 ■ 97

# Chapter 3
# Review and Test Preparation

## Focus Skill: Compare and Contrast

Copy the following graphic organizer onto a separate sheet of paper. Use the information you have learned to compare and contrast early peoples in South Carolina.

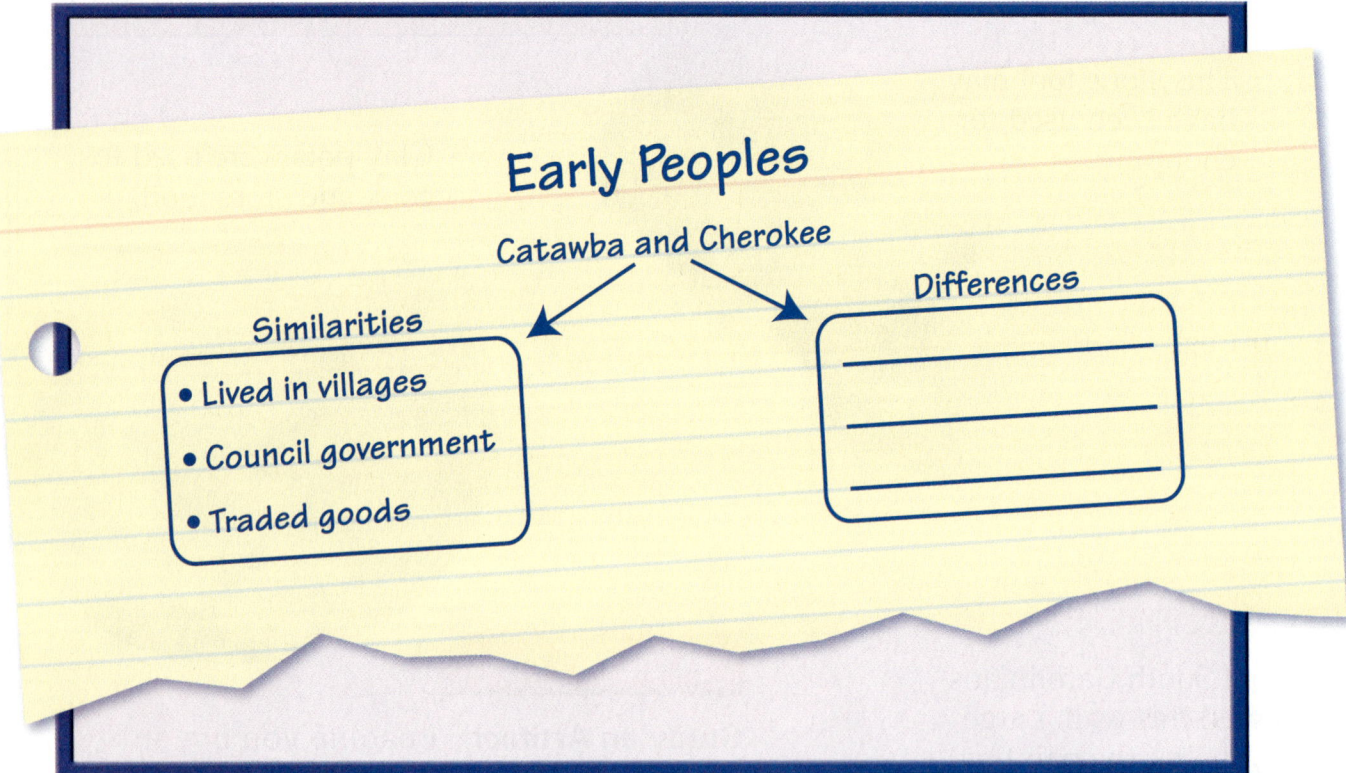

### Early Peoples
#### Catawba and Cherokee

**Similarities**
- Lived in villages
- Council government
- Traded goods

**Differences**

## THINK & WRITE

**Write a Short Story** Life in a Cherokee village was very busy. People grew crops, made pottery, and traded goods. Write a short story telling about a day in the life of a Cherokee person.

**Write Questions and Answers** Imagine you are visiting a child your age in a Cusabo village. Write a list of three questions you could ask. Then write answers that the Cusabo child might give.

98 ■ Unit 2

## Use Vocabulary

Write the correct term from the list to complete each sentence.

agriculture (p. 76)    clan (p. 83)
tradition (p. 77)      ancestor (p. 85)
council (p. 78)        confederation (p. 93)

1. The raising of crops, or ___, was important to the Cherokee people.

2. In Catawba villages, a ___ made decisions for the whole village.

3. The passing of rubbing stones from potter to potter was one Catawba ___.

4. The Cusabo formed a ___ to protect one another from other tribes.

5. An ___ is an early family member.

6. A large group of related families is called a ___.

## Recall Facts

Answer the questions.

7. What kind of climate does South Carolina have?

8. What crops did the Cherokee people grow?

9. Where did the Cusabo move their villages in summer?

10. Why did the Cherokee call themselves the principal people?

Write the letter of the best choice.

11. The Cusabo lived near the—
    A Blue Ridge Mountains.
    B fall line.
    C Catawba River.
    D Atlantic Ocean.

## Think Critically

12. Why were rivers important to early people?

13. Why do you think people keep traditions?

14. Why was trade so important to early Native Americans?

15. How did early people make use of natural resources?

## Apply Skills

**Find Intermediate Directions**

16. Use the map on page 81. Is Newberry northwest or northeast of Orangeburg?

**Use a Cultural Map**

17. Use the map on page 89. The Pee Dee were part of which culture?

**Use a Distance Scale**

18. Use the map on page 95. About how many miles is Greenville from Columbia?

### Boone Hall Plantation, Mt. Pleasant

These small brick houses were built about 300 years ago. Each year, many visitors come to Boone Hall Plantation to see how people lived long ago.

**LOCATE IT**

SOUTH CAROLINA

Mt. Pleasant

# Chapter 4

# Newcomers Arrive

> " The country is . . . full of . . . dainty brooks and rivers of running water . . . delightful forests . . . "
> 
> —Joseph I. Waring, 1970

## Generalize

When you **generalize,** you make a statement that groups facts or ideas. A generalization tells how the facts or ideas are related.

**As you read this chapter, make generalizations.**

- Collect ideas about new people in South Carolina.
- Make generalizations about why new people came to this land.

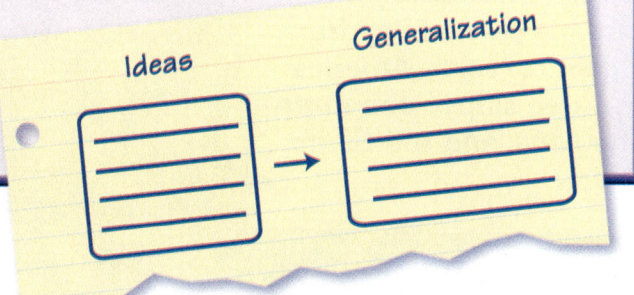

Chapter 4 ▪ 101

## Lesson 1

**Big Idea**
New people came looking for riches, lands, and honors.

**Vocabulary**
explorer
route
claim
religion
slave
settlement
settler
biography

# Cultures Meet

About 500 years ago, the famous Italian explorer Christopher Columbus sailed from Spain. An **explorer** is a person who goes to find out about a place.

Columbus thought he could sail west around the world to Asia. Instead, he reached a part of the world that Europeans did not know about. Today, we know these lands as North America and South America.

## Europeans Look West

Columbus was looking for a western route to the continent of Asia. A **route** is a path between one place and another. Columbus thought sailing west to Asia would be much faster than traveling east on land. He wanted to take Asian trade goods back to Spain.

**FAST FACT**
No one knows for sure where Columbus first landed. Some people think it was San Salvador Island, in the Caribbean Sea.

Christopher Columbus and his crew sailed from Spain to North America in three ships—the *Pinta*, the *Niña*, and the *Santa Maria*.

Columbus claimed the lands he visited for Spain. To **claim** something is to say it belongs to you. Soon ships from other European countries also sailed west. Most explorers hoped to find riches. Some wanted to tell Native Americans about their religions. A **religion** is a set of beliefs about a god or gods.

The explorers claimed new lands "for king and country." New lands brought honor to the explorers and their countries. Explorers helped make their kings very rich and powerful.

**Review** Why might a new route to Asia be important to other Europeans? **GENERALIZE**

## A Closer Look
### Early European Ships

Early ships used huge cloth sails to catch the wind. The wind helped the ships move more quickly through water. To steer the ship, sailors in the steerage room worked a long lever. The lever moved the ship's rudder. Sailors lived on the lower deck.

1. Mainmast
2. Quarterdeck
3. Upper deck
4. Steerage room
5. Lower deck
6. Storage

? How many levels are below the upper deck?

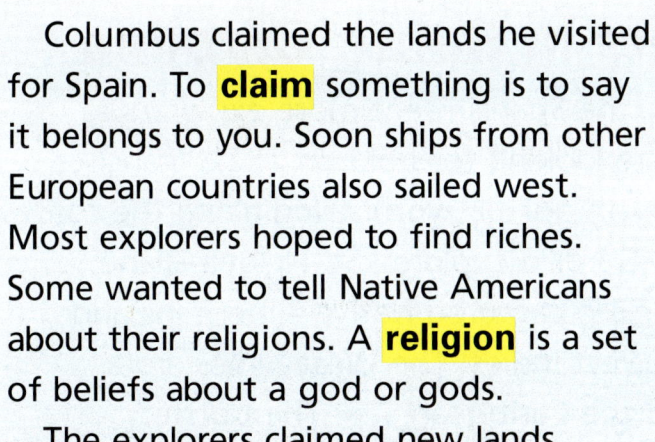

Chapter 4 ■ 103

# Explorers in South Carolina

After Columbus, the Spanish sent more explorers to the west. They were looking for gold. In 1521, Francisco Gordillo (fran•SEES•koh gor•DEE•yoh) sailed along the coast of South Carolina. Gordillo explored St. Helena Island.

While there, Gordillo captured Native Americans and took them to the West Indies. The West Indies are a group of islands in the Caribbean Sea. The Native Americans were to be used as slaves. A **slave** is a person kept against his or her wishes and made to work for no pay.

In 1526, the Spanish explorer Lucas Vásquez de Ayllón (VAS•keth day eye•LYON) sailed along the southern coast of North America. He explored lands near present-day Georgetown for a settlement. A **settlement** is a village built by the first people to live in a place.

De Ayllón and about 600 settlers tried to start a settlement. **Settlers** are the first people to live in a place. De Ayllón got sick and died within a few months. Other settlers died, too.

St. Helena Island is near Beaufort, South Carolina. St. Helena Island is made up of flat grasslands, salt marshes, and forests of pine, palmetto, and moss-covered oak trees.

LOCATE IT

SOUTH CAROLINA

St. Helena Island

**European explorers sometimes battled Native Americans.**

Soon, problems with neighboring Native American tribes led to war. One of the problems was disease. The explorers brought diseases that killed many Native Americans. The 150 settlers who were still alive after the war sailed back to the West Indies. The first European settlement in South Carolina had failed.

**Review** Why did de Ayllón's settlement in South Carolina fail?

## Exploring Inland

Most Europeans explored coastal lands. Hernando de Soto wanted to see lands that were away from the coast. In 1540, de Soto led a Spanish army of about 600 men. A few women traveled with them. The group traveled north from Florida on foot and on horseback. They were looking for gold and slaves.

De Soto's group traveled overland into South Carolina. They followed the Congaree River to a Catawba village near present-day Columbia. The village chief was a woman. She welcomed de Soto with gifts of pearls. De Soto called her "the Lady of Cofitachequi" (koh•fee•tah•CHAY•kwee).

**Review** How was de Soto treated by Native Americans he met? **GENERALIZE**

### · BIOGRAPHY ·

## Hernando de Soto   1500?–1542
### Character Trait: Perseverance

Hernando de Soto was a Spanish explorer. A **biography**, or life story, about de Soto shows he was a strong leader. After exploring in South America, he was the governor of the island of Cuba. For more than three years, de Soto explored North America, looking for riches. He did not find silver and gold. Yet, de Soto continued to explore the forests, rivers, and mountains in his search.

**MULTIMEDIA BIOGRAPHIES**
Visit The Learning Site at www.harcourtschool.com to learn about other famous people.

# Explorers in South Carolina

### Francisco Gordillo
**Location**
St. Helena Island
**Climate**
Average temperature 67 degrees. Average yearly rainfall 48 inches.
**Natural Resources**
marshes, forests, fish, mammals

### Lucas Vásquez de Ayllón
**Location**
Georgetown
**Climate**
Average temperature 65 degrees. Average yearly rainfall 52 inches.
**Natural Resources**
rivers, forests, fish, mammals

### Hernando de Soto
**Location**
Columbia
**Climate**
Average temperature 65 degrees. Average yearly rainfall 48 inches.
**Natural Resources**
rivers, forests, fish, mammals

**Analyze Tables** These three explorers went to three different parts of South Carolina.
- Which natural resource did Gordillo find that de Ayllón and de Soto did not find?

## LESSON 1 Review

 **Generalize** What does "for king and country" mean?

**1 Big Idea** Why did explorers first come to North America?

**2 Vocabulary** Write a sentence using the words **claim** and **explorer**.

**3 Geography** Where was de Ayllón's settlement?

 **Performance—Write a Journal Entry** Imagine that you are exploring with Hernando de Soto. Write a short journal entry telling about meeting the Catawba people.

# Skills: Follow Routes on a History Map

**Vocabulary**
history map

### ▶ Why It Matters

You have read about people from Europe exploring South Carolina. You can learn more by using a history map. A **history map** shows how a place looked in an earlier time.

A history map can show where an event, such as a battle, took place. It can show the journey of a traveler or routes used for trading.

### ▶ What You Need to Know

The title of a history map gives clues that can help you read it. The title often tells what the map is about. It may also tell when events shown on the map took place.

The map key tells you more. For example, the map on page 109 shows the routes of seven explorers. The map key gives their names. To find a route, check the color of the arrow beside an explorer's name. Then find the same color arrow on the map.

Ships like this one brought explorers to North America.

## Early European Explorers in South Carolina

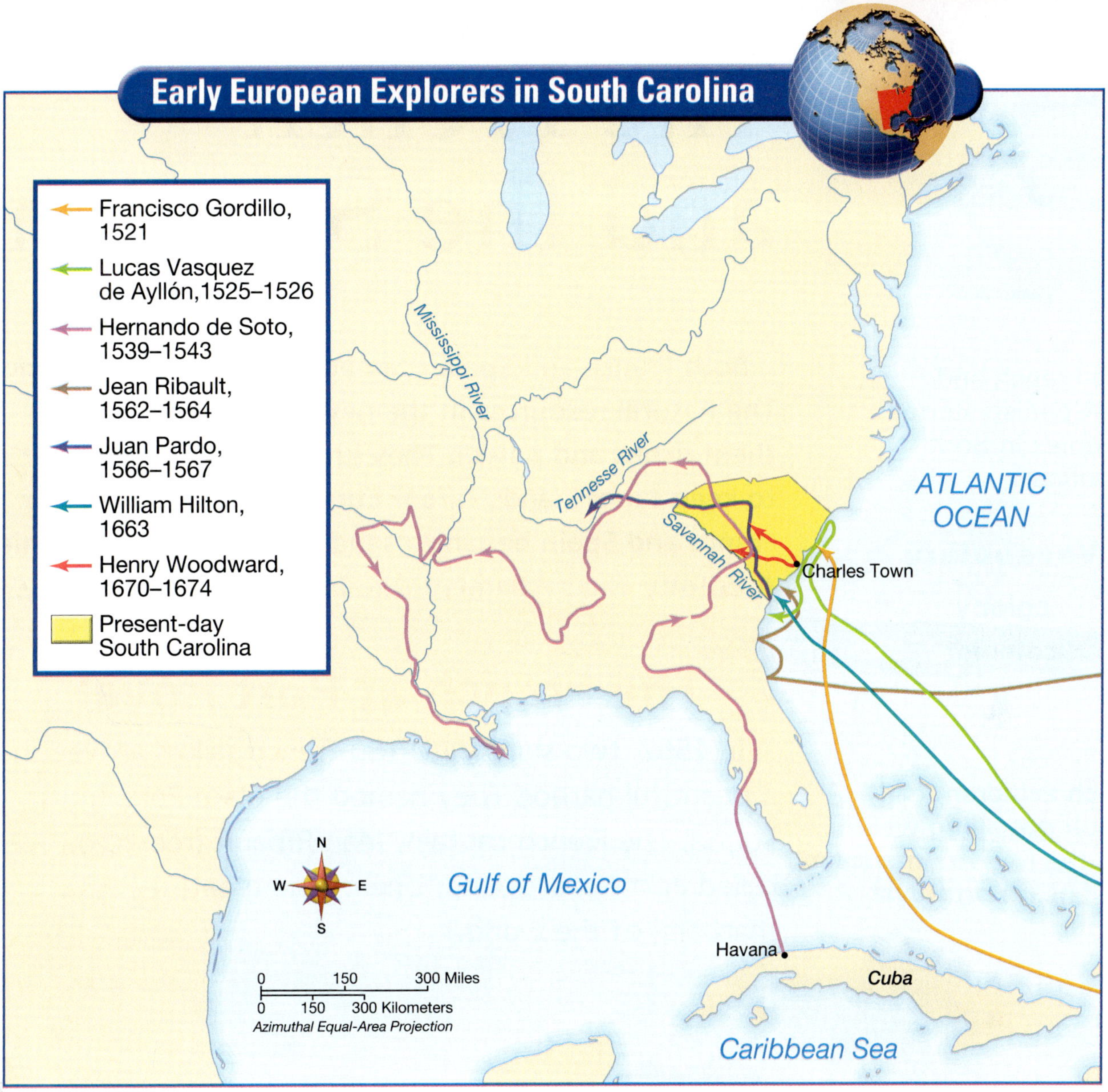

- Francisco Gordillo, 1521
- Lucas Vasquez de Ayllón, 1525–1526
- Hernando de Soto, 1539–1543
- Jean Ribault, 1562–1564
- Juan Pardo, 1566–1567
- William Hilton, 1663
- Henry Woodward, 1670–1674
- Present-day South Carolina

## Practice the Skill

Use the map to follow each explorer's route. Then answer these questions.

1. Which explorer sailed first?
2. Which explorer sailed last?
3. Which explorer started from Charles Town?
4. Which explorer traveled overland to reach South Carolina?

## Apply What You Learned

Write one more question about the routes of these explorers that can be answered by using this map. Trade papers with a partner, and answer each other's questions. Then tell how you used the map to answer your partner's question.

Practice your map and globe skills with the **GeoSkills CD–ROM**.

Chapter 4 ■ 109

# Lesson 2

# The French and the Spanish

**Big Idea**
The French and the Spanish started colonies in South Carolina.

**Vocabulary**
colony
colonist

Both France and Spain claimed lands in North America. The natural resources in the new lands would give them riches and power. They knew it would be easier to keep far-off lands safe if Europeans lived there. So France and Spain began to send people to build colonies. A **colony** is a settlement ruled by a country far away.

## The French at Port Royal

In 1562, two ships with 150 French sailors arrived in a beautiful harbor. They named the place Port Royal Sound. The French captain, Jean Ribault (ree•BOH), called Port Royal Sound "one of the greatest . . . [harbors] of the world."

French explorer Jean Ribault got along well with the Native Americans living near Port Royal Sound.

The **colonists**, or people living in a colony, spent the next five days cutting down trees. They built a fort on present-day Parris Island. Inside the fort they built a large, strong house. The walls were made of wood and earth. The roof was straw. The strong house was used to store goods and gave colonists a protected place to sleep.

The colonists named their settlement Charlesfort. On a nearby island, Captain Ribault put up a large stone column. It was carved with the symbols of France. It was a sign that the French meant to stay.

**Review** Why did colonists build a fort? **GENERALIZE**

## GEOGRAPHY

### Port Royal Sound

**Understanding Places and Regions**

Port Royal Sound is a wide body of water that flows into the Atlantic Ocean. There are many islands in Port Royal Sound. These include Parris Island, Hilton Head Island, Dawes Island, and Phillips Island.

Chapter 4 ■ 111

# Charlesfort

After a few months, Ribault left for France. He planned to return in a few months. Both ships and most of the colonists went with him.

Time passed, and food supplies ran low. The 27 people left in the settlement started to worry that a ship from France would not come back for them. So the colonists built a ship. The Charlesfort colonists built the first ship ever made in North America. In early 1563, they sailed away from Charlesfort. That was the end of the colony.

Most of the colonists died crossing the ocean. Near England, the last seven Charlesfort colonists were rescued.

**Review** How did the last settlers leave Charlesfort?

## Getting Food Supplies

### Analyze Primary Sources

The 27 colonists who stayed in Charlesfort needed more food. They had not been in the colony long enough to grow their own food. This painting shows how they met their needs.

❶ The colonists asked the Native Americans to give them some food. The Native Americans agreed to help out.

❷ The Native Americans helped the settlers load food onto a dugout.

❸ The colonists and Native Americans traveled back to Charlesfort in a dugout filled with food.

◆ What do you see in this painting that could be a food source?

By carefully digging away the soil and sand, experts learn how the French and Spanish colonists lived on Parris Island.

## Santa Elena

When the Spanish king heard about Charlesfort, he sent Pedro Menéndez de Avilés (Me•NEN•dez day ah•vee•LAYS) to guard Spanish lands. Menéndez sailed to Florida and built a fort at St. Augustine in 1565. The next year, he sailed north to Parris Island. There he built a small colony. He called it Santa Elena.

That summer, the Spanish explorer Juan Pardo brought 250 Spanish soldiers to Santa Elena. They built Fort San Felipe (SAHN fay•LEE•pay) to keep the colony safe. Soon farmers and craftsworkers arrived. In three years, nearly 200 settlers lived in 40 houses near the fort.

**Review** Where was Santa Elena?

### BIOGRAPHY

### Juan Pardo
**Character Trait: Responsibility**

Juan Pardo was a Spanish military officer who was sent to explore and claim land for Spain. In December 1566, Pardo led a group of 125 Spanish soldiers north from Port Royal Sound. Pardo was hoping to find silver mines or a route to Mexico. He and his soldiers visited many native towns in South Carolina. Pardo built several forts to protect his soldiers and to store food. Pardo didn't find silver, so the Spanish king stopped supporting Pardo's efforts.

**MULTIMEDIA BIOGRAPHIES**
Visit The Learning Site at
www.harcourtschool.com
to learn about other famous people.

**GO ONLINE**

Chapter 4 ■ 113

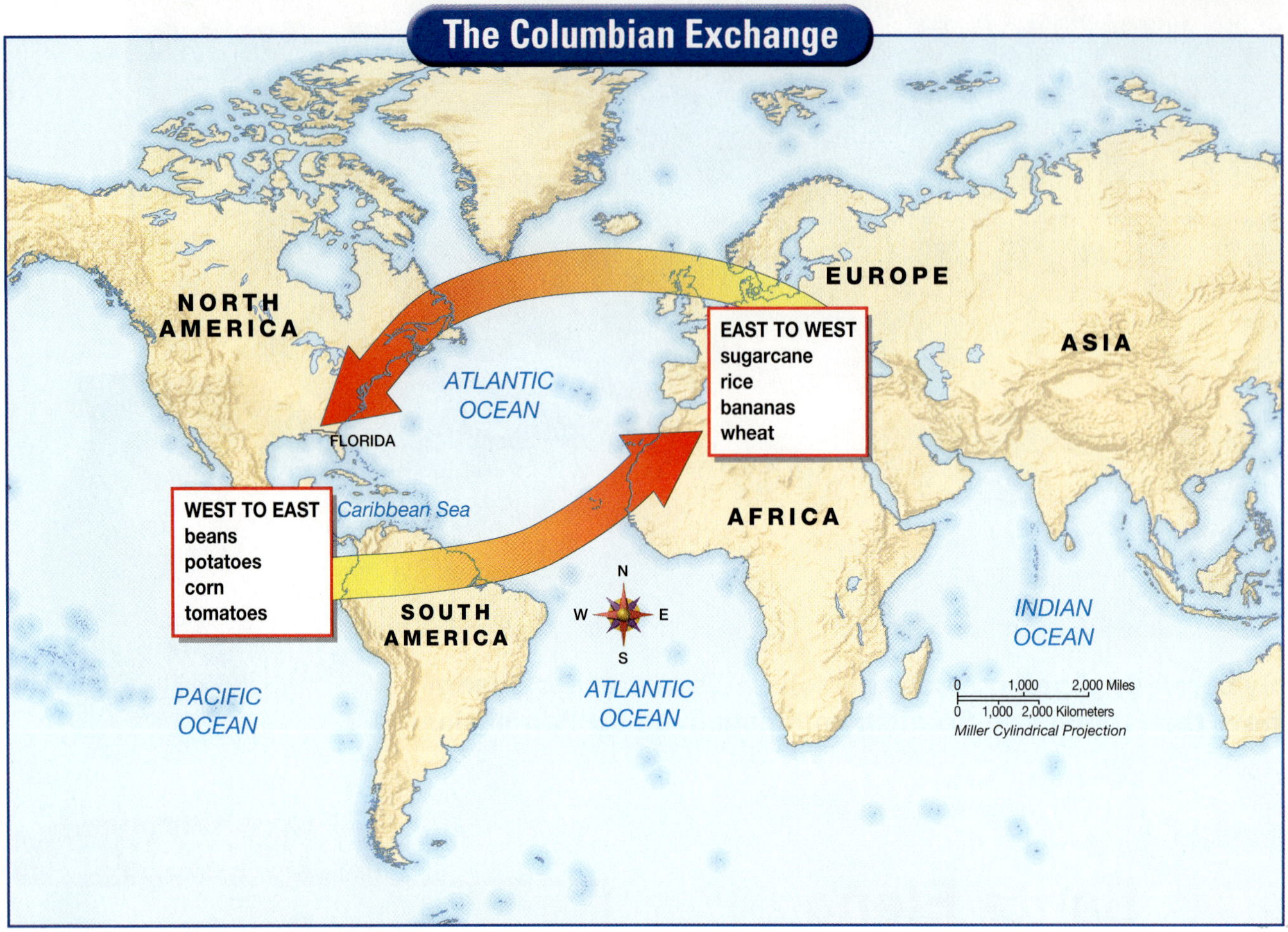

## The Columbian Exchange

Map showing West to East: beans, potatoes, corn, tomatoes; East to West: sugarcane, rice, bananas, wheat.

**Movement** When Christopher Columbus came from Europe, he brought foods and other resources to the colonies. Columbus found new foods in the colonies and brought those back to Europe. This trade of resources is known as the Columbian Exchange.

❓ What new foods did explorers bring to Europe?

## Spanish Florida

Menéndez named Santa Elena as the capital of Florida. *Florida* was the Spanish name for all of present-day Florida, Georgia, and South Carolina.

In 1571, Menéndez brought his wife and others to Santa Elena. By then, colonists were raising corn, grapes, hogs, and other foods.

Menéndez died three years later. The colony's leaders began to mistreat the Native Americans. The Native Americans attacked the settlement, killing many colonists. After ten years, the Spanish left Santa Elena.

**Review** What crops and animals did the Santa Elena colonists raise?

## Return to Santa Elena

In 1577, the Spanish went back to Santa Elena. They built a new fort and called it Fort San Marcos. New settlers arrived, and the colony at Santa Elena was rebuilt.

For ten years, Santa Elena grew. Then Spain went to war against England. The English attacked St. Augustine. Colonists feared they would attack Santa Elena, too. The Spanish could not protect both Santa Elena and St. Augustine. In 1587, settlers at Santa Elena were told to go to St. Augustine for safety.

**Review** Why did the settlers leave Santa Elena?

Fort San Marcos is located in St. Augustine, the oldest permanent European settlement in North America.

### LESSON 2 Review

**Generalize** Why did European countries want colonies?

**1 Big Idea** Which two countries started a colony on Parris Island?

**2 Vocabulary** Tell the difference between a **colonist** and a **colony** in a sentence about Charlesfort.

**3 History** Why did the Spanish king send Menéndez to Florida?

**Performance—Give a Speech** Imagine that you are a Spanish farmer going to live in Santa Elena. Write a speech telling others why they may want to go, too. Share your speech with your classmates.

Chapter 4 ■ 115

# Skills: Read a Time Line

**Vocabulary**
time line          sequence

## ▶ Why It Matters
You are learning about South Carolina's history. To understand history, you need to know the order of events. A **time line** can help. A time line is a drawing that shows when and in what order events took place.

## ▶ What You Need to Know
Read the time line below from left to right. The events at the left happened earlier. Events to the right of them happened later.

As you move from left to right, you follow the events in sequence. **Sequence** is the order in which events take place.

### Time Line of South Carolina Exploration

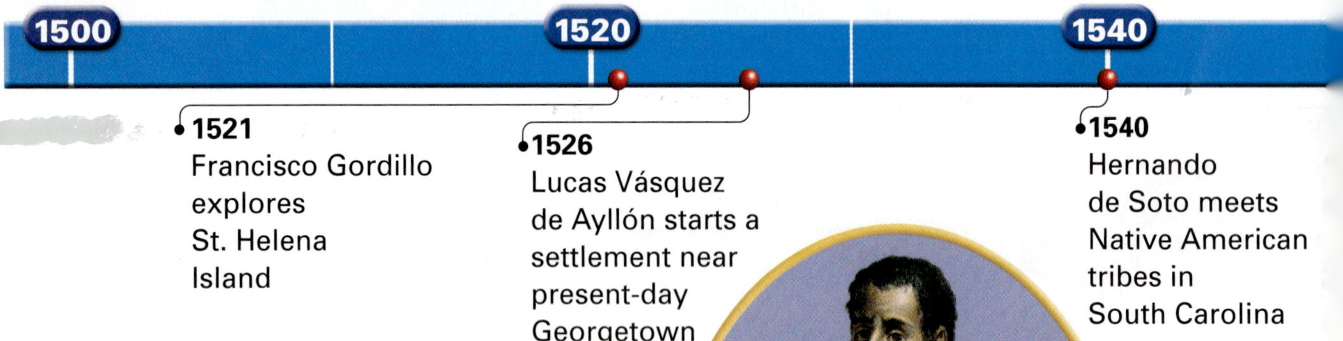

**1500**

**1520**

**1540**

- **1521** Francisco Gordillo explores St. Helena Island
- **1526** Lucas Vásquez de Ayllón starts a settlement near present-day Georgetown
- **1540** Hernando de Soto meets Native American tribes in South Carolina

Hernando de Soto

116 ■ Unit 2

▶ **Practice the Skill**

Use the time line to answer these questions.

① When did Francisco Gordillo explore St. Helena Island?

② In what year did de Soto and the Native Americans meet?

③ When was Charlesfort built?

④ Which happened first—Charlesfort was built or de Soto explored in South Carolina?

▶ **Apply What You Learned**

Make a time line about your life. Show your date of birth and when you started school. Then add a milestone for each year after that. A milestone is something important that you did or that happened to you.

1562 Jean Ribault builds Charlesfort at Port Royal Sound

Ribault's column

1565 Pedro Menéndez de Avilés arrives in Florida

1587 The Spanish leave Santa Elena colony

Pedro Menéndez

# Lesson 3

# An English Colony

**Big Idea**
Carolina became an English colony in the 1600s.

**Vocabulary**
raw material
plantation
planter
charter
Lords Proprietors

By about 1600, the English had land claims in North America. Their economy was based mainly on the making and selling of goods.

## The English

The English wanted to trade with Native Americans for raw materials. A **raw material** is a natural resource, such as wood, that can be used to make a product. Raw materials could be sent back to England and used to produce goods.

In 1627, a colony was started on Barbados Island in the Caribbean Sea. The English colonists there called themselves Barbadians.

In 1607, the first permanent English colony was started at Jamestown, Virginia. Today, reenactors show what it was like to live at Jamestown.

LOCATE IT
VIRGINIA
Jamestown National Historic Site

The colony was known as Little England. Barbadians were proud of their English heritage and of their island. Sugarcane crops were grown on huge farms called **plantations**. The rich landowners were known as **planters**. Their crops were grown by slaves.

By 1660, England had many colonies in North America. The colonies traded with one another and with England.

**Review** Why did the English want colonies in North America?

GENERALIZE

## English Products MADE FROM Colonial Materials

**1** Trees were cut down in the colonies, and the wood was sent to England.

**2** Factories in England made the wood usable.

**3** The usable wood was made into fine furniture.

## A Carolina Colony

In 1663, a group of Barbadian planters decided to start a new colony. They called themselves Barbadian Adventurers. They were interested in a place called Carolina.

The Barbadians hired William Hilton. They wanted him to explore the coast of Carolina. In 1663, Hilton explored places such as Cape Fear and Port Royal Sound. He wrote a report about his trip. In it, he described Carolina as a very pleasant place. The Barbadians wanted to move there.

England's King Charles II agreed to start a colony in Carolina. The king wrote a charter. A **charter** is a paper that gives permission to start a colony. The king's charter named the eight landowners as the Lords Proprietors of Carolina. The **Lords Proprietors** were the first to rule the Carolina Colony.

### · BIOGRAPHY ·

#### Anthony Ashley Cooper
#### 1621–1683

**Character Trait: Responsibility**

In 1663, the king of England gave Anthony Ashley Cooper and seven other men a large land grant in North America. The land was called Carolina. The eight men were called the Lords Proprietors of the colony.

Cooper worked hard for Carolina. He asked his friend John Locke to write a constitution. It was never adopted by the colony. He also designed the street plan for Charles Town. The nearby Ashley and Cooper rivers were named in his honor.

**MULTIMEDIA BIOGRAPHIES**
Visit The Learning Site at www.harcourtschool.com to learn about other famous people.

GO ONLINE

In 1669, the Lords Proprietors wrote the Fundamental Constitutions of Carolina. This plan for the colony's government promised settlers religious freedom and the right to own land. These promises brought colonists, like the Barbadians, to Carolina. However, the constitution was never used to rule the colony.

The Lords Proprietors could collect taxes from the colonists. They also controlled trade. In 1669, the Lords Proprietors bought ships and supplies. They used ships to bring raw materials to England and to bring back goods to the colonies.

**Review** Which two groups wanted to start a Carolina colony? **GENERALIZE**

**Analyze Diagrams** The Lords Proprietors started a Carolina settlement even though none of them ever visited South Carolina.

❓ How many Lords Proprietors were there?

Chapter 4 ▪ 121

The *Carolina* carried 130 settlers. Most were from England. There were also some English people from the West Indies and five African slaves.

# Charles Town

On May 15, 1670, a ship named the *Carolina* landed at Bulls Bay. The leaders of the settlers on board were Joseph West, William Sayle, and Dr. Henry Woodward. They built a village at Albemarle Point on the Ashley River. This first permanent Carolina settlement was called Charles Town to honor the king.

At first, many colonists came from England. Soon one-half of the new settlers were planters who came from Barbados. They brought their way of life to Carolina, including their use of African slaves. Slaves cleared the land and built the plantations. They also worked the fields as they had in Barbados.

In 1680, after ten years, leaders moved Charles Town to where it is today. They chose a location across the Ashley River on Oyster Point. There they laid out streets in a grid, with a public square and a market.

At this time, there were about 1,000 colonists. People had brought their languages and cultures to the colony. Many English settlers were from the West Indies. Many others were African slaves. Still others came from Ireland, Scotland, and Wales.

French Huguenots (HYOO•guh•natz) also joined the Carolina colony. They wanted to practice their religion, which was against the law in France.

**By 1680, Charles Town was growing.**

**Review** When did the Charles Town settlement move to Oyster Point?

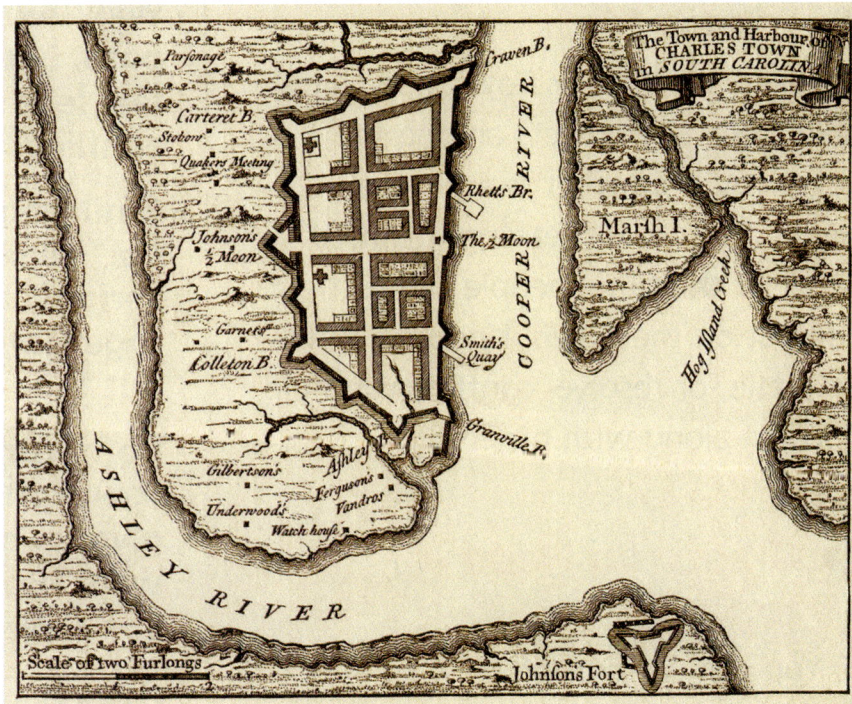

# LESSON 3
## Review

 **Generalize** How was life in Charles Town shaped by the Barbadian planters?

**1 Big Idea** What group was given a charter for a colony in Carolina?

**2 Vocabulary** Use **planter** and **plantation** in a sentence about Barbados.

**3 Economics** How did slaves help start the settlement of Charles Town?

 **Performance—Draw a Scene** Draw a scene showing the first colonists arriving at Charles Town in 1670. Show the ship *Carolina* in your scene. Be sure to include Europeans, Barbadians, and African slaves.

Chapter 4 ■ 123

# Skills

# Resolve Conflict

**Vocabulary**
conflict
compromise
mediator

## ▶ Why It Matters

Leaders in Charles Town had to be able to settle conflicts among the colonists. A conflict is a disagreement. Sometimes settling it is hard. Most of the time, people can settle a conflict on their own. Knowing how to settle, or resolve, conflicts can help you get along with others.

## ▶ What You Need to Know

You can use one of these solutions when you are in a conflict. The same solution may not work each time. You may need to try more than one solution.

- **Walk Away**—Let some time pass. Later, both people may feel less strongly about the conflict.

- **Smile About It**—Try to "lighten up." Make the conflict less serious. People who can smile together can more easily work out their problem.

- **Compromise**—In a compromise (KAHM•pruh•myz), both people give up some of what they want. Both people also get some of what they want.

- **Ask for Help**—A mediator (MEE•dee•ay•tor) helps people settle disagreements. She or he may show the people a new way of looking at their problem.

124 ■ Unit 2

### ▶ Practice the Skill

Work with a partner to practice resolving conflicts. For example, you and your partner could imagine a disagreement about what to do after school. Role-play ways to settle the conflict, using the solutions on page 124. Then think about what happened, and answer the questions.

1. What happened when one person walked away?
2. What happened when one person tried to compromise?
3. What happened when one person asked for help?

### ▶ Apply What You Learned

Write some ways that people at your school settle conflicts. Think about ways that they compromise or ask for help. Then talk with a teacher or a family member. Compare those ways with the four solutions that you learned.

## Lesson 4

# Early Plantations

**Big Idea**
In the 1700s, rice and indigo became major cash crops in Carolina.

**Vocabulary**
cash crop
self-sufficient
textile
indigo

The Barbadian planters shipped their crops from Charles Town to England to be sold. Because the English government controlled trade, the planters wanted to control the colony's government.

## The Carolina Plantations

In Barbados, the planters made the laws. They wanted control of the Carolina government. The colony had a governor and a council. The Lords Proprietors, in England, chose the governor. Colonists with at least 500 acres of land were allowed to vote for the council. So the Barbadian planters elected the council.

**Review** Which colonists could vote for council members?

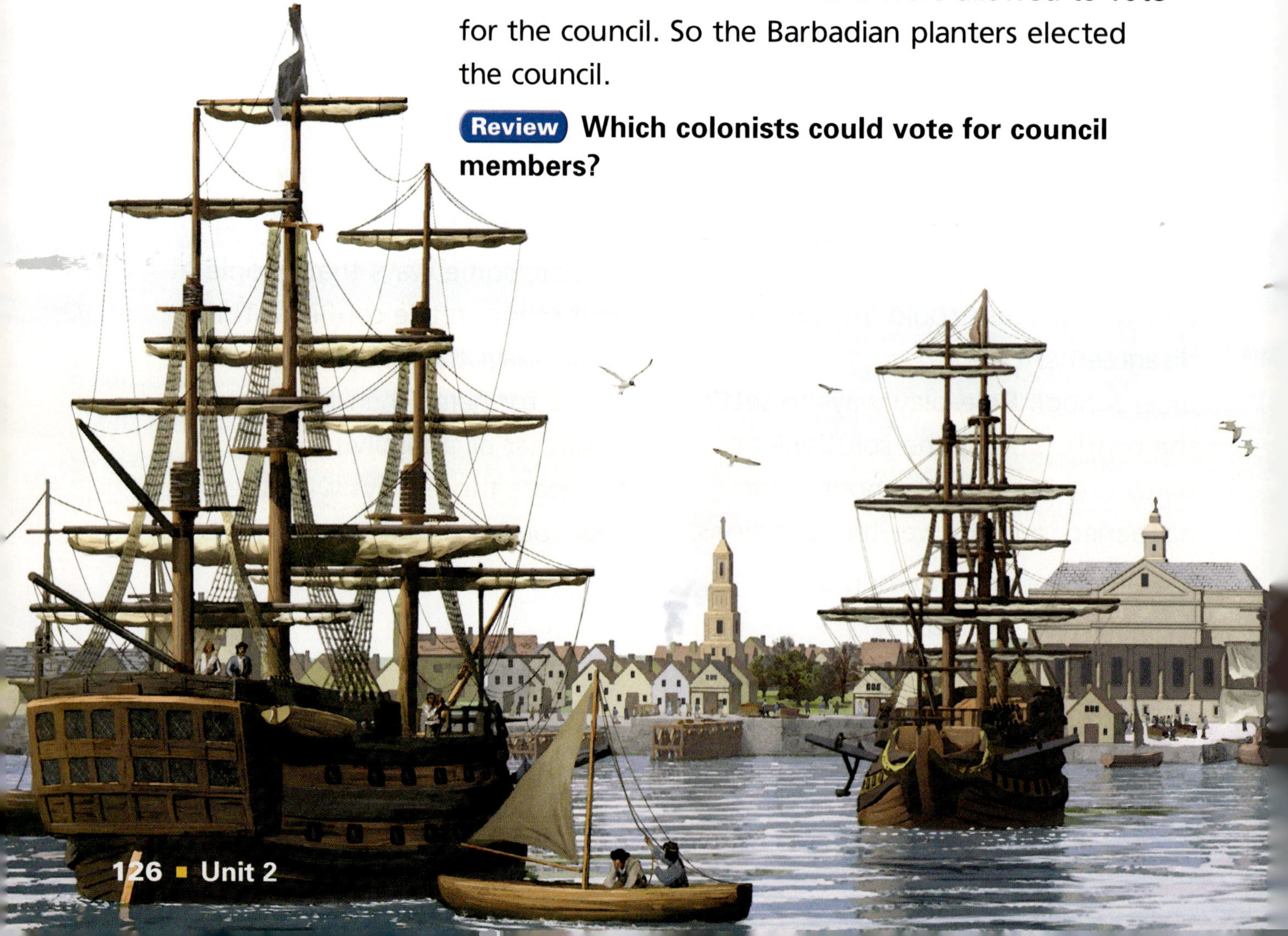

## Agriculture

Most of the colony's agriculture was on the plantations. On these huge farms, planters grew cash crops. A **cash crop** is a crop that people grow to sell, not to use themselves. Slaves from West Africa showed the planters how to grow rice in the wetlands along the rivers. Rice became Carolina's cash crop.

Rice plantations needed many workers. Soon there were not enough workers in the colony. The planters decided to buy more slaves from West Africa.

**Review** Why did planters grow a cash crop? GENERALIZE

The soil, water, and climate of South Carolina's lowcountry is just right for growing rice.

At the port in Charles Town, rice was shipped out for sale to other colonies and to England.

Chapter 4 ■ 127

During the 1700s, there were about 100 rice plantations in Carolina. The area was the second-largest rice producer in the world.

Planters had many fine objects, such as this harp, in their homes.

## Plantation Life

Early plantations were small communities. People living there were **self-sufficient**—they met their own needs by making or growing nearly everything they used. The plantations raised hogs and corn for food. Nearly all of the work was done by slaves.

Rice, the largest crop, was grown to be sold. Planters used the money from selling rice to buy fine clothing for their families and beautiful furniture for their homes.

The planters hired tutors to teach their children to read and write. The tutors often came to the colony from England. They lived with the planter's family. The planter's children learned to read the Bible and other books.

**Review** How was a plantation like a small community? **GENERALIZE**

## A Closer Look
### A Plantation

Plantations made or grew most of the things they needed. Each plantation was different, but they all had some things in common.

1. Kitchen
2. Planter's house
3. Barn
4. Loading dock
5. Slave cabins
6. Stables
7. River

❓ Why do you think plantations were built near the rivers?

These objects were used by slaves to make flour from grain, such as wheat.

## Plantation Work

African slaves were a large part of Carolina's population. Planters brought them from the West Indies. Soon many more people were needed to work on the rice plantations. Merchants, called slave traders, brought slaves from West Africa to Charles Town. The slaves were sold there in the slave markets.

A slave's life was harsh. Most lived in small cabins that had dirt floors. They rarely got meat to eat. They owned nothing.

Working in the rice fields was hard. Slaves drained swamps and cut down trees. They stood in deep, muddy water to plant, grow, and harvest the rice. They worked as long as the daylight lasted.

**Review** Who were the slave traders?

Slaves on plantations in the West Indies (above) used the rivers and streams to remove dye from indigo plants.

Today, dye made from indigo plants is used to make blue jeans blue.

# A New Cash Crop

In 1739, Eliza Lucas was a young woman in Charles Town. Her family owned several plantations. She was creative and curious.

Eliza knew that the business of making **textiles**, or cloth, was growing in England. Factories needed dyes, or colors. Eliza developed a new and better indigo plant. **Indigo** is a plant used to make a blue dye. Soon many planters were growing indigo. Indigo became the colony's most important cash crop, after rice.

**Review** Why did Lucas develop new indigo plants?

## BIOGRAPHY

### Eliza Lucas Pinckney
### 1722–1793

**Character Trait: Inventiveness**

Eliza Lucas was born in England in 1722. When Eliza was young, her family moved to Carolina. Soon after, her father was called away for business. Eliza took care of her family and the family's plantations.

In 1739, Eliza began working with indigo plants. The dye that came from her indigo plants was better than earlier dyes. Her inventive, or creative, work made indigo an important cash crop.

In 1744, Eliza married Charles Pinckney. Eliza continued her work with plants. She was well liked and respected. When she died in 1793, President George Washington came to her funeral.

**GO ONLINE — MULTIMEDIA BIOGRAPHIES**
Visit The Learning Site at www.harcourtschool.com to learn about other famous people.

## LESSON 4 Review

 **Generalize** How did the plantations help make Carolina a successful colony?

**1 Big Idea** How did planters learn to grow rice?

**2 Vocabulary** Use **cash crop** and **indigo** in a sentence about plantations.

**3 Geography** What kind of land is used for growing rice?

 **Performance—Write an Article** Write an article about a Carolina plantation in 1690. Tell how different people on the plantation live and work.

Chapter 4 ■ 131

## Lesson 5

# Settlers and Settlements

**Big Idea**
As Carolina grew, there were conflicts between settlers and other groups of people living nearby.

**Vocabulary**
ally
frontier
pioneer

Rice and indigo plantations made their owners very rich. Trade with Native Americans was making merchants rich, too. Other people began to think that they would succeed in the Carolina colony. Charles Town soon became an important colonial city.

## Charles Town and Beyond

New settlers continued to come to Carolina from Europe. Many were craftworkers who set up shops in Charles Town. Some people began to think about starting another settlement away from Charles Town. Henry Erskine, Lord Cardross of Scotland, was the first to try.

The new settlement was called Stuart's Town. The first settlers moved there in 1684. They found that life was very hard. Many died from the disease malaria. Many of those who lived returned to Charles Town.

This man is making wheels the way craftworkers did in colonial times.

This early map of the English colonies in North America shows that Carolina had no western border. North Carolina and Georgia are shown as regions of the South Carolina colony.

## Colonial Government

From its beginning, Carolina was ruled by a governor and a council. In 1691, planters were determined to have a larger say in government. The Lords Proprietors agreed to form the Commons House. The planters elected its members to represent them.

The arrival of new settlers and fear of Native Americans led to changes in the colony's government. In 1712, the colony was divided into North Carolina and South Carolina. The Commons House also wanted a colony south of the Savannah River for protection from the Spanish. The Lords Proprietors refused, so colonists asked the king for protection. In 1729, King George II made South Carolina a royal colony. Now the colony was ruled by the king.

**Review** Who elected members of the Commons House?

# The Township Plan

The Commons House wanted new settlers to move to the frontier. A **frontier** is the edge of the wilderness. Leaders believed that more settlements could protect Charles Town.

In 1730, the leaders made a plan to set up new townships. Each township had a town and 20,000 acres of farming land. **Pioneers**, or people who help settle frontier lands, were given 50 acres of land, as well as tools and supplies.

Leaders in Charles Town also asked the king for protection. The next year, 1731, the king chartered the new colony of Georgia. Lands south of the Savannah River were no longer a part of South Carolina. Settlers came from France, Germany, Ireland, and other countries.

**Review** Why did the Commons House set up townships?

German baptismal certificate, courtesy of the Museum of Early Southern Decorative Arts, Winston-Salem, NC

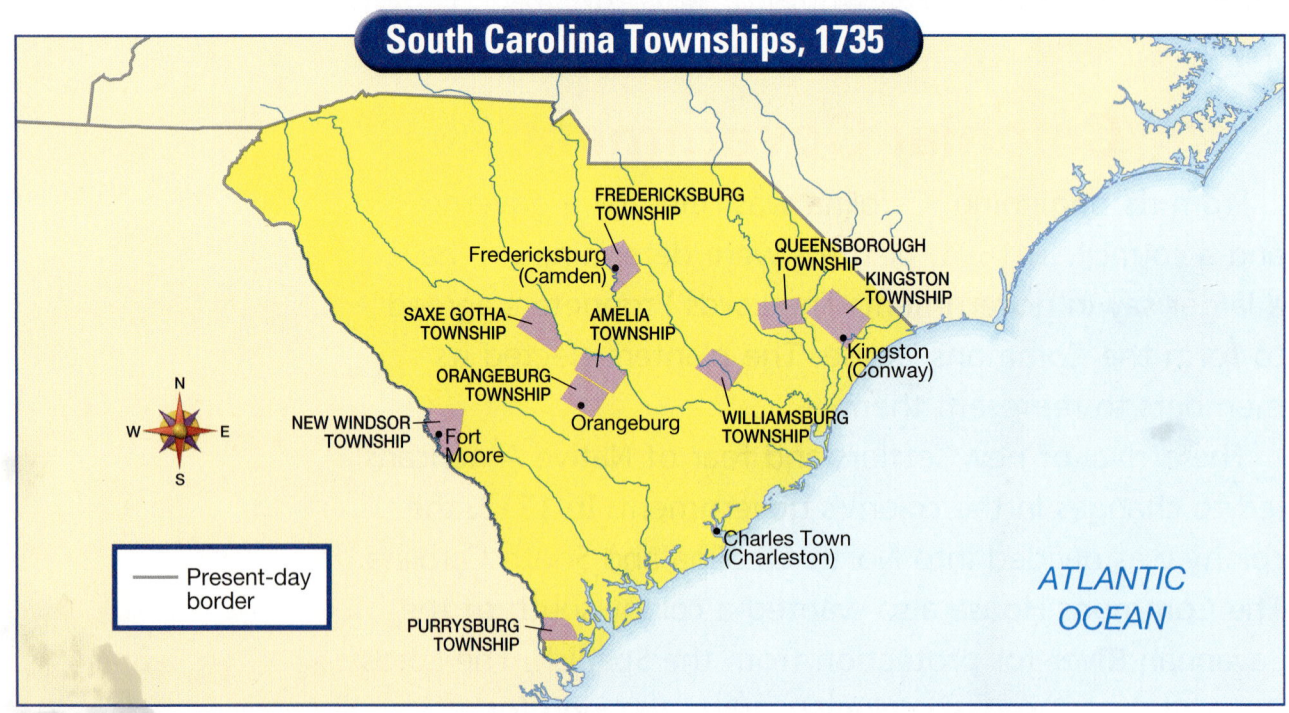

**Place** By 1735, there were nine townships in present-day South Carolina. Most of them were located in the central part of the state.

❖ In what township was Fort Moore located?

136 ▪ Unit 2

## The Stono Uprising

By 1700, the colony had more African slaves than European settlers. Some planters used harsh treatment to make the slaves work. Many slaves ran away. If they were caught, runaway slaves were punished.

In 1739, a group of slaves attacked a store near the Stono River. They killed the store owners. Then they headed for Florida. As they traveled, more runaway slaves joined them.

Slave owners caught up to the slaves. There was a battle. More than 20 colonists and 40 slaves were killed. The Stono Slave Uprising caused leaders to pass harsher slave laws.

**Review** What caused the Stono Slave Uprising?

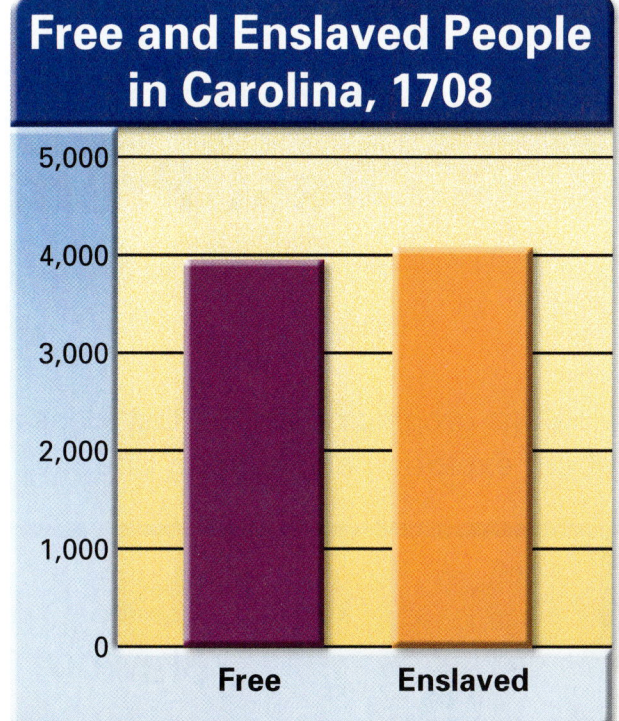

**Analyze Bar Graphs** This bar graph shows that there were more enslaved people than free people, in 1708.

● About how many people were living in Carolina in 1708?

## LESSON 5 Review

**Generalize** Why did the colonists want South Carolina to become a royal colony?

❶ **Big Idea** Why were there conflicts between the settlers and other groups of people?

❷ **Vocabulary** Write a sentence using the word **ally**.

❸ **History** Why did Carolina's leaders want townships?

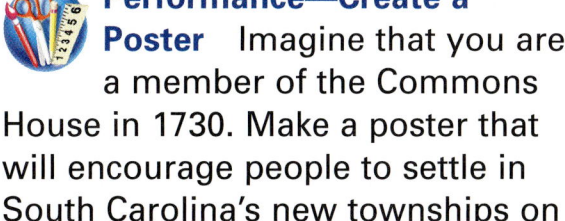

**Performance—Create a Poster** Imagine that you are a member of the Commons House in 1730. Make a poster that will encourage people to settle in South Carolina's new townships on the frontier.

Chapter 4 ■ 137

# Chapter 4 Review and Test Preparation

**Time Line**

1500

• 1540 Hernando de Soto explores inland South Carolina

## Generalize

Use this graphic organizer. List ideas and make generalizations about exploring and settling South Carolina.

### Newcomers Arrive

**Ideas** → **Generalization**

- Explorers from Europe looked for new lands.
- France, Spain, and England all wanted a permanent settlement in Carolina.
- Plantation owners became rich by growing rice and indigo.

## THINK & WRITE

**Write a Short Story** Imagine you are with the first settlers aboard the *Carolina* in 1670. Write a short story about settling a new town. Tell what you think it will be like to land and start a new town.

**Write a Persuasive Letter** Write a letter to King George II from a soldier living in South Carolina after the Yemassee War. Tell why you think the king should make a new colony south of the Savannah River.

138 ■ Unit 2

1600 — 1700 — 1800

- 1670 English settlement started at Charles Town
- 1712 Carolina becomes North Carolina and South Carolina
- 1729 South Carolina becomes a royal colony

## Use The Time Line

Use the chapter summary time line to answer these questions.

1. In what year did Hernando de Soto explore South Carolina?
2. In what year was Charles Town started?

## Use Vocabulary

Write the term that best matches each definition.

**slave** (p. 104)

**settlement** (p. 104)

**raw material** (p. 118)

**cash crop** (p. 127)

3. a person held against his or her will and forced to work for no pay
4. a crop that is grown to be sold
5. a village built by the first people to live in a new place
6. a resource that can be used to make a product

## Recall Facts

Answer these questions.

7. Who founded the Spanish settlement Santa Elena?

Write the letter of the best choice.

8. Problems between Native Americans and settlers caused the—
   A Stono Uprising.
   B Yemassee War.
   C pioneers to arrive.
   D settlement of Beaufort.

## Think Critically

9. Why do you think Native Americans sometimes helped the settlers?

## Apply Skills

**Follow Routes on a History Map**

10. Use the map on page 109. Which explorer traveled along the Carolina coast in 1521?

**Read a Time Line**

11. Use the time line on pages 116–117. How many events shown happened before 1562?

**Resolve Conflict**

12. Look at the information on pages 124–125. What four solutions can you use to help resolve conflicts?

Chapter 4 ■ 139

# VISIT HISTORIC BRATTONSVILLE

## Get Ready

Historic Brattonsville is a living-history museum. The Bratton family first settled here more than 200 years ago. Their plantation grew to be the village of Brattonsville. Today, visitors learn about life on an early South Carolina plantation.

Visitors can explore 29 historic buildings and see workers practicing traditional crafts. Brattonsville is also home to some special farm animals. Animal care experts here protect farming history by keeping animals such as Ossabaw Island pigs and Cotswold sheep.

**Locate It**
South Carolina

Brattonsville

## What to See

This cabin was once home to a slave family.

Horses, mules, or oxen pulled heavy loads in this farm wagon.

The Bratton children had their own schoolroom.

People reenact events from long ago.

## Take a Field Trip

**A VIRTUAL TOUR**
Visit The Learning Site at www.harcourtschool.com to take virtual tours of other historic sites.

# Unit 2 Review and Test Preparation

## Use Vocabulary

For each group of underlined words, write the term from the list below that has the same meaning.

tribe (p. 75)
council (p. 78)
charter (p. 120)
cash crop (p. 127)
pioneer (p. 136)

1. The large building in the Cherokee village was where the group who made decisions for everyone met.

2. The group of families that shares the same language and customs gathered for the Green Corn Festival.

3. The settler decided to grow a crop to sell instead of only growing food for himself.

4. Each new settler on the frontier was given land and tools.

5. The king gave the Lords Proprietors a paper giving them permission to rule Carolina.

## Recall Facts

Answer these questions.

6. Catawba is a part of which language family?

7. What does the name *Cherokee* mean?

8. What did Eliza Lucas do?

9. Which event caused harsh slave laws to be passed?

Write the letter of the best choice.

10. What is the name today of the place where Charlesfort was built?
    A Parris Island
    B Pawley's Island
    C Hilton Head Island
    D Dawes Island

11. What was the name of the first permanent Carolina settlement?
    F Barbados
    G England
    H Charles Town
    J Santa Elena

142 • Unit 2

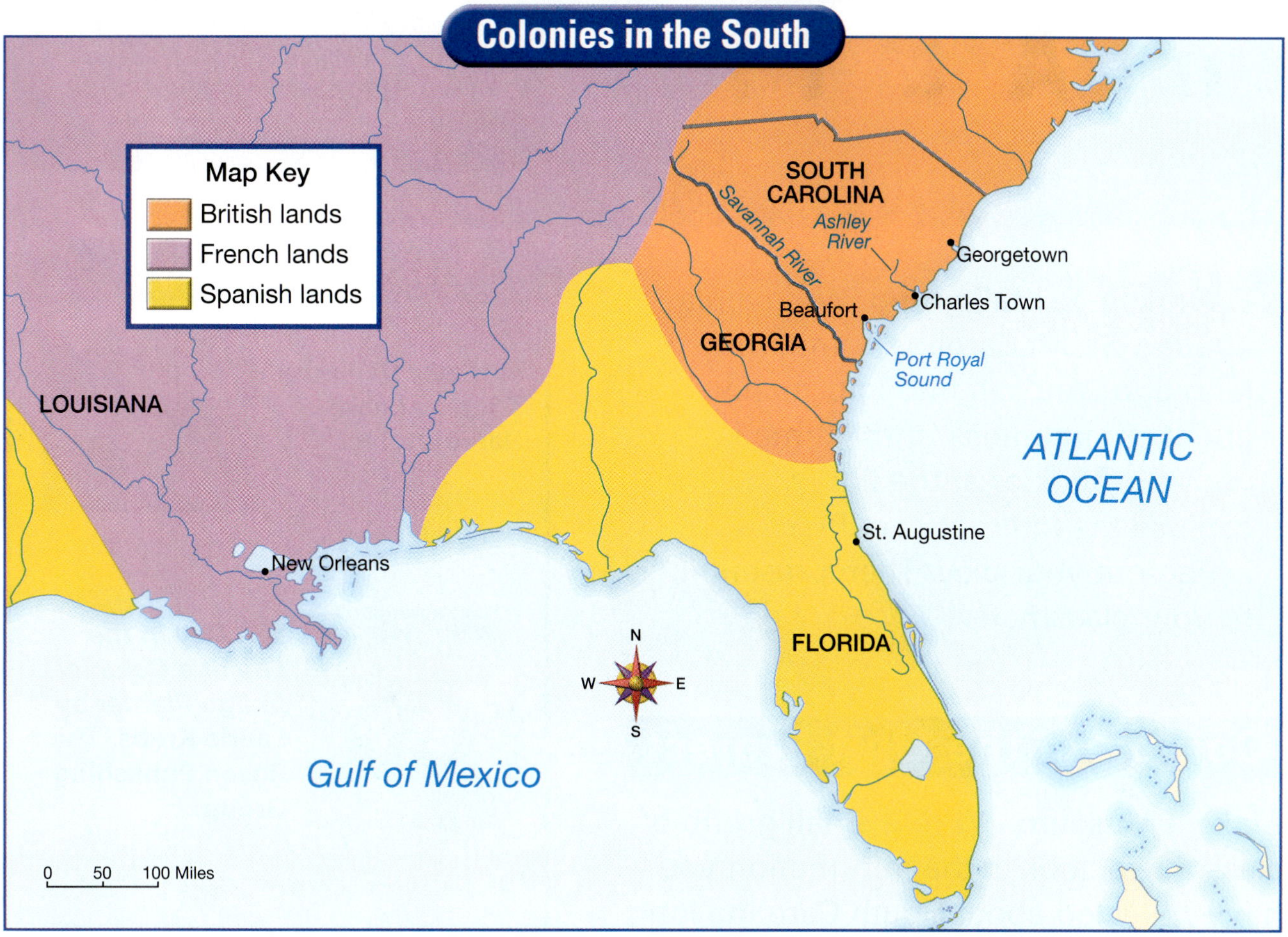

## Colonies in the South

**Map Key**
- British lands
- French lands
- Spanish lands

## Think Critically

12. How was life among the Catawba and Cusabo different? How were the two tribes the same?

13. How did the government of Carolina change during the 1700s?

14. What was the role of rice and indigo in the economy of Carolina?

15. How did settling the inland frontier help strengthen the colony of South Carolina?

## Apply Skills

**Use a Distance Scale**
Use the map above to answer the questions.

16. About how far is Beaufort from St. Augustine?

17. About how far is Georgetown from Charles Town?

18. About how far is New Orleans from St. Augustine?

Unit 2 ■ 143

# Unit Activities

 Visit The Learning Site at www.harcourtschool.com for additional activities.

## Present a Play

Work in a small group. Write a play about a South Carolina community of long ago. You can find information about communities of that time in your textbook or at the library. You can use the Internet, too. Practice acting out your play. Then present it to your classmates.

## Complete the Unit Project

**Make a Museum** With a small group of classmates, look at the information you have collected about South Carolina long ago. Use maps, portraits, photographs, time lines, and models to present the people, places, and events you have chosen to show in your museum. Display these items on a table or bulletin board in your classroom. Invite other classes to visit your museum.

### Visit Your Library

- *Water Dance* by Thomas Locker. Harcourt, Inc.

- *A Day in the Life of a Colonial Indigo Planter* by Laurie Krebs. The Rosen Publishing Group.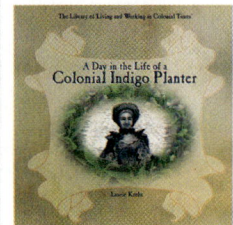

- *The South Carolina Colony* by Tamara L. Britton. ABDO Publishing Company.

# An Independent Spirit

Jackson Vase, 1817

A fife and drum parade in Camden, South Carolina

# Unit 3

# An Independent Spirit

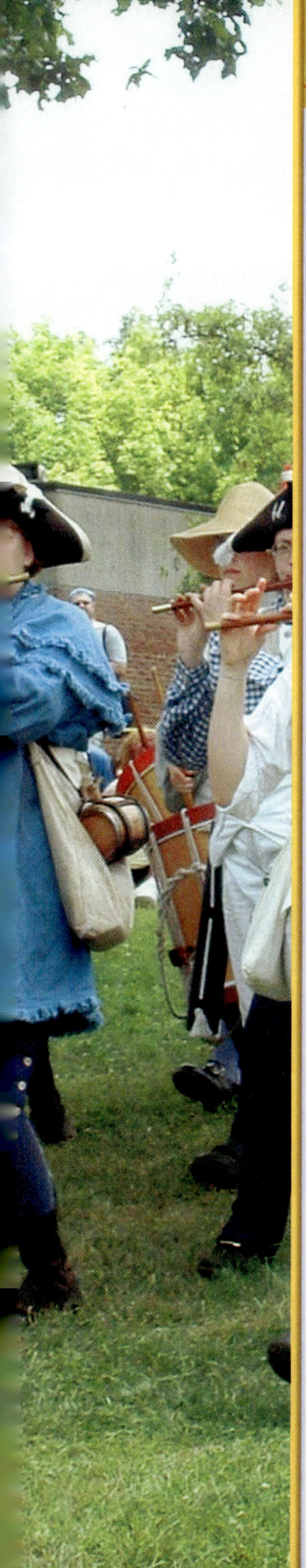

" We may be led, but we never will be driven. "

—Eliza Yonge Wilkinson, Charles Town, about 1780

## Preview the Content

Quickly read over the headings, captions, graphs, maps, and charts in the lesson. Then write predictions about what you will learn in the unit. Do this by answering the "five **W**s." **Who** and **What** will the unit be about? **Where** are the locations you will study? **When** did the events happen? **Why** are they important? After you have read the unit, review your predictions.

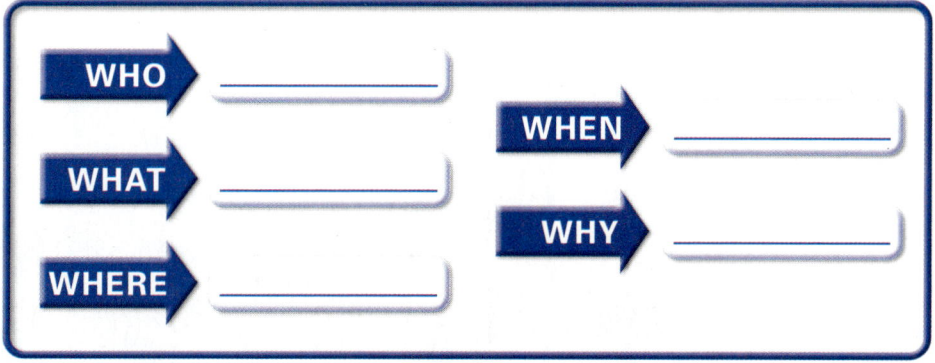

Unit 3 ▪ 145

# Unit 3 Preview

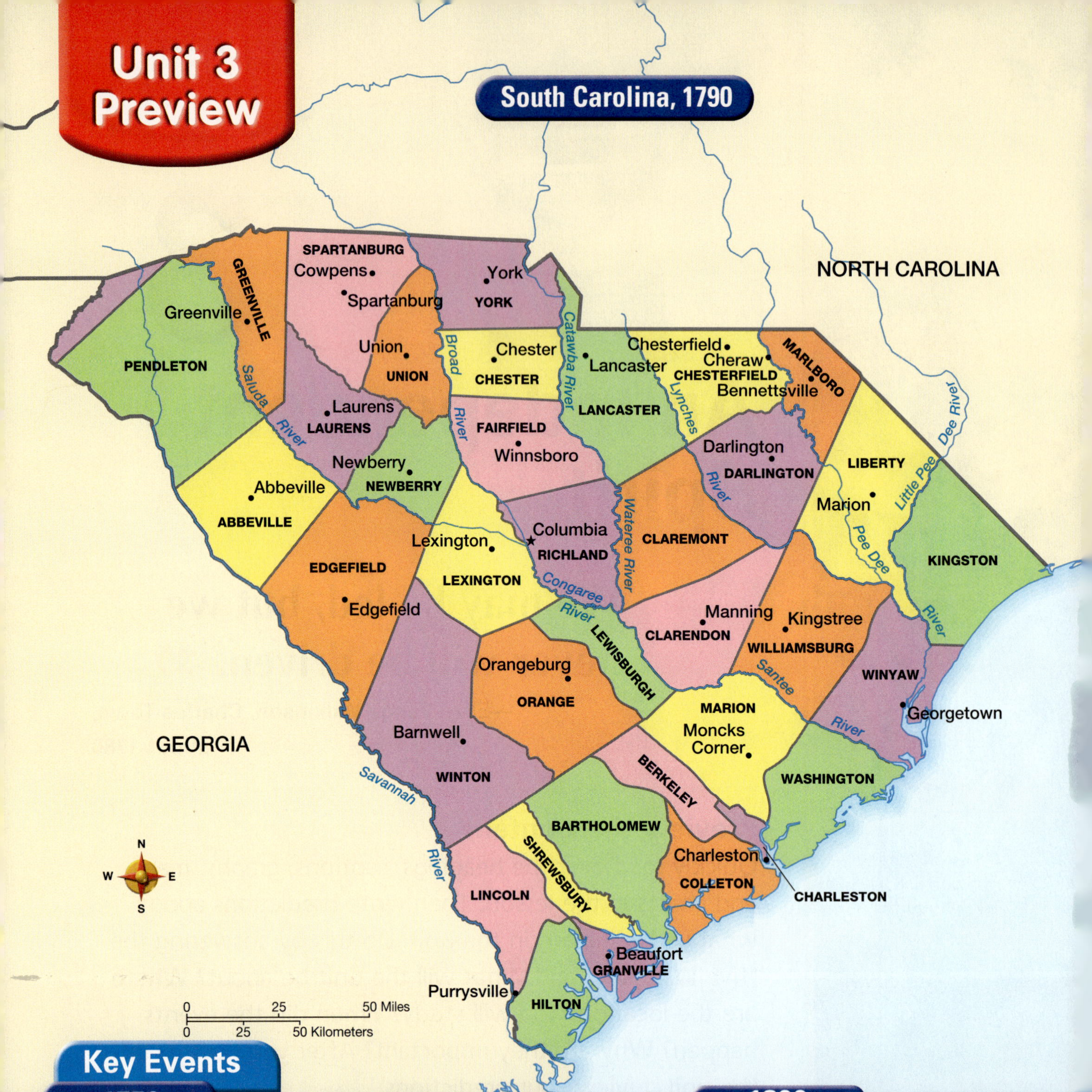

## South Carolina, 1790

## Key Events

**1750**

**1800**

**1750** Settlers start coming to South Carolina. p. 158

**1775** The American Revolution begins. p. 166

**1790** South Carolina's first State House opens. p. 179

## Population of South Carolina 1760–1880

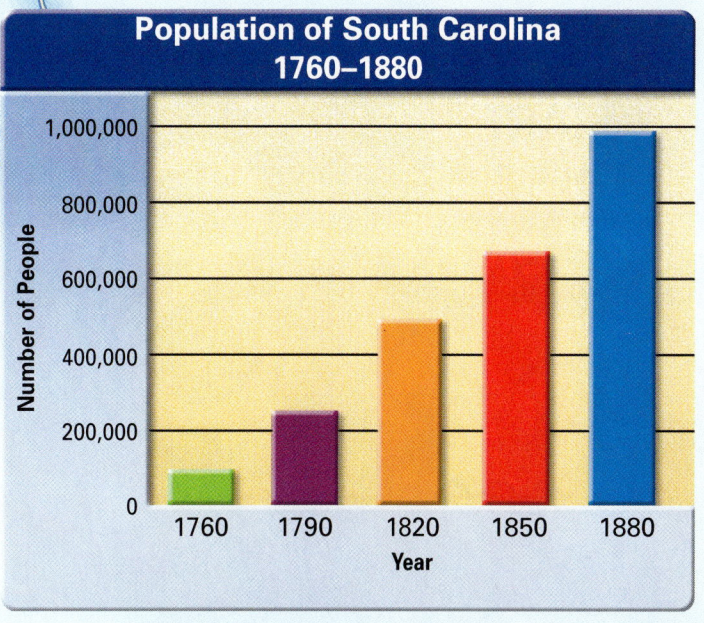

## The Thirteen Colonies

| COLONY | DATE FOUNDED |
|---|---|
| Virginia | 1607 |
| Massachusetts | 1629 |
| Maryland | 1634 |
| Connecticut | 1639 |
| Rhode Island | 1644 |
| New York | 1644 |
| South Carolina | 1670 |
| New Hampshire | 1680 |
| Pennsylvania | 1681 |
| New Jersey | 1702 |
| Delaware | 1704 |
| North Carolina | 1729 |
| Georgia | 1733 |

ATLANTIC OCEAN

**Map Key**
— Present-day state border
— County border
★ State capital

**1850** — **1900**

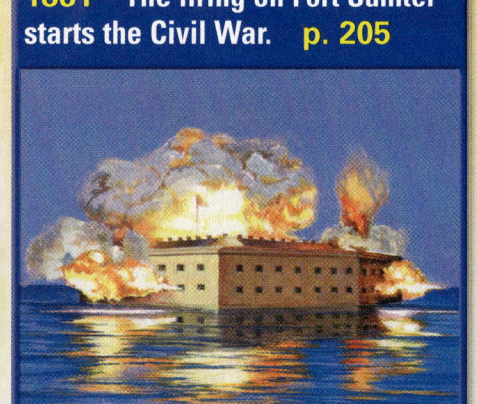

**1861** The firing on Fort Sumter starts the Civil War. p. 205

**1865** Freedman's Bureau schools begin to open. p. 212

**1868** African Americans vote for the first time. p. 211

147

**START with a LEGEND**

# THE SWAMP FOX

BY PLEASANT DeSPAIN
ILLUSTRATED BY RICK FARRELL

A legend is a story about a real person that is handed down over time. Often legends include real places and important events, too. Because of its long history, South Carolina has many legends.

In 1775 the colonies went to war against England. The war was called the American Revolution. Many colonial leaders became heroes. One legend tells how a South Carolina hero earned his famous nickname. Read now to learn how Francis Marion came to be called "The Swamp Fox."

Francis Marion was born in 1732 in the colony of South Carolina. A small, sickly boy, he loved to explore the marshes along the seacoast. He hunted and fished, and grew to love the mystery and danger of the swamplands. Here he was judged by his survival skills, not his small size.

Francis became a sailor at age fifteen but quit after his first voyage. A whale struck the ship and made it sink! The crew survived in a lifeboat with little food and water. They were lost at sea for six days. Francis discovered that he could be scared and brave at the same time.

He joined the army at seventeen and fought against the Native Americans. Francis admired the way the Cherokee won battles with surprise attacks and quick escapes. He learned it was the best way for a small army to defeat a much larger enemy force.

The American Revolution began and England sent a fleet of warships to capture the city of Charles Town. Francis gathered a band of brave men called Patriots. They saved the city with lightning quick strikes and escaped each time by hiding in the swamps.

Francis Marion was made a general. England sent even more troops and Charles Town finally fell to the Redcoats. But they didn't capture General Marion. He and his men stole weapons and horses, and freed 150 American prisoners during one of their many raids. This made English officer Colonel Tarleton extremely angry. He swore he'd capture the American general, swamps or no!

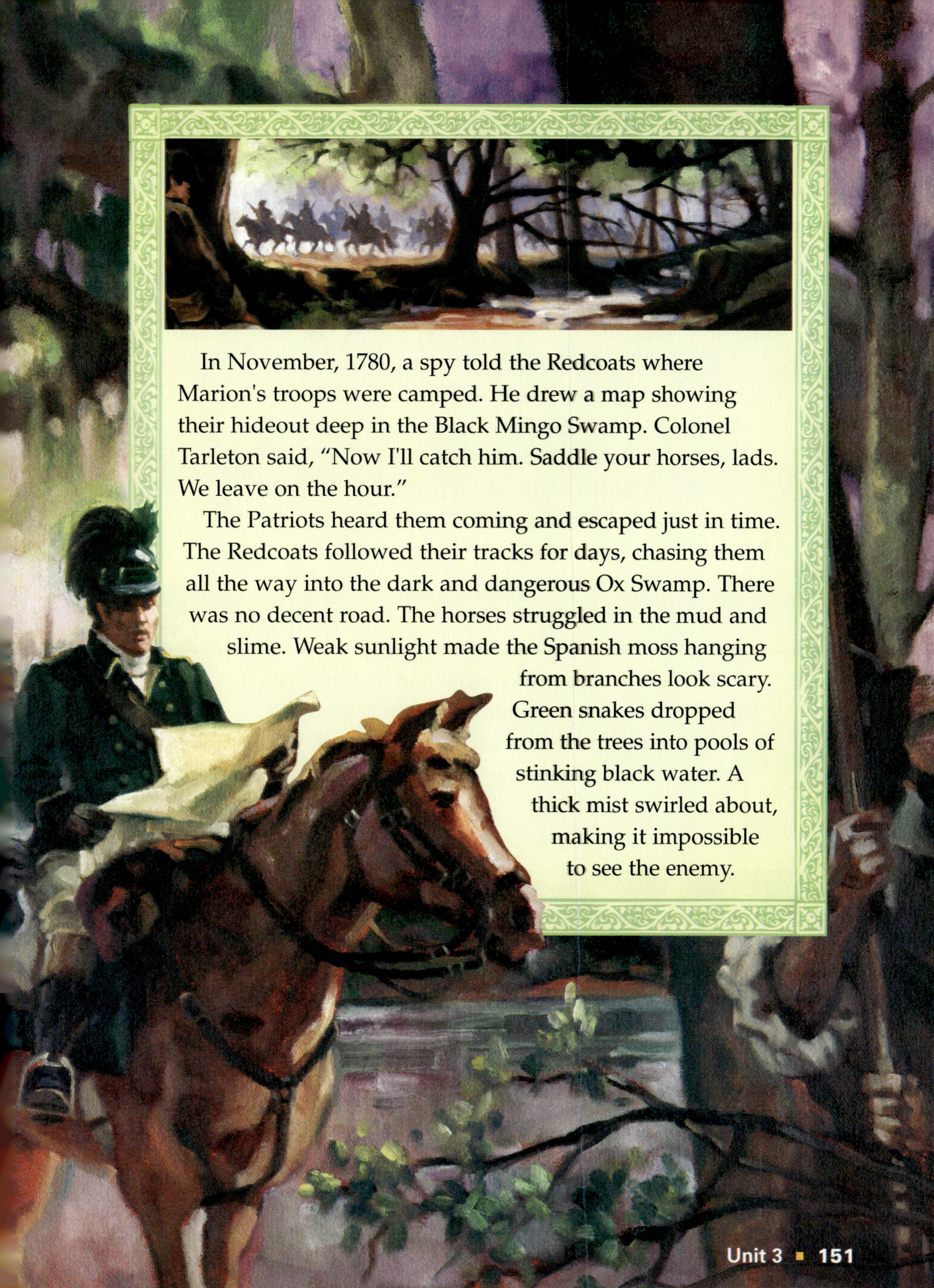

In November, 1780, a spy told the Redcoats where Marion's troops were camped. He drew a map showing their hideout deep in the Black Mingo Swamp. Colonel Tarleton said, "Now I'll catch him. Saddle your horses, lads. We leave on the hour."

The Patriots heard them coming and escaped just in time. The Redcoats followed their tracks for days, chasing them all the way into the dark and dangerous Ox Swamp. There was no decent road. The horses struggled in the mud and slime. Weak sunlight made the Spanish moss hanging from branches look scary. Green snakes dropped from the trees into pools of stinking black water. A thick mist swirled about, making it impossible to see the enemy.

General Marion's troops were close by. Hidden behind thick trees, they watched the Redcoats swat at hungry mosquitoes. They heard them complain about the terrible heat and pesky flies.

Colonel Tarleton got down from his horse and stepped on a fallen tree trunk. The long, greenish log next to it suddenly began to move. It was an alligator slipping quietly into a deep pool.

Tarleton said, "Come my boys! Let us go back. No one could catch this old swamp fox."

That's how General Francis Marion was given his famous nickname. He and the Patriots used the cleverness of the fox to help win the Revolutionary War. The Swamp Fox was an American hero who became a legend. He will never be forgotten.

## Think About It

1. Why was Francis Marion called "The Swamp Fox"?
2. How is a legend different from other stories?

## Read a Book

## Start the Unit Project

**Honor a Hero** With your classmates, honor a hero from South Carolina history. As you study this unit, take notes about the important people and events. Your notes will help you decide which person you want to honor.

## Use Technology

Visit the Learning Site at **www.harcourtschool.com** for additional activities, primary sources, and other resources to use in this unit.

### Star Fort at Old Ninety Six

In 1730, a fort was built at Ninety Six to protect settlers. The place was named by early European traders. They mistakenly thought it was 96 miles to the Cherokee town of Keowee (kee•OH•wee).

# Chapter 5

# From Colony to State

" **The American colonies are now... independent states.** "
—South Carolina General Assembly, 1776

 **Sequence**

Noticing the sequence of events helps you understand what you read. **Sequence** is the order in which events happen. Words such as *first, next, then,* and *last* help you put events in order.

As you read about how South Carolina changed from a colony into a state, write important events in a sequence chart.

- Use the words *first, next, then,* and *last*.

# Lesson 1

## The Colonies Grow

**Big Idea**
Many new people came from Europe to live in the colonies.

**Vocabulary**
migrate
crossroads
Parliament

In the early 1700s, England came to be called Britain. South Carolina was one of the thirteen colonies Britain had in North America. Britain encouraged Europeans to move to the colonies.

### The Thirteen Colonies

The colonies offered settlers new opportunities. In Europe, many areas were crowded. Most people did not have their own land to farm. For this reason, many people from Europe chose to **migrate**, or move.

New settlers arrived, from France, Germany, and Holland. Even so, most of the newcomers came from England, Scotland, and Ireland.

Port cities, such as Charles Town and Boston, soon became crowded with new people. Lands near these coastal cities were already settled. The newcomers would have to make their homes farther inland.

**Review** Where did the new settlers come from?

**FAST FACT** During the 1700s, hundreds of ships came to Charles Town each year. Most of South Carolina's trade was with London, not with the other colonies.

## Into the Frontier

New settlers did not have highways to travel on to reach their frontier homes. They used Native American paths, as the Indian traders did. Traders were the first European settlers in South Carolina's Upcountry. A few built trading posts at **crossroads**, where one path crossed another.

A fort and trading post were built on the Cherokee Path in 1730. The place was called Ninety Six. A village was also settled at Winnsboro around 1755.

**Review** Who were the first settlers in the Upcountry?

SEQUENCE

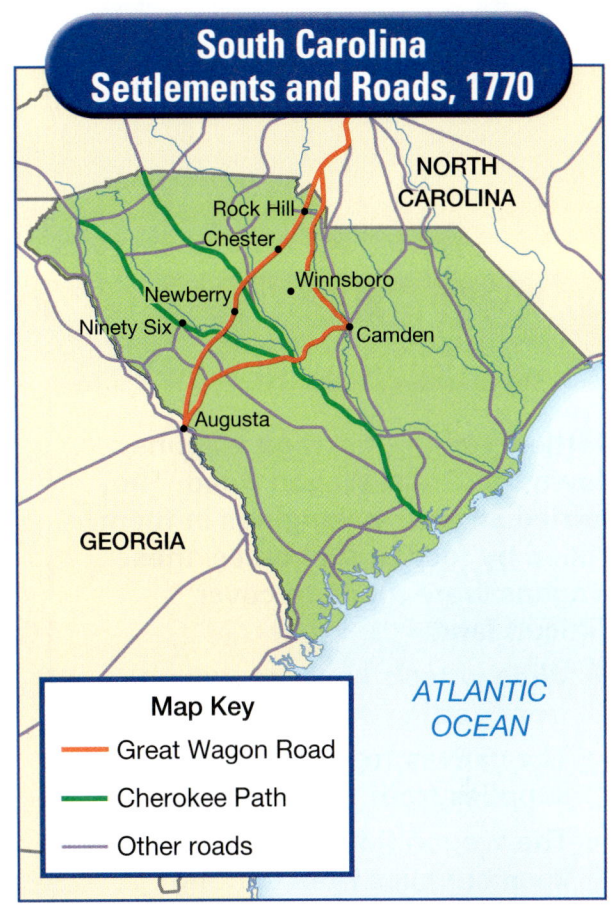

**Movement** In the 1700s, many settlers came to South Carolina on the Great Wagon Road.

As they traveled south, what was the first town settlers came to in South Carolina?

Chapter 5 • 157

# Wagon Roads

Many new settlers who came south first landed in Philadelphia, Pennsylvania. There were so many people traveling on Native American paths that the paths soon became colonial wagon roads.

The busiest road was the Great Wagon Road. It followed parts of the Great Indian Trading Path. The Great Wagon Road ran from Philadelphia to Camden. Colonists built many towns along the road. York and Abbeville were started alongside the Great Wagon Road.

**Review** Where did the Great Wagon Road start?

## A Closer Look
### Conestoga Wagon

Settlers took Conestoga wagons down the Great Wagon Road. They carried all their belongings in them. Pulled by four to six horses, these wagons were made to cover difficult land.

1. Wide wheels kept the wagon from getting stuck in the mud.
2. The canvas top protected supplies from the weather.
3. The wagon floor was curved to keep supplies from shifting when going up and down hills.
4. The ends were higher than the middle to keep the load from falling out. The wagon could hold up to 15,000 pounds.

❖ Why was the wagon floor curved?

## Frontier Troubles

Colonists were settling on Native Americans' lands. Sometimes they traded for the land. Often, they took land by force.

In 1754, the problem turned into a war. Some Native American tribes forced settlers to leave the frontier. The French helped these tribes.

The colonists wanted to build homes and farms. They wanted Britain to protect them from attacks. **Parliament**, or British lawmakers, agreed to send soldiers. This conflict was called the French and Indian War.

Many colonists fought alongside the British soldiers. In 1763, the war ended. The British had won.

**Review** Who won the French and Indian War?

Virginia colonist George Washington learned to be a strong leader during the French and Indian War.

## LESSON 1 Review

**Sequence** Which happened first—trading posts were built in the Upcountry or Native American paths became roads?

**1 Big Idea** What countries did many new colonists come from?

**2 Vocabulary** Write two sentences, one using the word **migrate** and another using **crossroads**.

**3 Geography** What town marked the southern end of the Great Wagon Road?

 **Performance—Write a List** Make a list of ten things you and your family might need to bring along if you were traveling in a Conestoga wagon. The things must all fit in the wagon and must not use electricity or batteries.

Chapter 5 ■ 159

# Skills

# Identify Cause and Effect

**Vocabulary**
cause
effect

## ▶ Why It Matters

Changes take place each day. To understand these changes, you need to identify cause and effect. A **cause** is what makes something happen. What happens is the **effect**. You can use a graphic organizer to help you identify causes and effects.

## ▶ What You Need to Know

History is made up of events. Part of learning history is understanding what caused events to happen.

Use the following steps to help you understand an event.

**Step 1** Look for the cause or causes of the event.

**Step 2** Look for the effect or effects of the event.

**Step 3** Think about how the causes and effects are connected.

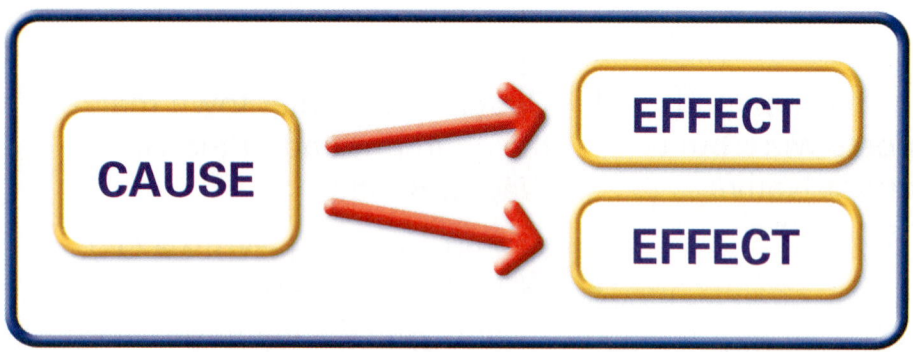

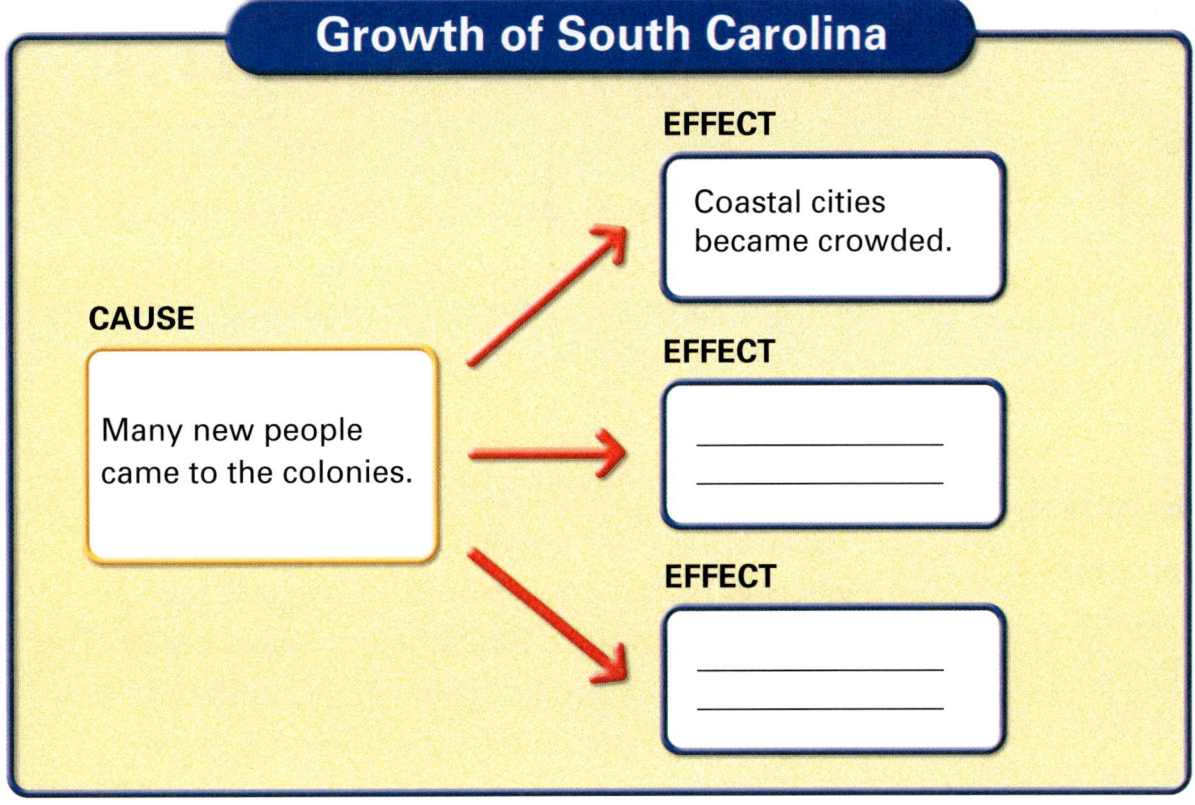

### ▶ Practice the Skill

Read the following paragraph. Copy the graphic organizer above. Use information in the paragraph to complete the graphic organizer.

In the 1700s, many people came to the colonies from Europe. As more people arrived, coastal cities became crowded. Settlers had to travel on wagon roads into the frontier. Some pioneers started towns along the wagon roads.

### ▶ Apply What You Learned

Imagine that a new school has opened in your neighborhood. What might have caused the need for a new school? What might be some effects of adding a school to the community? Use the chart above as a model to help you answer the questions. Share your answers with a partner.

# Lesson 2

## Colonies Unite

**Big Idea**
Some colonists wanted freedom from Britain.

**Vocabulary**
congress
Loyalist
Patriot
revolution
independence

After the French and Indian War, the colonies had hard times. Selling prices for colonial products were low. Yet, Parliament said colonists should pay for the costs of the war. Many colonists were upset.

### The Acts of Parliament

Only British citizens living in England voted for leaders in Parliament. Colonists wanted leaders to represent them, too. When new tax laws called "The Acts" were made, colonists grew angry. They said someone should represent them in government.

In 1765, Parliament passed the Stamp Act. All legal papers and newspapers were to be marked with a tax stamp. Colonists refused to pay the stamp taxes.

In October, the tax stamps arrived in Charles Town. A group called the Sons of Liberty planned to destroy the stamps. To prevent this, a British ship agreed to take the stamps away. This event became known as the South Carolina Stamp Party.

**Review** What was the Stamp Act?

This official government stamp (above) showed a tax had been paid. Angry colonists (below) protested against the Stamp Act.

162 • Unit 3

Boston colonists disguised themselves as Indians and boarded three tea ships in the harbor. A large crowd looked on as they threw the tea into Boston Harbor.

## The Tea Tax

In 1773, Parliament decided to tax tea. In Boston, Massachusetts, another group of the Sons of Liberty took action. They tossed tea boxes from a British ship into the harbor. Their protest was called the Boston Tea Party.

As punishment, the British closed the port in Boston. British soldiers were sent to keep order. Colonists called these laws "The Intolerable Acts." Intolerable means "unbearable."

Leaders in Charles Town worried the British might block their harbor, too. Leaders from South Carolina met in Charles Town to discuss their problems.

This tea chest was said to have washed ashore just one day after the Boston Tea Party.

**Review** What event led to the Boston Tea Party? SEQUENCE

# Philadelphia

In 1774, leaders decided to have a meeting in Philadelphia for all the colonies. It was the First Continental Congress. A **congress** is a group of elected leaders who meet to discuss problems.

South Carolina elected five men to go to the congress. The group included John and Edward Rutledge, Christopher Gadsden, Thomas Lynch, and Henry Middleton. Gadsden and others said the colonies should unite, or join together.

At this meeting, the colonies began to unite. However, they could not all agree on what to do about the British.

**Review** Where did the First Continental Congress meet?

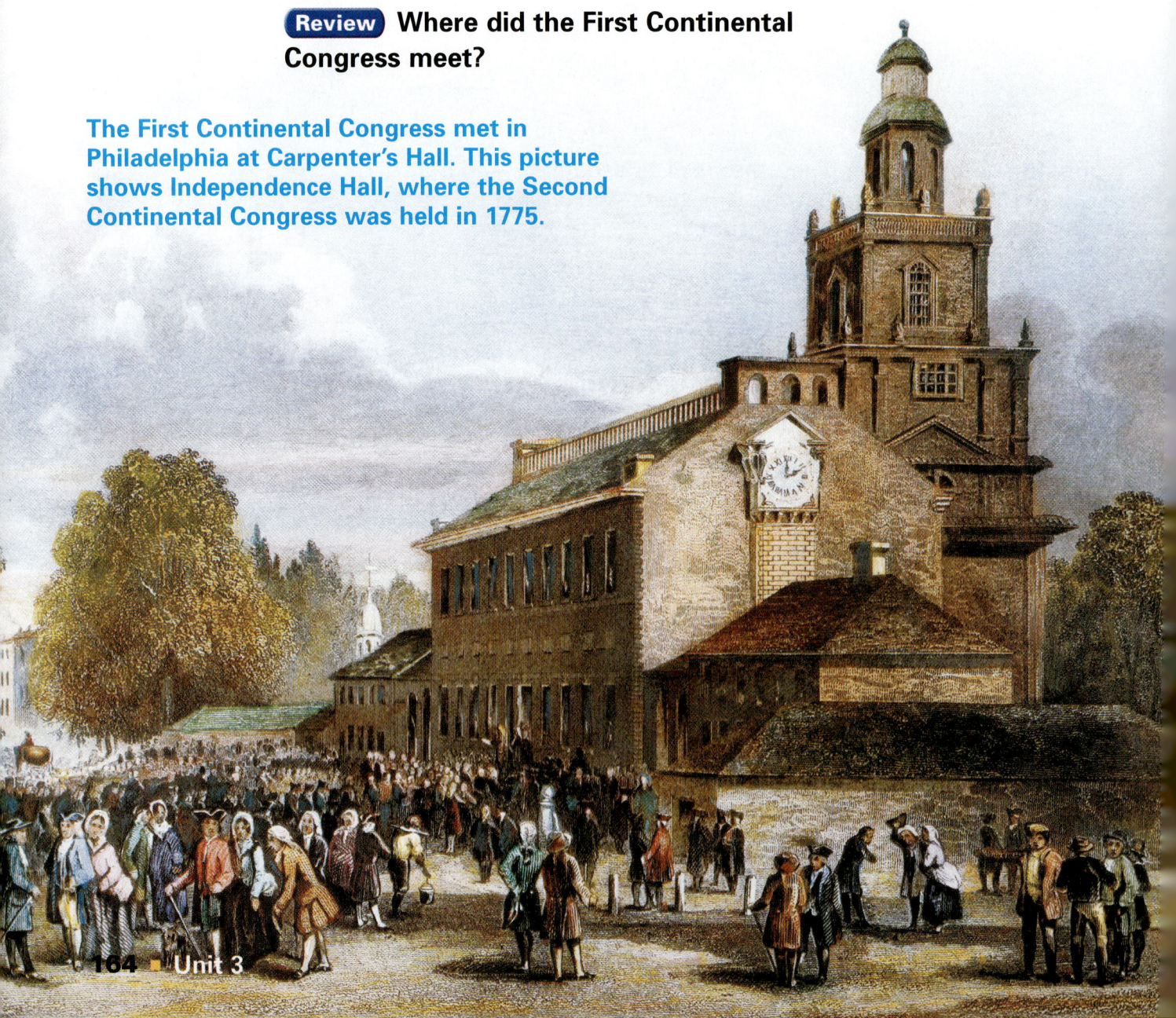

The First Continental Congress met in Philadelphia at Carpenter's Hall. This picture shows Independence Hall, where the Second Continental Congress was held in 1775.

## Points of View
### Loyalist vs. Patriot

**COLONEL THOMAS FLETCHALL—**
Loyalist, August 17, 1775

❝... would never take up arms against his king or his countrymen and that the proceedings of the Congress at Philadelphia were impolitic, disrespectful, and irritating to the King.❞

**CHRISTOPHER GADSDEN—**
Patriot, September 7, 1782

❝Our cause is good; the cause of humanity itself . . . These were my sentiments at the time of the Stamp Act, the beginning of our dispute, they have continued to be so ever since, and with the blessing of God, I am ready and willing to undergo anything Heaven may still think proper to call me to suffer in support of it.❞

### Analyze the Viewpoints
1. How did each man view British rule?
2. Imagine you are either Fletchall or Gadsden. Write a letter to your family explaining your point of view toward the British. Tell why you think the colonies should gain independence or remain under British rule.

A tricornered hat and button from a Revolutionary War uniform.

## Colonists Take Sides

People in the colonies began to take sides. In South Carolina's Upcountry, many people were **Loyalists**. They wanted the colonies to stay under British rule. The British had defended frontier settlers from Native American attacks. They allowed people to own farms and worship according to their own religions. Most Upcountry people wanted things to stay the same.

In the Lowcountry, most people were Patriots. **Patriots** were colonists who opposed British rule. They wanted to have their own government. Many Patriots were rich merchants and planters. British taxes and trade laws hurt their businesses. If the colonies separated from Britain, they would have their own government.

**Review** Where did most of South Carolina's Patriots live?

# War Breaks Out

After the meeting in Philadelphia, things grew worse. In April 1775, British soldiers in Massachusetts fought with colonists at the Battle of Lexington. This event started the American Revolution. A **revolution** is a fight for a change in government.

Soon, fighting began in South Carolina. Lowcountry Patriots tried to get Upcountry Loyalists to join them. Few Loyalists changed their minds.

In October, a Loyalist leader was arrested and taken to Charles Town. Soon other Loyalists attacked the Patriots at Ninety Six. After days of fighting, Captain Andrew Pickens spoke with the Loyalists. They agreed to move away from the fort.

**Review** What was the American Revolution?

A painting of the Battle of Lexington

## BIOGRAPHY

### Andrew Pickens   1739–1817
**Trait: Trustworthiness**

Early in the American Revolution, Patriot leader Andrew Pickens was captured. Because Pickens gave his word not to fight again, the British let him go home.

Loyalists later wrecked Pickens's house and frightened his family. Pickens felt that he could no longer keep his promise not to fight. To be fair and honorable, Pickens went to the British leader. He explained why he had to begin fighting the Loyalists again.

**MULTIMEDIA BIOGRAPHIES**
Visit The Learning Site at www.harcourtschool.com to learn about other famous people.

## Great Snow Campaign

When leaders in Charles Town learned of the attack on Ninety Six, they sent help. Colonel Richard Richardson and his Patriots marched south from Camden. Captain Pickens and other Patriots joined Richardson's group.

On December 21, 1775, the Patriots surprised the Loyalists near present-day Greenville. The Patriots won. They called this conflict the Great Snow Campaign, because they had come through bad weather.

By January, the Patriots were in control. They decided it was time for **independence**, or freedom, from Britain. On March 26, 1776, South Carolina's first constitution was adopted. The new government did not answer to Britain.

Winters in the Upcountry can be very cold and snowy.

**Review** Who won the Great Snow Campaign?

## LESSON 2 Review

 **Sequence** Which happened first—the Battle of Lexington or the South Carolina Stamp Party?

1. **Big Idea** Why did some colonists want freedom from Britain?

2. **Vocabulary** How was a **Patriot** different from a **Loyalist**?

3. **Geography** Why did people in the Upcountry stay loyal to British rule?

 **Performance—Write a News Story** Imagine you are interviewing a South Carolinian in 1775. Is he or she a Patriot or a Loyalist? Write a news story about the person. Then, put it in a class newspaper.

## Lesson 3

# The American Revolution

**Big Idea**
South Carolinians helped to win the American Revolution.

**Vocabulary**
blockade
turning point

In the spring of 1776, British ships sailed towards Charles Town. They planned to **blockade**, or shut off trade, at the harbor. Charles Town Patriots planned to keep the British out. They had a fort on James Island, but needed another fort on Sullivan's Island.

## The Palmetto Fort

William Moultrie, a Patriot army colonel (KER•nuhl), and his soldiers set to work. Time was short, so they built the fort with palmetto logs cut on the island.

On June 28, 1776, the British ships arrived and fired their cannons at the log fort. The cannonballs sank into the soft sand and wood. Patriots inside the fort fired their cannons and sunk four ships. That night, the British sailed from Charles Town Harbor.

The Patriots had won an important battle. The palmetto fort was given the new name, Fort Moultrie.

**Review** What did the Patriots use to build the fort?

A palmetto tree was added to South Carolina's flag to honor the battle and Colonel Moultrie (below).

Colonial leaders Benjamin Franklin, John Adams, and Thomas Jefferson work to write the Declaration of Independence. Members of Congress signed the Declaration (above) with this silver inkwell and quill pen.

## Declaring Independence

By the summer of 1776, the colonies wanted to be independent. Members of the Second Continental Congress decided to write a declaration, or formal statement, of the reasons they wanted to be free from Britain.

On July 4, 1776, the Continental Congress approved the Declaration of Independence. It states that people have a right to "Life, Liberty, and the pursuit of Happiness." On that day, the American colonies were no longer British. They were 13 free and independent states.

**Review** What is the Declaration of Independence?

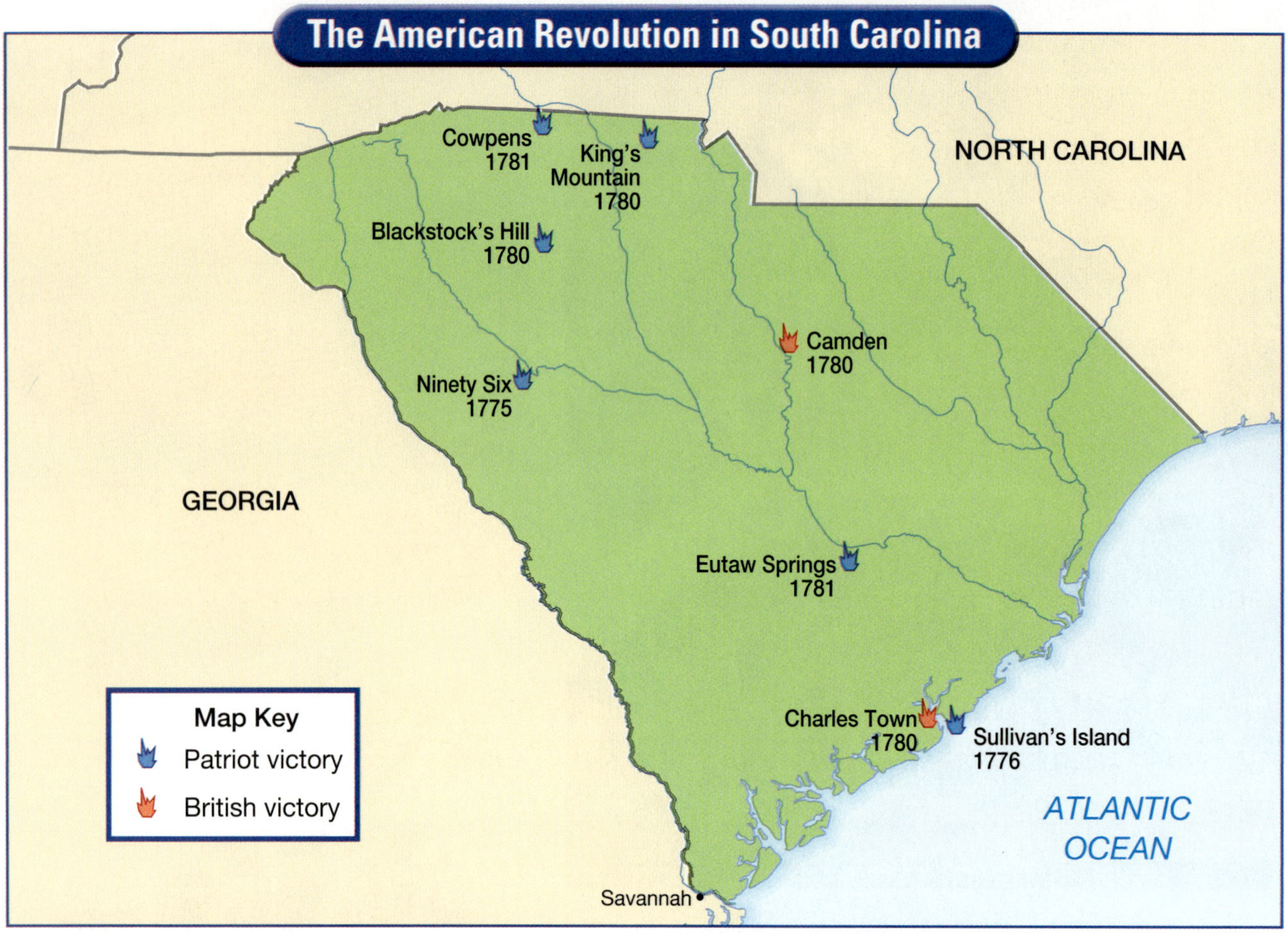

### The American Revolution in South Carolina

**Place** Battles during the American Revolution took place all over South Carolina. This map shows some important battles.

❓ Does this map show more Patriot victories or more British victories?

## Charles Town Blockade

The British returned to the southern coast in 1778. They still wanted to blockade Charles Town. The British also hoped to capture, or make prisoners of, Patriot leaders.

The British quickly took over Savannah, Georgia. From there, they marched north. The British army surrounded Charles Town on land. Their ships blockaded the harbor. In May 1780, the British took the city.

Important Patriot leaders were captured and sent to St. Augustine, Florida. Patriot Henry Laurens had served as the president of the Continental Congress. For this reason, he was sent to prison in Britain.

This British cannonball was recently found in a Charleston backyard.

**Review** Which city did the British capture first—Charles Town or Savannah? **SEQUENCE**

## War in the Upcountry

As they moved across South Carolina, British soldiers destroyed homes, farms, and plantations. They took food and everything of value.

One British officer was especially hated. Banastre Tarleton (BAN•us•ter TARL•tun) told his soldiers not to show mercy to Patriots. He even killed Patriots who tried to surrender. Some Loyalists joined the Patriots because of Tarleton.

Patriots Francis Marion and Thomas Sumter were experts at surprising the British and escaping quickly. Sumter's army fought Tarleton at Blackstock's Hill and won. Congress honored Sumter as a hero.

**Review** What did the British do as they moved through South Carolina?

Francis Marion inviting a British soldier to share his simple meal of sweet potatoes.

## · BIOGRAPHY ·

### General Thomas Sumter
#### 1734–1832

**Character Trait: Heroic Deeds**

In 1780, the British raided Sumter's home. After that, he became a leader in the Patriot army. He led his few soldiers against the British. Often, he did not win. In one battle, Sumter was nearly killed. However, his actions kept the British from regaining land in South Carolina. Fort Sumter in Charleston Harbor, a city, and a county all are named for this South Carolina hero.

**MULTIMEDIA BIOGRAPHIES**
Visit The Learning Site at www.harcourtschool.com to learn about other famous people.

Chapter 5 ■ 171

The Battle of King's Mountain was fought on horseback.

## King's Mountain to Cowpens

Two important battles in South Carolina helped end the war. At the Battle of King's Mountain, the British and Loyalists fought Patriots from the western frontier. The Patriots were called the Overmountain Men.

About 1,000 Patriots met the British at King's Mountain in October 1780. The battle lasted one hour. Most of the British and Loyalists were killed. It was a **turning point**, or big change, in the war. The Patriots began to believe they would win the war.

Patriot General Daniel Morgan brought his army to the Upcountry. Patriot soldiers, led by General Andrew Pickens and Colonel William Washington, soon joined Morgan.

On January 17, 1781, the two armies battled at Cowpens. The Patriots forced the British to leave South Carolina's Upcountry.

**Review** Why was the Battle of King's Mountain a turning point?

## The United States

A few months after the Battle of Cowpens, the Patriots won the war. British General Cornwallis surrendered to Patriot General George Washington in October 1781.

The British in Charles Town got ready to leave. Most Loyalists wanted to go, too. Thousands went to Britain, the West Indies, and Canada. Thousands of slaves were forced to go along.

The British had ruled South Carolina for more than one hundred years. Now, people would govern themselves in a new country—the United States of America.

**Review** Why did the British leave Charles Town?

British General Charles Cornwallis surrendered to General George Washington at Yorktown, Virginia.

## LESSON 3 Review

 **Sequence** Which event happened first—the Charles Town blockade or the Battle of Cowpens?

**1 Big Idea** How did South Carolinians help to win the war?

**2 Vocabulary** Write two sentences about the **blockade** of Charles Town.

**3 History** Which South Carolina battle was a turning point in the war?

**Performance—Write a Biography** Visit the library or use the Internet to learn more about South Carolina's Patriot leaders. Write a short biography of the person's life. Tell when he or she was born and died. Read your biography to a classmate.

Chapter 5 ■ 173

# Skills: Compare History Maps

**Vocabulary**
history map

## ▶ Why It Matters

The maps on page 175 show a part of North America at two different times in the past. You can see what has changed and what has stayed the same by comparing history maps. A **history map** shows how a place looked in an earlier time.

## ▶ What You Need to Know

Often colors on a map help you understand the information. Colors can help you tell water from land. They can show you special areas. The maps on page 175 use the color orange for colonies and states.

In the past, mapmakers used these instruments for measuring land and drawing maps.

## ▶ Practice the Skill

Look at each map key to see what each color shows. Then use the maps to complete the activities.

1. List the 13 colonies in 1775.
2. By 1800, what were the former colonies now called?
3. Compare the maps. Tell which new states were added to the United States by 1800.

## ▶ Apply What You Learned

Find an old map of a place, such as your community. Find a newer map of the same place. Compare and contrast the two maps. What has changed? What has stayed the same?

 Practice your map and globe skills with the **GeoSkills CD-ROM**.

## Lesson 4

# South Carolina Statehood

**Big Idea**
South Carolina set up a state government.

**Vocabulary**
Bill of Rights
federal

The American Revolution ended in 1783. After the war, many people had hard times. Many of South Carolina's farms and plantations were ruined in the fighting.

## Building a New State

People had to work together to make things better. Lowcountry planters and merchants had held most of the power under the British. People in the Upcountry wanted a state government that would represent their voices, too.

In 1786, leaders agreed to move the state government away from Charleston. They chose to build a new capital in the center of the state. The new location allowed more people in the Upcountry to take part in state government. The new capital city was named Columbia.

**Review** Why was the capital moved to Columbia?

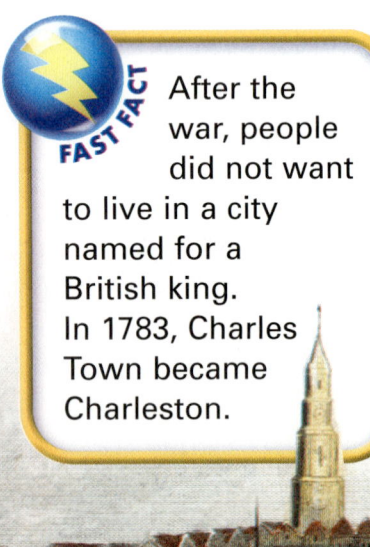

**FAST FACT** After the war, people did not want to live in a city named for a British king. In 1783, Charles Town became Charleston.

John Rutledge

Pierce Butler

Charles Cotesworth Pinckney

## Building a New Nation

Citizens in each of the former colonies wrote state constitutions. The 13 new states would also have to work together to write a constitution for the country.

In 1787, the Constitutional Convention met in Philadelphia. South Carolina was represented by John Rutledge, Pierce Butler, Charles Cotesworth Pinckney, and Charles Pinckney.

Leaders from some states wanted a strong national government that could protect business and trade. Leaders from other states disagreed. They worried that a strong national government might take away the rights of the states.

Each state would have to decide. In 1788, South Carolina became the eighth state to accept the United States Constitution.

**Review** Which came first—South Carolina statehood or the Constitutional Convention?

 SEQUENCE

Charles Pinckney

Chapter 5 ■ 177

George Washington was one of the group who wrote the United States Constitution.

## The Bill of Rights

The United States Constitution was a good plan for government. Yet, some people worried that a strong national government would mean fewer rights for citizens. Others felt that larger states might make laws that hurt smaller states. Promises of protection needed to be added to the Constitution.

In 1791, a list was added to the Constitution. The **Bill of Rights** listed some of the rights and freedoms that belonged to all Americans. It said that citizens may choose their religion. It said that citizens have the right to speak in public and print their ideas. It also said that citizens have a right to be heard in court.

The Bill of Rights was written in ten parts. For leaders of South Carolina's Upcountry, the last part was the most important. It said the **federal**, or national, government had certain powers. Except for those, all powers were reserved, or held, for the states.

**Review** Why was the Bill of Rights added to the Constitution?

# Columbia

By 1790, 2 out of 3 South Carolinians lived in the Upcountry. For many, moving the state's capital to Columbia was an important sign of change.

The new town was carefully planned. Streets were named for state heroes, such as Pickens, Gadsden, and Sumter. The South Carolina government met in the new State House for the first time in 1790.

Lawmakers decided to rewrite the state constitution that was written during the American Revolution. South Carolina's new constitution made a few important changes. People in the Lowcountry and the Upcountry would share the power of government more evenly.

**Review** Why was the state constitution rewritten?

**Columbia today has many reminders of our state's history.**

**Lawmakers met in the first South Carolina State House in Columbia in 1790.**

# Cotton Is King!

Upcountry farms had suffered during the war. Many farmers had fought as soldiers. When they returned, their farms were in poor condition. South Carolina needed a new cash crop.

In 1793, Eli Whitney invented the cotton gin. In the past, cotton was costly to grow as a cash crop because the seeds had to be removed from the plants one at a time, by hand. Whitney's machine easily removed the cotton seeds. Then the cotton fibers could be spun into thread and made into cloth.

The cotton gin made it easier to clean and sell cotton. Many people in South Carolina decided to try growing cotton. Soon, cotton replaced rice as the state's most important cash crop. In the early years of the state, people said, "Cotton is king!"

**Review** How did the cotton gin help cotton farmers?

Slaves did the hard work of growing fields of cotton.

These tools were used to make cotton cloth.

### The Cotton Gin

**Analyze Primary Sources**

In 1793 Eli Whitney invented the cotton gin. This machine could clean more cotton in one hour than several workers could in one day.

1. Freshly picked cotton was put into the cotton gin.
2. Turning the handle rolled the cotton between thin, hook-shaped wires.
3. The seeds fell into one section. The clean cotton fiber fell into another.

◆ What was the main purpose of the cotton gin?

## LESSON 4 Review

 **Sequence** What events led to cotton becoming the most important crop?

1. **Big Idea** How did changes in government give the Upcountry more power?

2. **Vocabulary** Write a sentence that tells how the **Bill of Rights** and the **federal** government are connected.

3. **Economics** How did the cotton gin change farming?

 **Performance—Make a Venn Diagram** Make a Venn diagram. On the left side, list what you learned about people and life in the Lowcountry after the Revolution. On the right side, list what you learned about people and life in the Upcountry. In the middle, list what the two areas had in common.

Chapter 5 ■ 181

# Skills: Use a Map Grid

**Vocabulary**
exact location
grid system

## ▶ Why It Matters

One way to find exact location is to use a map that has a grid system. **Exact location** is the point where two lines meet, or cross, on a map. A **grid system** is a set of lines the same distance apart that cross one another to form boxes. Knowing how to use a grid makes it easier to find locations on a map. For example, you can find the exact location of a street on a city map. You can find out exactly how far north, south, east, and west a place is on a world map.

## ▶ What You Need to Know

Look at the grid on this page. Find the row labels—the letters along the sides of the grid. Now look for the column labels—the numbers along the top and bottom of the grid.

Put your finger on the purple box. Now slide your finger to the left side of the grid. You will see that the purple box is located in row C. Go back to the purple box. Slide your finger to the top of the grid. The purple box is in column 3. To describe the exact location of the purple box, you would say that it is at C-3.

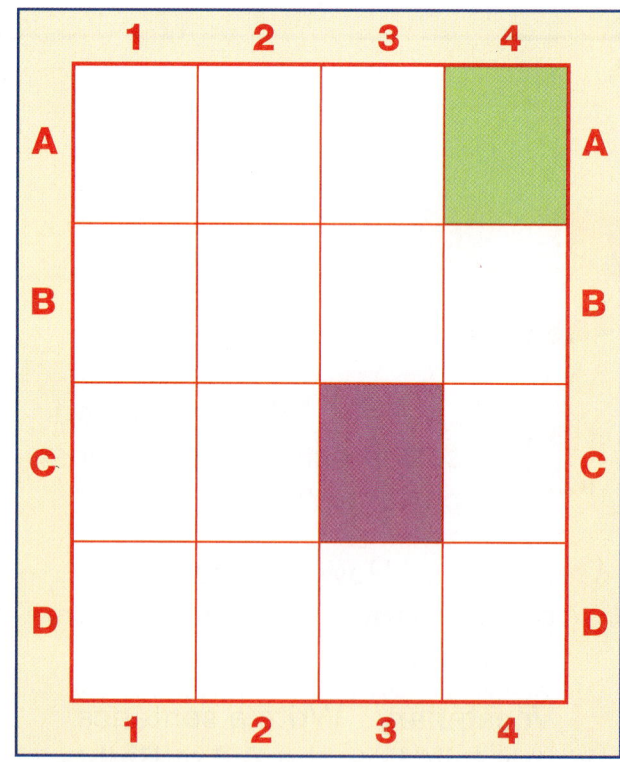

182 • Unit 3

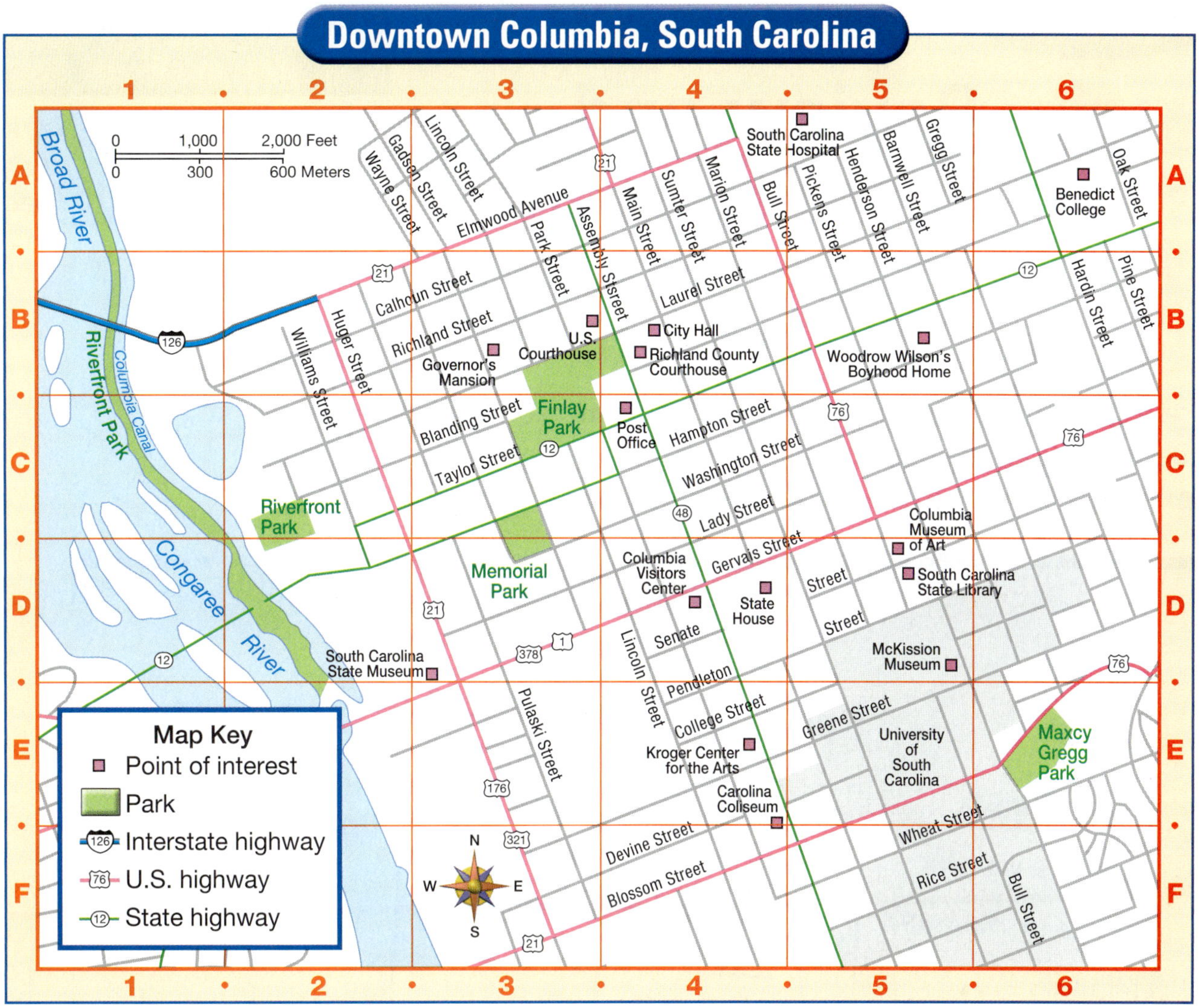

## Downtown Columbia, South Carolina

### ▶ Practice the Skill

Look at the map of Columbia, South Carolina, above. It has a grid system. Use the map and its grid system to answer these questions. Use a letter and a number for each place.

1. Where is the State House building?
2. What point of interest is found at B-5?
3. Where is Maxcy Gregg Park?

### ▶ Apply What You Learned

Draw a map of a place you know. It can be your neighborhood, home, school, or classroom. Add a grid so you can find places on your map. Share your map with a classmate or family member. Have him or her find a place by using the grid.

 Practice your map and globe skills with the **GeoSkills CD-ROM**.

Chapter 5 ■ 183

# Chapter 5
## Review and Test Preparation

**Time Line**

1750 — 1760

• 1760 Parliament passes the Stamp Act

### Focus Skill: Sequence

Copy the graphic organizer onto a separate sheet of paper. Use what you learned to put the events of the American Revolution in South Carolina in sequence.

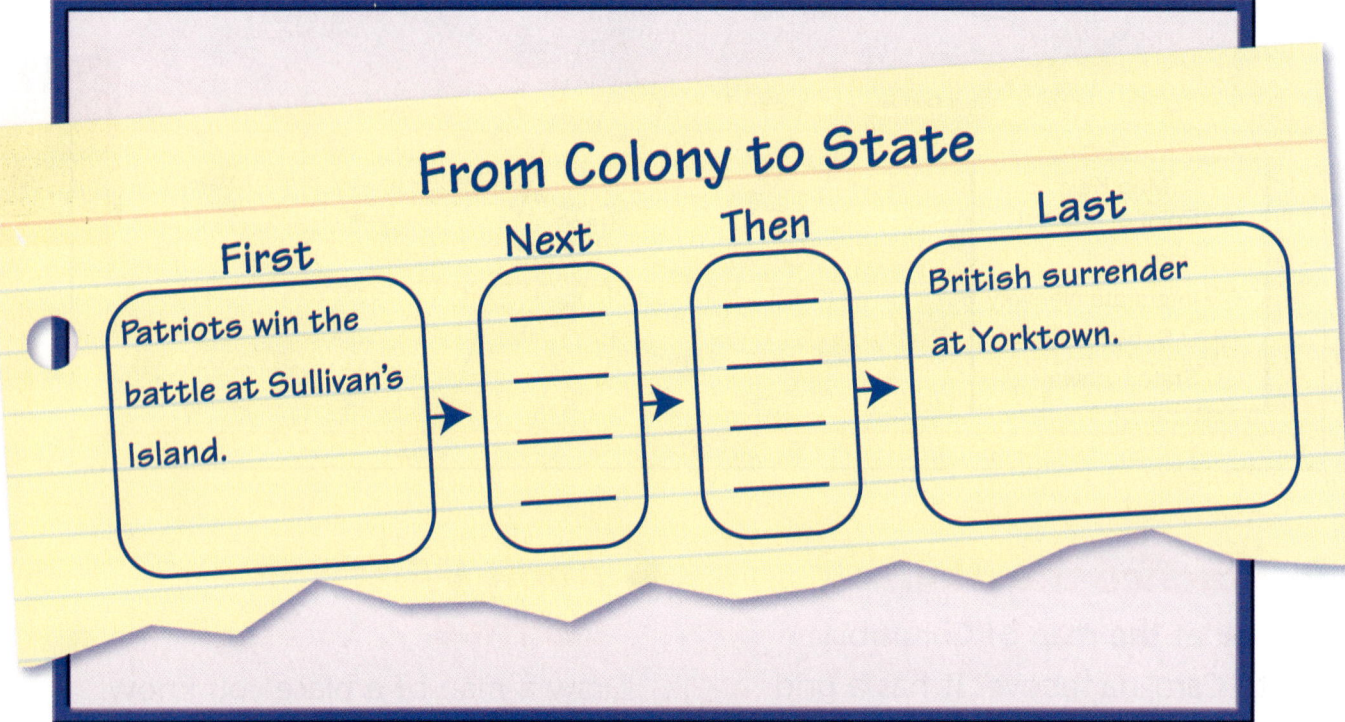

From Colony to State

- **First:** Patriots win the battle at Sullivan's Island.
- **Next:** ___
- **Then:** ___
- **Last:** British surrender at Yorktown.

## Think & Write

**Write a Speech** Imagine you live in the Upcountry when South Carolina is still under its first constitution. Write a speech that tells why people in your area should have more power in the state government.

**Write a Journal Entry** Imagine you are visiting the new state capital in 1790. Write a journal entry telling what the new capital is like. Include what you see and what you do while you are there.

- 1775 American Revolution begins
- 1780 British take Charles Town
- 1781 British surrender at Yorktown, Virginia
- 1788 South Carolina becomes the eighth state

## Use The Time Line

Use the chapter summary time line to answer these questions.

1. How many years passed between Parliment passing the Stamp Act and the start of the American Revolution?
2. In what year did the British take Charles Town?

## Use Vocabulary

Write the term from the list that best completes each sentence.

Loyalist (p. 165)   revolution (p. 166)
Patriot (p. 165)   turning point (p. 172)

3. A ___ is a big change in the war.
4. A ___ wanted South Carolina to separate from Britain.
5. A fight for a change in government is a ___.
6. A ___ wanted South Carolina to stay a British colony.

## Recall Facts

Answer these questions.

7. Who won the American Revolution?
8. What new cash crop grew in South Carolina after 1793?

Write the letter of the best choice.

9. Why was Columbia built?
   A to give more power to people in the Lowcountry
   B to let people from the Upcountry share in state government
   C to build a new State House
   D to celebrate the victory over the British

## Think Critically

10. How did ways of life in the Upcountry differ from those in the Lowcountry?

## Apply Skills

**Identify Cause and Effect**

11. Follow the steps on page 160. Explain the increase in cotton production in the early 1800s.

**Compare History Maps**

12. Use the maps on page 175. Name one territory added to the United States between 1775 and 1800.

**Use a Map Grid**

13. Look at the map on page 183. Where is the Governor's Mansion?

**Fort Sumter National Monument**

Fort Sumter was built by the United States to protect Charleston's harbor. It was named for Thomas Sumter, a hero of the American Revolution.

Chapter

6

# Civil War and Reconstruction

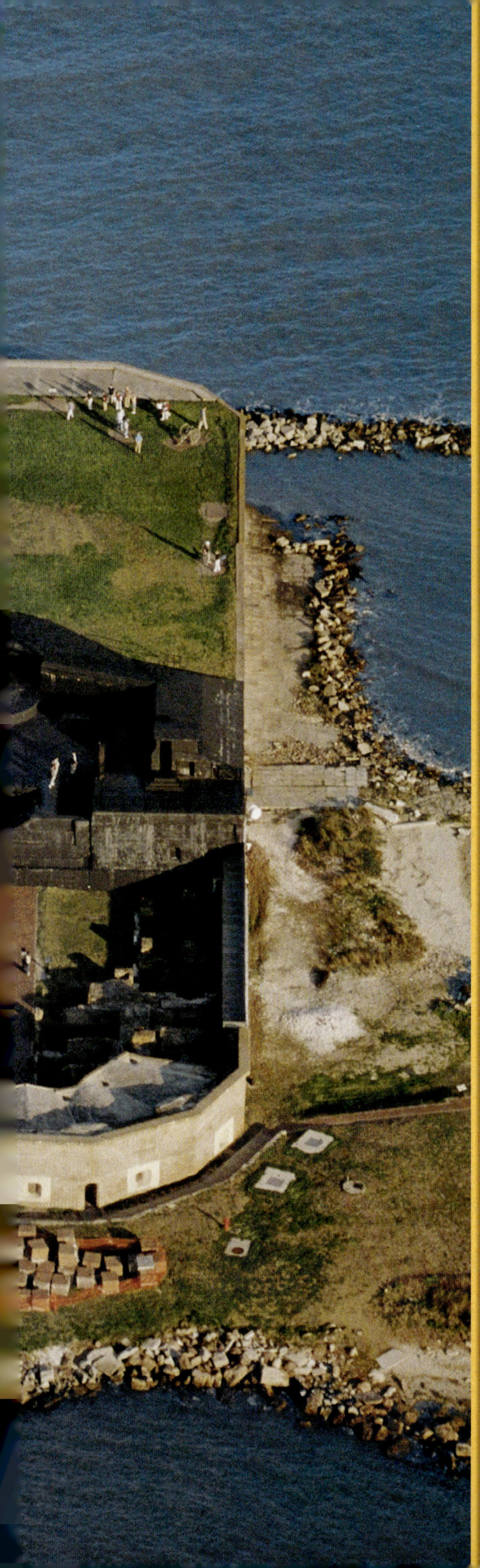

**"Honor and patriotism require me to stand by my state"**

—Benjamin Perry, 1860

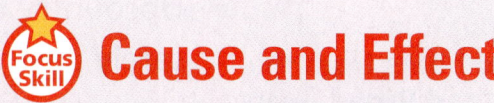

## Cause and Effect

Focus Skill

A **cause** is something that makes another thing happen. An **effect** is the thing that happens.

**As you read this chapter, look for clue words such as *because* and *as a result*. They will help you identify the causes and effects of important events.**

- **Make a list of causes and effects.**

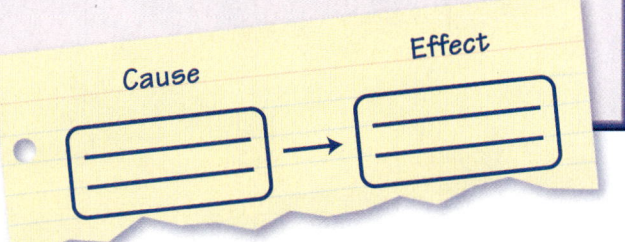

# Lesson 1

## Southern Life

**Big Idea**
South Carolina kept many of its colonial ways of life.

**Vocabulary**
canal
class system

South Carolina and the United States were changing in the early 1800s. New ways of farming changed life for many people, especially in the South.

### Changing Days

New inventions, such as the cotton gin, were changing the way people lived. Many people in the Upcountry started to grow cotton. In the past, most had grown just enough food for their families. Now they were growing a cash crop. In order to sell the cotton, they had to get it to Charleston.

Farmers near the Santee River wanted a **canal**, or human-made waterway, to shorten the trip to Charleston. When it was finished in 1800, the Santee River Canal made the trip to market faster. Other Upcountry canals were built to help boats travel safely past the fall line.

Leaders in Charleston wanted to improve travel to the city. In 1830, South Carolina opened its first railroad. It was called The Best Friend of Charleston.

**Review** How did the Santee River Canal improve trade? **CAUSE AND EFFECT**

The Columbia Canal allowed boats from the Saluda and Broad rivers to get to the Congaree River.

**Seven generations of the same family lived at Drayton Hall, which was built in 1738.**

**FAST FACT** Drayton Hall is the only plantation house on the Ashley River to survive since the American Revolution. The house is a National Historic Landmark.

## Southern Ways

When South Carolina was a colony, rich Lowcountry planters and merchants had controlled the government and society. In the new state government, those powers were shared. However, old colonial ideas about society continued.

The life of South Carolinians mostly depended on the family they were born into. Each family and the kind of work it did determined its place in society. South Carolina had a class system. In a **class system**, people are grouped in a rank. Those at the top, the planters, had the most money and power.

**Review** What determined a family's place in the class system?

**Cotton fibers come from the boll, or seed pod.**

Chapter 6 ▪ 189

## The Planter Class

South Carolina's planter class was at the top of society. It had the fewest members. Only the families of rich planters belonged to this class. Planters also owned most of the slaves in the state.

The planters were men who led in government and business. Their sons went to English schools. The planters enjoyed hunting and other sports.

Women in the planter class supervised their homes and children's education. Girls learned how to read and sew. Some learned how to paint or play music. A few became well-known artists and writers. In 1832, Caroline Gilman helped make the first children's newspaper in the country. It was called "The Rose Bud."

Planter families lived in beautiful homes. One family often had several houses. In spring and fall, they lived on their plantations. In the hottest part of the summer, families went to the Sea Islands. After Christmas, they gathered in Charleston. The times in the city were exciting. There were many dances and parties.

**Review** Who was in the planter class?

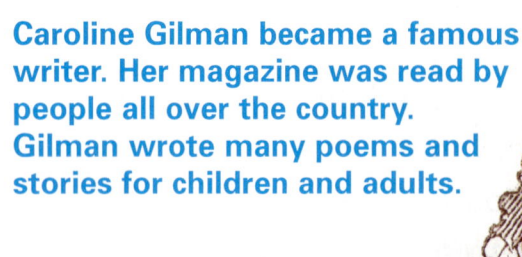

Caroline Gilman became a famous writer. Her magazine was read by people all over the country. Gilman wrote many poems and stories for children and adults.

Charleston was an important market city. Many people made, bought, and sold goods.

## The Middle Class

In the 1800s, most South Carolinians still lived on farms. Families living and working their own farms made up most of the middle class. Unlike the planters, most middle class families owned few slaves.

Skilled workers were also in the middle class. Charleston became well known for its lovely handmade products. Woodworkers, such as Thomas Elfe, made fine furniture for the planters. Other artists made and sold beautiful silver dishes and cups.

In most middle class families, everyone worked. Few children went to school beyond the eighth grade. Often, children were trained to do the same work as their parents.

**Review** Where did most people live in the 1800s?

Charleston was famous for its silversmiths. In the early 1800s, there were more than seventy at work in the city.

Chapter 6 ■ 191

Many lower class families lived in simple log cabins.

Early farm tools

## The Lower Class

Most people were not part of the planter class or the middle class. The largest class in South Carolina society was the lower class.

Most people in the lower class lived on small farms scattered across the state. Often, large families lived in houses with just one or two rooms. They had little money and made or grew everything they needed. Usually, people in the lower class could not read or write.

Everyone in the family worked on the farm. They needed to grow enough food to feed their families. They tried to grow extra crops to sell. People in the lower class worked hard, and many died at a young age. Poor farmers were at the bottom of South Carolina's white society.

**Review** What kind of work did most of the lower class do?

## Free African Americans

South Carolina's class system ranked African Americans, too. Some free African Americans earned a good living. Most of them lived in Charleston.

Most free African Americans in Charleston were skilled craftworkers. Denmark Vesey was a former slave. He earned enough money to buy his freedom working as a skilled woodworker. Later, he led a group of slaves to revolt.

South Carolina laws kept free African Americans from having the same rights as white citizens. They could not travel freely. Free African Americans in Charleston had to pay a yearly "head tax" to keep their freedom.

**Review** What kind of work did most free African Americans do?

Some free African Americans worked as silversmiths. Freedom papers showed that African Americans were free. (below)

### • BIOGRAPHY •

### Denmark Vesey 1767?–1822

**Trait: Courage**

Denmark Vesey (VEE•zee) was brought to Charleston as a slave in the 1780s. In 1800, Vesey paid for his own freedom. However, none of his children were free. Vesey thought that all African Americans should be free.

In 1822, Vesey tried to get a group of slaves to fight for their freedom. Sadly, their plans were discovered by the planters. The revolt was stopped. Vesey and some others were harshly punished.

**MULTIMEDIA BIOGRAPHIES**
Visit The Learning Site at www.harcourtschool.com to learn about other famous people.

These slave quarters in Charleston were crowded, but better than those on most plantations.

## African American Slaves

Under South Carolina's laws, enslaved African Americans were the property of the slaveowners. The owners decided every part of a slave's life. They decided where a slave lived and the kind of work he or she did.

Slaves had no rights or power. Laws said they could not learn how to read or write. An owner could sell a slave at any time, and to anyone. It was nearly impossible for slave families to stay together.

In their own society, slaves were ranked by the work they did. At the top were skilled workers, and those who worked in the planters' homes. They cleaned, cooked, cared for children, and served meals. Field workers were at the lowest social rank.

Slaves who worked on plantations had a hard life. They worked six days a week, usually from sunrise to sunset. They lived in small houses, crowded together. Their food was simple. Most slaves got a set of clothes twice a year. They had a new pair of shoes once a year.

**Review** How were slaves ranked?

Slaves who were hired out had to wear badges like this one.

### A Dave Jar

**Analyze Primary Sources**

Dave the Potter's jars and jugs are famous for being so large. They are also famous for their decoration. However, they are most famous for being made by a slave. Dave is the only slave known to have signed his art. He wrote poems and signed his name on many of his jars.

1. This jar is a kind of pottery called stoneware.
2. On this jar, Dave wrote the date and signed his name in large letters.

◆ When did Dave make this jar?

## LESSON 1 Review

 **Cause and Effect** How did more cotton trade cause changes in transportation?

1. **Big Idea** In what ways did South Carolina keep its colonial ways of life?

2. **Vocabulary** Use the terms **canal** and **class system** in two sentences about South Carolina life in the 1800s.

3. **Economics** What determined a family's place in society?

 **Performance—Make a Table** Think about how people on small farms and African American slaves lived and worked. Make a table comparing the two groups. Think about what kinds of houses they lived in and the work they did each day.

Chapter 6 ■ 195

# Skills Reading

# Determine Point of View in Pictures

**Vocabulary**

point of view

### ▶ Why It Matters

Two pictures with the same subject may be quite different. If you know how to study a picture, you can understand the artist's point of view. A **point of view** is the way a person feels about something.

### ▶ What You Need to Know

There are many reasons why people have different points of view. Some things can help you understand an artist's point of view.

1. How does the picture make you feel? Does the artist make the subject look good or bad? Is it funny or sad?
2. Think about the message of the artwork. What does the artist want you to know about this subject?
3. Compare two pictures of the same subject. What is different or the same about how the artists show their subject?

### ▶ Practice the Skill

Look at the pictures on page 197. Both show a scene of life on a farm. Each picture shows a different point of view.

1. What is happening in Picture A? What feelings does it show?
2. What is happening in Picture B? What feelings does it show?
3. What kind of feelings does each picture give you about farm life?
4. What do you think is the point of view of each artist?

### ▶ Apply What You Learned

Look through this chapter for a picture that gives you strong feelings. Describe how this picture makes you feel. What is the point of view? How did the artist show his or her point of view? Do you agree with this point of view?

**Picture A (above):** *Ready for Harvest,* **by Alice Ravenel Huger Smith**
**Picture B (below):** *Spring Planting,* **by Jonathan Green**

# Lesson 2

## Differences Divide the Nation

**Big Idea**
People in the nation were divided over slavery.

**Vocabulary**
industry
abolitionist
secede

In early 1820, the United States had grown to include 23 states. The nation expanded west as each new state was added. As in the other states, most people in these new states were farmers.

### Southern Cotton, Northern Factories

In the South, cotton farming depended on slavery. Some states in the North no longer allowed slavery. The North and South had different ways of life, too.

In the North, new industries were started. An **industry** includes all the businesses that make one kind of product or provide one kind of service. The textile industry was growing fast during this time.

Textile factories used large machines called looms to make cotton into cloth. As the textile industry grew, so did the need for more cotton from the South.

**Review** Why did the South grow more cotton?
**CAUSE AND EFFECT**

New York City was a major shipping and industrial center in the 1800s.

## • BIOGRAPHY •

### John C. Calhoun
### 1782–1850

**Character Trait: Loyalty**

John Calhoun was elected Vice President of the United States in 1824 and 1828. Yet, he cared most about events in his home state. He thought that President Jackson's ideas were bad for South Carolina. He quit as Vice President and became a Senator instead. As a Senator, Calhoun tried to stop laws that hurt the slave states.

 **MULTIMEDIA BIOGRAPHIES**
Visit The Learning Site at www.harcourtschool.com to learn about other famous people.

## States' Rights

The seventh United States President was born in South Carolina. Andrew Jackson believed that Congress made laws for the good of all the states. Senator John C. Calhoun disagreed.

South Carolina Senator Calhoun believed that it was a state's right to decide what is best. Calhoun did not want Congress to pass laws that took away the rights of his state.

In 1832, Calhoun led South Carolina to throw out a federal law that lowered cotton prices. President Jackson said that soldiers would force the state to follow the law. In the end, South Carolina went along. However, many people still felt strongly about states' rights.

**Review** Why did Senator Calhoun want states to make their own decisions?

**President Andrew Jackson was born in Waxhaw, South Carolina, in 1767.**

Chapter 6 ■ 199

# The Underground Railroad

One group, called the **abolitionists** (a•buh•LIH•shun•ists), wanted to end all slavery. They knew slavery was wrong. Sisters Angelina and Sarah Grimke (GRIM•kee) grew up in South Carolina. They moved to the North to join the abolitionists.

Abolitionists helped slaves who wanted to escape to the North. They offered safe hiding places. The secret trails and safe houses became known as the Underground Railroad.

Harriet Tubman, an escaped slave, led many people to freedom. If she had been caught, she would have been returned to her owner. Yet, Tubman bravely returned to the South many times to help others escape.

**Review** What was the Underground Railroad?

**Harriet Tubman is believed to have led 300 slaves to freedom.**

**Many people helped slaves escape to freedom along the Underground Railroad.**

# South Carolina Leaves the Union

The North and South disagreed about many things. The South thought some laws favored the North. The two sides struggled over equal power in the federal government.

Abolitionists in the North were calling for an end to slavery. Cotton planters in the South insisted on keeping their way of life. In 1860, President Abraham Lincoln was elected. Lincoln said he would not allow slavery in any more new states.

South Carolina said it would **secede** (seh•CEED), or leave, the United States. On December 20, 1860, leaders at a special Secession Convention voted to leave the United States of America.

An 1860 election poster for Abraham Lincoln. Some states in the South did not put Lincoln on the election ballot.

**Review** Why did South Carolina vote to secede?

## LESSON 2 Review

**Cause and Effect** How did the textile industry lead to a need for more cotton?

1. **Big Idea** Why did some people want to end slavery?
2. **Vocabulary** Write two sentences using the words **abolitionists** and **secede**.
3. **Civics and Government** What did President Jackson say he would do if South Carolina did not follow federal law?

**Performance—Do Research** Learn more about the Underground Railroad. Use an encyclopedia or the Internet. Write a paragraph about what you learned. Read your paragraph to your classmates.

# Skills: Compare Bar Graphs

## ▶ Why It Matters

Bar graphs are an easy way to show changes over time. You can see how things, like cotton production or slavery, changed over a set length of time.

## ▶ What You Need to Know

Each bar graph has a title. The title tells what the graph shows. A bar graph also has a scale. The scale is the row of numbers that runs along one side of the bar graph. The scale lets you measure the bars on the graph. For example, on Graph A on page 203, the scale goes from 0 to 4 million. You can use it to see how many bales of cotton the North and South had.

You can use Graph A to see how many bales of cotton were produced every ten years. You can use Graph B to see how the number of enslaved people grew every ten years.

## ▶ Practice the Skill

Use the graphs to answer the following questions.

1. Look at Graph A. In which ten-year period did the greatest increase in cotton production take place?
2. Approximately how many bales of cotton were produced in 1840?
3. Now look at Graph B. In which year were there about 2,000,000 enslaved people?
4. Approximately how many people were enslaved in 1850?

## ▶ Apply What You Learned

Bar graphs can be used to compare numbers of things. For example, you might want to compare the number of students in each grade at your school. Collect the information. Use the information to make a bar graph. Share your bar graph with your family.

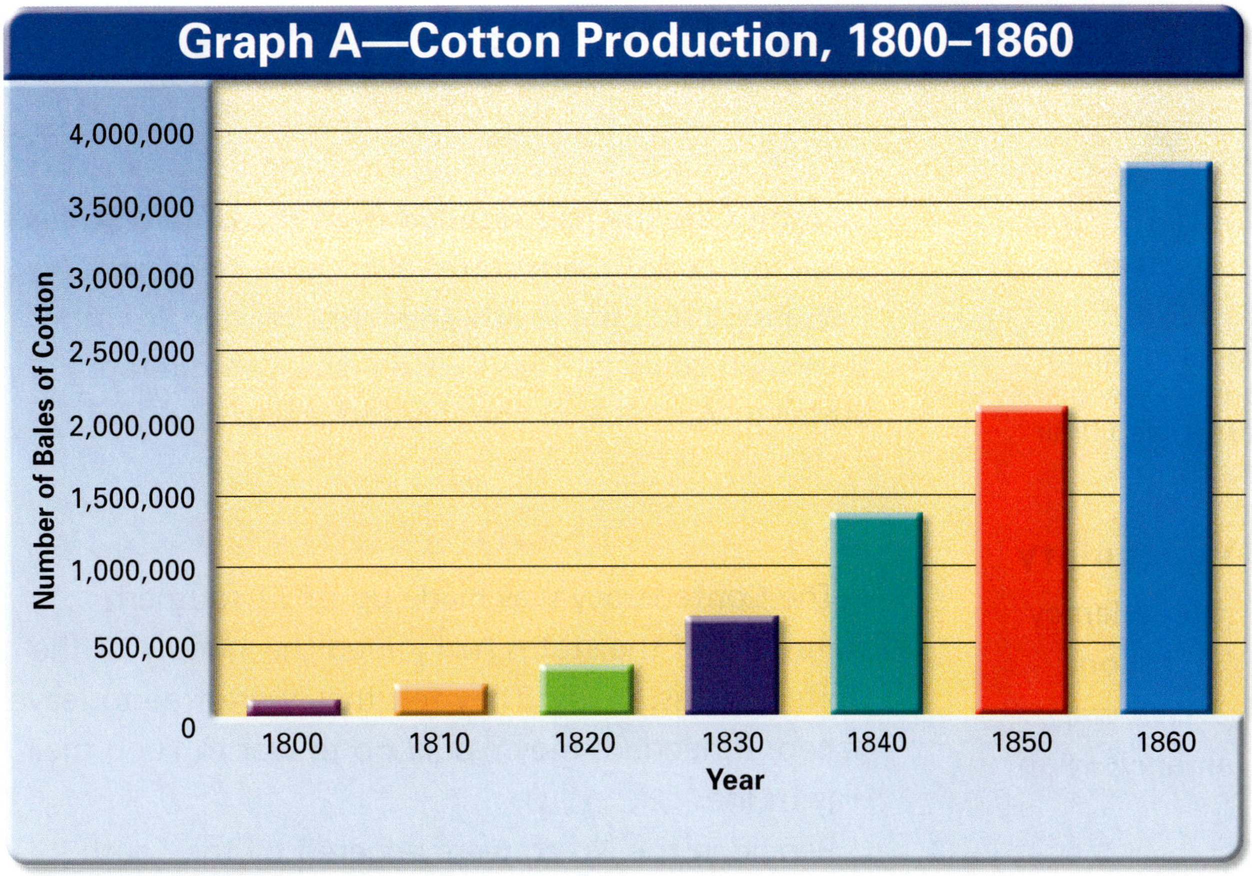

## Graph A—Cotton Production, 1800–1860

*Number of Bales of Cotton* vs *Year*

| Year | Bales of Cotton (approx.) |
|---|---|
| 1800 | ~100,000 |
| 1810 | ~200,000 |
| 1820 | ~350,000 |
| 1830 | ~700,000 |
| 1840 | ~1,400,000 |
| 1850 | ~2,100,000 |
| 1860 | ~3,800,000 |

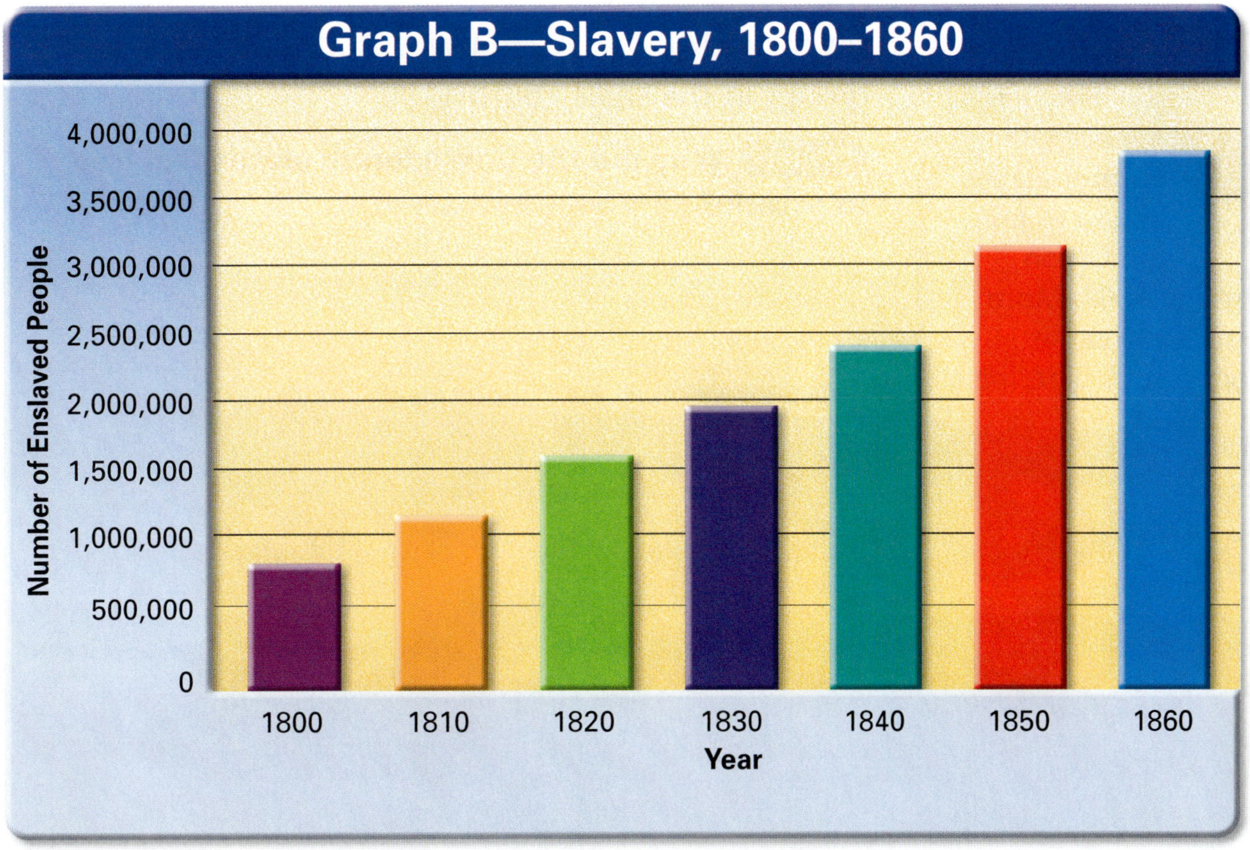

## Graph B—Slavery, 1800–1860

*Number of Enslaved People* vs *Year*

| Year | Enslaved People (approx.) |
|---|---|
| 1800 | ~800,000 |
| 1810 | ~1,100,000 |
| 1820 | ~1,600,000 |
| 1830 | ~1,950,000 |
| 1840 | ~2,400,000 |
| 1850 | ~3,150,000 |
| 1860 | ~3,850,000 |

CHART AND GRAPH SKILLS

## Lesson 3

**Big Idea**
People of South Carolina went to war to keep their way of life.

**Vocabulary**
Confederacy
Union
civil war
emancipation

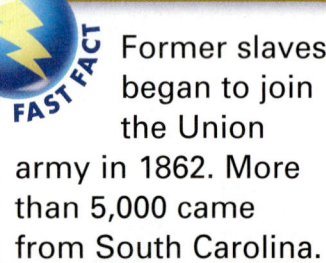

**FAST FACT** Former slaves began to join the Union army in 1862. More than 5,000 came from South Carolina.

# The Civil War

South Carolina had seceded from the United States. Soon, other Southern states also chose to secede. In February 1861, the southern states decided to form their own country. They called it the Confederate States of America, or the **Confederacy**.

## The Confederacy

The Confederacy was made up of 11 southern states. All of the states had joined the **Union**, or the United States, freely. They felt they were free to leave it, too. If needed, they would go to war to keep their way of life.

People in the North were angered by the South. There were still 19 states in the Union. They would fight to keep the Union together. The two sides were set for a civil war. A **civil war** is a fight between groups in the same country.

**Review** Why did the Confederate states feel free to secede? **CAUSE AND EFFECT**

John Ross Key (1837–1920), Bombardment of Fort Sumter, Siege of Charleston Harbor, 1863, circa 1865 (oil on canvas)

## Fort Sumter

States in the Confederacy took over the post offices, forts, and other government property in the South. Fort Sumter, in Charleston Harbor, was one of the few forts that stayed in Union control.

Early on the morning of April 12, 1861, Confederate soldiers, led by General P. G. T. Beauregard (BO•ree•gard), attacked Fort Sumter. They fired their cannons all day without stopping. The next day, Union Major Robert Anderson surrendered the fort. The South had won the first battle of the Civil War.

**Review** Where was the first battle of the Civil War?

### GEOGRAPHY

## Charleston Harbor
### Understanding Places and Regions

Charleston Harbor was a major port. It was especially important during the Civil War. It was one of the routes for supplying the Confederacy with food and supplies. Fort Sumter was built to protect the harbor. There were also many other forts and locations for cannons on the small islands and along the shore. Many battles were fought in Charleston Harbor during the Civil War.

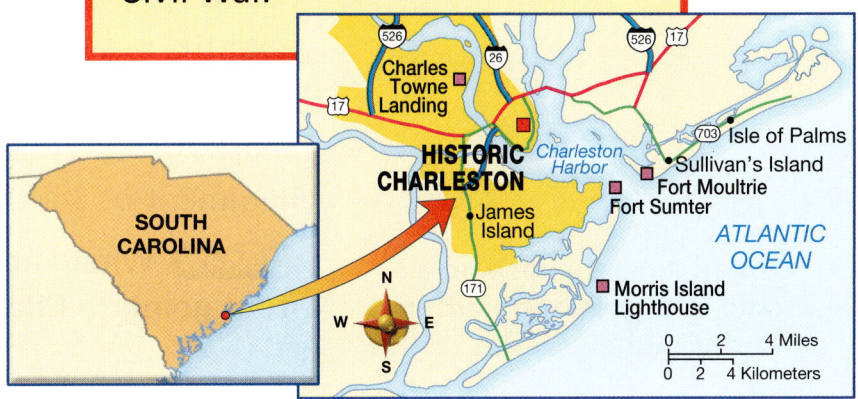

This painting shows how the firing on Fort Sumter looked from James Island.

# War Between the States

Most people, on both sides, thought that the Civil War would be a short war. Each side felt they were right, and that they would win. At first, it seemed the South might win the "War Between the States."

Many South Carolinians joined the Confederate army. Most were not slave owners. Yet, they all wanted to protect their state, their families, and their way of life.

The Union set up a blockade of Charleston Harbor. Confederate supply ships could not get through. Soon, the South ran short of food and other important items.

The Union took over Port Royal Sound and Beaufort in November 1861. They stayed there until the war ended. Slaves in the area were freed. Many wanted to join the Union army. These African American soldiers were the First Regiment of South Carolina Volunteers.

**Review** What kept Confederate supply ships from going to Charleston?

A Confederate cap and water canteen

Union soldiers pose on a ship in Charleston Harbor during the blockade.

Confederate hospitals treated many wounded soldiers.

# War Years

The blockade of Charleston made life hard for Confederate soldiers. It also hurt people at home. Most of South Carolina's farmland was used to grow cotton, not food. Many people struggled to get food, clothing, and medicine.

Those who were not in the army helped in other ways. Louisa McCord, from Columbia, started the Soldiers' Relief Association. Supplies went to the soldiers first. Families went without meat, and reused old clothes in order to help.

In 1862, a Confederate hospital was set up near Columbia. Sallie Hampton and Susan Preston Hampton cared for about 75,000 soldiers there. They worked as nurses. South Carolina's doctors, such as Julian Chisholm, tried to save the lives of injured soldiers.

A Union camp in Hilton Head

**Review** How did the war affect life for people in South Carolina? **CAUSE AND EFFECT**

Chapter 6 ■ 207

## SCIENCE AND TECHNOLOGY

### CSS *Hunley*

In 1864, in Charleston Harbor, the *Hunley* became the first submarine to sink an enemy ship. All of the *Hunley's* Confederate sailors died in the first battle when their ship sank.

In 1994, the *Hunley* was discovered 28 feet below the surface of the Atlantic Ocean. Six years later, on August 8, 2000, a team of experts lifted the submarine out of the water. Since then, they have been trying to piece together what happened on the night when the *Hunley* sank.

## Freedom

The Union army was larger than the Confederate army. The North had more factories and railroads, too. President Lincoln believed that the war would end more quickly if slaves were encouraged to fight for their freedom.

On January 1, 1863, a document called the "Emancipation Proclamation" became the law. **Emancipation** means to be set free. This document stated that all enslaved people in the Confederacy were free. Wherever the Union army went, newly freed slaves joined them.

**Review** What made the North a stronger force than the South?

Confederate General Robert E. Lee surrenders to Union General Ulysses S. Grant at a private home in Appomattox, Virginia, on April 9, 1865.

## An End to the War

On February 1, 1865, Union soldiers entered South Carolina. The Union army destroyed many towns, farms, and plantations. On February 17, 1865, Union General Sherman captured Columbia. Much of the city was burned down.

The Confederates left Charleston the same day. Fires destroyed many buildings there, too. In April 1865, the South could no longer fight. The Union won the war.

**Review** Who won the Civil War?

### LESSON 3 Review

**Cause and Effect** How did the blockade of Charleston Harbor make life hard for Confederate soldiers?

**1 Big Idea** Why did people in South Carolina fight a civil war?

**2 Vocabulary** Write a sentence telling the difference between the **Confederacy** and the **Union**.

**3 History** Why was the Emancipation Proclamation important?

**Performance—Write Newspaper Headlines** Write two newspaper headlines about the firing on Fort Sumter. Write one headline that might have appeared in a Union newspaper. Write another headline that might have run in a Confederate newspaper.

Chapter 6 ■ 209

# Lesson 4

## After the Civil War

**Big Idea**
South Carolina faced many challenges after the Civil War.

**Vocabulary**
Reconstruction
Black Codes
Freedmen's Bureau

More than 71,000 soldiers from South Carolina had fought in the Civil War. Columbia and Charleston were nearly destroyed. It would take many years for the people of South Carolina to rebuild the state. The time of rebuilding was called **Reconstruction**.

### Reconstruction

Just a few days after the Civil War ended in April 1865, President Lincoln was killed. The new president, Andrew Johnson, had to rebuild the South.

President Johnson chose leaders for each of the southern states. However, many leaders in the South would not give rights to African Americans. Instead, they wrote laws that limited the freedoms of former slaves. Those laws were called the **Black Codes**.

**Review** Why did the South have to be rebuilt?
**CAUSE AND EFFECT**

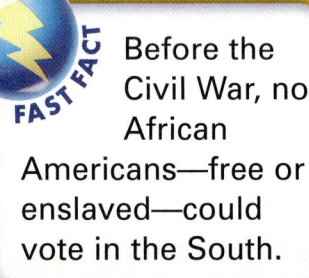

**FAST FACT**
Before the Civil War, no African Americans—free or enslaved—could vote in the South.

210 • Unit 3

## A New Constitution

Members of the United States Congress were angry over the Black Codes. They sent the army into the South. The states were told they could not rejoin the Union until they had written a new state constitution. Congress decided that the new constitution would have to give all adult men the right to vote.

In 1868, South Carolina had a new constitution and rejoined the Union. For a short time, African American voters outnumbered white voters in the South. This was partly because so many white voters had fought and died in the war.

Many African Americans voted in 1868. In South Carolina, more than half of the newly elected leaders were African American.

**Review** What did southern states have to do to rejoin the Union?

**This newspaper drawing from 1871 shows African Americans voting in the South.**

# The Freedmen's Bureau

After the Civil War, people worried about the former slaves, or freedmen. Congress created the **Freedmen's Bureau**. This group passed out food, clothing, and medicine. The Bureau tried to protect African Americans' rights.

The Freedmen's Bureau started schools. Many African Americans wanted to learn how to read and write. In order for them to be good citizens, they needed to be educated.

Some people from the North came to the South to make money or to work for the government. Others wanted to help people. Richard "Daddy" Cain was an African American from New York. He moved to South Carolina and ran a newspaper called the *Missionary Record*. He also served as a state senator and a Congressman.

**Review** How did the Freedmen's Bureau help former slaves?

Richard "Daddy" Cain wanted to improve life for African Americans.

This is one of the nearly 3,000 schools that was started by the Freedmen's Bureau.

Sharecroppers used simple farming tools such as this seeder.

## Sharecropping

Before the Civil War, slaves had done most of the plantation farming in the South. After the war, planters had to find a way to farm their land without slaves. At the same time, former slaves needed work to live.

The planters came up with sharecropping. In this system, African Americans rented small plots of land from the planters. When the crops were sold, workers had to share part of the money with the planter in exchange for using the land. The worker, or sharecropper, also paid for tools and supplies. Sharecroppers could keep whatever money was left. Usually, it was not much.

Many former slaves became sharecroppers. Their lives were hard. Some people found sharecropping to be little better than slavery.

**Review** How did sharecroppers pay for the land that they farmed?

Chapter 6 ▪ 213

## The End of Reconstruction

Ending slavery was very hard. Some people tried to ignore the changes. Others tried to punish people who had owned slaves or fought for the South. A few tried to get everyone to work together.

In 1876, Reconstruction ended. However, South Carolina had changed. The future would be different from the past.

**Review** How did Reconstruction change life in South Carolina?

**CAUSE AND EFFECT**

This monument in Columbia shows important events in African American history in South Carolina.

### LESSON 4 Review

**Cause and Effect** How did the Freedmen's Bureau affect Reconstruction?

**1 Big Idea** What challenges did the South face after the war?

**2 Vocabulary** Write a sentence telling how **Reconstruction** and the **Black Codes** are related.

**3 Economics** How did sharecropping help both planters and former slaves?

**Performance—Make a Poster** Research the Freedmen's Bureau. Choose one service that you think was important. Make a poster telling about this service. Share your poster with classmates. Tell why you chose that service.

# Skills: Make a Thoughtful Decision

| Vocabulary | |
|---|---|
| decision | consequence |

### Why It Matters

You make many decisions every day. A **decision** is a choice. Making careful, or thoughtful, decisions is important. To make a thoughtful decision, think of the consequences before you act. **Consequences** are what happens because of a choice.

### What You Need to Know

After the Civil War, newly freed African Americans faced many decisions—where to live, what work to do, and who to vote for. To make the best decisions, they may have followed steps like these.

**Step 1** Identify your choices.

**Step 2** Think of consequences for each choice.

**Step 3** Make a decision.

### Practice the Skill

Mark must decide when to do his homework—before or after playing basketball. Make a chart to help Mark decide. Copy the chart below and list two consequences for each choice.

### Apply What You Learned

Think about a decision you made. Make a chart that shows the choices and consequences you faced.

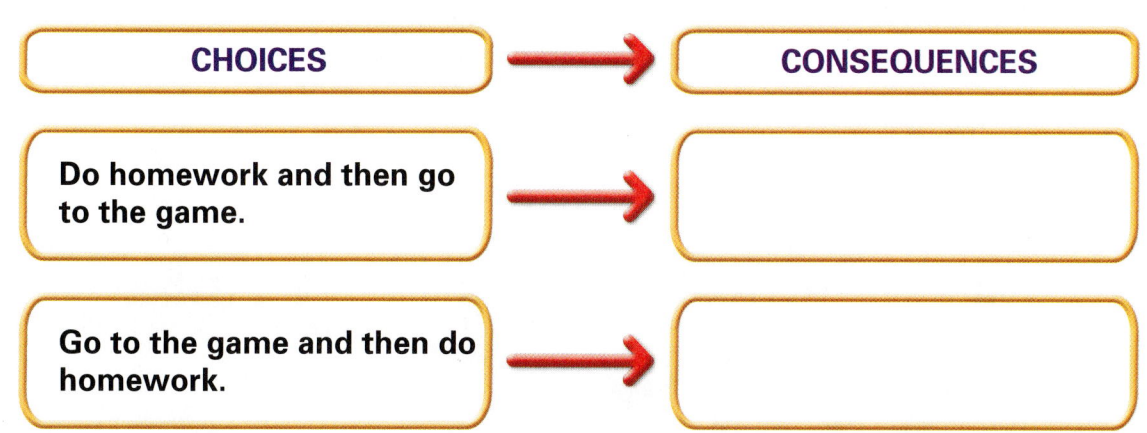

Chapter 6 ■ 215

## Examine Primary Sources

# Charleston's Children

The lives of children in Charleston varied greatly in the 1800s. Young children from wealthy families were educated at home. Middle-class children went to school or learned a skill or trade. Poor children went to work when they were very young. But all children, then as now, loved games, music, and play.

Robert and Elizabeth Gilcrest

 **From the Charleston Museum**

Toy horses that children could ride were very popular. They were also known as hobbyhorses.

### Analyze the Primary Source

1. How do you think the rider made the hobbyhorse move?
2. What do you think the board game shows?

Children used mapping games to help them understand world events.

George Washington's childhood cup.

### Activity

**Create a Toy Museum Display** Working in small groups, write a story about a child in Charleston in the 1800s. Choose one of the artifacts, and describe how its first owner played with it.

### Research

 Visit The Learning Site at www.harcourtschool.com to research other primary sources.

Chapter 6 ■ 217

# Chapter 6

## Review and Test Preparation

**Time Line**
- 1800: Santee River Canal is built
- 1822: Denmark Vesey leads slave revolt

### Focus Skill: Cause and Effect

Copy this graphic organizer onto a separate sheet of paper. Use what you have learned in Chapter 6 to show some causes and effects of the Civil War and Reconstruction.

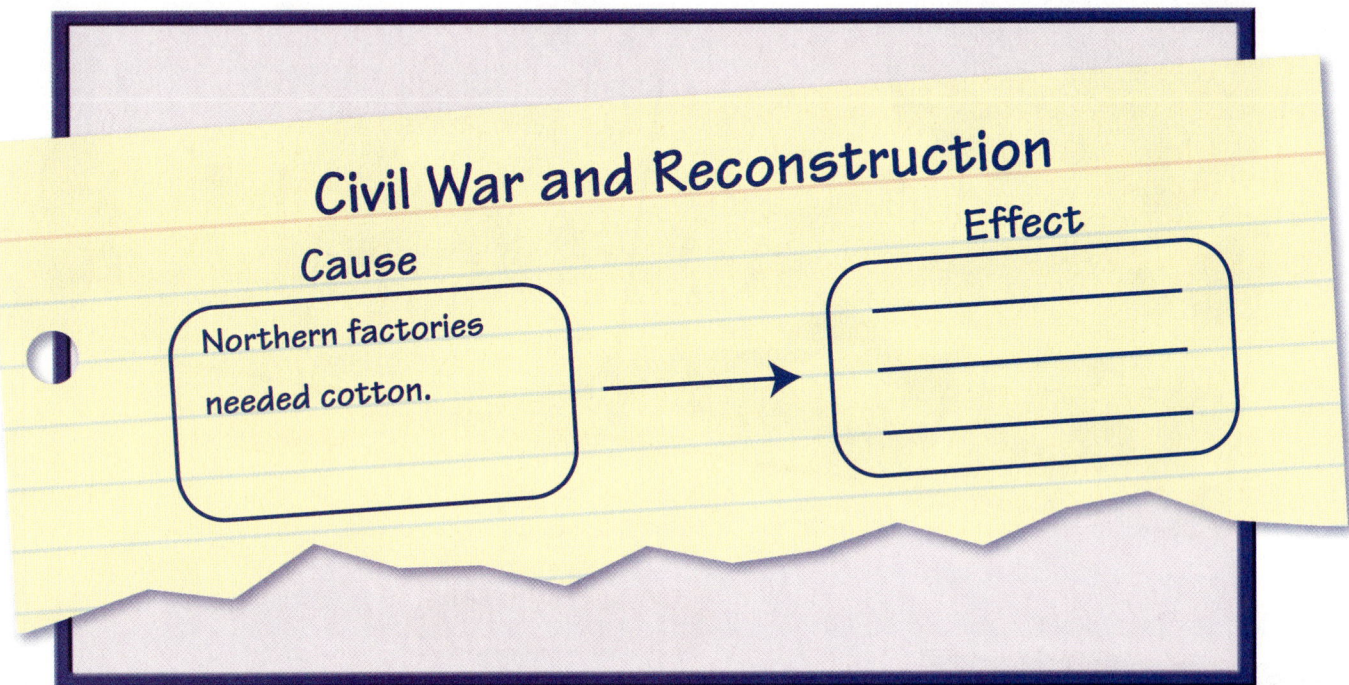

## THINK & WRITE

**Cause and Effect** Write three sentences describing how the need for more cotton affected South Carolina.

**Write a Letter** Imagine that you work for the Freedmen's Bureau in 1865. Write a letter to a newspaper explaining why all people should be able to go to school.

Timeline: 1850 — 1900
- 1860 South Carolina secedes
- 1861 Civil War begins
- 1863 Emancipation Proclamation enacted
- 1865 Civil War ends
- 1876 Reconstruction ends

## Use The Time Line

1. When did the Civil War begin?
2. When did the Reconstruction end?

## Use Vocabulary

Use each term in a sentence that tells its meaning.

3. **class system** (p. 189)
4. **industry** (p. 198)
5. **abolitionists** (p. 200)
6. **secede** (p. 201)
7. **Confederacy** (p. 204)
8. **Black Codes** (p. 210)

## Recall Facts

Answer these questions.

9. In 1832, ___ led South Carolina to ignore a federal law.
   A Andrew Jackson
   B John Calhoun
   C Abraham Lincoln
   D Richard Cain
10. Where was the first battle of the Civil War?
11. What happened to the CSS *Hunley*?
12. What was the purpose of the Freedmen's Bureau?
13. What did sharecroppers do?

## Think Critically

14. How did the textile industry in the North affect the South?
15. Why was the Freedmen's Bureau important?

## Apply Skills

**Determine Point of View in Pictures**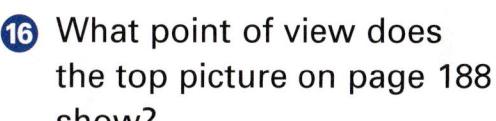

16. What point of view does the top picture on page 188 show?

**Compare Graphs**

17. In Graph B, on page 203, about how many people were enslaved in 1810?

**Make a Thoughtful Decision**

18. Imagine that your family lives on a farm in South Carolina at the end of the Civil War. How would you help get your family farm back in working order?

Chapter 6 ▪ 219

# VISIT

# THE OLD EXCHANGE & PROVOST DUNGEON

## Get Ready

The Old Exchange and Provost Building was built in Charleston in 1771. It was called the Royal Exchange and Custom House then. The elegant building was a business center and a meeting place.

In 1776, South Carolina proclaimed its independence from Great Britain in this building. Fifteen years later, President George Washington visited Charleston. He stood on the front steps of the Exchange Building. Crowds lined the streets and cheered. Soldiers fired guns in his honor.

Today, reenactors help visitors to imagine life in Charleston at the time of the American Revolution.

### Locate It
**South Carolina**

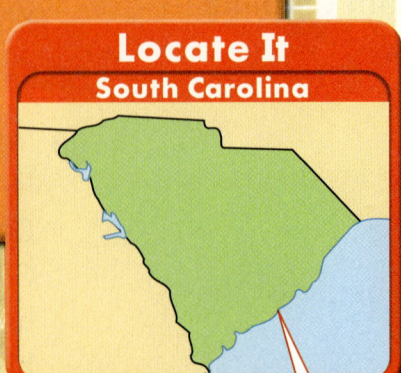

Charleston

## What to See

During the American Revolution, the lower level was used to hold prisoners.

President Washington was once honored at a dinner in the Great Hall.

An reenactor greets visitors.

Life-size figures show where captured Patriots were held.

## Take a Field Trip

**A VIRTUAL TOUR**
Visit The Learning Site at **www.harcourtschool.com** to take virtual tours of other sites in South Carolina.

Unit 3 • 221

# Unit 3 Review and Test Preparation

## Use Vocabulary

For each group of underlined words, write the term from the list below that has the same meaning.

> migrate (p. 156)
> congress (p. 164)
> independence (p. 167)
> Bill of Rights (p. 178)
> emancipation (p. 208)
> reconstruction (p. 210)

1. When President Lincoln signed the document that freed slaves, he showed his belief in setting people free.

2. During the early 1700s, many people from European countries decided to move to the colonies.

3. 3. After the United States Constitution was written, the drafters added a list that stated the rights and freedoms of all Americans.

4. After the Civil War, there was a period when the South was rebuilt.

5. 5. When South Carolina Patriots decided they wanted freedom from Britain, they wrote the state's first constitution.

6. When a meeting took place in Philadelphia in 1774, there was a group of elected leaders who discussed problems with the British.

## Recall Facts

Answer these questions.

7. Which act required colonists to pay taxes on legal papers and newspapers?

8. What is a major change in government?

9. What material did South Carolina Patriots use to make Fort Moultrie?

10. Where did most South Carolinians live in the 1800s?

11. What was the name of the network of secret trails and houses that helped slaves escape to freedom?

12. Which crop kept the South Carolina economy strong throughout the 1800s?

## Eastern South Carolina

[Map of Eastern South Carolina with grid coordinates A-F vertically and 1-6 horizontally]

### Think Critically

**13** What were some of the good reasons for migrating to the colonies? What were some of the ways that moving to the colonies was difficult?

**14** What were some of the reasons why people wanted to join the Underground Railroad? What were the challenges of getting involved with the Underground Railroad?

### Apply Skills

**Use a Map Grid** Use the map grid of Eastern South Carolina to answer the following questions.

**15** Where is the town of Conway?

**16** What point of interest is found in D-3?

**17** Where is Congaree National Park?

Unit 3 ■ 223

# Unit Activities

 Visit The Learning Site at www.harcourtschool.com for additional activities.

## Make a Poster

Work in a small group to make a poster advertising something from this unit. Look through Chapters 5 and 6 for ideas. Once you choose an idea, decide on an image to use in your poster. Then work together to create a slogan to go with your picture. When you finish your poster, hang it in your classroom along with the other posters that your classmates have made.

## Visit Your Library

- ■ *A Picture Book of George Washington* by David A. Adler. Holiday House.

- ■ *Fort Sumter* by Charles W. Maynard. The Rosen Publishing Group.

- ■ *Spunky Revolutionary War Heroine* by Idella Bodie. Sandlapper Publishing Co.

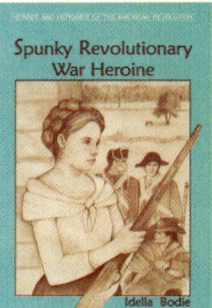

## Complete the Unit Project

**Honor a Hero** With a small group of classmates, look at your notes about important people and events in South Carolina history. Choose one person to honor. Then decide how your group will honor this person. You might do research to find pictures, writings, and other materials related to your person. Gather your materials and put them together into a visual display. Plan a presentation and share it with your classmates.

# Into Modern Times

Cooper River Bridge Medallion, 1929

An aerial view of the Grand Strand

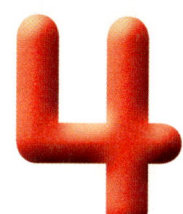

# Into Modern Times

**❝ You really can change the world if you care enough. ❞**

—Marian Wright Edelman

## Preview the Content

Before you study the unit, read the lesson titles for both chapters. Then make a web for each chapter. Write the chapter's main topic in the center of the web. As you read, fill in the webs with supporting details. Use words and phrases that relate to the chapter's main topic.

# Unit 4 Preview

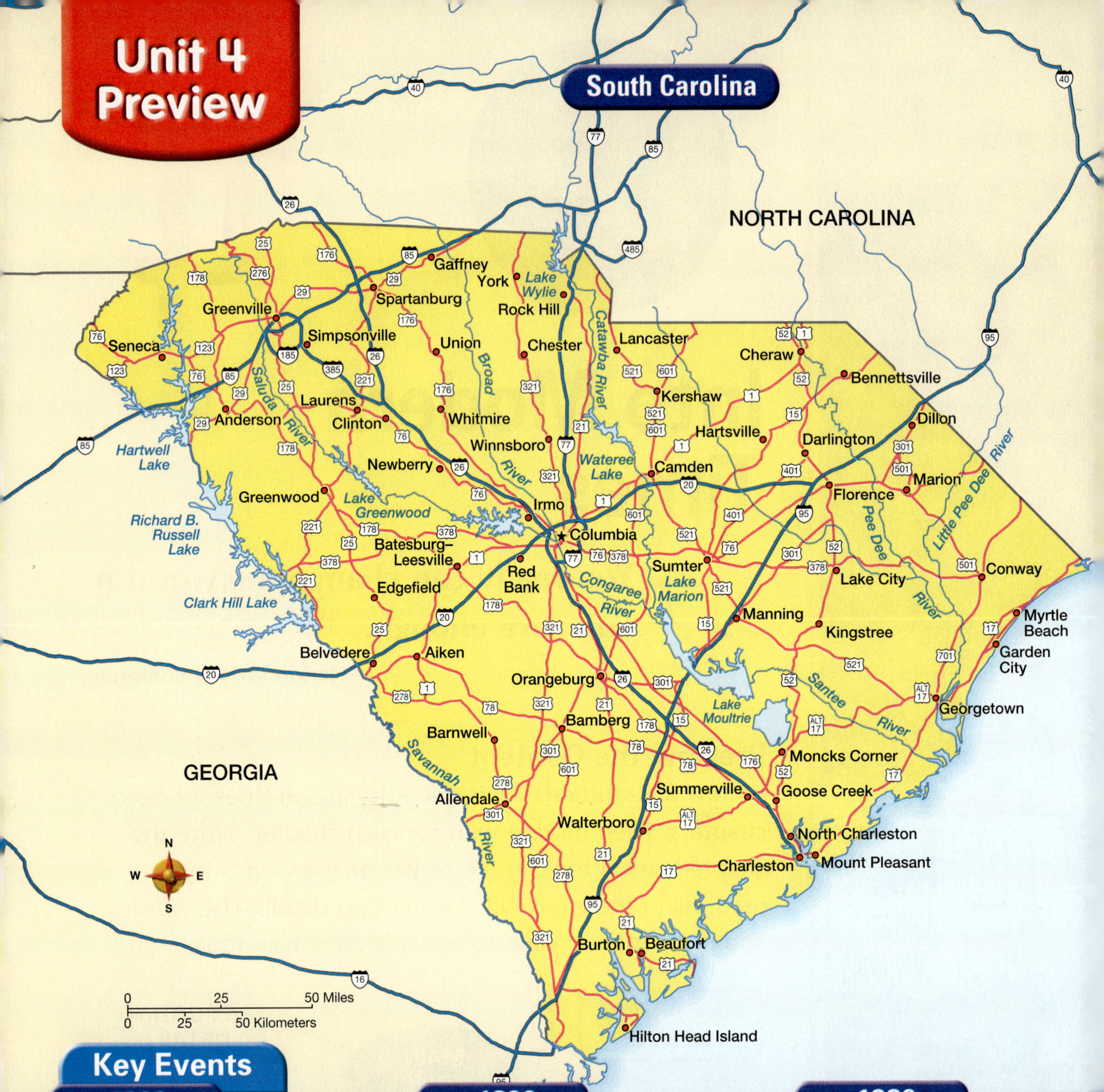

## South Carolina

## Key Events

**1860** — **1890** — **1920**

**1899** Clemson College was founded. p. 237

**1917** Soldiers trained for World War I at Camp Jackson. p. 252

**1920** Women get the right to vote. p. 257

## South Carolina Population 1900–2000

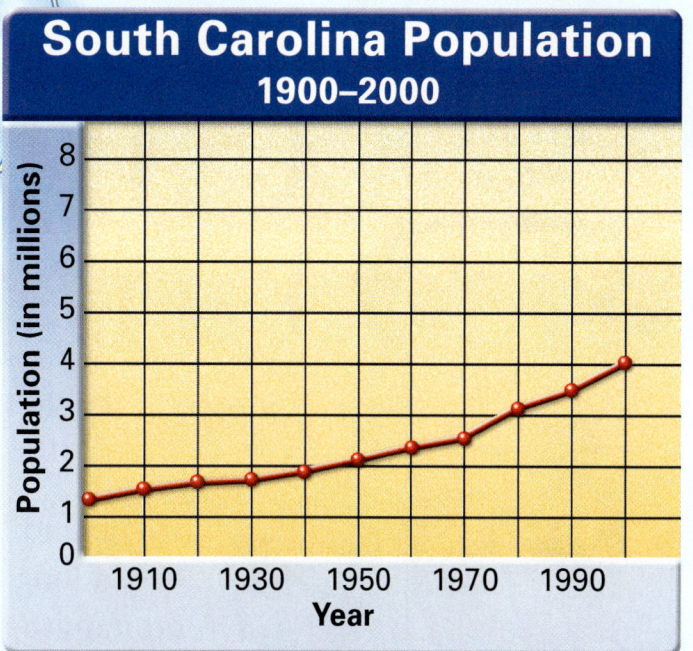

### Age Groups in South Carolina

| Age Group | Population |
|---|---|
| Under 20 years old | 👤👤👤👤👤👤👤👤👤👤 |
| 20-39 | 👤👤👤👤👤👤👤👤👤👤 |
| 40-59 | 👤👤👤👤👤👤👤👤👤👤 |
| 60-79 | 👤👤👤👤👤 |
| Over 80 years old | 👤 |

👤 =100,000 persons

**Map Key**
- 26 Interstate highway
- 52 U.S. highway
- ★ State capital
- ● Other city

ATLANTIC OCEAN

**1950** — **1980** — **2010**

**1941** Tuskegee Airmen fought in World War II. **p. 265**

**1964** Martin Luther King, Jr. spoke out for civil rights. **p. 275**

**PRESENT** People have fun at festivals. **p. 292**

**START with a STORY**

# Circle Unbroken

by Margot Theis Raven   illustrated by E. B. Lewis

The tradition of making baskets from grass began long ago. People from western Africa brought the craft to South Carolina. Today these baskets are known as sweetgrass baskets.

In Circle Unbroken, one family's history is sewn into the sweetgrass baskets they make. Each basket begins with a center knot. A young girl learns that her family had a beginning too. A basket grows larger and stronger with each spiral of grass added to it. The family's story has also grown and changed over time. Read now as Grandma tells how times have changed since the end of slavery.

Now it was the times after slavery,
when your great-great-great grandfather
worked shares on this land of marsh, sea, and sky,
where the creek beds rose high on the old rice fields,
melting them away like shadows into shade.

He built a boat of wood and took it to the sea,
far past the shores where the sweetgrass grows.
Rowing in, he had fish for his family and fish to sell.
Then, long night after long day,
he told children tales of Br'er Rabbit and Br'er Fox,
till their laughing eyes danced
like sunlight on the water,
stars above the creek.

Your great-great-great-grandmamma heard the stories, too.
Next day, she carried fish and wares
to market in the basket she'd made,
toting her burdens and cares high on her head.

And the circle went out and out:
like the stone that milled their corn,
and the net that caught their shrimp,
and the Ring Shout that praised their Lord.

*Just as I give praise for you . . .*

Then their children had children, and their children, too,
until one day across the great wide ocean, a war began.
The men of the island went away like the tide,
while the women waited and sewed, long night after long day.

When the man came home again,
the bridge builders came, too,
tying islands to land with steel-arching hands.
"What's coming, Grandma?" the yard children cried.
"Tomorrow," she sighed.

And the porch children watched as the bridges brought cars,
and the cars brought people.
And the basket children lay looking up at the sky,
    not knowing the old ways were leaving
    as fast as the cars passing by.

But some folks at night sat around the lamplight,
showing the young ones the road ahead was
over and through—as new hands talked to old friends:
the bulrush, the sweetgrass, palmetto, and pine.

Then those children had children
who put up wooden stands to show their basket
along the highways and in the marketplace
where the tourists came through—
and thought the beauty of old basket was something new.

*Just as my baskets are new to you . . .*

While the women sat behind their stands, their sacred place,
sewing and sharing with daughters all they knew,
the men took the boys to their sacred place—
the dunes and marshes by the creeks and the sea—
to cut the bulrush, and pull the sweetgrass,
and dry it in the sun as it had long been done.
And so it has always been, time flowing like a river,
circle going out like a pebble in a pond,
until I came along—your mamma—and you.

And time has come now, child,
for you to learn the knot that ties us all together—
The circle unbroken.
And when your fingers talk just right
that circle will go out and out again—
past slavery and freedom, old ways and new,
and your basket will hold the past—

*Just as surely and tightly
as my arms now hold and circle you . . .*

## Think About It

1. Why does Grandma say that baskets "hold the past"?
2. Imagine you are a basket maker. Make a list of three things you would put into your basket.

## Read a Book

## Start the Unit Project

**South Carolina Heritage Fair**
As you read, think of a topic for a display at a class fair. Displays at your South Carolina Heritage Fair will celebrate the culture, people, history, government, and economy of our state. You may use your textbook, books from the library, and the Internet to help you plan your display.

## Use Technology

Visit the Learning Site at **www.harcourtschool.com** for additional activities, primary sources, and other resources to use in this unit.

Unit 4 • 233

### Clemson University

Thomas Clemson gave the land and money to start a college to teach people how to farm better. Today, Clemson University is known and respected across the country and around the world.

**LOCATE IT**

Clemson
SOUTH CAROLINA

# Chapter 7

# A Changing World

> " America is . . . like a quilt—many patches, many pieces, many colors, many sizes, all woven and held together by a common thread. "
>
> —Rev. Jesse Jackson, 1984

## Focus Skill: Draw Conclusions

A **conclusion** is something you figure out from clues in what you read.

**As you read this chapter, list the clues and conclusions about changes in South Carolina.**

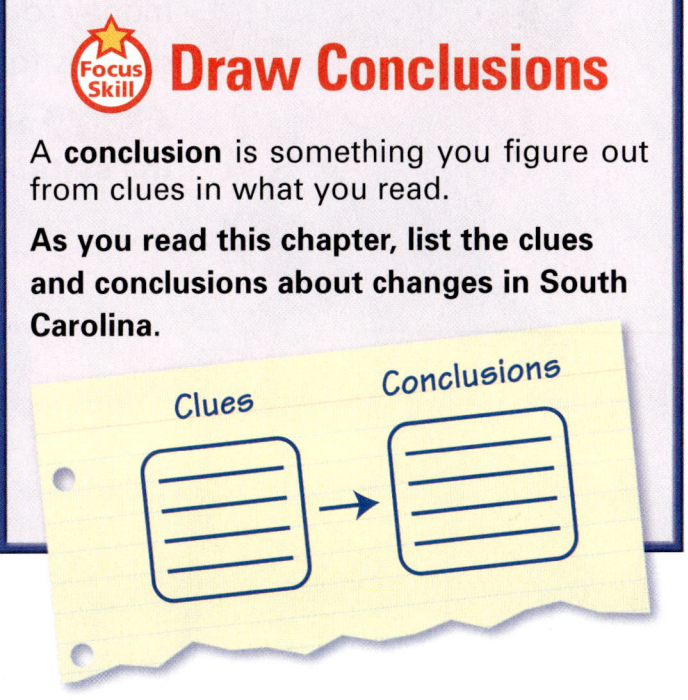

# Lesson 1

## Old Ways and New

**Big Idea**
Changes in our state in the late 1800s affected society in South Carolina.

**Vocabulary**
racism
prejudice
Jim Crow
segregation
urban
discrimination
rural

In the late 1800s, South Carolina was under the control of white leaders. Many of them wanted a return to old ways. These leaders changed the state laws in ways that took away the rights of African Americans.

### Wade Hampton III

In 1876, Reconstruction ended in South Carolina. That same year, Wade Hampton III was elected governor. He was a Confederate hero from a powerful South Carolina family. His grandfather was a leader in the American Revolution and had served in Congress.

Governor Hampton encouraged industry to grow. To do this, he kept state taxes low. However, less tax money meant there was little money to pay for schools, hospitals, and public services for the poor.

**Review** How did low taxes hurt some people in the state? **DRAW CONCLUSIONS**

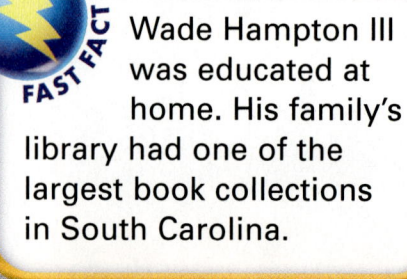

**FAST FACT** Wade Hampton III was educated at home. His family's library had one of the largest book collections in South Carolina.

236 • Unit 4

Not everyone agreed with leaders in the State House. Congressman Robert B. Eliot spoke out against old ways.

## Ben Tillman

Most people in South Carolina still lived on farms at the end of the 1800s. It was a very hard life. Many people blamed the government. They thought the state's leaders did not care about them.

One farmer, Ben Tillman, wanted to use education to improve farmers' lives. He said farmers could learn how to be better farmers. He helped start Clemson College, a school that taught about farming.

Tillman believed that only white South Carolinians should have power in government. He did not want African Americans to vote or go to school. Many people supported Tillman. In 1890, he was elected governor. Tillman's ideas were based on **racism**. This is the belief that one group of people is better than another. Racism is a form of prejudice (PRE•juh•dis). **Prejudice** is an unfair hatred of another group based on their culture, skin color, or religion.

Ben Tillman

**Review** What school did Ben Tillman help start?

## Jim Crow Laws

During these years, the General Assembly passed laws that were unfair to African Americans. They were called Jim Crow laws. **Jim Crow** was an African American character from a song.

One Jim Crow law was the "eight-box law." Voters were given eight different ballots, or voting papers. Each ballot went into a different box. If the wrong box was used, the vote did not count. This way of voting was hard for people who did not know how to read.

During elections, officials helped white voters who could not read. They would not help African Americans. This kept many African American votes from being counted.

This is an image of Jim Crow, a musical entertainer.

These women are selling cakes to travelers at the train station in Alston, South Carolina.

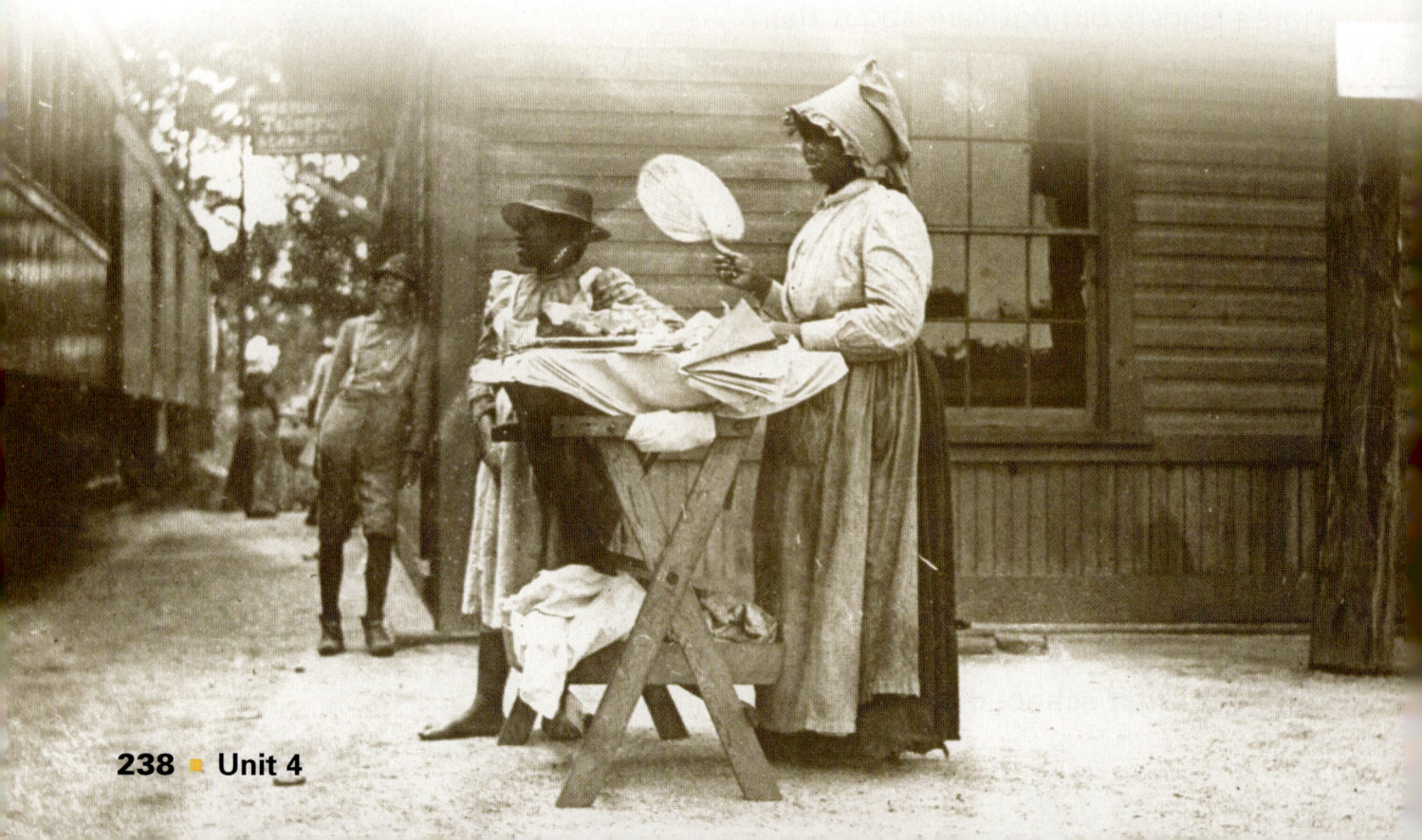

## BIOGRAPHY

### Robert Smalls
### 1839–1916

#### Character Trait: Courage

Robert Smalls was a brave man with an amazing story. On May 13, 1862, during the Civil War, Smalls hid his family on a Confederate ship called the *Planter*. Smalls then took over the boat and sailed it into Charleston Harbor. Then he hoisted a flag of truce and sailed the *Planter* to the commanding Union officer. Smalls said his action was a contribution by black Americans to the cause of freedom.

**GO ONLINE**

**MULTIMEDIA BIOGRAPHIES**
Visit The Learning Site at www.harcourtschool.com to learn about other famous people.

White leaders were not able to keep all African Americans from voting. Some African Americans were elected to office. Robert Smalls and Thomas Miller were elected to Congress from the Beaufort area.

Jim Crow laws did not just keep African Americans from voting. They also kept African Americans and whites apart. African Americans and whites went to separate schools. They sat in different railroad cars. They used different drinking fountains. Separating people in society by skin color is called **segregation**.

**Review** What did Jim Crow laws do?
 DRAW CONCLUSIONS

These women, in Belton, used brooms made from palmetto and straw.

# Schools and Churches

African American and white children went to different schools. The state government would not provide much money for schools. Schools were small and crowded. In many schools, all grades were taught in one room. There were few books. Many had no heat or running water.

Religion was important to people in South Carolina. Most churches in white communities supported the Jim Crow laws. Many churches also helped people who were poor. Many churches sent missionaries to help people in other countries.

Churches were very important to African Americans, too. They were places where people could gather. They provided food and clothing. Many served as schools for African American children. The ministers were strong leaders. They helped African Americans deal with racism and prejudice.

**Review** Why were schools small and crowded?

Children line up outside the Beaufort school in 1865.

## Farms and Factories

It was hard to make money on a small farm. Seed and fertilizer were costly. Most farmers did not know how to farm well. They were not paid much for their crops.

Industry was growing in the South. New factories started to be built in urban areas. **Urban** areas are cities or towns. The factories needed many workers.

Some people gave up farming to work in a factory. Most of them were white and poor. Often they went to work in textile factories called cotton mills.

When hiring workers, most factories practiced **discrimination**, or unfair treatment based on prejudice. African Americans were not hired by the new factories. Most stayed in rural areas. A **rural** area is away from cities and large towns.

**Review** Why did people move to urban areas?

This photograph, taken in the 1860s, shows a general store in Beaufort.

### LESSON 1 Review

 **Draw Conclusions** How did Jim Crow laws affect voting?

1. **Big Idea** How did changes in state government after Reconstruction affect society?

2. **Vocabulary** Write a sentence telling the difference between **urban** and **rural**.

3. **Culture** What did the churches do to help people?

**Performance—Prepare Interview Questions**
Imagine that you are interviewing a South Carolina farmer in the late 1800s. Write five questions that you would ask. Try to find out if the farmer is giving up farming and moving to an urban area. Ask why he or she wants to move.

Chapter 7 ■ 241

**Lesson 2**

# A New Century Brings Change

**Big Idea**
South Carolina's economy changed in the 1900s.

**Vocabulary**
transportation
consumer
producer
invention
tourism
exposition

The economy in South Carolina began to change around 1900. Some of the older industries continued. New railroads helped other industries grow.

## Old Industries and New

Some of the small industries in South Carolina did not change much in the 1800s. Edgefield potters kept making pottery. Loggers still cut trees and sold them to be used for lumber.

The biggest growth was in transportation. **Transportation** is moving people and goods from one place to another. The South Carolina Railroad Company laid many miles of new track.

Railroads made it easier for people to travel and move. New towns grew up along the railroad lines.

Cotton and other goods moved easily around South Carolina. Goods could also be sent to other states in the North and South. People and news traveled more quickly. Each day, 144 trains went in and out of Columbia.

**Review** How did railroads affect the economy? **DRAW CONCLUSIONS**

**Railroads and Factory Towns**

**Place** In the early 1900s, factory towns grew alongside the railroads.

❓ Why do you think some of the railroads went to the coast?

### A Closer Look
#### Steam Locomotive

Steam locomotives run on steam from boiling water.

① Coal is fed into the firebox. As the coal burns, smoke and heat move through the boiler tubes and out the chimney pipe.

② Water is heated by the hot boiler tubes, making steam.

③ The steam pushes the main rods. The main rods turn the locomotive's wheels.

❓ What natural elements are used to run a steam locomotive?

Chapter 7 ▪ 243

## The Cotton Mills

The largest growth in industry was the new cotton mills. In the past, most South Carolina cotton was shipped out of the state. Far away factories made clothing to sell to **consumers**, or people who buy things.

For the first time, South Carolina became a main **producer**, or maker, of textiles. Cotton mills were built near cities such as Columbia and Greenville. Other new mills were started near such towns as Newberry, Union, and Rock Hill.

The growing textile industry changed life for many South Carolinians. The mills were seen as a chance to get away from the hard life of farming. The cotton mills hired thousands of workers. Many poor farmers went to work in the mills. New jobs brought workers from other states, too.

In 1908, Hattie Hunter had already worked for three years at this cotton mill in Lancaster. She worked long hours for 50 cents a day.

When it was built in 1898, Olympia Mills in Columbia was the largest cotton mill inside one building.

Mill owners wanted workers to live near work. New communities called mill villages were built. Mill stores let workers borrow against their pay. Workers ended up giving most of what they earned to repay the mill store.

The mill controlled life in the village. A loud whistle marked the start of the day for everyone. Some mills had schools for the village children. However, most children went to work in the mill at a young age. Many workers were less than ten years old.

**Review** What is a mill village?

**Except for the mother, this entire family worked in the Maple Mills in Dillon.**

South Carolinians were happy to drive Anderson automobiles.

## SCIENCE AND TECHNOLOGY

### Anderson Automobiles

John Gary Anderson founded the Rock Hill Buggy Company. His company began to make automobiles. Anderson also started the Rock Hill Telephone Company so that he would know when his supplies came in at the train depot. By 1920, Anderson's factory was making 35 cars per day. Anderson was very successful for ten years. Then the company had some trouble. Anderson's company went out of business in 1926.

## Cars

In the late 1800s, a small engine that ran on gasoline was invented. An **invention** is something made for the first time. The gasoline engine was soon used in automobiles, or cars.

By the early 1900s, cars were very popular. Soon, they changed the way people lived. People could travel more quickly over long distances. They could live farther away from work and stores.

Many people in South Carolina wanted to own cars. However, few people could afford them. People in the cities had them first. In Columbia, there were about 50 cars by 1904.

The roads were a problem for cars. Few roads outside of cities were paved. People often got stuck in mud.

**Review** How did cars change the way people lived?

## Tourism

Travel was easier for people in the 1900s. Some people began to travel for fun. **Tourism** is the business of serving travelers on vacation.

Visitors came to the state for its beauty. Some wanted to explore the mountains. Others came for the warm weather and beaches. Coastal towns, such as Myrtle Beach, became popular vacation places.

Many cities began to have expositions. An **exposition** (EHKS•puh•zih•shuhn) is a large fair or show. Charleston hosted an exposition in 1901. It was called the South Carolina Interstate and West Indian Exposition. Special buildings went up. Thousands of people came, some from other countries. President Theodore Roosevelt also attended.

**Review** Why did the business of tourism grow?

This building and the Ferris wheel below were built in 1901. The building was called the Palace of Agriculture.

### LESSON 2 Review

 **Draw Conclusions** How did the textile industry affect people in South Carolina?

1. **Big Idea** How did the state's economy change around 1900?
2. **Vocabulary** Write a sentence that tells how **transportation** helps **tourism**.
3. **Geography** Why did people go to Myrtle Beach?

 **Performance—Write an Advertisement** Find out more about the South Carolina Interstate and West Indian Exposition in 1901. Imagine that you have to help tell people about it. Write a short advertisement that tells why people should come. Draw a picture for your advertisement.

# Skills: Use a Line Graph

**Vocabulary**
line graph

## Why It Matters

Using a **line graph** helps you see how information changes over time. South Carolina's textile industry changed between 1910 and 1922. A line graph can show the changes.

The diagram below shows the parts of a line graph. It also shows how to read the information on the line graph.

## What You Need to Know

To make a line graph, you mark dots on a grid. Then, you connect the dots with lines. Find the main parts of a line graph on the diagram below.

**A** horizontal direction (across)

**B** vertical direction (up and down)

**C** dots that mark the amounts of something at given times

**D** lines that show the change from one dot to the next

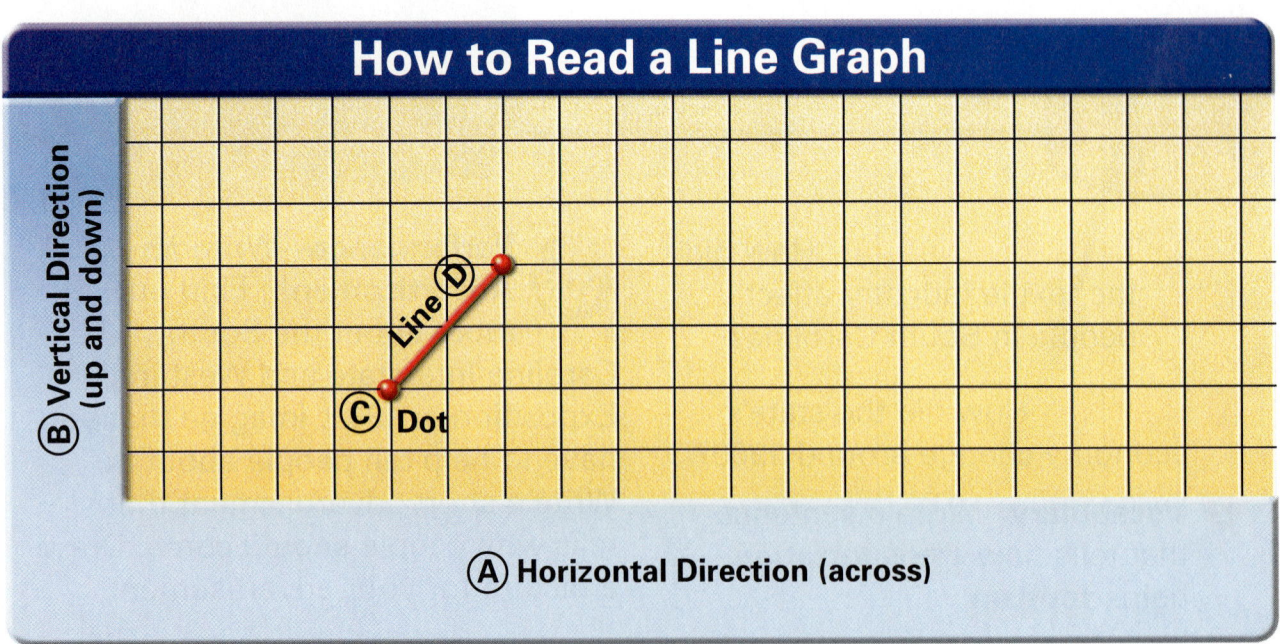

How to Read a Line Graph

### ▶ Practice the Skill

Use the line graph below to answer these questions.

1. What does the vertical direction show?
2. What does the horizontal direction show?
3. In what year was the most cotton produced? In what year was the least cotton produced?

### ▶ Apply What You Learned

Work in a small group. Think of some information you could show on a line graph. It should be something that changes over time. For example, you could graph the temperature at the start of each school day. Make a line graph to show the information you gather. Share your line graph with your classmates.

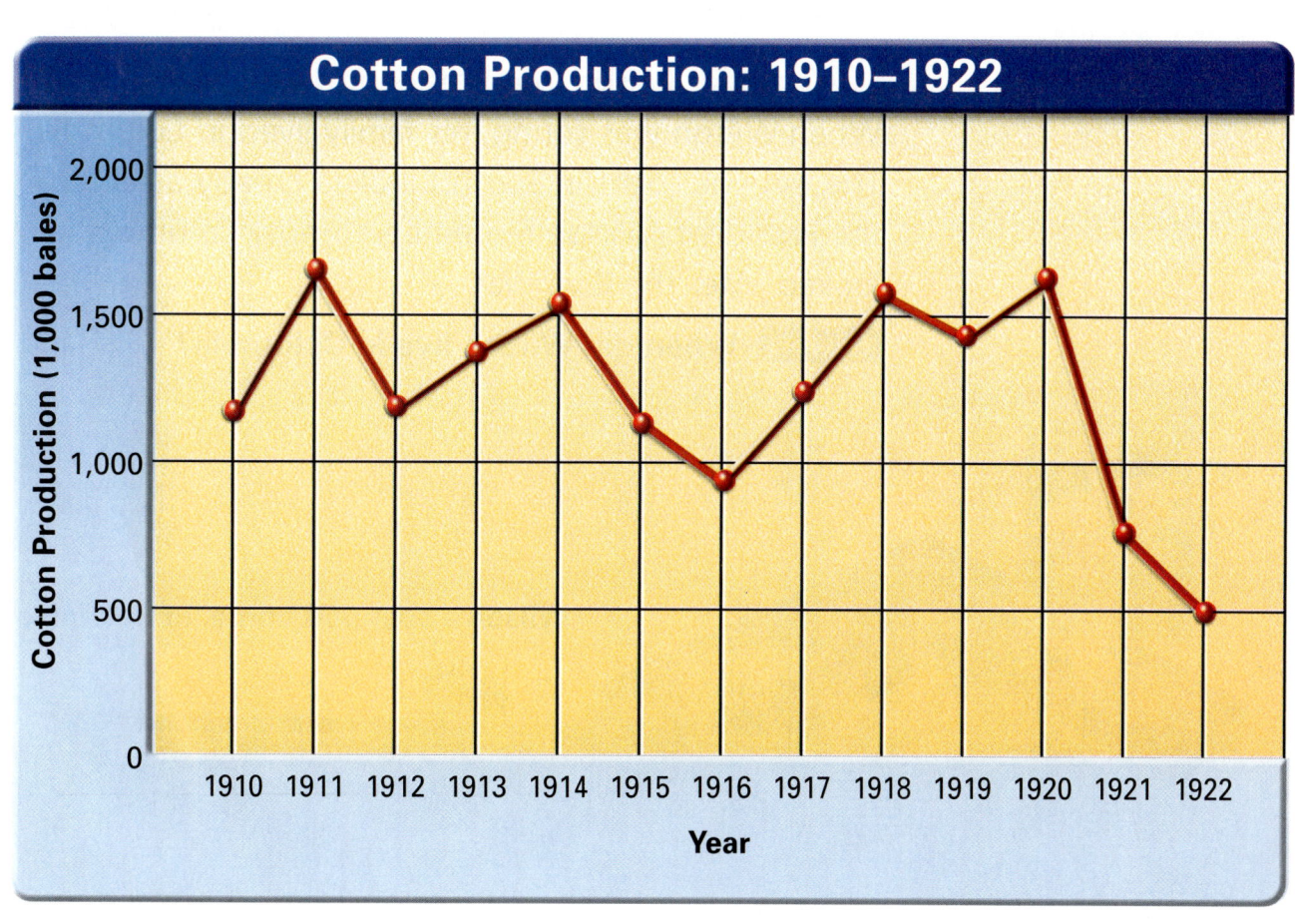

# Lesson 3

## South Carolina and the World

**Big Idea**
Events in Europe affected people in South Carolina and around the world.

**Vocabulary**
war bonds

In 1914, World War I began in Europe. France and Britain were fighting Germany and its allies. The United States joined the war after Germany attacked American ships.

### President Woodrow Wilson

Woodrow Wilson was President during World War I. When Wilson was young, his family lived in Columbia. The time he spent in South Carolina greatly affected the President. Wilson remembered how Columbia looked after the Civil War.

**Review** When did Wilson live in Columbia?

LOCATE IT — Columbia, SOUTH CAROLINA

Wilson's boyhood home, in Columbia

250 • Unit 4

## · BIOGRAPHY ·

### Woodrow Wilson
### 1856–1924

**Character Trait: Cooperation**

Woodrow Wilson grew up in the South. He was a child during the Civil War. As an adult, he tried to get countries to cooperate instead of fighting. After World War I, he helped form the League of Nations. It was the first time countries around the world tried to work together to stop wars. The League did not last, but Wilson's ideas did. In 1945, the United Nations was formed.

**GO ONLINE**

**MULTIMEDIA BIOGRAPHIES**
Visit The Learning Site at www.harcourtschool.com to learn about other famous people.

## World War I

The United States entered World War I in 1917. This was the first time American soldiers would fight a war in Europe. Young men from every state joined the United States Army. Many South Carolinians went to fight. About 62,000 served in all.

**Review** When did the United States join World War I?

Posters like this one, told people about the war.

## HERITAGE

### Fort Jackson

At the beginning of World War I, the army needed places to train new soldiers. The citizens of Columbia gave the land for a new training camp. It was named in honor of President Andrew Jackson. Thousands of soldiers were trained at Camp Jackson. United States Army soldiers still train there. Today, it is called Fort Jackson.

## Fighting a War

Many soldiers trained at camps in Columbia, Greenville, and Spartanburg. Marines trained at Parris Island. The Charleston Navy Yard built warships.

African Americans served in separate groups in the army. Some African Americans served as cooks and workers. Many fought in the war. However, African American soldiers were not allowed to serve with white soldiers.

Many South Carolinians fought in France. Some won special medals. Seven men from the state won the Medal of Honor. This is the highest war honor in the United States. One of the seven men was Corporal Freddie Stowers. He was an African American.

**Review** Where did many soldiers from South Carolina fight?

A marker in France honors Freddie Stowers. Marines train for World War I on Parris Island (below).

## The Home Front

People at home wanted to help fight the war. They were asked not to waste food or fuel. Many South Carolinians did not heat their homes on Mondays. People also bought war bonds. **War bonds** allowed people to loan money to the government.

Many men were away in the army. Factories still needed workers to make goods and weapons for the war. So for the first time, factories hired women and African Americans to do skilled work. For many of the new workers, it was their first job.

World War I ended in 1918. The United States and its allies in Europe won the war.

**Review** Why did factories hire women and African Americans to do skilled work?

**DRAW CONCLUSIONS**

These colorful posters asked people to buy war bonds.

This painting shows African Americans leaving the South. It was painted by artist Jacob Lawrence.

The United States Postal Service honored Dr. Ernest E. Just with a stamp.

## The Great Migration

Around 1910, African Americans started leaving the South. They wanted to find a better way of life and better jobs. This movement to the North is called the Great Migration. Strong African American communities formed in many northern cities. Many people continued to move north into the 1960s.

About two million African Americans left the South in the Great Migration. About 500,000 came from South Carolina. Many African Americans who left were strong leaders. Some were well educated. Dr. Ernest E. Just was born in Charleston. He went to the North for school and stayed there. Later, he became a famous scientist.

Teacher Mary McLeod Bethune also left her home in South Carolina. However, Bethune did not go north. She moved to Florida and started a school for African American girls.

**Review** Why did many African Americans leave South Carolina for the North? DRAW CONCLUSIONS

## BIOGRAPHY

### Mary McLeod Bethune 1875–1955

**Character Trait: Responsibility**

Mary McLeod Bethune grew up in South Carolina. Her parents had been slaves. She knew that a good education was important for everyone. She started an African American school in Florida. Today it is Bethune-Cookman College. Bethune worked all her life for equal rights and to improve the lives of African Americans.

**MULTIMEDIA BIOGRAPHIES**
Visit The Learning Site at
www.harcourtschool.com
to learn about other famous people.

GO ONLINE

## LESSON 3 Review

**Draw Conclusions** Why did the Great Migration happen?

**1 Big Idea** How did World War I affect South Carolina?

**2 Vocabulary** Write a sentence that tells how  helped the war.

**3 Economics** Why did factories need new workers during World War I?

**Performance—Make a Poster** Draw a poster with a message about helping at home during World War I. Your poster might ask people to buy war bonds. You might ask people not to waste food or not to use heat on Mondays. Display your poster in your classroom.

Chapter 7 ■ 255

## Lesson 4

### Big Idea
People in South Carolina began to want changes in their society.

### Vocabulary
suffrage
preservation
renaissance

# Changing Times

After World War I, people began to think about things differently. Women in the United States were calling for a voice in government.

## Women Get the Vote

Women worked hard during World War I. They did jobs usually done by men. They produced goods to support the war. Many felt they should have the same voting rights as men.

The right to vote is called **suffrage** (SUH•frij). Suffrage leaders, such as Anita Pollitzer, gave speeches and wrote articles. Suffrage workers had meetings and marched in parades.

**FAST FACT** In 1869, Wyoming became the first state to allow women to vote. Utah was the second, in 1870.

Women marched in the streets to speak out for their right to vote.

## Women's Suffrage Map

**MONTANA, 1916** — First woman elected to serve in Congress

**WYOMING, 1869** — First state to give women the vote

**NEW YORK, 1848** — Women speak out for the right to vote

**WASHINGTON, D.C. 1913** — 5,000 women march for a voice in government

**SOUTH CAROLINA, 1917** — Women in Aiken hold a suffrage parade

**Analyze Diagrams** This diagram shows some major events in the suffrage movement.

❖ How many years passed between the women's march in Washington and the first suffrage parade in South Carolina?

Finally, in 1920, a federal law gave women in all states the right to vote. Women in South Carolina had the same right to vote and serve in government as men. Sadly, Jim Crow laws kept African American women from voting.

Women began to take part in elections and government. In 1928, Mary Gordon Ellis was elected to the South Carolina Senate. She became the first woman to serve in the General Assembly.

**Review** Why did women think they should have voting rights? **DRAW CONCLUSIONS**

Mary Gordon Ellis

Chapter 7 ■ 257

## BIOGRAPHY

### Susan Pringle Frost
### 1873–1960

**Character Trait: Responsibility**

Susan Pringle Frost wanted to save South Carolina's historic places. In 1920, she started a group to save Charleston's most important old homes. Frost also helped save the street called Rainbow Row. She wanted people to feel proud of Charleston's past. Today, Frost's group is called the Preservation Society of Charleston.

**MULTIMEDIA BIOGRAPHIES**
Visit The Learning Site at www.harcourtschool.com to learn about other famous people.

**GO ONLINE**

## Preserving the Past

Many beautiful buildings in South Carolina were destroyed in the Civil War. Many others were damaged. Some people wanted to replace the old buildings with new ones. Others loved the memories of their past. These people worked to save, or preserve, buildings that had been built long ago.

Susan Pringle Frost started a group to show how Charleston's heritage could be saved by preservation. **Preservation** means to maintain or keep up. People in Columbia and across the state started their own preservation groups.

**Review** Why did people in South Carolina want to save old buildings?

**DRAW CONCLUSIONS**

The colorful houses that make up Rainbow Row are still in Charleston today.

The painter Alice Ravenel Huger Smith created many works of art set in the Lowcountry like the one above.

This is the original Playbill for *Porgy and Bess.* Dubose Heyward (left) wrote stories about South Carolina.

## The Charleston Renaissance

In the 1920s and 1930s, South Carolina artists and writers began creating new and popular works. Many lived in Charleston. This new burst of artistic activity was called the Charleston Renaissance (REN•nuh•sawnce). A **renaissance** is a rebirth of art and culture.

Dubose Heyward became famous when he wrote a book and set the story in Charleston. He then wrote a play based on his story. It was called *Porgy and Bess.* The play was performed first in 1927. Later, it was made into a musical play and a movie.

The artists and writers of the Charleston Renaissance made works of all kinds. They wrote poetry and novels. They created paintings, sculptures, and photographs. Many Charleston Renaissance artists became famous around the world.

**Review** What was the Charleston Renaissance?

# The Great Depression

The economy of the United States fell on hard times at the end of the 1920s. These hard times were called the Great Depression. People had little money. Everyone suffered.

People in South Carolina had an especially bad time. One reason was the boll weevil (BOHL WEE•vill), an insect that eats cotton. In the early 1920s, they ruined about one half of the cotton crop. Cotton prices were low, and crops were poor. Many farmers could no longer make a living by farming.

**People all over the nation had to line up for food handouts, during the Great Depression.**

In 1932, Franklin D. Roosevelt was elected President. His plan to help the country was called the New Deal.

The New Deal put people to work. One program was called the Civilian Conservation Corps, or CCC. Workers built Table Rock State Park. In other government programs, workers built a new airport, post office, and high school in Greenville. They built parks at Hunting Island and Myrtle Beach.

**Review** What was the New Deal?

*During the Great Depression, everyone in the family had to help harvest the cotton crop.*

## LESSON 4 Review

**Draw Conclusions** How did women's suffrage change society?

1. **Big Idea** What kinds of changes happened after World War I?

2. **Vocabulary** Write two sentences that tell about the **renaissance** in Charleston.

3. **History** Who was Mary Gordon Ellis?

**Performance—Make a Bulletin Board** Work in a small group. Find more information about South Carolina during the 1920s and the 1930s. You can use the Internet and the library to help. Each group member should find one or two pictures from the time. Group the pictures to make a bulletin board display. Include labels and information about each picture.

# Skills Reading: Tell Fact from Opinion

**Vocabulary**
fact　　opinion

## ▶ Why It Matters

You get information from many sources. You watch television. You read books. You talk with other people. To make good decisions, you need to be able to tell facts from opinions.

## ▶ What You Need to Know

Some of the information you get has both facts and opinions. A **fact** is a statement that can be proved. An **opinion** is something that a person believes. An opinion may be supported by facts, but it cannot be proved.

## ▶ Practice the Skill

Many advertisements contain both facts and opinions. Look at the advertisements on the next page. Then use the information in the advertisements to answer these questions.

1. Look at the statement "extra fancy" in Advertisement B. Is "extra fancy" a fact or an opinion? How can you tell?
2. Make a list of facts and opinions you find in each advertisement.
3. Compare lists with a partner. Discuss any differences you find. Make changes together, and create a new list to share with the class.

## ▶ Apply What You Learned

Create an advertisement and share it with your class. Include facts and opinions. Trade advertisements with your classmates. Practice finding the facts and the opinions in each other's advertisements.

Advertisement A

Advertisement B

Chapter 7 ■ 263

# Lesson 5

## South Carolina in World War II

**Big Idea**
South Carolina's economy grew quickly during World War II.

**Vocabulary**
suburban

Jack H. Williams (below right) was killed in the Japanese attack on Pearl Harbor. (below) Williams and others were given a Purple Heart for bravery.

The start of World War II brought an end to the Great Depression. Once again, people all over the nation and the state helped to fight the war.

### World War II

Japan attacked Pearl Harbor, Hawaii in 1941. This brought the United States into World War II. The United States joined with England, France, and Russia. They fought against Germany, Italy, and Japan.

Thousands of soldiers trained in South Carolina. About 184,000 people from South Carolina served during World War II. These included both African American and white men and women. Jack H. Williams was a sailor from Columbia. He died in the attack on Pearl Harbor.

Many people call the Tuskegee Airmen heroes.

Ernest Henderson, Sr. grew up on a South Carolina farm. He learned how to fly in the army. He helped train a famous group of African American pilots in Tuskegee (tuhs•KEE•gee), Alabama. These pilots earned many awards during the war.

Charity Adams Earley was one of 4,000 African American women who served in the war. At the end of the war, she was a Lieutenant Colonel. This made her the highest-ranking African American woman in the army.

**Review** Why was Charity Adams Earley important? **DRAW CONCLUSIONS**

Charity Adams Earley

Images like these show women working in jobs that once belonged to men.

## On the Home Front

World War II caused the economy to grow faster than ever before. Industries had to produce many more goods to support the soldiers. Factories ran for longer hours. Many more workers were needed. People who had lost work in the Great Depression found jobs again.

When the United States joined the war, many workers went off to fight. To keep factories going for the war, the owners once again began to hire African Americans and women.

Review How did the war affect industries?

DRAW CONCLUSIONS

## After the War

The United States and its allies won the war in 1945. After the war, the economy continued to grow. People had more money to spend.

People were changing where they lived. Many began to leave urban areas. New **suburban** communities sprang up around the cities.

The suburbs grew quickly. People wanted a house with a yard where children could play. Many people bought a new car to drive to work in the cities.

**Review** What areas grew up around cities after World War II?

Restaurants and movies often used the term "Drive-in" to attract new customers.

### LESSON 5 Review

 **Draw Conclusions** How did World War II help end the Great Depression?

**1 Big Idea** Why did South Carolina's economy grow during World War II?

**2 Vocabulary** Write sentences that tell the difference between urban and **suburban**.

**3 History** Why did the United States enter World War II?

 **Performance—Write a Newspaper Story** Find out more about the Tuskegee Airmen. Use the Internet or books from the library to help. Write a short newspaper story that tells what the Airmen did in World War II.

## Skills: Read a Product Map

**Vocabulary**
product map

### ▶ Why It Matters

The map on page 269 shows where some products in South Carolina are grown or raised on farms. When you can read a **product map**, you learn where different products come from.

### ▶ What You Need to Know

Picture symbols are important on product maps. Each symbol stands for a different product. To find out what product each symbol stands for, look at the map key.

Some products that the map shows are from agriculture. Agriculture is the raising of crops and farm animals for sale. Look at the map key to find the products from agriculture.

### ▶ Practice the Skill

Use the map to answer these questions.

1. In which part of the state are most beef cattle raised?
2. Are more vegetables grown in the north or the south?
3. Which products are raised near Florence?

### ▶ Apply What You Learned

Draw a map of your county. Find out what kinds of products are made or grown in your county. They may be farm goods, textiles, or other products. Draw a product map to show where they are made or grown. Be sure to include a map key with symbols for the different products. Share your map with a classmate or family member.

Practice your map and globe skills with the **GeoSkills CD-ROM**.

## Lesson 6

### The Struggle for Equal Rights

**Big Idea**
People began to work for equal rights for African Americans and others.

**Vocabulary**
civil rights
equality

After World War II, people were working to make life better for everyone in South Carolina. Jim Crow laws kept African Americans from having civil rights. **Civil rights** are rights given to all citizens by the Constitution.

## Separate but Equal

Schools for African Americans did not get as much money from the state as schools for whites did. Often they did not have good buildings or enough books. Hospitals for African Americans also got less money. Some people wanted to change things, so that everyone in South Carolina would be equal.

Children gather at the water pump at a segregated school in South Carolina in the 1960s.

270 ▪ Unit 4

Children line up outside their school in Orangeburg in 1954.

African Americans had fewer opportunities. Leaders, such as Modjeska Monteith Simkins, had much to overcome. Simkins believed in education for all people. Despite Jim Crow laws, Simkins became a teacher, a leader in business, and a strong voice for civil rights.

Other African American leaders wanted to improve health care. Anna DeCosta Banks worked to become a nurse and a teacher. For over 30 years, she cared for people who were sick or hurt. Banks felt everyone should have the best doctors, nurses, and hospitals.

**Review** Why did people want civil rights?
**DRAW CONCLUSIONS**

# Making Changes

The struggle for civil rights began with better schools. In Clarendon County, there were about three times more African American children than white children. White children rode to their school in buses. African American children walked to their school. Some walked nine miles each way. African American children were not treated fairly.

African American parents wanted to help their children. Led by Reverend Joseph DeLaine (dee•LAYN), they went to court. They asked the court to provide school buses for their children. The court said no, but it was a start.

Several years later, Reverend DeLaine encouraged the parents to try again. An African American lawyer named Thurgood Marshall represented the parents. He showed the court that separate schools cannot be equal.

**Thurgood Marshall**

**People in Summerton went to court to get school buses for their children.**

## BIOGRAPHY

### Reverend Joseph Armstrong DeLaine
#### 1898–1974

**Character Trait: Courage**

Joseph DeLaine was a minister, a teacher, and a school principal in South Carolina. He wanted all people to be able to get a good education. So he helped a group of parents that wanted to end separate schools for African American and white children.

In 2003, Reverend DeLaine was awarded the Congressional Gold Medal. Congress said that he showed great courage. He helped African Americans to get their civil rights.

 **MULTIMEDIA BIOGRAPHIES**
Visit The Learning Site at www.harcourtschool.com to learn about other famous people.

In 1954, the United States Supreme Court decided that segregation in public schools was against federal law. According to this decision, there could no longer be separate schools for African Americans and whites.

Many people in the South did not agree with the Supreme Court decision. They tried to hold on to the old ways. Some people even tried to close all public schools in South Carolina.

The struggle for equality went on for many years. Things changed slowly. Finally, in 1970, all children in South Carolina were allowed to go to the same schools.

Reverend DeLaine was awarded a Congressional Gold Medal.

**Review** What was not equal about the schools in South Carolina?

Dr. Martin Luther King, Jr. and his wife, Coretta Scott King, led marches for civil rights.

## Civil Rights Movement

In the 1950s and 1960s, all of society in the South was segregated. African Americans could not sit where whites did in public buildings, such as airports and restaurants. Leaders, such as Martin Luther King, Jr., wanted to change things.

King organized the civil rights movement. African Americans held peaceful protests. At lunch counter sit-ins, African Americans sat at the section for white people. They wanted others to see that they did not have the same opportunities as whites.

Throughout the 1960s, there were many protests all across the South. African Americans rode in buses and sat in bus stations. In 1963, they held a big rally in Washington, D.C. Jesse Jackson, born in Greenville, worked as an assistant to King. Jackson and others marched for the right to vote. Eventually, all Jim Crow laws were ended.

South Carolinian Jesse Jackson is an important civil rights leader.

**Review** What did Martin Luther King, Jr. do that was important?

## Civil Rights Laws

The federal government passed laws in the 1960s. They forced the states to have equality for all. **Equality** means having the same rights. The Civil Rights Act of 1964 said that laws keeping whites and African Americans separate were not legal. It said that everyone should have the same chances to live, work, or go to school where they want.

The Voting Rights Act said that all adults have the right to vote. Officials in the South had to make voting fair. Now the number of African American voters grew quickly. In 1958, there were 58,000 African American voters in South Carolina. In 1970, there were 220,000.

**Review** How did the Voting Rights Act change things for African Americans?
 DRAW CONCLUSIONS

### · BIOGRAPHY ·

## James Strom Thurmond   1902–2003

**Character Trait: Citizenship**

Strom Thurmond spent most of his long life in public service. Thurmond set two records as a United States senator. At 100 years old, he was the oldest person to serve in the Senate. He served in the Senate for more than 47 years, longer than any other senator. Thurmond was well loved by many South Carolinians.

**MULTIMEDIA BIOGRAPHIES**
Visit The Learning Site at
www.harcourtschool.com
to learn about other famous people.

**GO ONLINE**

Chapter  ■ 275

# South Carolina Votes for Change

In 1970, three African Americans were elected to the South Carolina General Assembly. They were Herbert Fielding, James Felder, and I.S. Leevy Johnson. They were the first African Americans elected since the 1890s.

In 1992, James Clyburn was elected to the United States House of Representatives. He was the first African American to represent South Carolina in the federal government since 1897.

**Review** Who is James Clyburn?

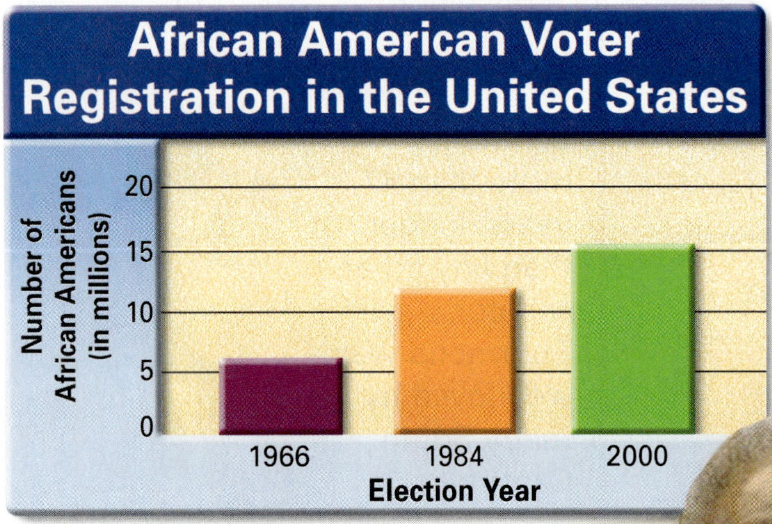

### African American Voter Registration in the United States

| Election Year | Number of African Americans (in millions) |
|---|---|
| 1966 | ~6 |
| 1984 | ~12 |
| 2000 | ~16 |

**Analyze Bar Graph** This bar graph shows the number of African Americans who registered to vote in the United States in three different election years.

- How many more African Americans registered to vote in 2000 than in 1966?

James Clyburn

## Equal Rights for Others

Civil rights laws helped women, too. Today, they hold many important government offices.

For example, in 1974, Juanita Willmon-Goggins became the first African American woman to serve in the South Carolina General Assembly.

Immigrants help lead South Carolina, too. For example, Terry Dozier (DOH•zhee•er) was named National Teacher of the Year in 1985. She came to South Carolina from Vietnam.

**Review** Who was the first African American woman elected to the General Assembly?

As a young teacher, Terry Dozier made learning fun for her students.

### LESSON 6 Review

**Draw Conclusions** How did the civil rights movement change government?

1. **Big Idea** What actions did people take to bring about equality in the schools?

2. **Vocabulary** Write a sentence about **civil rights**.

3. **Civics and Government** Who worked hard to make schools equal in South Carolina?

**Performance—Make a Collage** Find out more about the civil rights struggle in South Carolina. Pick a person who worked for civil rights in South Carolina. Use old magazines, newspapers, and the Internet to find pictures of the person. Write a paragraph about the person. Use the text and pictures to make a collage.

# Chapter 7

## Review and Test Preparation

**Time Line**

1875 — 190[0]

• 1895 New South Carolina Constitution

### Focus Skill: Draw Conclusions

Copy the following graphic organizer onto a separate sheet of paper. Use the information to show what you have learned about changes in South Carolina.

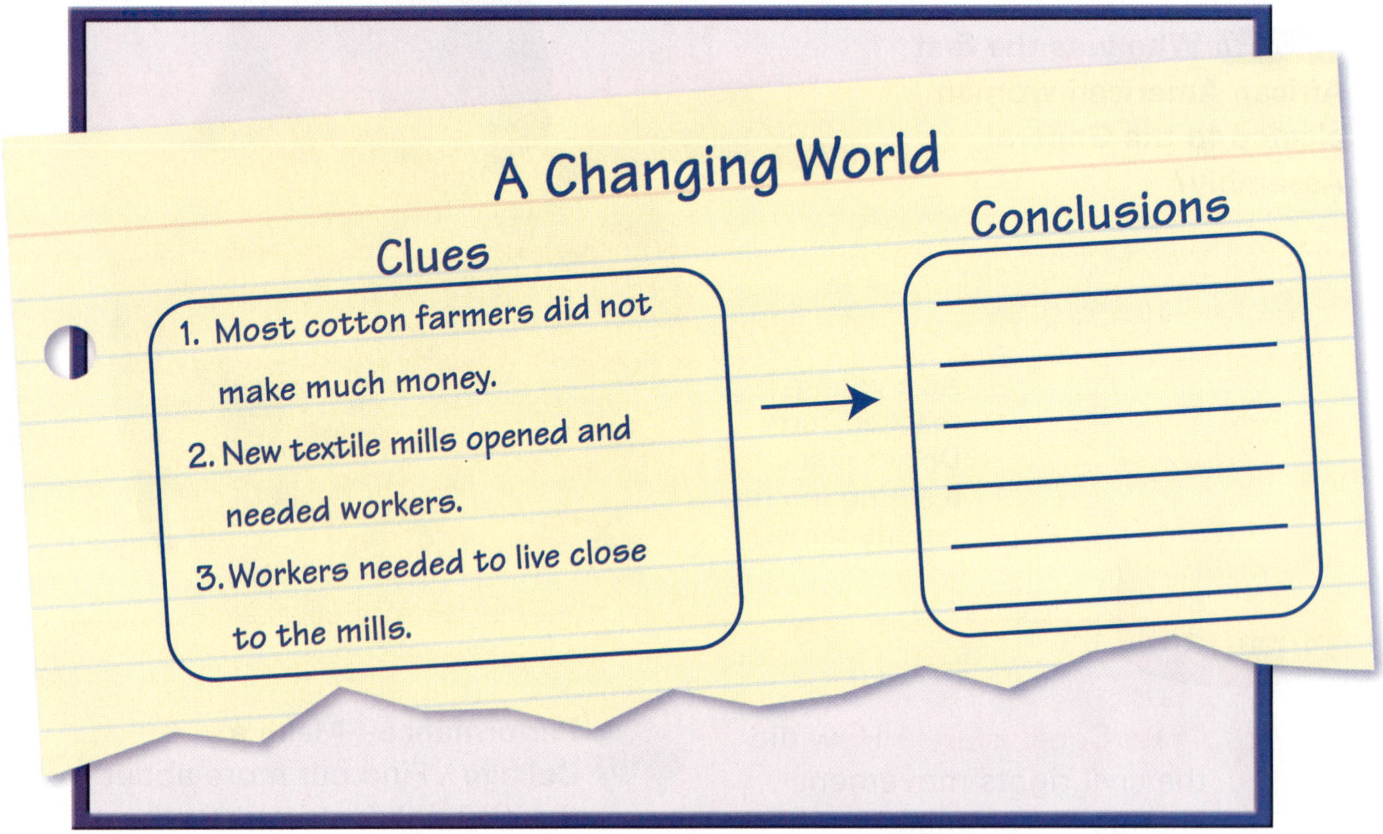

**A Changing World**

Clues:
1. Most cotton farmers did not make much money.
2. New textile mills opened and needed workers.
3. Workers needed to live close to the mills.

→ Conclusions: _____

## Think & Write

**Write a Letter** Until 1917, many children worked in cotton mills. Write a letter to a newspaper. Persuade readers it would be better for children to go to school than to work long hours in a mill.

**Write a Short Play** Choose one of the people you read about in this chapter. Write a short play that shows why the person you chose is important to South Carolina history.

278 ▪ Unit 4

**1925** | **1950** | **1975** | **2000**

- **1917** United States joins World War I
- **1920** Women get the right to vote
- **1964** The Civil Rights Act is passed

## Use The Time Line

Use the chapter summary time line to answer these questions.

1. Did women get the right to vote before or after the United States joined World War I?

2. When was the Civil Rights Act passed?

## Use Vocabulary

Identify the word that correctly matches each definition.

3. laws that took away African Americans' rights

   **Jim Crow** (p. 238)
   **rural** (p. 241)

4. something made for the first time

   **exposition** (p. 247)
   **invention** (p. 246)

## Recall Facts

Answer these questions.

5. What industry grew the most in the early 1900s?

6. How did the federal government help South Carolina during the Great Depression?

Write the letter of the best choice.

7. Joseph Armstrong DeLaine won the Congressional Gold Medal because he—
   A wanted to become famous.
   B helped end school segregation.
   C was a minister.
   D worked in a school.

## Think Critically

8. How did Jim Crow laws affect schools?

## Apply Skills

**Use a Line Graph**

9. Use the line graph on page 249. What is the difference between the number of cotton bales produced in 1914 and 1922?

**Tell Fact from Opinion**

10. Look at the advertisements on page 263. Choose one. Rewrite to change any opinions into facts.

**Read a Product Map**

11. Look at the product map on page 269. In what areas are shellfish harvested?

Chapter 7 ■ 279

### Freedom Weekend Aloft

Each year, visitors come to Anderson on Memorial Day to watch hot-air balloons. The event is called Freedom Weekend Aloft.

**LOCATE IT** — Anderson, SOUTH CAROLINA

Chapter

# Today and Tomorrow

❝ Opportunities can only come if we make the changes that prepare us . . . ❞

—Governor Mark Sanford, Inaugural Address, 2003

 **Summarize**

When you **summarize**, you retell main events and ideas in your own words.

**As you read this chapter, summarize what you learned.**

- List the topic, or main idea, of each lesson.
- List the events and ideas.
- Use the list to summarize what you have read.

Chapter 8 ■ 281

## Lesson 1

# A Modern Economy

**Big Idea**
Today, people in South Carolina work in many industries.

**Vocabulary**
technology
high-tech
service industry
interdependent
import
export

In the past, much of South Carolina's economy was based on cotton and textiles. Some people still farm, but not as many as before. The textile industry still provides jobs, too. People today also work in many other kinds of jobs.

## Agriculture

In the early 1900s, most farmers grew cotton or other crops. Today, chickens are the most valuable farm product. Many other farmers grow trees and flowers. They also produce vegetables, eggs, milk, and peaches. Some grow pecans, rice, or cotton.

South Carolina is the only place in the United States where tea is grown as a cash crop. The first tea plants were brought to Wadmalaw Island about two hundred years ago. It is just south of Charleston.

**Review** What crops do farmers grow in South Carolina today? **SUMMARIZE**

**FAST FACT**
Gaffney hosts the South Carolina Peach Festival every year. South Carolina is the nation's second-largest producer of peaches. Only California grows more peaches. There are 16,000 acres of peach orchards in South Carolina.

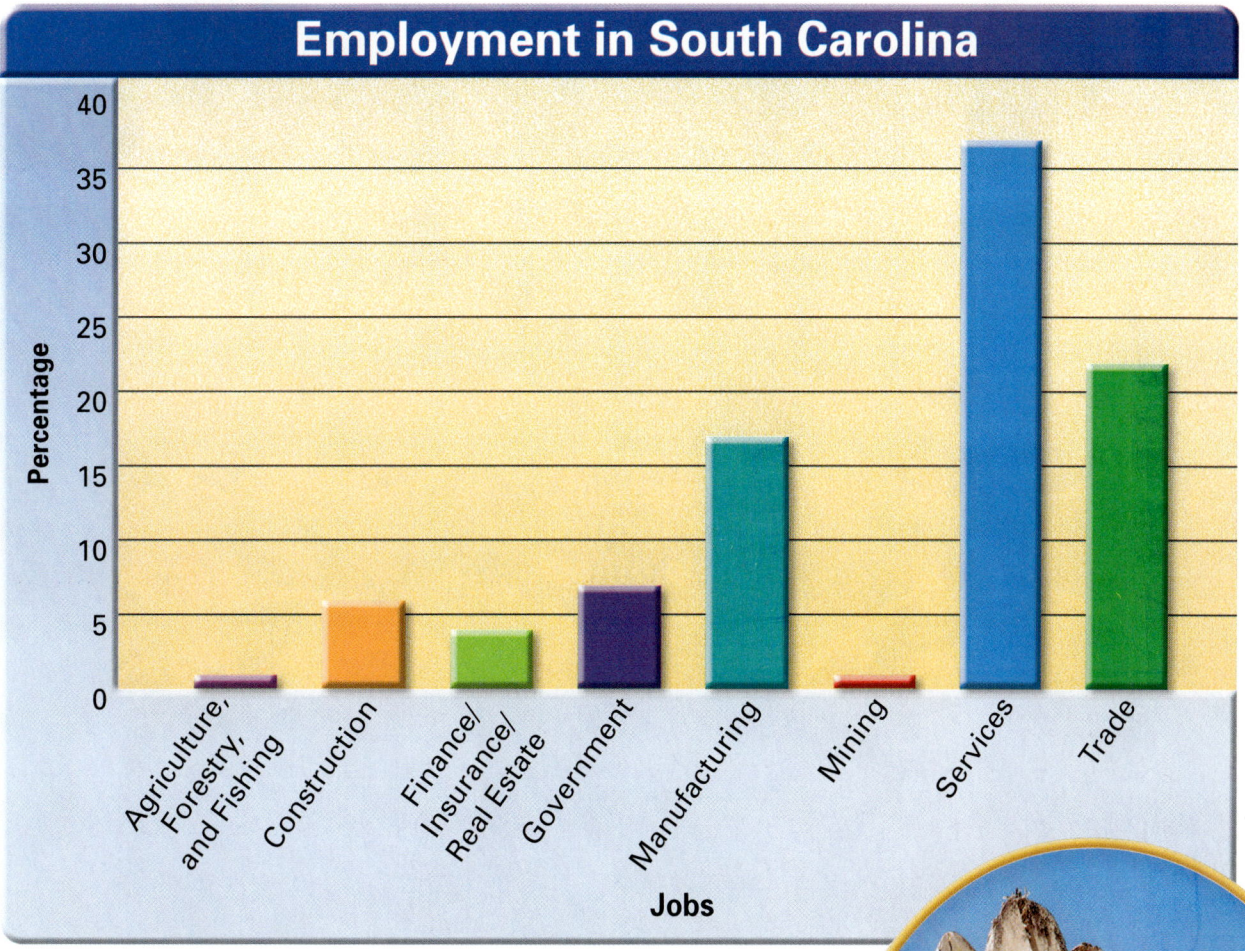

**Analyze Bar Graphs** This bar graph shows what the people in South Carolina do for a living.
◆ Which industry has the most workers? Which industry has the least?

## Making Products

Most factory workers in South Carolina have jobs in cotton mills. **Technology**, or new inventions people use in everyday life, has changed the mills. Mills can now make more cloth with fewer workers.

Several companies make high-tech products. **High-tech** industries invent, make, or use computers and other kinds of electronic equipment. Some companies make cars. Others make furniture and wood products. Some also make paper or print books.

Today, forestry is an industry that has few workers.

**Review** How has technology changed cotton mills?

People in service industries help others.

## Service Industries

Today, most people in South Carolina work in service industries. A **service industry** is a business that does work for others. Service industries include tourism, transportation, and health care.

In South Carolina today, most service jobs are in tourism. People work helping visitors at airports, hotels, restaurants, museums, and parks.

Education is a service industry, too. Lawyers, bankers, and people who fix cars all provide services. Over all, about six of every ten workers in South Carolina are in a service industry.

**Review** Where are most service jobs in South Carolina?

# South Carolina's Port Cities

Today, economies around the world are **interdependent**. That means they need each other. South Carolina has many trade partners. The ports at Charleston, Georgetown, and Port Royal Sound handle both imports and exports. **Imports** are goods that come into a country. **Exports** are goods that go out of a country.

Companies from everywhere in South Carolina ship goods from these ports. So do companies from more than 20 other states. Goods from all over the world come into South Carolina's ports.

**Review** What are imports?

Boats tie up near the lighthouse at Hilton Head.

## LESSON 1 Review

 **Summarize** Summarize how factory jobs have changed in South Carolina.

**1 Big Idea** What is one new industry that people work in today?

**2 Vocabulary** Write a sentence that tells the difference between **imports** and **exports**.

**3 Economics** What kind of work do most people do in South Carolina today?

 **Performance—Give a Speech** Find out more about one product made or raised in South Carolina today. Use what you learn to give a report to your classmates about that product. Tell where the product comes from, what kind of industry makes it, and what it is used for. If possible, show a picture or sample of your product as you give your report.

Chapter 8 ■ 285

## Skills Citizenship

# Make an Economic Choice

**Vocabulary**
trade-off  opportunity cost

### ▶ Why It Matters

When you buy something at a store, you are making a choice about how to spend your money. You cannot buy everything you want, so you must spend your money wisely.

### ▶ What You Need to Know

Here are some steps that can help you make a wise choice.

**Step 1** Think about the trade-off. To buy or do one thing, you have to give up the chance to buy or do something else. This is called a trade-off.

**Step 2** Think about the opportunity cost. What you give up to get what you want is called an opportunity cost.

### ▶ Practice the Skill

Imagine that you have $35.00 to spend. You need a new bike helmet. You will have to make a choice about how to spend your money.

Helmet A is the latest style. It has a fun design. It costs $30.00. Helmet B is just as safe as Helmet A, but it is an older model. It only comes in pink. It costs $15.00.

**Helmet A**

**Helmet B**

1. If you buy Helmet A, what is the trade-off? What is the trade-off if you buy Helmet B?
2. What is the opportunity cost if you buy Helmet A? What is the opportunity cost if you buy Helmet B?
3. What choice would you make? Why?

▶ **Apply What You Learned**

Think about a recent choice you made to buy something. What was the trade-off? Think about it. What was the opportunity cost? Think about that, too. Do you think you made the right choice? Write a paragraph telling why.

Chapter 8 ■ 287

## Lesson 2

## South Carolina Today

**Big Idea**
South Carolinians are proud of our state.

**Vocabulary**
recreation

The citizens of South Carolina are proud of our state. We honor our past. We also look forward to our future.

### Smiling Faces and Beautiful Places

People come to South Carolina from around the world for recreation. **Recreation** is what people do to have fun. There is something in South Carolina for everyone.

One of the most popular places to go is the Grand Strand. It includes beaches along the coast. They stretch for more than 60 miles. The city of Myrtle Beach is at its center.

**Review** Why do people go to the Grand Strand?

A view of Myrtle Beach from the ocean

**FAST FACT** Today, the city of Myrtle Beach is one of the country's fastest-growing urban areas.

The Speedy Gonzales roller coaster is in the Family Kingdom Amusement Park in Myrtle Beach.

## GEOGRAPHY

### Myrtle Beach

#### Environment and Society

Myrtle Beach has been a vacation place for a long time. Before the Civil War, plantation families went there in the summers because it was cooler and breezier. In 1926, a businessman built a large hotel and laid out streets. Myrtle Beach's first golf course was built at about that time, too. In the 1960s, many golf courses were built. People began to come year-round. Today, Myrtle Beach is a growing city.

# Museums and More

You can learn a lot about history in our state. You can enjoy southern food and culture. Still, there are many other activities all across our state.

Jones Gap State Park near Cleveland offers camping and hiking opportunities. In Greenville, you can learn about the stars at the Hooper Planetarium. Riverbanks Zoo and Garden in Columbia is home to more than 2,000 animals.

Jones Gap State Park

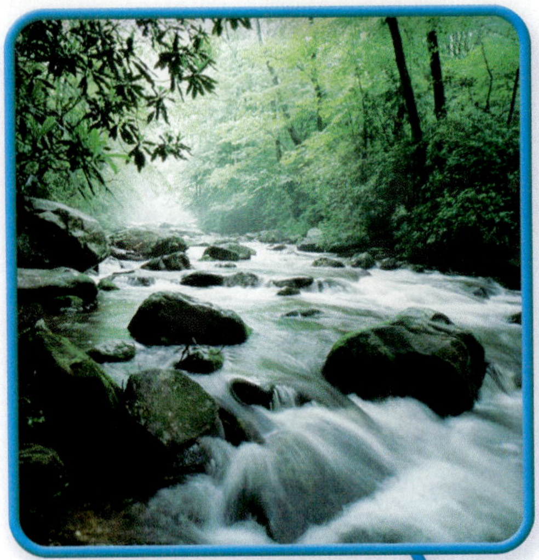

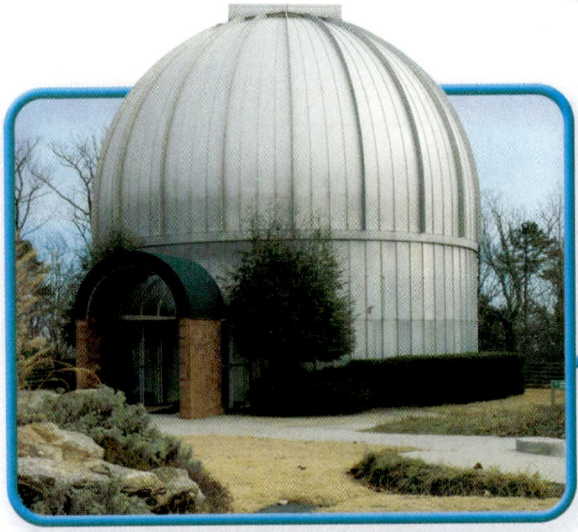

T. C. Hooper Planetarium

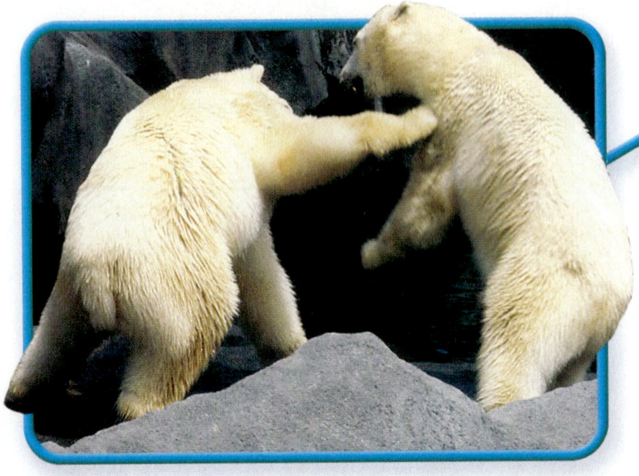

Riverbanks Zoo and Garden

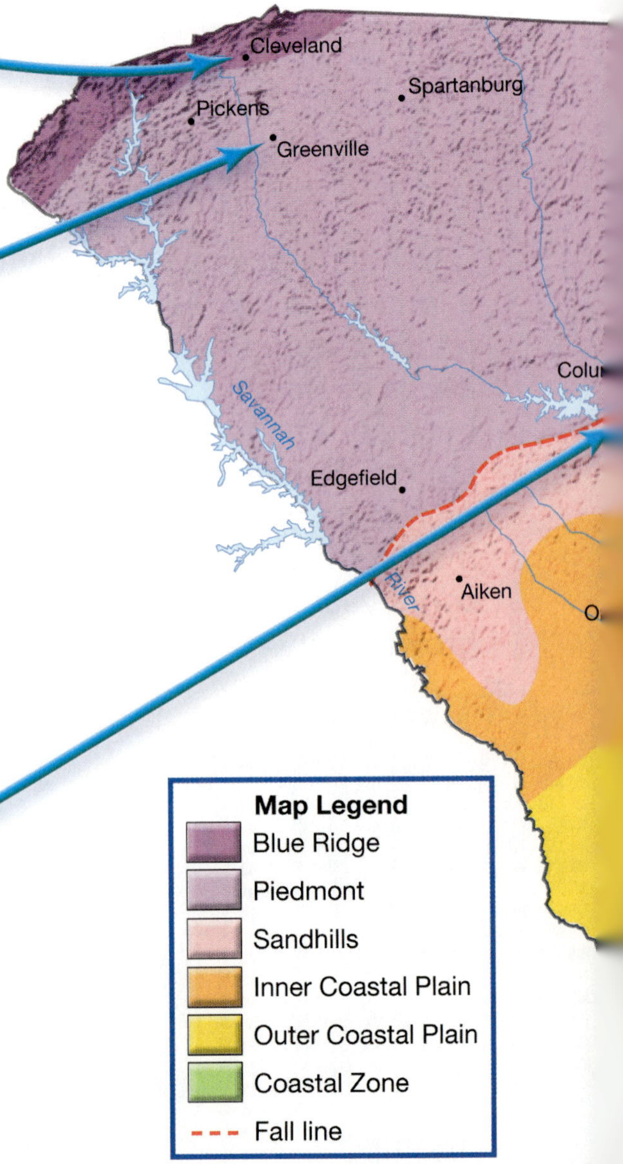
Cleveland
Spartanburg
Pickens
Greenville
Colu
Savannah
Edgefield
River
Aiken
Map Legend
Blue Ridge
Piedmont
Sandhills
Inner Coastal Plain
Outer Coastal Plain
Coastal Zone
Fall line

Car racing fans go to Darlington Raceway. The South Carolina Artisans Center in Walterboro preserves traditional arts and crafts for the future. In Charleston, the South Carolina Aquarium lets visitors learn about ocean life up close.

**Review** Which activity is nearest to your community?

**Darlington Raceway**

**South Carolina Artisans Center**

**South Carolina Aquarium**

Chapter 8 ■ 291

# Festivals Are Fun!

Festivals are times when people get together to have fun. The South Carolina State Fair has rides, concerts, plays, and food. Storytellers come from around the country to the Stone Soup Storytelling Festival in Woodruff. In spring, you could go to Rock Hill for the Come-See-Me Festival. You can visit York, in October, for an apple picking festival.

**Review** Where does the State Fair take place?

You might see Glen and Glenda, the frog mascots of the Come-See-Me Festival.

The South Carolina State Fair is held each October in Columbia.

## Palmetto Pride

One reason people love South Carolina is its beauty. But sometimes people litter. This destroys the beauty of a place. It is also dangerous for animals and people.

Palmetto Pride is a state program that works to keep South Carolina clean. Each year, thousands of volunteers clean up the state. One year, they picked up more than 2 million pounds of trash! By keeping South Carolina clean, citizens keep it beautiful. They show their pride, too.

Every fall, people pick up trash in the Beach Sweep/River Sweep. This group helped clean up a beach on Hilton Head Island.

**Review** What is Palmetto Pride?

### LESSON 2 Review

**Summarize** Why is it important to keep South Carolina clean?

1. **Big Idea** How do the people of South Carolina show pride in our state?

2. **Vocabulary** Use the word **recreation** in a sentence about people in South Carolina.

3. **Culture** What kinds of activities bring visitors to South Carolina?

**Performance—Make a Map** Draw a map of South Carolina. On your map, show locations where festivals and other special events take place. Make a map key with a symbol for each event. Display your map.

Chapter 8 ■ 293

# Skills: Use Latitude and Longitude

### Vocabulary
latitude      longitude

## ▶ Why It Matters

Mapmakers draw lines of latitude and longitude on maps and globes to form a grid system. You can give the exact location of a place if you know its latitude and longitude.

## ▶ What You Need to Know

Lines of **latitude** run east and west around the globe. They measure distances in degrees (°) north and south of the equator.

Lines of latitude go from 0° at the equator to 90° at each pole. They are labeled *N* for *north* and *S* for *south*.

Lines of **longitude**, also called meridians, run north and south from pole to pole. They measure distances east and west of the prime meridian near London, England. Lines of longitude go from 0° at the prime meridian to 180° halfway around the globe. They are labeled *E* for *east* and *W* for *west*.

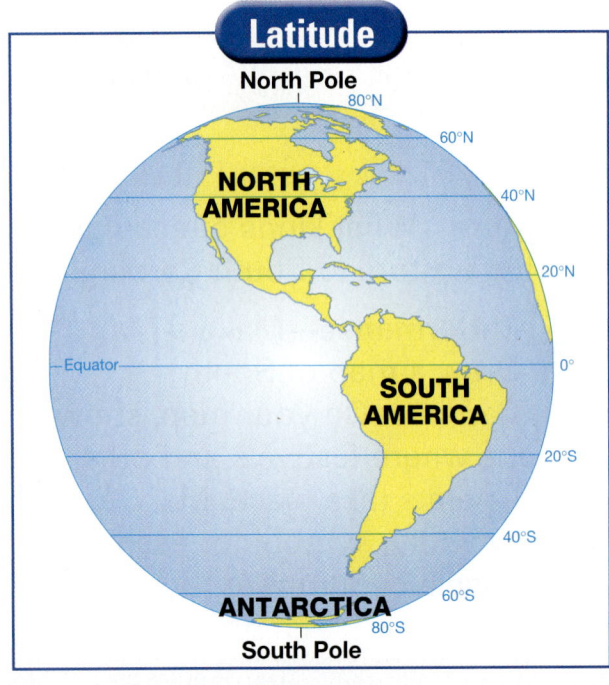

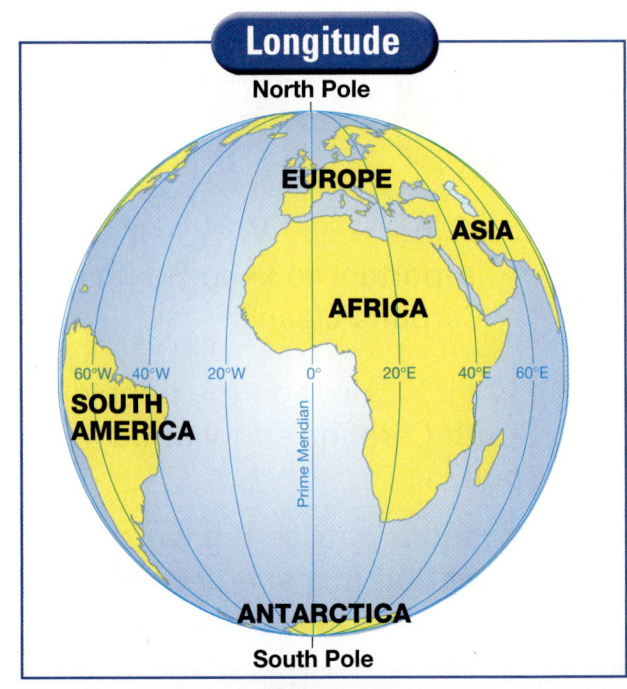

▶ **Practice the Skill**

Use the map of South Carolina to answer these questions.

1. On which line of latitude is Allendale?
2. Which line of longitude is near Conway?
3. Which lines of latitude and longitude are closest to Spartanburg?
4. What city is located near 35°N and 81°W?

▶ **Apply What You Learned**

Use an atlas or another map to find the latitude and longitude of your town. Work with a partner to find three cities or towns in the world with the same latitude. Then find three with the same longitude. Make lists of the cities. Compare your lists.

Practice your map and globe skills with the **GeoSkills CD–ROM**.

**South Carolina Latitude and Longitude**

Chapter 8 ■ 295

# Examine Primary Sources

## Communication Artifacts

Imagine life without the telephone, television, or recorded music. These things are part of our daily lives, but they did not exist 150 years ago. Then, around 1900, inventions began to change the way we all see, hear, and send information. The John Rivers Communication Museum in Charleston has a large collection of items that shows the history of these changes.

 **FROM THE JOHN RIVERS COMMUNICATION MUSEUM**

This children's record player was easy to use.

## Analyze the Primary Source

1. In what ways does the record player look like a child's toy?
2. How does the radio on this page differ from the ones you have used?
3. Look at the telephone. How do you think it works?

Radios brought news, music, and popular shows into our homes.

This gramophone was powered by turning a crank handle.

Telephones, like this one from the 1920s, were large and heavy.

### Activity

**Write an Advertisement**  Pick one artifact from this spread. Write an advertisement for the object. Tell how people can use and enjoy the object.

### Research

 Visit The Learning Site at www.harcourtschool.com to research other primary sources.

Chapter 8 ■ 297

# Chapter 8

# Review and Test Preparation

## Focus Skill: Summarize

Copy the following graphic organizer onto a separate sheet of paper. Use what you have learned to summarize the information about modern industries in South Carolina.

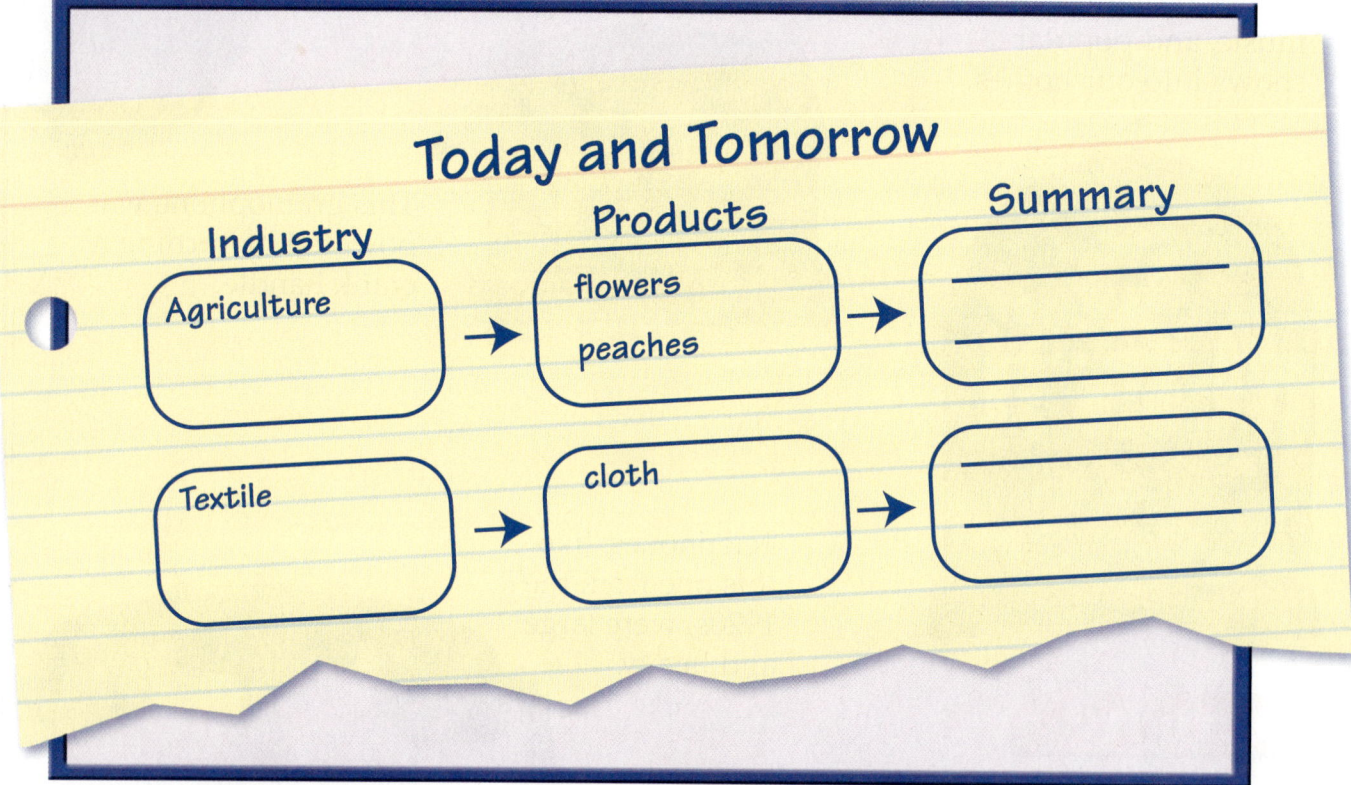

## THINK & WRITE

**Write a Letter** Imagine that you have a pen pal in another state. Write a letter to your pen pal and tell what your favorite thing is about South Carolina and why.

**Write a Paragraph** Write a paragraph that tells about tourism in South Carolina. Use information from the chapter to help you.

## Use Vocabulary

Write the word that correctly completes each sentence.

**technology (p. 283)**
**interdependent (p. 285)**
**import (p. 285)**
**export (p. 285)**
**recreation (p. 288)**

1. An ___ is a product from another country.
2. ___ is what people do for fun.
3. People use new inventions, or ___, to improve their lives.
4. When economies need each other, they are ___.
5. A product sent out of the country is called an ___.

## Recall Facts

Answer the questions.

6. The most valuable farm product in South Carolina today is—
   A tea.
   B pecans.
   C cotton.
   D chickens.

7. Most factory workers in South Carolina today have jobs in—
   F automobile plants.
   G cotton mills.
   H the high-tech industry.
   J the furniture industry.

8. Where is Myrtle Beach?
   A Blue Ridge
   B Upcountry
   C Grand Strand
   D The Piedmont

## Think Critically

9. How have new industries affected the economy of South Carolina?
10. How does South Carolina's location near the Atlantic Ocean have an effect on its economy?

## Apply Skills

**Make an Economic Choice**

11. Imagine that you want to buy a new CD. You have $20.00. One CD that you want costs $10.00. It contains your favorite song, but has only 10 songs. Another CD you want costs $20.00, has 20 songs, but does not have your favorite song. If you buy the CD for $20.00, what is the trade-off?

**Use Latitude and Longitude**

12. Use the map of South Carolina on page 295. What city is near 34°N and 79°W?

Chapter 8 ▪ 299

# VISIT

# CONGAREE NATIONAL PARK

## Get Ready

Congaree National Park contains some of the tallest trees in the United States. Many types of animals and birds live in the park, too. The Congaree River is at the heart of the 22,000-acre park. It is surrounded by the Congaree Swamp, where many of the old trees grow.

**Locate It**
South Carolina

Congaree National Park

## What to See

Visitors can hike along several trails to see the mighty trees up close.

Children who visit the park can become Junior Rangers.

People who want to canoe along the swamp can use the Cedar Creek Trail. It takes about a day to complete the trail.

Barred Owl

Comma Butterfly

Carolina Anole

### Take a Field Trip

**A VIRTUAL TOUR** Visit The Learning Site at **www.harcourtschool.com** to take virtual tours of other parks and scenic areas.

River Otter

# Unit 4
# Review and Test Preparation

## Use Vocabulary

Write the term that matches the definition.

1. the moving of people or goods

   **suffrage** (p. 256)
   **transportation** (p. 243)

2. describing a city area

   **urban** (p. 241)
   **suburban** (p. 267)

3. the business of serving visitors

   **recreation** (p. 288)
   **tourism** (p. 247)

4. a rebirth of art and culture

   **exposition** (p. 247)
   **renaissance** (p. 259)

5. someone who makes something

   **consumer** (p. 244)
   **producer** (p. 244)

6. an unfair hatred for a group

   **prejudice** (p. 237)
   **preservation** (p. 258)

## Recall Facts

Answer these questions.

7. Who was Wade Hampton III?
8. What was the Great Migration?

Write the letter of the best choice.

9. In the early 1900s, the new form of transportation was—
   A the railroad.
   B the automobile.
   C cruise ships.
   D wagons.

10. Reverend DeLaine worked hard to—
    F start a school.
    G build more churches.
    H end segregation.
    J build a mill village.

## Think Critically

11. How did the civil rights movement affect life in South Carolina?

12. How can keeping South Carolina clean help our economy?

## Apply Skills

**Use Latitude and Longitude**

Use the map of the Southeastern United States on page 303 to answer these questions.

13. Near which lines of longitude does Tennessee begin and end?

14. What city is near 36°N and 80°W?

302 • Unit 4

# Unit Activities

Visit The Learning Site at www.harcourtschool.com for additional activities.

### Create a Diary

Find out more about an event that happened in South Carolina in the past 100 years. You can use books in the library or the Internet. Imagine that you lived through this event or took part in it. Create a historical diary to tell about the event. Draw pictures and write diary entries. Show how the event affected you, your family, and your friends.

## Complete the Unit Project

**South Carolina Heritage Fair** Work with a partner to make a display for a South Carolina Heritage Fair. Use information from your textbook, the library, or the Internet. Make a poster or a display that includes pictures and facts about your topic. Work with your teacher to choose a day for the fair. Look at all the displays and ask questions. Be ready to answer questions about your display.

## Visit Your Library

- **All Around Town** by Dinah Johnson. Henry Holt and Company.

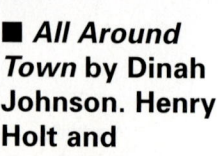
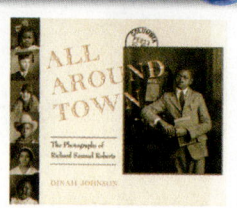

- **The Island Child** by Monica Simmons. Today's Kids Publishers, Inc.

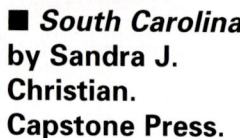

- **South Carolina** by Sandra J. Christian. Capstone Press.

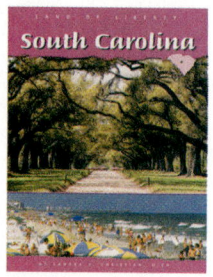

# For Your Reference

## Almanac
R2 Facts About South Carolina Counties
R4 Facts About South Carolina Governors

## Biographical Dictionary
R7

## Gazetteer
R10

## Glossary
R15

## Index
R20

# Almanac

## Facts About South Carolina Counties

| County Name | Population* | County Seat |
|---|---|---|
| Abbeville | 26,167 | Abbeville |
| Aiken | 142,552 | Aiken |
| Allendale | 11,211 | Allendale |
| Anderson | 165,740 | Anderson |
| Bamberg | 16,658 | Bamberg |
| Barnwell | 23,478 | Barnwell |
| Beaufort | 120,937 | Beaufort |
| Berkeley | 142,651 | Moncks Corner |
| Calhoun | 15,185 | St. Matthews |
| Charleston | 309,969 | Charleston |
| Cherokee | 52,537 | Gaffney |
| Chester | 34,068 | Chester |
| Chesterfield | 42,768 | Chesterfield |
| Clarendon | 32,502 | Manning |
| Colleton | 38,264 | Walterboro |
| Darlington | 67,394 | Darlington |
| Dillon | 30,722 | Dillon |
| Dorchester | 96,413 | St. George |
| Edgefield | 24,595 | Edgefield |
| Fairfield | 23,454 | Winnsboro |
| Florence | 125,761 | Florence |
| Georgetown | 55,797 | Georgetown |
| Greenville | 379,616 | Greenville |
| Greenwood | 66,271 | Greenwood |
| Hampton | 21,386 | Hampton |
| Horry | 196,629 | Conway |
| Jasper | 20,678 | Ridgeland |
| Kershaw | 52,647 | Camden |
| Lancaster | 61,351 | Lancaster |
| Laurens | 69,567 | Laurens |
| Lee | 20,119 | Bishopville |
| Lexington | 216,014 | Lexington |
| McCormick | 9,958 | McCormick |
| Marion | 35,466 | Marion |

R2 ■ Reference

| County Name | Population* | County Seat | County Name | Population* | County Seat |
|---|---|---|---|---|---|
| Marlboro | 28,818 | Bennettsville | Saluda | 19,181 | Saluda |
| Newberry | 36,108 | Newberry | Spartanburg | 253,791 | Spartanburg |
| Oconee | 66,215 | Walhalla | Sumter | 104,646 | Sumter |
| Orangeburg | 91,582 | Orangeburg | Union | 29,881 | Union |
| Pickens | 110,757 | Pickens | Williamsburg | 37,217 | Kingstree |
| Richland | 320,677 | Columbia | York | 164,614 | York |

# Almanac

## Facts About South Carolina Governors, 1776–2003

| Governor | Term |
|---|---|
| John Rutledge | 1776–1778 |
| Rawlins Lowndes | 1778–1779 |
| John Rutledge | 1779–1782 |
| John Mathews | 1782–1783 |
| Benjamin Guerard | 1783–1785 |
| William Moultrie | 1785–1787 |
| Thomas Pinckney | 1787–1789 |
| Charles Pinckney | 1789–1792 |
| William Moultrie | 1792–1794 |
| Arnoldus Vander Horst | 1794–1796 |
| Charles Pinckney | 1796–1798 |
| Edward Rutledge | 1798–1800 |
| John Drayton | 1800–1802 |
| James Burchill Richardson | 1802–1804 |
| Paul Hamilton | 1804–1806 |
| Charles Pinckney | 1806–1808 |
| John Drayton | 1808–1810 |
| Henry Midddleton | 1810–1812 |
| Joseph Alston | 1812–1814 |
| David Rogerson Williams | 1814–1816 |
| Andrew Pickens | 1816–1818 |
| John Geddes | 1818–1820 |
| Thomas Bennett Jr. | 1820–1822 |
| John Lyde Wilson | 1822–1824 |
| Richard Irvine Manning I | 1824–1826 |
| John Taylor | 1826–1828 |
| Stephen Decatur Miller | 1828–1830 |
| James Hamilton Jr. | 1830–1832 |
| Robert Young Hayne | 1832–1834 |
| George McDuffie | 1834–1836 |
| Pierce Mason Butler | 1836–1838 |
| Patrick Noble | 1838–1840 |
| Barnabus Kelet Henagan | 1840 |
| John Peter Richardson | 1840–1842 |
| James Henry Hammond | 1842–1844 |
| William Aiken | 1844–1846 |
| David Johnson | 1846–1848 |
| Whitemarsh Benjamin Seabrook | 1848–1850 |

R4 ■ Reference

| Governor | Term |
|---|---|
| John Hugh Means | 1850–1852 |
| John Lawrence Manning | 1852–1854 |
| James Hopkins Adams | 1854–1856 |
| Robert Francis Withers Allston | 1856–1858 |
| William Henry Gist | 1858–1860 |
| Francis Wilkinson Pickens | 1860–1862 |
| Milledge Luke Bonham | 1862–1864 |
| Andrew Gordon Magrath | 1864–1865 |
| Benjamin Franklin Perry | 1865 |
| James Lawrence Orr | 1865–1868 |
| Robert Kingston Scott | 1868–1872 |
| Franklin J. Moses Jr. | 1872–1874 |
| Daniel Henry Chamberlain | 1874–1877 |
| Wade Hampton III | 1877–1879 |
| William Dunlap Simpson | 1879–1880 |
| Thomas Bothwell Jeter | 1880 |
| Johnson Hagood | 1880–1882 |
| Hugh Smith Thompson | 1882–1886 |
| John Calhoun Sheppard | 1886 |
| John Peter Richardson | 1886–1890 |
| Benjamin Ryan Tillman | 1890–1894 |
| John Gary Evans | 1894–1897 |

| Governor | Term |
|---|---|
| William Haselden Ellerbe | 1897–1899 |
| Miles Benjamin McSweeney | 1899–1903 |
| Duncan Clinch Heyward | 1903–1907 |
| Martin Frederick Ansel | 1907–1911 |
| Coleman Livingston Blease | 1911–1915 |
| Charles Aurelius Smith | 1915 |
| Richard Irvine Manning III | 1915–1919 |
| Robert Archer Cooper | 1919–1922 |
| Wilson Godfrey Harvey | 1922–1923 |
| Thomas Gordon McLeod | 1923–1927 |
| John Gardiner Richards | 1927–1931 |
| Ibra Charles Blackwood | 1931–1935 |
| Olin Dewitt Talmadge Johnston | 1935–1939 |
| Burnett Rhett Maybank | 1939–1941 |
| Joseph Emile Harley | 1941–1942 |
| Richard Manning Jefferies | 1942–1943 |
| Olin Dewitt Talmadge Johnston | 1943–1945 |
| Ransome Judson Williams | 1945–1947 |
| James Strom Thurmond | 1947–1951 |
| James Francis Byrnes | 1951–1955 |
| George Bell Timmerman, Jr. | 1955–1959 |

| Governor | Term |
| --- | --- |
| Ernest Frederick Hollings | 1959–1963 |
| Donald Stuart Russell | 1963–1965 |
| Robert Evander McNair | 1965–1971 |
| John Carl West | 1971–1975 |
| James Burrows Edwards | 1975–1979 |
| Richard Wilson Riley | 1979–1987 |
| Carroll Ashmore Campbell, Jr. | 1987–1995 |
| David Muldrow Beasley | 1995–1999 |
| James Hovis Hodges | 1999–2003 |
| Mark Sanford | 2003– |

# Biographical Dictionary

The Biographical Dictionary lists many of the people introduced in this book. The page number tells where the main discussion of the person starts. See the Index for other page references.

## A

**Anderson, John Gary** *(1861–1937)* The founder of an automobile company called Rock Hill Buggy Company and the Rock Hill Telephone Company. p. 246

**Ayllón, Lucas Vásquez de** *(1475?–1526)* A Spanish explorer who was the first European to start a colony in what is now South Carolina. p. 104

## B

**Banks, Anna DeCosta** *(1869–1930)* An African American nurse who won awards for her work. p. 271

**Bethune, Mary McLeod** *(1875–1955)* An educator who left South Carolina to start a school for African Americans in Florida. p. 255

**Butler, Pierce** *(1744–1822)* A South Carolinian elected to the Constitutional Convention in 1787. p. 177

## C

**Cain, Richard "Daddy"** *(1825–1887)* An African American who moved to South Carolina, ran a newspaper called the *Missionary Record,* and served in state and federal government. p. 212

**Calhoun, John C.** *(1782–1850)* Elected as Vice President of the United States in 1824 and 1828; quit to become a South Carolina senator. p. 199

**Chisholm, Julian** *(1830–1903)* A South Carolina doctor who cared for Confederate soldiers during the Civil War. p. 207

**Clemson, Thomas** *(1807–1888)* The man who donated land and money to start Clemson University. p. 234

**Clyburn, James** *(1940–)* A United States Congressman from South Carolina, elected in 1992, the first African American since 1897. p. 276

**Columbus, Christopher** *(1451–1506)* An Italian explorer who in 1492 claimed North America for Spain. p. 102

**Cooper, Anthony Ashley** *(1621–1683)* One of the eight Lords Proprietors who was given a large area of land in North America. p. 120

**Cornwallis, General Charles** *(1738–1805)* A British general who surrendered to General George Washington in October 1781. p. 173

## D

**DeLaine, Rev. Joseph** *(1898–1974)* A South Carolina minister who led parents of African American students in a legal argument against the separate but equal conditions of schools. p. 272

**de Soto, Hernando** *(1500?–1542)* A Spanish explorer who came to the area near Columbia, South Carolina p. 106

**Dozier, Terry** *(1953– )* A South Carolina teacher named Teacher of the Year in 1985. p. 277

## E

**Earley, Charity Adams** *(1918–2002)* An African American woman who became the highest ranked African American female in the army during World War II. p. 265

**Elfe, Thomas** *(1719–1775)* A woodworker from South Carolina's middle class in the 1800s. p. 191

**Ellis, Mary Gordon** *(–A.D.1934)* The first woman to serve in the South Carolina General Assembly, elected in 1928. p. 257

## F

**Ferguson, Major Patrick** *(1744–1780)* The Patriot leader who won the battle at King's Mountain, the turning point in the American Revolution. p. 172

**Frost, Susan Pringle** *(1873–1960)* A woman who started a group to save Charleston's historic buildings and homes. p. 258

## G

**Gadsden, Christopher** *(1724–1805)* One of five men elected to represent South Carolina at the First Continental Congress. p. 164

**Gilman, Caroline** *(1794–1888)* An artist and writer from South Carolina who helped create the first children's newspaper in the country in 1832. p. 190

**Grant, Ulysses S.** *(1822–1885)* The eighteenth President of the United States and commander of Union forces during the Civil War. p. 209

**Grimke, Angelina** *(1805–1879)* **and Sarah** *(1792–1873)* Sisters who grew up in South Carolina and moved to the North to end slavery. p. 200

## H

**Hampton III, Wade** *(1818–1902)* A Confederate Civil War hero who became the first governor of South Carolina after Reconstruction. p. 236

**Henderson Sr., Ernest** *(1917– )* A pilot in World War II who trained a group of African American pilots called the Tuskegee Airmen. p. 265

**Henry, Lord Cardross** *(1650?–1693)* An English settler who founded Stuart's Town on Port Royal Sound in 1684. p. 133

**Heyward, Dubose** *(1885–1940)* An author who wrote a book set in Charleston called *Porgy*. He wrote a popular play called *Porgy and Bess* based on the book. p. 259

**Hilton, William** *(1617–1675)* An explorer who was hired by the Barbadian Adventurers to explore the coast of Carolina in 1663. p. 120

## J

**Jackson, Andrew** *(1767–1845)* The seventh President of the United States. Born in South Carolina. p. 199

**Jefferson, Thomas** *(1743–1826)* The third President of the United States and author of the Declaration of Independence. p. 169

**Johnson, Andrew** *(1808–1875)* The seventeenth President of the United States. p. 210

**Johnson, I.S. Leevy** *(1942– )* One of three African Americans elected to the South Carolina General Assembly in 1970. p. 276

**Just, Dr. Ernest E.** *(1883–1941)* A scientist from Charleston who became famous for his studies in biology. p. 254

## K

**King, Martin Luther, Jr.** *(1929–1968)* A civil rights leader who used nonviolent methods to win civil rights. p. 274

## L

**Laurens, Henry** *(1724–1792)* President of the Continental Congress. p. 170

**Lee, Robert E.** *(1807–1870)* A general of the Confederacy during the Civil War. p. 209

**Lincoln, Abraham** *(1809–1865)* The sixteenth President of the United States. p. 201

**Lynch, Thomas** *(1749–1779)* One of the five men elected to represent South Carolina at the First Continental Congress. p. 164

## M

**Marion, Francis** *(1732–1795)* An American Revolutionary war hero, nicknamed "The Swamp Fox." p. 148

**Marshall, Thurgood** *(1908– )* An African American lawyer who represented parents in the Briggs v. Elliot case in Clarendon County. p. 272

**McCord, Louisa** *(1810–1879)* A woman from Columbia, South Carolina, who started the Soldiers' Relief Association during the Civil War. p. 207

**Menéndez de Avilés, Pedro** *(1519–1574)* Spanish explorer who built forts in St. Augustine, Florida, and Santa Elena, South Carolina. p. 113

**Middleton, Henry** *(1770–1846)* One of the five men elected to represent South Carolina at the First Continental Congress. p. 164

**Miller, Thomas** *(1849–1938)* An African American elected to Congress during the Jim Crow era. p. 239

**Morgan, General Daniel** (1736–1802) Patriot leader whose army helped win the battle against the British at Cowpens in 1781. p. 172

**Moultrie, William** (1730–1805) A colonel in the Patriot army who helped build a fort on Sullivan's Island. p. 168

### P

**Pickens, Andrew** (1739–1817) A Patriot leader in the American Revolution. p. 166

**Pinckney, Charles** (1757–1824) South Carolinian elected to the Constitutional Convention in 1787. p. 178

**Pinckney, Charles Cotesworth** (1746–1825) South Carolinian elected to the Constitutional Convention in 1787. p. 178

**Pinckney, Eliza Lucas** (1722–1793) An English settler in Carolina whose indigo dye became an important cash crop. p. 131

**Pollitzer, Anita** (1894–1975) A leader in the women's suffrage movement. p. 256

### R

**Ribault, Jean** (1520–1565) French explorer and ship captain who landed in Port Royal Sound in South Carolina in 1562. p. 110

**Richardson, Colonel Richard** (1704–1780) A Patriot leader during the American Revolution. p. 167

**Roosevelt, Franklin D.** (1882–1945) The thirty-second President of the United States in 1932. His plan to end the Great Depression was called the New Deal. p. 261

**Roosevelt, Theodore** (1858–1919) The twenty-sixth President of the United States. p. 247

**Rutledge, Edward** (1749–1800) One of the five men elected to represent South Carolina at the First Continental Congress. p. 164

**Rutledge, John** (1739–1800) One of the five men elected to represent South Carolina at the First Continental Congress. p. 164

### S

**Sayle, William** (A.D. 1671) A leader of the settlers of Charles Town. p. 122

**Sherman, William Tecumseh** (1820–1891) A Union General who captured and set fire to Columbia, South Carolina, on February 17, 1865. p. 209

**Smalls, Robert** (1839–1916) An African American elected to Congress during the time of Jim Crow era. p. 239

**Stowers, Freddie** (1896–1918) An African American corporal who fought and died in France during World War I. p. 252

**Sumter, Thomas** (1734–1832) A general in the Revolutionary army who was honored by Congress as a hero. p. 171

### T

**Tarleton, Banastre** (1754–1833) A British officer during the American Revolution. p. 150

**Thurmond, James Strom** (1902–2003) A South Carolina senator who was the oldest and longest serving. p. 275

**Tillman, Ben** (1847–1918) A farmer who helped start Clemson University. He was elected governor of South Carolina in 1890. p. 237

**Tubman, Harriet** (1820–1913) An escaped slave who helped other slaves escape on the Underground Railroad. p. 200

### V

**Vesey, Denmark** (1767?–1822) A freed slave in Charleston who tried to organize slaves to fight for their freedom. p. 193

### W

**Washington, George** (1732–1799) A general in the Revolutionary army; first President of the United States. p. 173

**Washington, Colonel William** (1752–1810) Patriot colonel who was partly responsible for the victory against the British at Cowpens in 1781. p. 172

**Whitney, Eli** (1765–1825) Inventor of the cotton gin. p. 180

**Wilson, Woodrow** (1856–1924) The twenty-eighth President of the United States who helped form the League of Nations after World War I. p. 250

**Woodward, Dr. Henry** (1646–1686) An English explorer who settled Charles Town. p. 122

# Gazetteer

This gazetteer is a geographical dictionary that will help you locate places discussed in this book. The page number tells where each place appears on a map.

## A

**Africa** The second-largest continent, lying south of Europe between the Atlantic and Indian oceans. p. A3

**Aiken** A town in west central South Carolina. p. 81

**Alabama** A state in the southeastern United States. p. 63

**Alaska** A state in the United States in the extreme northwest North America. p. 32

**Albemarle Point** A piece of land along the coast of the Carolina colony. p. 66

**Amelia Township** A town in South Carolina settled by 1735. p. 136

**Anderson** A town in northwest South Carolina that hosts an event with hot air balloons on Memorial Day. p. 280

**Antarctica** A continent lying mostly within the Antarctic Circle and centered on the South Pole. p. 294

**Appalachian Mountains** Mountain system in eastern North America. p. 33

**Arkansas** A state in the south central United States. p. 63

**Ashley River** A river near Charleston named for Anthony Ashley Cooper, who owned land in the Carolina colony. p. 123

**Asia** The world's largest continent, occupying the eastern part of the Eurasian landmass. p. A3

**Atlanta** The capital of Georgia. p. 63

**Atlantic Ocean** The body of water that separates North and South America from Europe and Africa. p. 9

**Augusta** A settlement along the Great Wagon Road. p. 157

## B

**Beaufort** A town in the Carolina colony settled by people from Barbados. p. 146

**Biloxi** City in southeast Mississippi. p. 33

**Birmingham** City in north central Alabama. p. 33

**Black Hills** Group of mountains in western South Dakota and northeast Wyoming. p. 33

**Blackstock's Hill** The site of a Patriot victory during the American Revolution. p. 170

**Blue Ridge Mountain Region** A range of mountains that is part of the Appalachian Mountains. p. 31

**Boise** Largest city in Idaho. p. 32

**Boston** Capital of Massachusetts. p. 33

**Broad River** A river in northern South Carolina. p. 76

## C

**Camden** A settlement along the Great Wagon Road. p. 157

**Canada** Independent country in North America. p. 33

**Cape Fear** A point of land in the Carolina colony projecting into the Atlantic Ocean. p. 66

**Caribbean Sea** A part of the Atlantic Ocean. The West Indies and Central and South America form its boundaries on three sides. p. 109

**Cascade Range** A mountain range that extends across Oregon and Washington. p. 32

**Catawba River** A river in South Carolina named for the people living nearby. p. A15

**Charleston** The second largest city in South Carolina. p. 27

**Charleston Harbor** A major port that was especially important during the Civil War. p. 205

**Charles Town** The first permanent settlement in Carolina established in 1670. Today it is known as Charleston. p. 123

**Charlotte** A city in North Carolina. p. 33

**Cherokee County** A county in northern South Carolina. p. 146

**Chester** A settlement along the Great Wagon Road. p. 157

**Chicago** A city in northeast Illinois. p. 33

**Clemson** A town in western South Carolina. p. 295

**Cleveland** A town in northern South Carolina. p. 290

**Clinton** A town in central South Carolina. p. 243

**Coast Ranges** Mountains along the Pacific coast of North America. p. 32

**Coastal Zone** A long, narrow and sandy region of South Carolina on the Atlantic Ocean. p. 27

**Colorado River** A river in the southwestern United States. p. 33

**Columbia** The capital of South Carolina. p. 27

**Columbia River** A river in southwest Canada and northwest United States. p. 32

**Connecticut** A state in the northeastern United States. p. 175

**Conway** A town in eastern South Carolina. p. 81

**Cooper River** A river in South Carolina. p. 123

**Cowpens** Site of an important battle during the American Revolution. p. 170

**Cuba** An island country in the Caribbean Sea south of Florida. p. 109

**Currituck** A town in the Carolina colony. p. 66

### D

**Dallas** A city in northeast Texas. p. 33

**Darlington** A town in eastern South Carolina. p. 291

**Daufuskie Island** An island off South Carolina named for the Muskogean word meaning "land with a point." p. 91

**Dawes Island** An island in Port Royal Sound. p. 111

**Delaware** A state in the eastern United States. p. 175

**Dillon** A town in eastern South Carolina. p. 243

### E

**Edenton** A town in the Carolina colony. p. 66

**Edgefield** A town in central South Carolina. p. 290

**Edisto Island** An island off the coast of South Carolina. p. 2

**Edisto River** One of South Carolina's main river systems. p. A15

**Europe** The sixth-largest continent. p. A3

**Eutaw Springs** A town in southeast South Carolina. p. 170

### F

**Fall Line** A long, low cliff where rivers drop suddenly. p. 27

**Florence** A town in eastern South Carolina. p. 81

**Florida** A state in the southeastern United States. p. 63

**Fork Mountain** A mountain in northwest South Carolina. p. 2

**Fort Moultrie** A fort built in 1776 on Sullivan's Island named after a Patriot army colonel. p. 205

**Fort San Marcos** A fort built in 1577 in Santa Elena. p. 115

**Fort Sumter** A fort in Charleston, South Carolina. p. 205

**Fort Sumter National Monument** A fort built by the United States to protect Charleston Harbor. It was named for Thomas Sumter, a hero of the American Revolution. p. 186

**Fredericksburg** A South Carolina township settled in 1735. p. 136

### G

**Garden City** A town south of Myrtle Beach. p. 289

**Georgetown** A port city in South Carolina. p. 295

**Georgia** A state in the southeastern United States. p. 63

**Goose Creek** A town in southern South Carolina. p. 2

**Grand Strand** A recreation area along the coast of South Carolina that stretches for more than sixty miles. p. 289

**Graniteville** A town in south-central South Carolina. p. 243

**Great Basin** An elevated region including Nevada and parts of Utah, California, Idaho, Wyoming, and Oregon. p. 32

**Great Lakes** Chain of five lakes, Erie, Huron, Michigan, Ontario, and Superior, in central North America. p. 33

**Great Plains** The continental slope of central North America. p. 33

Gazetteer ■ R11

**Great Wagon Road** A road in the colonies that stretched from Philadelphia to Camden. p. 157

**Greenville** A town in northwest South Carolina. p. 81

**Greenwood** A town in central South Carolina. p. 243

**Gulf of Mexico** A body of water on the southeastern coast of North America. p. 63

**Havana** The capital and largest city in Cuba. p. 109

**Hilton Head Island** An island in Port Royal Sound. p. 111

**Inner Coastal Plain** A coastal region of South Carolina with rich soil for growing cotton, peanuts, and soybeans. p. 27

**Isle of Palms** An island near Charleston, South Carolina. p. 205

**Jackson** The capital of Mississippi. p. 303.

**James Island** The site of Fort Johnson. p. 205

**Jamestown** The first English settlement in America. p. 66

**Johns Island** The home of Angel Oak, one of the oldest living oak trees in the world. p. 6

**Kentucky** A state in the east central United States. p. 63

**King's Mountain** A battle during the American Revolution that became the turning point of the war. p. 170

**Kingston Township** A town in South Carolina settled by 1735. p. 136

**Knoxville** City in Tennessee. p. 33

**L**

**Lakemont** A town in northwest South Carolina. p. 30

**Lancaster** A town in northern South Carolina. p. 243

**Lexington** A town in central South Carolina. p. 243

**Louisiana** A state in the southeastern United States. p. 63

**Lowcountry** The region that is made up of Charleston, Beaufort, Myrtle Beach, and Hilton Head Island. p. 2

**Lynches River** A river in northern South Carolina. p. 76

**M**

**Maine** A state in the northeastern United States. p. 175

**Maryland** A state in the eastern United States. p. 63

**Massachusetts** A state in the northeastern United States. p. 175

**Mexico** Independent country in North America. p. 33

**Midlands** The central region of South Carolina. p. 2

**Minneapolis** City in southeast Minnesota. p. 33

**Mississippi** A state in the southeastern United States. p. 63

**Mississippi River** A river in the central United States. p. 33

**Moncks Corner** A town in southern South Carolina. p. 81

**Montgomery** The capital of Alabama. p. 303

**Mount Pleasant** A town on the South Carolina coastline. p. 100

**Myrtle Beach** A popular vacation place with golf courses and beaches on the Atlantic Ocean. p. 289

**N**

**Nashville** The capital of Tennessee. p. 303

**Newberry** A settlement along the Great Wagon Road. p. 157

**New Hampshire** A state in the northeastern United States. p. 175

**New Jersey** A state in the northeastern United States. p. 175

**New York** A state in the eastern United States. p. 175

**New Orleans** A city in southeast Louisiana. p. 33

**New Windsor Township** A town in South Carolina settled by 1735. p. 136

**Nimmons** A town in northwest South Carolina. p. 30

**Ninety Six** A town in northwest South Carolina. p. 154

**Norfolk** A town in Virginia. p. 66

**North America** The continent that includes the United States, Canada, Mexico, and some countries in Central America. p. 22

**North Carolina** A state in the southeastern United States. p. 63

**North Charleston** A town in southern South Carolina. p. 2

**North Pole** The northern end of the earth's axis of rotation, a point in the Arctic Ocean. p. 294

### O

**Oconee County** A county in northwest South Carolina. p. A14

**Ohio River** A river that flows through Pennsylvania, Ohio, Indiana, and Illinois. p. 33

**Oklahoma** A state in the south central United States. p. 63

**Orangeburg** A town in central South Carolina. p. 81

**Orlando** A city in central Florida. p. 63

**Outer Coastal Plain** A coastal region of South Carolina where the land rises gently and steadily. p. 27

### P

**Parris Island** An island in Port Royal Sound. p. 111

**Pee Dee River** A river that flows south from North Carolina, through South Carolina, to the Atlantic Ocean. p. 8

**Pennsylvania** A state in the northeastern United States. p. 175

**Phillips Island** An island in Port Royal Sound. p. 111

**Phoenix** Capital of Arizona. p. 32

**Pickens** A town in northwest South Carolina p. 290

**Piedmont** A large area of land rich in natural resources that lies at the edge of the Blue Ridge Mountains. p. 27

**Port Royal Sound** A harbor in South Carolina. p. 111

**Portland** A city in northwest Oregon. p. 32

**Pumpkintown** A town in northwest South Carolina. p. 30

**Purrysburg Township** A town in South Carolina settled by 1735. p. 136

### Q

**Queensborough Township** A town in South Carolina settled by 1735. p. 136

### R

**Raleigh** The capital of North Carolina. p. 303

**Reno** City in northwest Nevada. p. 32

**Rhode Island** A state in the northeastern United States. p. 175

**Richmond** The capital of Virginia. p. 303

**Ridgeland** A town in southern South Carolina. p. 81

**Rio Grande River** A river in the southwest United States and northern Mexico. p. 33

**Rock Hill** A city in northern South Carolina. p. 72

**Rocky Mountains** Mountain system in western North America. p. 33

### S

**Sacramento** Capital of California. p. 32

**St. Augustine** A city in northeast Florida. p. 115

**St. Helena Island** An island in southern South Carolina. p. 104

**St. Louis** City in eastern Missouri. p. 33

**Salt Lake City** Capital of Utah. p. 33

**Saluda County** A county in west central South Carolina. p. A14

**Saluda River** A river in northwest South Carolina. p. 76

**Sandhills Region** Hills of rough, sandy soil in the Midlands of South Carolina. p. 27

**Santa Fe** Capital of New Mexico. p. 33
**Santee River** One of South Carolina's main river systems. p. 76
**Sassafras Mountain** The tallest mountain in South Carolina, located in the Blue Ridge. p. 2
**Savannah** A city in southeast Georgia. p. 303
**Savannah River** A river in South Carolina that starts in the Piedmont. p. 2
**Saxe Gotha Township** A town in South Carolina settled by 1735. p. 136
**Seneca** A town in northwest South Carolina. p. 243
**Sierra Nevada** Mountain range in eastern California. p. 32
**Socastee** A town near Myrtle Beach. p. 289
**South America** The continent that lies southeast of North America. p. A31
**South Pole** The southern end of the earth's axis of rotation, a point in Antarctica. p. 294
**Spartanburg** A town in northern South Carolina. p. 2
**Sullivan's Island** An island in the harbor at Charlestown. p. 170
**Summerville** A town in southern South Carolina. p. 2
**Sumter** A town in central South Carolina. p. 2
**Sunset** A town in northwest South Carolina. p. 30

**Table Rock Mountain** A mountain in the Blue Ridge Mountains, near the border of North Carolina. p. 30
**Tallahassee** The capital of Florida. p. 303
**Tennessee** A state in the southeast central United States. p. 63
**Tennessee River** A river of the southeast United States. p. 109
**Texas** A state in the southern United States. p. 63

**Upcountry** The upper third of South Carolina. p. 2

**Vermont** A state in the northeastern United States. p. 175
**Virginia** A state in the eastern United States. p. 63

**Walterboro** A town in southern South Carolina. p. 291
**Washington, D.C.** The capital city of the United States. p. 33
**Wateree River** A river in north central South Carolina. p. 76
**West Virginia** A state in the eastern United States. p. 63
**Williamsburg** A town in Virginia. p. 66
**Williamsburg Township** A town in South Carolina settled by 1735. p. 136
**Winnsboro** A village in South Carolina settled around 1755. p. 157

# Glossary

This glossary contains important social studies words and their definitions. Each word is respelled as it would be in a dictionary. When you see the ´ mark after a syllable, pronounce that syllable with more force than the other syllables. The page number at the end of the definition tells you where to find the word in your book. The boldfaced letters in the examples that follow show how these letters are pronounced in the respellings after each glossary word.

add, āce, câre, pälm; end, ēqual; it, īce; odd, ōpen, ôrder; to͝ok, po͞ol; up, bûrn; yo͞o as u in fuse; oil; pout; ə as a in above, e in sicken, i in possible, o in melon, u in circus; check; ring; thin; this; zh as in vision

## A

**abolitionist** (a•bə•li´shən•ist) A person who wanted to end all slavery. (p. 200)
**agriculture** (a´grə•kul•chər) The raising of crops and farm animals. (p. 76)
**ally** (a´lī) A friend. (p. 134)
**ancestor** (an´ses•tər) An early family member. (p. 85)
**artifact** (är´tə•fakt) A human-made object from the past that can be a map, a tool, or a photograph. (p. 42)

## B

**bar graph** (bär graf) A graph that uses bars of different lengths to stand for numbers. (p. 24)
**barrier island** (bar´ē•ər ī´lənd) A long, sandy island between the ocean and the mainland. (p. 27)
**Bill of Rights** (bil əv rīts) An addition to the constitution that lists some of the rights and freedoms that belong to all Americans. (p. 178)
**biography** (bī•ä´grə•fē) A life story. (p. 106)
**Black Codes** (blak kōdz) Laws that limited the freedom of former slaves after the Civil War. (p. 210)
**blockade** (blä•kād´) To shut off trade by using ships to stop other ships from entering or leaving a port. (p. 168)
**border** (bôr´dər) A line on a map that shows where a state or nation ends. (p. 22)

## C

**canal** (kə•nal´) A human-made waterway. (p. 188)
**cardinal directions** (kär´də´nəl di•rek´shənz) The four main directions—*north, south, east,* and *west*. (p. 16)
**cash crop** (kash krop) A crop that people grow to sell, not to use themselves. (p. 127)
**cause** (côz) An action or event that makes something happen. (p. 160)
**charter** (chär´tər) A paper that gives permission to start a colony. (p. 120)
**citizen** (sit´ə•zən) A person who lives in and belongs to a community. (p. 13)
**civil rights** (si´vəl rīts) Rights given to all citizens by the constitution. (p. 270)
**civil war** (si´vəl wôr) A fight between groups in the same country. (p. 204)
**claim** (klām) To say that something belongs to you. (p. 103)
**clan** (klan) A large group of related families. (p. 83)
**class system** (klas sis´təm) A system where people are grouped in ranks; the top rank has the most money and power. (p. 189)
**climate** (klī´mət) The weather in a place over time. (p. 74)
**coastal plain** (kōs´təl plān) An area of flat land along a sea or ocean. (p. 28)
**colonist** (kä´lə•nist) A person living in a colony. (p. 111)
**colony** (kä´lə•nē) A settlement ruled by a country far away. (p. 110)
**common good** (kä´mən go͝od) Something that meets the needs of all people in a community. (p. 44)
**community** (kə•myo͞o´nə•tē) A group of people who live or work in the same place. (p. 13)
**compass rose** (kum´pəs rōz) A drawing on a map with the letters *N, S, E,* and *W* which stand for north, south, east, and west. (p. 16)
**compromise** (kom´prə•mīz) A solution to a conflict in which both sides give up some of what they want. (p. 124)
**Confederacy** (kən•fe´də•rə•sē) The Confederate States of America; formed by the southern states that had seceded from the United States. (p. 204)

Glossary ■ R15

**confederation** (kən•fe•də•rā´shən) A group of tribes that agree to help one another. (p. 93)

**conflict** (kän´flikt) A disagreement. (p. 124)

**congress** (kong´grəs) A group of elected leaders who meet to discuss problems. (p. 164)

**consequence** (kän´sə•kwens) What happens because of a choice. (p. 215)

**constitution** (kän•stə•tōō´shən) A written plan for government. (p. 50)

**consumer** (kən•sōō´mər) A person who buys things. (p. 244)

**continent** (kän´tən•ənt) One of the seven largest land areas on Earth. (p. 22)

**council** (koun´səl) A group of people who make laws. (p. 78)

**county** (koun´tē) A part of a state. (p. 46)

**county seat** (koun´tē sēt) A city or town that serves as the center of the county government. (p. 46)

**crossroads** (krôs´rōdz) A place where one path crosses another. (p. 157)

**cultural region** (kul´chə•rəl rē´jən) An area where people have the same way of life. (p. 88)

**culture** (kul´chər) A way of life shared by a group of people. (p. 14)

**custom** (kus´təm) A way of doing something. (p. 38)

### D

**decision** (di•si´zhən) A choice. (p. 215)

**discrimination** (dis•kri•mə•nā´shən) Unfair treatment based on prejudice. (p. 241)

**distance scale** (dis´təns skāl) A feature that shows that a certain length on a map equals a real distance on Earth. (p. 16, 94)

**diversity** (də•vûr´sə•tē) A rich mixture of cultures. (p. 38)

**dugout** (dug´out) A boat made from a log hollowed-out by burning and scraping the wood. (p. 79)

### E

**economics** (ek•ə•nä´miks) The way people use resources to meet their needs and wants. (p. 12)

**effect** (i•fekt´) The result of something that has happened. (p. 160)

**election** (i•lek´shən) A time when citizens vote, or make a choice. (p. 45)

**emancipation** (i•man•sə•pā´shən) To be set free from slavery. (p. 208)

**equality** (i•kwä´lə•tē) Having the same rights. (p. 275)

**equator** (i•kwā´tər) A made-up line that runs around the globe, halfway between the North Pole and the South Pole. (p. 20)

**ethnic group** (eth´nik grōōp) A group of people with the same culture, or way of life. (p. 39)

**exact location** (ig•zakt´ lō•kā´shən) The point where two lines meet, or cross, on a map. (p. 182)

**executive** (ig•ze´kyə•tiv) The branch of government that sees that the laws are obeyed. (p. 50)

**explorer** (ik•splôr´ər) A person who goes to find out about a place. (p. 102)

**export** (eks´pôrt) Goods that go out of a country. (p. 285)

**exposition** (eks´pə´zi´shən) A large fair or show. (p. 247)

### F

**fact** (fakt) A statement that can be proved. (p. 262)

**fall line** (fôl līn) A long, low cliff where rivers drop suddenly. (p. 29)

**federal** (fe´də•rəl) National; the federal government is made up of the whole nation. (p. 178)

**Freedmen's Bureau** (frēd´menz byûr´ō) A group created by Congress that helped former slaves by passing out food, clothing, and medicine. (p. 212)

**frontier** (frən•tir´) The edge of the wilderness. (p. 136)

### G

**geography** (jē•ä´grə•fē) The study of Earth's features. (p. 8)

**globe** (glōb) A model of Earth. (p. 20)

**government** (guv´ərn•mənt) A group of leaders who solve problems and make laws. (p. 13)

**governor** (guv´ər•nər) The head of the state's executive branch of government. (p. 55)

**grid system** (grid sis´təm) A set of lines the same distance apart that cross one another to form boxes. (p. 182)

## H

**harbor** (här´bər) A protected place with deep water where large ships can come close to shore. (p. 27)

**hemisphere** (hem´ə•sfir) One half of the globe. (p. 20)

**heritage** (her´ə•tij) A set of beliefs and customs handed down from people who lived earlier. (p. 41)

**high-tech** (hī tek) Having to do with inventing, making, or using computers and other kinds of electronic equipment. (p. 283)

**history** (his´tə•rē) The story of what has happened in a place. (p. 10)

**history map** (his´tə•rē map) A map that shows how a place looked in an earlier time. (p. 108, 174)

## I

**immigrant** (im´ə•grənt) A person who comes to live in a country from somewhere else in the world. (p. 38)

**import** (im´pôrt) Goods that come into a country. (p. 285)

**indigo** (in´di•gō) A plant used to make a blue dye. (p. 130)

**independence** (in•də pen´dəns) Freedom from the rule of another country. (p. 167)

**industry** (in´dəs•trē) All the businesses that make one kind of product or provide one kind of service. (p. 198)

**interdependent** (in•tər•də•pen´dənt) Needing each other; depending on each other for goods and services. (p. 285)

**intermediate directions** (in•tər•mē´dē•ət di•rek´shənz) The directions between the cardinal directions—*northeast, southeast, northwest,* and *southwest.* (p. 80)

**invention** (in•ven´shən) Something made for the first time. (p. 246)

## J

**Jim Crow** (jim krō) An African American character in a popular song. A series of unfair laws against African Americans were named after this character. (p. 238)

**judicial** (jōō•di´shəl) The branch of government that decides if laws are fair or unfair. (p. 50)

**jury** (joor´ē) A group of citizens who listen to the facts of a case in court. (p. 54)

## L

**landform** (land´fôrm) A shape on the land, such as a mountain or a river. (p. 26)

**landform map** (land´fôrm map) A map that shows the physical features of a place. (p. 32)

**language group** (lang´gwij grōōp) A group of people who speak similar languages. (p. 75)

**latitude** (la´tə•tōōd) A line that runs east and west around the globe. (p. 294)

**law** (lô) A rule for living together. (p. 13)

**legislative** (le´jəs•lā•tiv) The branch of government that makes laws. (p. 50)

**line graph** (līn´graf) A graph that uses a line that helps you see how information changes over time. (p. 248)

**location** (lō•kā´shən) Where a place is. (p. 18)

**longhouse** (lông´hous) A long, narrow building with a curved roof. (p. 83)

**longitude** (lon´jə•tōōd) A line that runs north and south from pole to pole; also called a meridian. (p. 294)

**Lords Proprietors** (lordz prə•prī´•ə•tərz) The eight landowners named in the charter written by King Charles II. They were the first to rule the Carolina colony. (p. 120)

**Loyalist** (loi´ə•list) A person who wanted the colonies to stay under British rule. (p. 165)

## M

**map key** (map kē) The part of the map that tells what the map symbols mean; also called the map legend. (p. 16)

**map symbol** (map sim´bəl) A symbol that stands for something real on Earth. (p. 16)

**map title** (map tī´təl) A title that tells what the map is about. (p. 16)

**mediator** (mē´dē•ā•tər) A person who helps people settle disagreements. (p. 124)

**migrate** (mī´grāt) To move from one place to another. (p. 156)

**museum** (myōō•zē´əm) A place where objects from other times and places can be seen. (p. 11)

## N

**nation** (nā´shən) A country. (p. 50)

**natural resource** (na´chə•rəl rē´sôr•sə) A type of material from nature, such as wood, stone, and water. (p. 30)

## O

**opinion** (ə•pin´yən) Something that a person believes. (p. 262)

**opportunity cost** (ä•pər•tōō´nə•tē kôst) What you give up in order to get what you want. (p. 286)

## P

**Parliament** (pär´lə•mənt) The British lawmakers. (p. 159)

**Patriot** (pā´trē•ət) A colonist who opposed British rule. (p. 165)

**permanent** (pûr´mə•nənt) Long-lasting. (p. 91)

**physical region** (fi´zi•kəl rē´jən) A region that has the same kinds of physical features. (p. 26)

**picture graph** (pik´chər graf) A graph that uses small pictures or symbols to stand for numbers. (p. 24)

**pioneer** (pī•ə•nir´) A person who helps settle frontier lands. (p. 136)

**plantation** (plan•tā´shən) A huge farm. (p. 119)

**planter** (plan´tər) A plantation owner. (p. 119)

**point of view** (point uv vyōō) The way a person feels about something. (p. 196)

**prejudice** (pre´jə•dəs) An unfair hatred of another group based on their culture, skin color, or religion. (p. 237)

**preservation** (pre´sûr•vā´shən) Maintaining or keeping up. (p. 258)

**primary source** (prīmer•ē sôrs) A written or printed artifact made by a person who saw or took part in an event. (p. 42)

**problem** (prä´bləm) Something difficult or hard to understand. (p. 48)

**producer** (prə•dōō´sər) A maker of a product. (p. 244)

**product map** (prä´dukt map) A map that shows where different products come from. (p. 268)

**public service** (pub´lik sûr´vəs) Work that helps everyone. (p. 45)

## R

**racism** (rā´•si•zəm) The belief that one group of people is better than another. (p. 237)

**raw material** (rô mə•tir´ē•əl) A natural resource, such as wood, that can be used to make a product. (p. 118)

**Reconstruction** (rē•kən•struk´shən) The time of rebuilding after the Civil War. (p. 210)

**recreation** (rek•rē•ā´shən) What people do to have fun. (p. 288)

**region** (rē´jən) An area that has at least one feature that makes it different from other areas. (p. 22)

**religion** (ri•li´jən) A set of beliefs about a god or gods. (p. 103)

**renaissance** (re´nə•säns) A rebirth of art and culture. (p. 259)

**responsibilities** (ri•spän•sə•bil´ə•tēz) Things citizens should do because they are necessary and important. (p. 47)

**revolution** (re•və•lōō´shən) A fight for a change in government. (p. 166)

**rights** (rīts) Freedoms that all citizens share. (p. 47)

**river basin** (ri´vər bā´sən) Land drained by a river. (p. 30)

**river system** (ri´vər sis´təm) A system made of small rivers and streams flowing into larger ones. (p. 74)

**route** (rōōt) A path between one place and another. (p. 102)

**rural** (rûr´əl) An area away from cities and large towns. (p. 241)

## S

**secede** (si•sēd´) To withdraw from a country. (p. 201)

**secondary source** (se´kən•dâr•ē sôrs) A record written by someone who was not there when an event took place. (p. 43)

**segregation** (se•gri•gā´shən) Separating people in society by skin color. (p. 239)

**self-sufficient** (self•sə•fi´shənt) Being able to meet your own needs by making or growing nearly everything you use. (p. 128)

**sequence** (sē´kwəns) The order in which events take place. (p. 116)

**service industry** (sûr´vəs indəs•tre) A business that does work for others. (p. 284)

**settlement** (se´təl•mənt) A village built by the first people to live in a place. (p. 104)

**settler** (set´lər) One of the first people to live in a place. (p. 104)

**slave** (slāv) A person kept against his or her wishes and made to work for no pay. (p. 104)

**society** (sə•sī´ə•te) A human group. (p. 14)

**solution** (sə•lōō´shən) An answer to a problem. (p. 48)

**suburban** (sə•bûr´bən) A town or small city near a big city. (p. 267)

**suffrage** (su´frij) The right to vote. (p. 256)

**swamp** (swämp) A wet area where woody plants grow. (p. 26)

## T

**table** (tā´bəl) A drawing that is used to organize information. (p. 56)

**taxes** (tak•səs) Money that citizens pay to the government. (p. 53)

**technology** (tek•näl´ə•jē) New inventions people use in everyday life. (p. 283)

**textile** (tek´stīl) Cloth. (p. 130)

**time line** (tīm līn) A drawing that shows when and in what order events took place. (p. 116)

**tourism** (tōōr´i•zəm) The business of serving travelers on vacation. (p. 247)

**trade** (trād) The exchange of one thing for another. (p. 79)

**trade-off** (trād´ôf) The thing you give up in order to buy or do something else. (p. 286)

**tradition** (trə•di´shən) A custom or way of doing something that is passed on by families to their children. (p. 77)

**transportation** (trans•pər•tā´shən) The moving of people and goods from one place to another. (p. 242)

**tribe** (trīb) A group of related people who share a way of life. (p. 75)

**turning point** (tər´ning point) A big change. (p. 172)

## U

**urban** (ûr´bən) Relating to a city. (p. 241)

**Union** (yōōn´yən) The federal group of states during the U.S. Civil War. (p. 204)

## W

**war bond** (wôr bond) A way that allowed a person to loan money to the government. (p. 253)

**weir** (wir) A fence or net that can be put across a river to trap fish. (p. 92)

# Index

Page references for illustrations are set in italic type. An italic *m* indicates a map. Page references set in boldface type indicate the pages on which vocabulary words are defined.

## A

**Abbeville, South Carolina,** 158, R2
**Abbeville County,** R2
**Abolitionists, 200,** 200, 201
**"Acts, The"** (British tax laws), 162, *162*
**Adams, John,** 169
**Advertisements**
   telling fact from opinion in, 262–263, *263*, 279
   writing, 247
**African Americans**
   civil rights of, 270–275, *270, 271, 272, 273, 274, 275*
   in Civil War, 204, 206, 208, 239, *239*
   dance of, 40, *40*
   education of, 194, 212, *212*, 216, 237, 239, 240, 255, *255*, 270, *270*, 272–273, *272*
   enslavement of. *See* Slave(s)
   free, 193, *193*, 210
   Freedmen's Bureau and, 212, *212*
   in government, 239, 276, *276*
   in Great Migration to North, 254–255, *254, 255*
   "head tax" on, 193
   jobs of, 241, 253, 266, 271, *271*
   laws involving, 210, 211, 236, 238–239, *238*, 240, 257, 274
   as leaders, 254, *254*, 255, *255*, 272, *272*, 273, *273*, 274, *274*, 275, 276, *276*, 277
   in manufacturing, 241, 253, 266
   monument to, *214*
   music of, 40
   prejudice and, 237, 240
   racism and, 237, 240
   Reconstruction and, 210, 211, *211*, 212
   religion and, 240
   rights of, 194, 210, 211, *211*, 212, 236, 237, 238–239, 257, 270–276
   in rural areas, 241
   segregation of, 239, 240, 270–271, *270, 271, 272, 272*
   sharecropping by, 213, *213*
   voting rights of, 210, 211, *211*, 237, 238–239, 257, 274, 275, 276, *276*

women, 239, 255, *255*, 257, 265, *265*, 271, *271*, 274, 277
   in World War I, 252, *252*
   in World War II, 264, 265, *265*, 266
**Agriculture (farming), 76**
   after American Revolution, 176
   in Carolina, 127–131, *127, 128–129, 130*
   during Great Depression, 260, *260–261*
   jobs in, 282
   lower class in, 192, *192*
   of Native Americans, 76, 84, *84, 92*
   products from, 268, *m269*. *See also* Crops
   sharecropping in, 213, *213*
   small farmers in, 213, *213*, 241
   in Spanish Florida, 114
   tools used in, 180, *180, 181, 181*, 188, *192*, 213
   *See also* Plantation(s)
**Aiken County,** R2
**Alabama,** 265, R10
**Albemarle Point,** 122, R10
**"All Around Town" (Johnson),** 304
**Allendale County,** R2
**Ally, 134**
**Almanac,** R2–R6
**American Indians.** *See* Native Americans
**American Revolution,** 168–173, *m170, 171*
   battles in, 140, *141*, 146, 166, *166*, 168, *168, m170*, 172, *172, 173*, R10
   beginning of, 166, *166*
   British blockades in, 168, 170
   Declaration of Independence and, 169, *169*
   drummer in, *221*
   dungeon in, 220, *221*
   end of, 173, *173*
   events leading to, 146, 162–167, *162, 163, 164, 166*
   Great Snow Campaign in, 167
**Amusement parks,** *289*
**Ancestors, 85**
**Anderson, John Gary,** 246, R7
**Anderson, Robert,** 205
**Anderson, South Carolina,** *280–281*, R2, R10

**Anderson automobiles,** 246, *246*
**Anderson County,** R2
**Angel Oak,** *6–7, m6*
**Animals**
   in Native American stories, 68–71
   as state symbols, 3
   in swamps, *301*
   *See also individual animals*
**Anole, Carolina,** 301
**Answers,** writing, 98
**Appalachian Mountains,** 31, R10
**Appomattox, Virginia,** *209*
**Aquariums,** 291, *291, m291*
**Archaeological site (dig), 96,** *96*
**Archaeologist, 96,** *96*
**Arledge, Buzz,** 4–5
**Arrowhead,** *96*
**Art,** *97, 197*, 254, *259, 259*
**Articles,** writing, 131
**Artifacts, 43,** *43, 96, 97, 97,* 296–297, *296, 297*
**Ashley River,** *m17,* 66, 120, 122, 123, *m123,* R10
**Atlantic Ocean,** R10
**Atlas,** *mA1–A15*
   of South Carolina, *mA14–A15*
   of United States, *mA8–A13*
   of Western hemisphere, *mA6–A7*
   of world, *mA2–A5*
**Augusta, South Carolina,** *m157,* R10
**Automobiles,** 246, *246,* 283
**Avery Institute** (Charleston), 147
**Ayllón, Lucas Vásquez de,** 104, 107, *m109,* 116, R7

## B

**Balloons, hot-air,** *280–281*
**Ballot.** *See* Election; Votes and voting
**Banks, Anna DeCosta,** 271, R7
**Bar graph, 24,** *25, 35, 137, 147,* 202–203, *203,* 219, *276,* 283
**Barbadian Adventurers,** 120
**Barbados Island,** 40, 118–119, 120, 122
**Barnwell County,** R2
**Barrier island, 27,** 28, 29
**Basket weaving,** *41,* 72, 87, 92, *92,* 228–233, *228, 229, 230, 233*

**Battle of Cowpens,** *m170,* 172, 173, R11
**Battle of Huck's Defeat,** 140, *m140, 141*
**Battle of King's Mountain,** *m170,* 172, *172,* R12
**Battle of Lexington,** 166, *166*
**Battle of Sullivan's Island,** 146, 168, *168, m170,* R14
**Beach(es),** 2, 9, *9,* 26, *26,* 288–289, 289, *m289,* 293, *293,* R12
**Beach Sweep/River Sweep,** 293, *293*
**Beans,** 76, 84, 92
**Beaufort, South Carolina,** R2, R10
   attacks by Native Americans in, 134, *134*
   during Civil War, 206
   festival in, 3, 14, 40, *40*
   grocery store in, *241*
   school in, *240*
**Beaufort County,** R2
**Beauregard, P. G. T.,** 205
**Beef,** *m269*
**Beliefs.** *See* Religion
**Belton, South Carolina,** *239*
**Bennettsville, South Carolina,** R3
**Berkeley County,** R2
**Bethune, Mary McLeod,** 7, 255, *255,* R7
**Bike helmets,** choosing, 286–287, *286, 287*
**Bill(s),** 52, **55,** *55*
**Bill of Rights, 178**
**Biographical dictionary,** R7–R9
**Biographies, 106**
   Mary McLeod Bethune, 255, *255*
   John C. Calhoun, 199, *199*
   Anthony Ashley Cooper, 120, *120*
   Hernando de Soto, 106, *106*
   Reverend Joseph Armstrong DeLaine, 273, *273*
   Susan Pringle Frost, 258
   Juan Pardo, 113
   Andrew Pickens, 166, *166*
   Eliza Lucas Pinckney, 131, *131*
   Robert Smalls, 239, *239*
   Thomas Sumter, 171, *171*
   James Strom Thurmond, 275, *275*
   Denmark Vesey, 193
   Woodrow Wilson, 251, *251*
   writing, 173

R20 ■ Reference

**Birds,** 3, *301*
**Bishopville, South Carolina,** R3
**Black Codes, 210,** 211
**Blackstock's Hill, South Carolina,** *m170,* R10
**Blockades, 168**
  during American Revolution, 168, 170
  during Civil War, 206, 207
  effect in South Carolina, 207
**Blue Ridge Mountains,** 2, *m27,* 30–31, *31,* 66, 82, R10
**Board game,** 217
**Boats and ships**
  building, 112, *112,* 252
  canals and, 188, *188*
  in Civil War, 208
  dugouts, 79, *79,* 85, 87
  European, 102–103, *103, 108,* 127–128
  immigrants arriving by, 156, *156–157*
  sailing, *102–103, 103, 108,* 127–128
  submarines, 208
**Boll weevil,** 260–261
**Bonds, war,** 253
**Boone Hall Plantation,** *100–101*
**Border,** 22, *m22, m135*
**Boston, Massachusetts,** 156, 163, *163,* R10
**Boston Tea Party,** 163, *163*
**Brattonsville, South Carolina,** 140–141, *140–141, m140*
**Britain.** *See* England
**Britton, Tamara L.,** 144
**Broad River,** *m2,* 188, R10
**Bruchac, Joseph,** 68–71
**Bulletin boards,** making, 261
**Bull's Bay,** 122
**Business.** *See* Industries; Manufacturing; Trade
**Butler, Pierce,** 177, *177,* R4, R7
**Butterfly,** *301*

### C

**Caesars Head State Park,** 9
**Cain, Richard "Daddy,"** 212, *212,* R7
**Calhoun, John C.,** 199, *199,* R7
**Calhoun County,** R2
**Camden, South Carolina,** 145, *m157,* 158, 167, *m243,* R2, R10
**Canals,** 188, *188*
**Cannonball,** *170*
**Cape Fear,** 120, R10
**Capital, state.** *See* Columbia, South Carolina
**Car(s),** 246, *246,* 283
**Cardinal directions,** 16, *m17*
**Caribbean Sea,** 40, 118–119, R10

**Carolina,** 120–123, *121, 122, m66*
  agriculture in, 127–131, *127, 128–129, 130*
  attacks by Native Americans in, *105,* 133, 134, *134*
  Fundamental Constitutions of, 121
  government of, 126, 135
  land grant of, 120
  plantations in, 126–130, *128–129*
  western border of, *m135*
  *See also* North Carolina; South Carolina
**Cart,** *141*
**Cash crop,** 127, 130, *130,* 131, 180, 188, 282
**Catawba River,** *m2,* 66, 75, 91, R10
**Catawba tribe,** 66, 72, *m72,* 75–79, *m76, m95*
  government of, 78, *78*
  population of, 67, 75
  trading among, 79, *79*
  traditions of, 77, *77*
  village life of, 76, *76*
**Categorizing,** 37, 58
**Cattle,** *m269*
**Cause,** 160
**Cause and effect,** 160–161, *161,* 185, 187, 218
**Cave painting,** 97
**Cedar Creek Trail,** *301*
**Character traits**
  citizenship, 275
  cooperation, 251
  courage, 193, 239, 273
  heroic deeds, 171
  inventiveness, 131
  loyalty, 199
  perseverance, 106
  responsibility, 113, 120, 255
  trustworthiness, 166
**Charles II, king of England,** 67, 120, 135
**Charles Town,** R10
  after American Revolution, 176, *176*
  in American Revolution, 170, *m170*
  arrival of immigrants in, 156
  British blockade of, 168, 170
  changing name of, 176
  craftworkers in, 132, *132*
  in events leading to American Revolution, 163
  new townships around, 136, *m136*
  plan for, 120, 123, *m123*
  port of, *126–127,* 156, *156–157*
  settlement of, 3, 46, *46,* 120, 122–123, *122, m123,* 132, *132*
  slavery in, *67,* 127, 129
  *See also* Charleston, South Carolina

**Charlesfort,** 111, 112, *112,* 113, 117
**Charleston, South Carolina,** *m2,* 9, R2, R10
  after American Revolution, 176
  aquarium in, 291, *291, m291*
  Avery Institute in, 147
  children in 1800s, 216–217, *216, 217*
  Christmas gatherings in, 190
  in Civil War, 205, 210
  commercial activity in, *191*
  Drayton Hall in, *189*
  as early settlement. *See* Charles Town
  exposition in, 247, *247*
  festivals in, 15, 39
  free African Americans in, 193, *193*
  manners in, 284
  museums in, 11, *11,* 296–297, *296, 297*
  Old Exchange and Provost Dungeon in, 220–221, *220–221, m220*
  Palace of Agriculture in, *247*
  parade in, *14*
  population of, 25
  preservation work in, 258, *258*
  railroad in, 188
  slave quarters in, *194*
  state government moved from, 146, 176, 179, *179*
  street map of, *m17*
  as trade center, 188, *188*
**Charleston County,** R2
**Charleston Harbor,** 27, 168, *168,* 170, *204–205,* 205, *206,* 207, R10
**Charleston Museum,** 11, *11*
**Charleston Navy Yard,** 252
**Charleston Renaissance,** 259, *259*
**Chart and Graph Skills**
  bar graphs, comparing, 202–203, *203,* 219
  graphs, reading, 24, 25, 35
  line graphs, using, 248–249, *248, 249,* 279
  tables, reading, 56–57, *57,* 59
  time lines, reading, 116–117, *116–117,* 139
**Charter,** 120, 136
**Cherokee County,** R2
**Cherokee Falls,** 91, *m91*
**Cherokee Path,** 157
**Cherokee tribe,** 66, 82–87, *82, 83, m83, 86, m95*
  chiefs of, 86
  families of, 83
  festivals of, 84, 85
  population of, 67, 82
  as "principal people," 82
  village life of, 84, *84,* 85, *85*
  ways of, 84, *84,* 85, *85*
  in Yemassee War, 134
**Chester, South Carolina,** *m157, m243,* R2, R10

**Chester County,** R2
**Chesterfield County,** R2
**Chiefs,** 85, 86, *86*
**Children**
  in Charleston in 1800s, 216–217, *216, 217*
  education of, 128, *141,* 190, 191, 216
  middle class, 191, 216
  Native American, 84, 85, *85*
  in South Carolina colony, *136*
  toys of, *216, 217*
  working in mills, 245, *245*
**Chisholm, Julian,** 207, R7
**Choice, economic,** 286–287, *286, 287,* 299
**Christian, Sandra J.,** 304
**Christmas,** 190
**Churches,** 240. *See also* Religion
*Circle Unbroken* (Raven), 228–233
**Cities**
  in Civil War, 205, 209, 210
  expositions in, 247, *247*
  largest, 25
  population of, 25
  port, *126–127,* 156, *156–157,* 163, *163,* 285, *285*
  slave quarters in, *194*
  suburbs of, 267, *267*
  *See also* Communities; *individual cities*
**"Cities: Yesterday, Today, and Tomorrow"** (Ring), 5
**Citizens,** 13
  responsibilities of, 47
  rights of, 47, 178. *See also* Votes and voting
**Citizenship,** 275
**Citizenship Skills**
  decision making, 215, 219
  economic choice, making, 286–287, *286, 287,* 299
  problem solving, 48–49, *48, 49,* 59
  resolving conflict, 124–125, *124, 125,* 139
**Civil rights,** 270–277
  of African Americans, 270–275, *270, 271, 272, 273, 274, 275*
  in schools, 270, *270, 271, 272, 272*
  of women, 277, *277*
**Civil rights laws,** 275, *275*
**Civil rights movement,** 272, 273, *273, 274, 274*
**Civil War,** 147, 153, **204–209**
  African Americans during, 204, 206, 208, 239, *239*
  Confederacy in, 93, 204–209, *206, 209*
  divisions leading to, 197, 198–201, *200, 201*
  end of, 209, *209*
  Reconstruction period following, 210–214, *211, 212, 213*
  women in, 207

**Civilian Conservation Corps (CCC), 261**
**Claim, 103**
**Clan, 83**
**Clarendon County,** 272, R2
**Clark Hill Lake,** m2
**Class magazine,** 5, 64
**Class system, 189**–194, *191, 192, 193, 194*
**Clemson, Thomas,** 234, R7
**Clemson University,** 234–235, *m234,* 237
**Cleveland, South Carolina,** 290, *290, m290,* R11
**Climate, 74**
**Clinton, Bill,** 277
**Clinton, South Carolina,** *m243,* R11
**Closer Look**
  Cherokee village, 85, *85*
  Conestoga wagon, 158, *158*
  early European ships, *102–103,* 103
  landforms and bodies of water, 28, *28–29*
  plantations, 129, *129*
  pottery, 77, *77*
  steam locomotive, 242–243, *243*
**Clothing**
  Confederate, 206
  manufacturing of, 198, 244–245, *244–245,* 283
  Native American, 76, 77
  of slaves, 194
**Clyburn, James,** 276, *276,* R7
**Coastal Plain,** *m27,* 28, *28,* R12, R13
**Coastal zone,** 26–27, *m27,* R11
  Native Americans in, 90–93, *90–91, m91, 92, m93*
**Cofitachequi, Lady of,** 106
**Collage,** making, 277
**Colleges and universities,** 234–235, *m234,* 237
**Colleton County,** R2
**Colonies, 110**
  Carolina. *See* Carolina
  economics in, 118, *118–119*
  English, *3,* 46, *46,* 118–123, *118–119, 121, 122, 123, m135*
  French, 110–112, *m111, 112,* 117
  government of, 126, 135, 165
  growth of, 156–159, *156–157, m157*
  original thirteen, 147, 156, *m175*
  royal, 135
  Spanish, 104–105, 110, 113, 114, 115, *115,* 116, 117, 133
  trade with England, 118, 119, 126, *126–127*
  trade with other colonies, 119
  uniting of, 162–167, *162, 163, 164, 166*
**Colonists, 111**
  loyalists and patriots, 165, *166, 167,* 171, 172, 173

**Colorado,** 256
**Columbia, South Carolina,** *m2,* 179, *m226, m243,* R3, R11
  automobiles in, 246
  burning of, 209, *210–211*
  in Civil War, 209, 210, *210–211*
  Fort Jackson in, 252, *252*
  manufacturing in, 244, *244–245*
  parade in, 36, *36–37*
  planning of, 179
  population of, *25*
  preservation groups in, 258
  state fair in, 292
  state government moved to, *146,* 176, 179, *179*
  State House in, *2, 3, 13,* 51, 52, 60–61, *60–61, m60, 146,* 179, *179*
  Woodrow Wilson's home in, 250, *250*
  zoo in, 290, *290, m290*
**Columbia Canal,** 188, *188*
**Columbian Exchange,** *m114*
**Columbus, Christopher,** 102–103, *102–103,* R7
**Columns,** on tables, 56, *56,* 57
**Combahee River,** 133
**Come–See–Me Festival (Rock Hill),** 292
**Common good,** 44
**Commons House,** 135, 136
**Communication**
  artifacts used for, 296–297, *296, 297*
  by telephone, 246, *297*
**Communities, 13**
  government of, 44–45, *44, 45,* 48–49, *48*
  suburban, **267,** *267*
  *See also* individual communities
**"Community Helpers" (Doyle),** 5
**Compare and contrast paragraph,** writing, 34
**Compare and contrast skill,** 73, 98
**Compass rose,** 16, 80–81, *m80*
**Compromise,** 124
**Conclusion,** 235, 278
**Conestoga wagon,** 158, *158*
**Confederacy,** 93, **204**–209, *206, 209*
**Confederation,** 93
**Conflict,** 124
**Conflict resolution,** 124–125, *124, 125,* 139
**Congaree National Park,** 300–301, *300–301, m300*
**Congaree River,** *m2,* 91, 106, 188, 300
**Congaree Swamp,** 300, *300–301, m300*
**Congaree tribe,** *m95*
**Congress,** 164
  First Continental, 164, *164*
  Second Continental, 169, 170

**Congressional Gold Medal,** 273, *273*
**Consequences, 215**
**Constitution, 50**
  Bill of Rights added to, 178
  Fundamental Constitutions of Carolina, 121
  state, 50, 178, 179, 211
  of United States, 50, 177–178, *177, 178*
**Constitutional Convention,** 177–178, *177, 178*
**Consumers, 244**
**Continent, 22,** *m22*
**Conway, South Carolina,** R2, R11
**Cooper, Anthony Ashley,** 120, *120,* R7
**Cooper River,** *m17,* 120, *m123,* R11
**Cooperation, 251**
**Corn,** 76, 84, 92, 114, *m114,* 128, *m269*
**Cornwallis, General,** 172, *172,* R7
**Cost, opportunity, 286**
**Cotton,** 180, *180,* 188, *189,* 198, 199, 201, *203,* 243, 249, 260–261, *m269,* 282
**Cotton gin,** 180, 181, *181,* 188
**Cotton mills,** 241, 244–245, *244–245,* 283
**Council, 78**
  in colonial government, 126, 135
  in county government, 46
  in Native American governments, 78, *78,* 85, 86
**Council house,** 85, 86, 91
**County,** 46, *m146*
**County clerk,** 46
**County government,** 46, 48, *48*
**County records,** 46
**County seats,** 46, *m146*
**Courage,** 193, 239, 273
**Courts,** 51, 54, *54,* 57, 273
**Cowpens, Battle of,** *m170,* 172, 173, R11
**Crafts**
  basket weaving, 41, 72, 87, 92, *92,* 228–233, *228, 229, 230, 233*
  beadwork, 72
  pottery, 72, 77, *77,* 92, *97, 113, 195, 195,* 242
**Craftworkers**
  in Charles Town, 132, *132*
  free African Americans as, 193
  in middle class, 191, *191*
  silversmiths, 191, *191*
  slaves as, 193
  woodworkers, 191
**Crane, Carol,** 64
**Critical Thinking Skills,** 35, 59, 63, 99, 139, 143, 185, 219, 279, 299, 302
**Crops**
  beans, 76, 84, 92, *m114*
  cash, **127,** 130, *130,* 131, 180, 188, 282

  corn, 76, 84, 92, 114, *m114,* 128, *m269*
  cotton, 180, *180,* 188, *189,* 198, 199, 201, *203,* 243, 249, 260–261, *m269,* 282
  fruit, 114, *m269,* 282
  grapes, 114
  indigo, 126, 130, *130,* 131
  oats, *m269*
  peaches, 282
  peanuts, *m269*
  pecans, 282
  rice, *m114,* 126, 127, *127, 128, 128,* 129, 180, 282
  soybeans, *m269*
  squash, 76, 84, 92
  sugar cane, *m114,* 119
  tea, 282
  tobacco, *m269*
  wheat, *m114, m269*
  *See also* Agriculture (farming)
**Crossroads, 157**
**Crow, Jim,** 238, *238*
**Cultural maps,** 88–89, *m89,* 99
**Cultural regions,** 88, *m89*
**Culture, 14,** *14, 15*
  art, *97, 197,* 254, 259, *259*
  crafts. *See* Crafts
  diversity of, 38–40, *38, 39, 40*
  festivals, *3, 14, 15, 39,* 40, *40,* 41, 72, 84, 85, *282,* 292
  foods, *12,* 39, *39,* 72
  literature. *See* Literature
  museums, 11, *11,* 71, 144, 284
  music, 40
  parades, *14,* 36, *36–37,* 145
  village life of Native Americans, 76, *76,* 84, *84, 85, 85,* 90–91, *91*
**Cusabo tribes,** 66, 67, 90–93, 92, *m93*
  houses of, 90, *90–91*
  language of, 90
  population of, 90
  villages of, 90–91, *91*
  ways of, 92, *92*
**Customs, 38,** 41

## D

**Dairy products,** *m269*
**Dance**
  African American, 40, *40*
  Native American, 72, 76, 91
**Darlington County,** R2
**Darlington Raceway,** 291, *291, m291*
**Daufuskie Island,** *18,* R11
**Daufuskie Light,** 18
**Dave Jar,** 195, *195*
**Dawes Island,** 111, *m111,* R11
**"Day in the Life of a Colonial Indigo Planter, A" (Krebs),** 144

**Day of the Catawba Festival,** 72, *m72*
**de Soto, Hernando,** 106, *106, 107, m109,* 116, R7
**Decision(s), 215**
**Decision making,** 215, 219
**Declaration of Independence,** 169, *169*
**DeLaine, Reverend Joseph Armstrong,** 272, 273, *273,* R7
**Depression,** 260–261, *260–261,* 264
**DeSpain, Pleasant,** 148–153
**Details,** 7, 34
**Diagrams**
    analyzing, 23, *51, 77, 121, 257*
    Venn, 181
**Dig (archaeological site),** 96, *96*
**Dillon, South Carolina,** *m243,* 245, R2, R11
**Dillon County,** R2
**Dioramas,** 87
**Directions**
    cardinal, **16,** *m17*
    intermediate, **80–81,** *80, m81,* 99
**Discrimination,** 241
**Diseases**
    Native Americans and, 105
    settlers and, 132
**Distance scales, 16,** *m17,* **94–95,** *m95,* 99, 143, *m143*
**Diversity,** 38–40, *38, 39, 40*
**Dome, of State House,** 61
**Dorchester County,** R2
**Dozier, Terry,** 277, *277,* R7
**Drawing activities,** 15, 123
**Drayton Hall (Charleston),** *189*
**Drive-ins,** 267, *267*
**Dugouts,** 79, *79,* 85, 87
**Dungeon,** 220, *221*

### E

**Earley, Charity Adams,** 265, *265,* R7
**Eastern hemisphere,** 21, *m21*
**Economic choice,** 286–287, *286, 287,* 299
**Economics, 12,** *12*
**Economy**
    in colonies, 118, *118–119*
    employment and, *283*
    Great Depression and, 260–261, *260–261,* 264
    imports and exports in, 285
    interdependence in, 285
    jobs and, 282–284, *283, 284.* See also Jobs
    of Native Americans, 79, *79,* 87
    New Deal and, 261
    after World War II, 267
    World War II and, 264

*See also* Agriculture (farming); Industries; Manufacturing; Trade
**Edgefield County,** R2
**Edisto Island,** *m2,* R11
**Edisto River,** 74, 91, R11
**Edisto tribe,** *m95*
**Education**
    of African Americans, 194, 212, *212,* 216, 237, 239, 240, 255, *255,* 270, *270,* 272–273, *272*
    in colleges and universities, *234–235, m234,* 237
    of freedmen, 212, *212*
    of lower class, 192, 216
    of middle class, 191, 216
    on plantations, 128, *141,* 190
    as service industry, 284
    of slaves, 194, 216
    of women, 190
    *See also* School(s)
**Effect,** 160. *See also* Cause and effect
**"Eight–box law,"** 238
**Election, 45,** *45,* 46
    of governor, 57
    of members of British Parliament, 162
    *See also* Votes and voting
**Elfe, Thomas,** 191, R7
**Eliot, Robert B.,** 237
**Ellis, Mary Gordon,** 257, *257,* R7
**Emancipation,** 208
**Emancipation Proclamation,** 208
**Employment,** 283. *See also* Jobs
**England**
    in American Revolution, 168, 170, *m170,* 172, *172*
    blockading of colonies by, 168, 170
    factories in, 119, *119*
    in French and Indian War, 159, *159*
    government of, 159, 162, 165
    laws of, 162, *162,* 163, 165
    settlements of, 3, 46, *46,* 118–123, *118–119, 121, 122, m123, m135*
    trade with colonies, 118, 119, 126, *126–127*
**Environment,** keeping clean, 293, *293*
**Equal rights.** *See* Civil rights
**Equality, 275,** 276
**Equator,** 20, *m20*
**Erskine, Henry, Lord Cardross,** 132, R8
**Ethnic group,** 39. *See also* African Americans; Native Americans
**Europe,** R11
    diseases from, 105
    explorers' ships from, *102–103,* 103, *108*
    immigrants from, 40, 156
    in World War I, 250, 251–253, *251, 252, 253*

**Eutaw Springs, Battle of,** *m170,* R11
**Exact location, 182,** 294
**Examine Primary Sources.** *See* Primary Sources
**Executive branch of government,** 50, *51,* 55, *55*
**Explaining,** in paragraph, 58
**Exploration**
    of Carolina coast, 120
    French, 110–112, *110–111, m111,* 117, R9
    Spanish, 102–107, *102–103, 105, 106,* 110, 113, 114, 116, 117, 133, R7, R8
    time line of, 116–117, *116–117,* 139
**Explorers,** 102
    Lucas Vásquez de Ayllón, 104, 107, *m109,* 116, R7
    Christopher Columbus, 102–103, *102–103,* R7
    Hernando de Soto, 106, *106, 107, m109,* 116, R7
    Francisco Gordillo, 104, 107, *m109,* 116
    Pedro Menéndez de Avilés, 113, 114, 117, R8
    Jean Ribault, 110–111, *110, 112,* 117, R9
**Exports,** 285
**Exposition, 247,** *247*

### F

**Fact,** 262
    opinion vs., 262–263, *263,* 279
**Factories**
    discrimination in, 241
    in England, 119, *119*
    during World War I, 253
    during World War II, 266, *266*
    *See also* Manufacturing
**Factory towns,** *m243*
**Fair,** 233, *292,* 304
**Fairfield County,** R2
**Fall line,** *m27,* 28, **29,** *29,* R11
**Families**
    Cherokee, 83
    lower–class, 192, *192*
    middle–class, 191
    on plantations, 128, 190
    southern ways and, 189
    working in mills, 245
**Family Kingdom Amusement Park (Myrtle Beach),** *289*
**Farming.** *See* Agriculture (farming)
**Federal government,** 177–178, *177, 178*
**Felder, James,** 276
**Ferguson, Patrick,** 172, R7
**Festivals,** 3, 14, 15, 39, 40, *40,* 41, 72, 84, 85, 282, 292
**Field trips**
    Congaree National Park, 300–301, *300–301, m300*

**Historic Brattonsville,** 140–141, *140–141, m140*
**Old Exchange and Provost Dungeon,** 220–221, *220–221, m220*
**South Carolina State House,** 60–61, *60–61, m60*
**Fielding, Herbert,** 276
**Fife and Drum Parade (Camden),** *145*
**First Continental Congress,** 164, *164*
**First Regiment of South Carolina Volunteers,** 206
**Fish, as product,** *m269*
**Fishing,** by Native Americans, 74, 76, 84, 92, *92*
**Flag,** 37, *50,* 168
**Fletchall, Thomas,** 165
**Florence, South Carolina,** 46, R2, R11
**Florence County,** 46, R2
**Florida,** R11
    African American school in, 255
    during American Revolution, 170
    exploration of, 67
    Native Americans in, 134
    settlement of, 113, 115, *115*
    Spanish, 114, 133
**Focus Skills**
    categorize, 37, 58
    cause and effect, 187, 218
    compare and contrast, 73, 98
    draw conclusions, 235, 278
    generalize, 101, 138
    main idea and details, 7, 34
    sequence, 155, 184
    summarize, 281, 298
**Foods**
    in diversity of cultures, 39, *39*
    economics and, *12*
    Native American, 72
**Forestry,** 242, *m269,* 283
**Fork Mountain,** *m2,* R11
**Fort Jackson,** 252, *252*
**Fort Moultrie,** 168, R11
**Fort San Felipe,** 113
**Fort San Marcos,** 115, R11
**Fort Sumter,** *147,* 171, *186–187, m186,* 204–205, *205,* R11
**Fourth of July parade,** 36, *36–37*
**Fowler, Allan,** 64
**France**
    explorers sent from, 110–112, *110–111, m111,* 117, R9
    settlements of, 110–112, *m111, 112,* 117
    in World War I, 252, *252*
**Franklin, Benjamin,** *169*
**Free African Americans,** 193, *193,* 210
**Free enterprise.** *See* Agriculture (farming); Industries; Manufacturing; Trade
**Freedmen's Bureau,** 212, *212*

Index ▪ R23

# Freedom

**Freedom**
of religion, 178
of speech, 178
See also Votes and voting
**Freedom Weekend Aloft (Anderson),** 280–281
**French and Indian War,** 159, *159*
**French Huguenots,** 123
**Frontier,** 136, 157–159, *m157,* 165
**Frost, Susan Pringle,** 258, R8
**Fruit crops,** 114, *m269,* 282
**Fundamental Constitutions of Carolina,** 121
**Furniture makers,** 191, 283

## G

**Gadsden, Christopher,** 164, 165, R8
**Gaffney, South Carolina,** 282, R2
**Games**
of children in 1800s, 217
Native American, 68–71, 76, 85, *85,* 91
Scottish, 39
**General Assembly,** 52, *52,* 54, 78, 155, 257, 276
**Generalizing,** 101, 138
**Geography,** 8–9, *8–9*
Charleston Harbor, 204–205, *205*
human features in, 8
Myrtle Beach, 288–289, 289, *m289*
physical features in, 8, 9
Port Royal Sound, 110–111, *111, m111*
Table Rock Mountain, 30–31, *30–31, m30*
See also Atlas; Map(s); Map and Globe Skills; Physical regions
**Geography terms,** A16
**Georgetown, South Carolina,** *m295,* R2, R11
**Georgetown County,** R2
**Georgia,** 18, 22, 136, 170, R11
**Gilman, Caroline,** 190, *190,* R8
**Globe,** 20–21, *m20, m21*
**Golf courses,** 289
**Gordillo, Francisco,** 104, 107, *m109,* 116
**Gospel music,** 40
**Gourds,** 76
**Government,** 13
African Americans in, 239, 276, *276*
British, 159, 162
of Carolina, 126, 135
colonial, 126, 135, 165
community, 44–45, *44, 45,* 48–49, *48*
county, 46, 48, *48*
executive branch of, **50,** *51,* 55, *55*

federal, 177–178, *177, 178*
judicial branch of, **50,** *51,* 53, *53,* 54
legislative branch of, **50,** *51,* 52–53, *52, 57,* 237
local, 44–48, *44, 45, 48*
national, 177–178, *177, 178*
of Native Americans, 78, *78, 85, 86, 86*
offices in, 56, *57*
representative, 78
state. See State government
women in, 257, *257,* 277, *277*
**Governor,** 55, R4–R6
age of, 57
in colonial government, 126
election of, 57
role in passing laws, 52, 55, *55*
**Governor's Mansion,** 51
**Gramophone,** 297
**Grand Strand,** 288, *288–289,* R11
**Graniteville, South Carolina,** *m243,* R11
**Grant, U. S.,** 209
**Grapes,** 114
**Graph(s)**
bar, **24,** *25, 35, 137, 147, 202–203, 203, 219, 276, 283*
line, *227,* **248**–249, *248, 249, 279*
picture, **24,** *25, 35, 67, 229*
reading, 24, 25, 35
**Graphic organizer,** 160
*Great Ball Game: A Muskogee Story* (Bruchac), 68–71
**Great Britain.** See England
**Great Depression,** 260–261, *260–261,* 264
**Great Migration,** 254–255, *254, 255*
**Great Seal of South Carolina,** 13, 60
**Great Snow Campaign,** 167
**Great Wagon Road,** 146, 153, *m157,* 158, R12
**Green, Jonathan,** *197*
**Green Corn Ceremony,** 84
**Greenhouse products,** *m269*
**Greenville, South Carolina,** *m2,* 167, *m243,* R2, R12
Civilian Conservation Corps in, 261
manufacturing in, 244
military training camp in, 252
planetarium in, 290, *290, m290*
population of, 25
**Greenville County,** R2
**Greenwood, Lake,** *m2*
**Greenwood, South Carolina,** *m243,* R2, R12
**Greenwood County,** R2
**Grid system,** **182**–183, m183, 185, 294
**Grimke, Angelina,** 200, R8
**Grimke, Sarah,** 200, R8

**Grocery store,** 241
**Gullah Festival (Beaufort),** 3, 14, 40, *40*

## H

**Hampton, Sallie,** 207
**Hampton, Susan Preston,** 207
**Hampton, Wade, III,** 236, *236,* R5, R8
**Hampton County,** R2
**Handicrafts.** See Crafts
**Harbors,** 27, 28, 29, 168, 198
at Charleston, 27, 168, *168,* 170, 204–205, *205, 206, 207,* R10
Pearl Harbor, Japanese attack on, 264, *264*
**Hartwell Lake,** *m2*
**Hawaii,** 264, *264*
**Hay,** *m269*
**Healthcare industry,** 284
**Helmets,** choosing, 286–287, *286, 287*
**Hemisphere,** *mA6–A7,* **20**–21, *m20, m21*
**Henderson, Ernest, Sr.,** 265, R8
**Henry, Lord Cardross,** 132, R8
**Heritage,** 41
Fort Jackson, 252, *252*
Native American place names, 91, *m91*
**Heritage fair,** 233, 304
"Hermy the Hermit Crab Goes Shopping" (Weathers), 64
**Heroic deeds,** 171
**Heyward, Dubose,** 259, *259,* R8
**High-tech industries,** 283
**Hilton, William,** 120, R8
**Hilton Head Island,** 111, *m111,* 207, 285, 293, R12
**Historians,** 10, *10*
**Historic Brattonsville,** 140–141, *140–141, m140*
**Historical Center of York County,** 42
**History,** 10–11, *10, 11,* 140
**History maps,** 108, **174**
comparing, 174–175, *m175,* 185
following routes on, 108–109, *m109,* 139
**Hobbyhorse,** 216
**Hogs,** 114, 128, *m269*
**Holidays**
Christmas, 190
Independence Day (Fourth of July), 36, *36–37*
Martin Luther King, Jr. Day, 275
Memorial Day, 280–281
St. Patrick's Day, 14
South Carolina Day, 4
**Hooper Planetarium (Greenville),** 290, *290, m290*
**Horry County,** R2
**Horses,** *141, 172*

# "Intolerable Acts"

**Hospitals**
during Civil War, 207, *207*
segregation in, 270, *271*
**Hot-air balloons,** 280–281
**House(s)**
log cabins, *192*
longhouses, 83
Native American, *76,* 83, 90, *90–91*
on plantations, *189,* 190
roundhouses, *76*
for slaves, *141,* 194, *194*
**House of Representatives, state,** 52
**Huck's Defeat, Battle of,** 140, *m140, 141*
**Huguenots,** 123
*Hunley* (submarine), 208
**Hunter, Hattie,** 245
**Hunting**
by Native Americans, 75, 76, 84, 92
by planters, 190
**Hunting Island,** 261

## I

**Illustrations,** analyzing, 86, *86*
**Immigrants,** 38, 40, 156, *156–157*
**Imports,** 285
**Independence,** 167
**Independence Day parade,** 36, *36–37*
**Independence Hall (Philadelphia),** 164
**Indian(s), American.** See Native Americans
**Indigo,** 126, **130,** *130,* 131
**Industries,** 198
automobile, 246, *246,* 283
forestry, 242, *m269,* 283
high-tech, 283
in North, 198, *198*
service, 284, *284*
shipbuilding, 112, *112,* 252
in South, 241, 242–247, 244–245, 246, 247
textile, 198, 244–245, 244–245, 282, 283
tourism, 247, *247,* 284
in World War I, 253
in World War II, 266, *266*
See also Agriculture (farming); Manufacturing
**Inner Coastal Plain,** *m27,* 28, R12
**Interdependence,** 285
**Intermediate directions,** 80–81, *80, m81,* 99
**Interviews**
preparing questions for, 241
role-playing, 47
**"Intolerable Acts"** (British laws), 163

R24 ■ Reference

## Inventions

**Inventions, 246**
  car, 246, *246*, 283
  for communication, 296–297, *296*, *297*
  cotton gin, 180, 181, *181*, 188
  gramophone, *297*
  radio, *297*
  record player, *296*, *297*
  steam locomotive, 242–243, *243*
  telephone, 246, *297*
  textile industry and, 283
  *See also* Technology
**Inventiveness,** 131
**"Inventors and Their Inventions" (Martin),** 233
**Iroquoian language group,** 67, 82
**"Island Child, The" (Simmons),** 304

## J

**Jackson, Andrew,** 199, *199*, R8
**Jackson, Jesse,** 235, 274, *274*
**Jail,** 220–221, *220–221*, *m220*
**James Island,** 168, 205, R12
**Japan, in attack on Pearl Harbor,** 264, *264*
**Jasper County,** R2
**Jazz,** 40
**Jefferson, Thomas,** 169, R8
**Jim Crow laws, 238**–239, *238*, 240, 257, 274
**Jobs,** 282–284
  of African Americans, 241, 253, 266, 271, *271*
  in agriculture, 282
  employment in various, *283*
  in making products, 283, *283*
  in service industries, 284, *284*
  women and, 253, *253*, 255, *255*, 265, *265*, 266, *266*, 271, *271*, 277, *277*
**John Rivers Communication Museum (Charleston),** 296–297, *296*, *297*
**Johns Island,** 6–7, *m6*, R12
**Johnson, Andrew,** 210, R8
**Johnson, Dinah,** 304
**Johnson, I. S. Leevy,** 276, R8
**Jones Gap State Park,** 290, *290*, *m290*
**Journal entries,** 107, 184
**Judges,** 54, *54*
**Judicial branch of government, 50**, *51*, 53, *53*, 54
**Junior Rangers,** *300*
**Jury,** 54, *54*
**Just, Dr. Ernest E.,** 254, *254*, R8
**Justices,** 54, *54*, 57

## K

**Kahn, Gus,** 1
**Keowee,** 154
**Kershaw County,** R2
**King, Coretta Scott,** 274
**King, Martin Luther, Jr.,** 274, *274*, 275, R8
**King's Mountain, South Carolina,** *m170*, 172, R12
**Kingstree, South Carolina,** R3
**Krebs, Laurie,** 144
**K–W–L chart,** 65, *65*

## L

**Lacrosse,** 85, *85*
**Lakes,** *m2*
**Lancaster, South Carolina,** *m243*, R2, R12
**Lancaster County,** R2
**Land grants,** 120
**Landform(s), 26,** 28, *28–29*
  mountains and mountain ranges, 2, 9, 30–31, *30–31*
  plains, *m2*, *m27*, 28, *28*, R11
  plateaus, *m2*, 30
  rivers, *m2*, *m17*, 293
**Landform map,** reading, **32**–33, *m32–33*, 36, 63, *m63*
**Language groups,** 67, **75**
**Latitude, 294**–295, *m294*, *m295*, 299, 302, *m303*
**Laurens, Henry,** 170, R8
**Laurens County,** R2
**Law(s), 13**
  African Americans and, 210, 211, 236, 238–239, *238*, 240, 257, 274
  Black Codes, 210, 211
  British, 162, *162*, 163, 165
  on civil rights, 275, *275*
  on education of slaves, 194
  Jim Crow, **238**–239, *238*, 240, 257, 274
  judicial branch of government and, 54
  passage of, *52*, 55, *55*
  representative government and, 78
  slave states and, 199
  on voting rights, 238–239, 257, 275
**Lawrence, Jacob,** 254
**"Leaders for Peace" (Ahearn),** 233
**Leadership**
  by African Americans, 254, *254*, 255, *255*, 272, *272*, 273, *273*, 274, *274*, 275, 276, *276*, 277
  of civil rights movement, 272, *273*, *273*, 274, *274*
  by women, 106, 257, *257*, 274, 277, *277*
**League of Nations,** 251
**Lee, Robert E.,** *209*, R8

**Lee County,** R2
**Legends,** 148–153
**Legislative branch of government, 50**, *51*, 52–53, *52*, 57, 237
**Letter writing,** 58, 138, 218, 278, 298
**Lexington, Battle of,** 166, *166*
**Lexington, South Carolina,** *m243*, R12
**Lexington County,** R2
**Liberty.** *See* Freedom
**Lighthouses,** *18*, 285
**Lincoln, Abraham,** 201, *201*, 208, 210, R8
**Line graph,** 227, **248**–249, *248*, *249*, 279
**Literature,** 148–154
  *All Around Town* (Johnson), 304
  in Charleston Renaissance, 259, *259*
  *Circle Unbroken* (Raven), 228–233
  *Cities: Yesterday, Today, and Tomorrow* (Ring), 5
  *Community Helpers* (Doyle), 5
  *Day in the Life of a Colonial Indigo Planter, A* (Krebs), 144
  *Great Ball Game: A Muskogee Story* (Bruchac), 68–71
  *Hermy the Hermit Crab Goes Shopping* (Weathers), 64
  *Inventors and Their Inventions* (Martin), 233
  *Island Child* (Simmons), 304
  *Leaders for Peace* (Ahearn), 233
  legends, 148–153
  *Mound Builders, The* (Sweeny), 71
  *Mystery of Roanoke, The* (Goldman), 71
  *On the Great Wagon Road* (Prokos), 153
  *P Is for Palmetto: A South Carolina Alphabet* (Crane), 64
  *Pioneer Living* (Ring), 153
  *Pirates on the Prowl* (Garner), 71
  *Sites of the Civil War* (Price), 153
  *South Carolina* (Christian), 304
  *South Carolina Colony, The* (Britton), 144
  *Swamp Fox, The* (DeSpain), 148–153
  *Transportation Yesterday and Today* (Ring), 233
  *Water Dance* (Locker), 144
  *When a Storm Comes Up* (Fowler), 64
  *Where Water Comes From* (Ahearn), 5

## Map(s)

  women in, 64, 144, 190, *190*, 304
**"Little England" colony,** 118–119
**Little Pee Dee River,** *m2*
**Livestock,** 114, 128
**Local governments,** 44–48
  community, 44–45, *44*, *45*, 48–49, *48*
  county, 46, 48, *48*
**Location,** *18*–23, *m20*, 21, *m21*, *m76*, *m83*, *m93*
  exact, **182**, 294
**Locke, John,** 120
**Locker, Thomas,** 144
**Locomotives, steam,** 242–243, *243*
**Log cabins,** 192
**Logging,** 242, 283
**Longhouse,** 83
**Longitude,** 294–295, *m294*, *m295*, 299, 302, *m303*
**Lords Proprietors, 120**–121, *121*, 126, 135
**Lowcountry,** *m2*
  after American Revolution, 176
  Native Americans in, 90–93, *90–91*, 92, *m93*
  patriots in, 165, 166, 167
  representation in state government, 176, 179
**Lower class,** 192, *192*
**Loyalists, 165,** 166, 167, 171, 172, 173
**Loyalty,** 199
**Lucas, Eliza,** 130, 131, *131*, R9
**Lumber industry,** 242, 283
**Lynch, Thomas,** 164, R8
**Lynches River,** *m2*, R12

## M

**Magazine, class,** 5, 64
**Main idea and details,** 7, 34
**Malaria,** 132
**Manners,** 284
**Manning, South Carolina,** R2
**Manufacturing,** *m269*
  African Americans in, 241, 253, 266
  of clothing, 198, 244–245, *244–245*, 283
  discrimination in, 241
  in England, 119, *119*
  jobs in, 283, *283*
  in North, 198, *198*
  in South, 241, 242–246, *244–245*, 246
  women in, 253, 265, *265*
  during World War I, 253
  during World War II, 266, *266*
**Map(s)**
  cardinal directions on, **16**, *m17*

compass rose on, **16**, *m17*, 80–81, *80*
cultural, **88–89**, *m89*, 99
distance scale on, **16**, *m17*, **94–95**, *m95*, 99, **143**, *m143*
history. *See* History maps
intermediate directions on, **80–81**, *80*, *m81*, 99
landform, **32–33**, *m32–33*, 63, *m63*
making, 23, *174*, 293
product, **268**, *m269*, 279
reading, **16–17**, *m17*, 36
from satellite photographs, 19, *19*
**Map and Globe Skills**
cultural maps, using, **88–89**, *m89*, 99
distance scales, using, **94–95**, *m95*, 99, **143**, *m143*
history maps, comparing, **174–175**, *m175*, 185
history maps, following routes on, **108–109**, *m109*, 139
intermediate directions, finding, **80–81**, *80*, *m81*, 99
landform maps, reading, **32–33**, *m32–33*, 36, 63, *m63*
latitude and longitude, using, **294–295**, *m294*, *m295*, 299, 302, *m303*
map grids, using, **182–183**, *m183*, 185, 294
maps, reading, **16–17**, *m17*, 36
product maps, reading, **268**, *m269*, 279
*See also* Map(s)
**Map grid**, **182–183**, *m183*, 185, 294
**Map key**, **16**, *m17*, 108
**Map symbols**, **16**, *m17*
**Map title**, **16**, *m17*, 108
**Maple Mills (Dillon)**, 245
**Marion, Francis**, 148–153, **171**, *171*, R8
**Marion, Lake**, *m2*
**Marion County**, R2
**Marlboro County**, R3
**Marshall, Thurgood**, 272, *272*, R8
**Martin, Hank**, 4–5
**McCord, Louisa**, 207, R8
**McCormick County**, R2
**Medal(s)**, 252, 264, 273, *273*
**Mediator**, 124
**Meetinghouse**, 76, 78
**Memorial Day**, *280–281*
**Menéndez de Avilés, Pedro**, 113, 114, 117, R8
**Meridian**, 294, *m294*, *m295*
**Middle class**, **191**, *191*
**Middleton, Henry**, 164, R8
**Midlands**, *m2*, 29, R12. *See also* Sandhills Region
**Migration**, **156**, 254–255, *254*, *255*

**Mill(s)**
children working in, 245, *245*
cotton, 198, 241, **244–245**, *244–245*, 283
textile, 198, 241, **244–245**, *244–245*, 283
**Mill stores**, 245
**Mill villages**, 245
**Miller, Thomas**, 239, R8
*Missionary Record* (newspaper), 212
**Mississippian culture**, **96–97**, *96*, *97*
**Moncks Corner, South Carolina**, *m81*, R2, R12
**Money**, **12**, *12*
**Morgan, Daniel**, 172, R9
**Moultrie, Lake**, *m2*
**Moultrie, William**, 168, *168*, R4, R9
**Mound(s), village**, 71, 85
**"Mound Builders, The" (Sweeny)**, 71
**Mountains and mountain ranges**
Native Americans living in, 82–87, *82*, *83*, *m83*, *84*, *85*, *86*
in South Carolina, 2, 9, **30–31**, *30–31*
*See also individual mountains and mountain ranges*
**Movement**, *m87*, *m114*, *m157*
**Museums**, **11**, *11*
of communication artifacts, **296–297**, *296*, *297*
heritage, **42–43**, *42*
making, 71, 144
as service industry, 284
**Music**, 4–5, 40, 296, *296*, *297*
**Muskogean language group**, 67, 90
**Myrtle Beach, South Carolina**, 9, *9*, *m289*, R12
Civilian Conservation Corps in, 261
festival in, *15*
for recreation, *15*, 247, 288, **288–289**, *289*, *m289*
**"Mystery of Roanoke, The" (Goldman)**, 71

## N

**Nation**, 50
**National government**, **177–178**, *177*, *178*
**National park**, 300–301, *300–301*, *m300*
**Native Americans**, 40, **66**, *67*, 67
agriculture of, 76, 84, *84*, 92
art of, 97
attacks on settlers, 105, 133, 134, *134*, 159, 165
children, 84, 85, *85*
clans of, 83
clothing of, 76, 77
cultural regions of, 88, *m89*
dance of, 72, 76, 91

early, 96–97, *96*, *97*
economics of, 79, *79*, 87
European diseases and, 105
families of, 83
fishing and, 74, 76, 84, 92, *92*
French and, 159
games of, 68–71, 76, 85, *85*, 91
government of, 78, *78*, 85, 86, *86*
houses of, 76, 83, 90, *90–91*
hunting and, 75, 76, 84, 92
language groups of, 67
location of tribes, *m95*
in lowcountry, 90–93, *90–91*, 92, *m93*
in mountains, 82–87, *82*, *83*, *m83*, *84*, *85*, *86*
place names in South Carolina, 91, *m91*
population of, 67, 75, 82, 90
pottery of, 72, 77, *77*, 92, 97
religion and, 97, 103
along rivers, 66, 74–79, *74*, *75*, *76*, *77*, *78*
roads and trails of, *m87*, 157, 158
tools of, 77, 79, 97
trade among, 79, *79*, 87, *m87*
trade with settlers, 132, 133, *133*, 134, 157
traditions of, 77, *77*
village life of, 76, *76*, 84, *84*, 85, *85*, 90–91, 91
women, 76, 77, 78, 83, 84, *84*, 86, 106
in Yemassee War, 134, *134*
*See also individual groups*
**Natural resources**, **30**, 118, 119, *119*
**New Deal**, 261
**New York Harbor**, 198
**Newberry, South Carolina**, *m157*, *m243*, 244, R3, R12
**Newberry County**, R3
**Newspapers**, 212
for children, 190
freedom of speech and, 178
writing headlines for, 209
writing stories for, 167, 267
**Nimmons, South Carolina**, *m30*, R13
*Niña* (sailing ship), *102–103*
**Ninety Six, South Carolina**, 154–155, *m154*, 157, *m157*, 166, 167, *m170*, R13
**North**
in Civil War, 204–209, *207*, *209*
disagreements with South, 201
Great Migration to, 254–255, *254*, *255*
industry in, 198, *198*
on slavery, 201
**North Carolina**, 18, 22, 30, R13
**North Charleston, South Carolina**, population of, 25, R13
**North Pole**, 20, *m20*, 21, R13
**Northern hemisphere**, 20, *m20*

## O

**Oak tree**, 6–7, *m6*
**Oats**, *m269*
**Oconee County**, R3, R13
**Old Exchange and Provost Dungeon**, **220–221**, *220–221*, *m220*
**Olympia Mills (Columbia)**, 244–245
**"On the Great Wagon Road" (Prokos)**, 153
**Opinion**, **262**
fact vs., **262–263**, *263*, 279
**Opportunity cost**, **286**
**Orangeburg, South Carolina**, 271, R3, R13
**Orangeburg County**, R3
**Otter**, *301*
**Outer Coastal Plain**, *m27*, **28**, R13
**Over Mountain Men**, 172, *172*
**Owl**, *301*
**Oyster Point**, 123

## P

**"P Is for Palmetto: A South Carolina Alphabet" (Crane)**, 64
**Painting**, 97, 197, 254, 259, *259*
**Palace of Agriculture (Charleston)**, 247
**Palmetto fort**, 168, *168*
**Palmetto Pride program**, **293**, *293*
**Palmetto tree**, **3**, 50, *50*, 92, *92*, 168, 293
**Paper making**, 283
**Parades**, 14, 36, *36–37*, 145
**Paragraphs**, writing, 34, 58, 298
**Pardo, Juan**, 113
**Parks**
national, 300–301, *300–301*, *m300*
as service industry, 284
state, 9, 261, **290**, *290*, *m290*
**Parliament**, **159**, 162, 165
**Parris Island**, *m2*, 111, *m111*, 113, 252, *252*, R13
**Patriots**, **165**, 166, 167, 171, 172
**Peaches**, 282
**Peanuts**, *m269*
**Pearl Harbor, Hawaii**, 264, *264*
**Pee Dee River**, *m2*, 8, **8–9**, *m8*, 30, 74, 91, R13
**Pee Dee tribe**, *m95*
**Performance**
advertisements, writing, 247
articles, writing, 131
biographies, writing, 173
bulletin boards, making, 261
collages, making, 277
dioramas, making, 87
drawing, 15, 123
interviewing, 47, 241

journal entries, writing, 107
letter writing, 218, 298
map making, 23, 293
news stories, writing, 167, 267
newspaper headlines, writing, 209
postcards, making, 31
posters, making, 41, 137, 214, 255
researching and reporting, 55, 201
scenes, writing, 79
speeches, giving, 115, 285
symbols, designing, 93
tables, making, 195
Venn diagrams, 181
**Permanent village,** 91
**Perry, Benjamin,** 187, R5
**Perseverance,** 106
**Persuasive writing,** 58, 138
**Philadelphia, Pennsylvania,** 158
 Constitutional Convention in, 177–178, *177, 178*
 First Continental Congress in, 164, *164*
**Phillips Island,** 111, *m111*, R13
**Physical maps**
 of South Carolina, *mA15*
 of United States, *mA12–A13*
 of world, *mA4–A5*
**Physical regions,** 26–33
 Blue Ridge, 31, *31*
 coastal plains, 28, *28*
 coastal zone, **26–27,** *m27*, R10
 Piedmont, 30, *30*
 sandhills, *m2, m27, 29, 29,* R11
**Physical systems,** understanding, 30–31, *30–31, m30*
**Pickens, Andrew,** 166, *166,* 167, 172, R4, R7
**Pickens County,** *m30,* R3
**Picture(s),** determining point of view in, 196–197, *197,* 219
**Picture graph,** 24, *25, 35, 67,* 227
**Piedmont Plateau,** *m27,* 30, *66, 82,* R13
**Pinckney, Charles,** 177, R4, R9
**Pinckney, Charles Coatsworth,** 177, *177,* R9
**Pinckney, Eliza Lucas,** 130, 131, *131,* R9
**Pinta** (sailing ship), *102–103*
**Pioneer(s),** **136,** 153, 157–159, *158,* 161
**"Pioneer Living"** (Ring), 153
**"Pirates on the Prowl"** (Garner), 71
**Place,** *m136, m170, m243*
**Plains, Coastal,** *m27,* 28, **28,** R11
**Planetariums,** 290, *290, m290*
**Plantation(s),** 100–101, **119,** 126–131
 in Carolina, 126–130, *128–129*
 common things on, 129, *129*

families on, 128, 190
in Historic Brattonsville, 140–141, *140–141, m140*
slaves on, 118–119, 127, 128, 129, *141,* 180, 190, 194, 198
in West Indies, *130*
work on, 129
**Plantation house,** 189, 190
**Planters,** 119, 190, *190*
**Plays**
 Charleston Renaissance and, 259, *259*
 writing, 278
**Point of view,** 165, **196**
 determining in pictures, 196–197, *197,* 219
**Poles, North and South,** 20, *m20,* 21, *m21*
**Police,** 44, 46
**Political maps**
 of South Carolina, *mA14*
 of United States, *mA10–A11*
 of world, *mA2–A3*
**Pollitzer, Anita,** 256, R9
**Population**
 of largest cities, *25*
 of Native Americans, *67, 75, 82,* 90
 of slaves, 137, 203
 of South Carolina, 1760–1880, 147
 of United States in 1800s, 198
***Porgy and Bess,*** 259, *259*
**Port cities,** 126–127, 156, *156–157, 163, 163, 285, 285*
**Port Royal Sound,** 110–111, *110–111, m111,* 117, 120, 206, R13
**Postal Service,** 254
**Posters**
 making, 41, 137, 214, 255
 World War I, *251*
**Pottery,** 113
 Dave Jars, 195, *195*
 Native American, 72, 77, *77, 92,* 97
 as South Carolina industry, 242
**Poultry,** *m269*
**Prejudice,** 237, 240
**Preservation,** 258, *258*
**Primary Sources,** 42
 analyzing, 43, 97, 112, *112, 181, 181, 195, 195, 217,* 297
 Charleston's children, 216–217, *216, 217*
 communication artifacts, 296–297, *296, 297*
 cotton gin, 181, *181*
 Dave Jar, 195, *195*
 first Carolinians, 96–97, *96, 97*
 getting food supplies, 112, *112*
 heritage museum, 42–43, *42*
**Prime meridian,** 294, *m294*

**"Principal people,"** 82. See also Cherokee tribe
**Printing,** 283
**Problem,** 48
**Problem solving,** 48–49, *48, 49,* 59
**Producers,** 244
**Product(s),** *m269,* 283, *283*
**Product map,** 268, *m269,* 279
**Projects.** See Unit projects
**Public service,** **45,** *45,* 53
**Pumpkintown, South Carolina,** *m30,* R13
**Purry, Jean Pierre,** 65

## Q

**Questions and answers,** writing, 98, 241

## R

**Racism, 237,** 240
**Radio,** 297
**Railroads,** 188, 242–243, *243, m243*
**Rainbow Row (Charleston),** 258, *258*
**Raven, Margot Theis,** 228–233
**Raw material, 118,** 119, *119*
**Reading Skills**
 cause and effect, identifying, 160–161, *161,* 185
 fact vs. opinion, 262–263, *263,* 279
 point of view in pictures, determining, 196–197, *197,* 219
**Reading Your Textbook,** xii–xvi
**"Ready for Harvest"** (Smith), *197*
**Reconstruction, 210**–214
 end of, 214, 236
 farming during, 213, *213*
 Freedmen's Bureau and, 212, *212*
 racism following, 237
 rights of African Americans and, 210, 211, *211,* 212
**Record players,** 296, 297
**Recreation,** 247, **288**–293, *m290–291*
 amusement parks, 289
 aquariums, 291, *291, m291*
 beaches, *2, 9, 9, 26, 26, 288–289,* 289, *m289,* 293, *293,* R12
 fairs, 233, *292,* 304
 festivals, *3, 14, 15, 39,* 40, *40, 41, 72, 84, 85, 282, 292*
 golf, 289
 museums, 11, *11,* 71, 144, 284
 planetariums, 290, *290, m290*

raceways, 291, *291, m291*
 zoos, 290, *290, m290*
**Regions, 22,** *m2, m22, m27*
 cultural, **88,** *m89*
 physical, **26**–33, *26, m27, 28, 29, 30, 31,* R12, R13, *m290–m291*
**Religion,** 103
 African Americans and, 240
 freedom of, 178
 of French Huguenots, 123
 loyalists and, 165
 Native Americans and, 97, 103
 in South Carolina, 240, *240*
**Renaissance,** 259, *259*
**Report(s),** 55, 201
**Representative government,** 78
**Research,** 55, 201
**Reservoir,** *m30*
**Resources, natural,** 30, 118, 119, *119*
**Responsibilities,** of citizens, **47**
**Responsibility,** as character trait, 113, 120, 255
**Restaurant industry,** 284, *284*
**Revolution,** 166
**Revolutionary War.** See American Revolution
**Revolutionary War Reenactors,** 145
**Ribault, Jean,** 110–111, *110,* 112, 117, R9
**Rice,** 126, 127, *127,* 128, *128,* 129, 180, 282
**Richard B. Russell Lake,** *m2*
**Richardson, Richard,** 167, R9
**Richland County,** R3
**Ridgeland, South Carolina,** R2, R13
**Rights,** 47
 of African Americans, 194, 210, 211, *211,* 212, 236, 237, 257, 270–276
 Bill of, **178**
 of citizens, 47, 178
 of slaves, 194, 210
 of states, 178, 199
 voting. See Votes and voting
 of women, 256–257, *256, 257, 277, 277*
 *See also* Civil rights
**River(s),** *m2, m17,* 293
 Native Americans living along, *66,* 74–79, *74, 75, 76, 77, 78*
 *See also individual rivers*
**River basin,** 28, *29,* **30**
**River otter,** *301*
**River system,** 74
**Riverbank Zoo and Garden (Columbia),** 290, *290, m290*
**Rivers, John,** *296*
**Roads and trails,** *m157*
 cars and, 246
 Cedar Creek Trail, *301*
 in Charleston, *m17,* 258, *258,* R10
 Cherokee Path, 157, *m157*
 crossroads, 157

Great Indian Trading Path, 158
Great Wagon Road, 146, 153, *m157*, 158, R12
Native American, *m87*, 157, 158
Rainbow Row (Charleston), 258, *258*
Rock Hill, South Carolina, *m157*, R13
  festivals in, 72, *m72*, 292
  manufacturing in, 244
  population of, 25
Rock Hill Buggy Company, 246
Rock Hill Telephone Company, 246
Rocking horse, 216
Rocky Bottom, South Carolina, *m30*
Role–playing, 47
Roosevelt, Franklin D., 261, R9
Roosevelt, Theodore, 247, R9
"Rose Bud, The" (children's newspaper), 190
Roundhouses, 76
Routes, 102
  following on a history map, 108–109, *m109*, 139
Rows, on tables, 56, *56*, *57*
Royal colony, 135
Royal Exchange and Custom House, 220–221, *220–221*
Rural areas, 241
Rutledge, Edward, 164, R4, R9
Rutledge, John, 164, 177, *177*, R9

## S

St. Augustine, Florida, 113, 115, *115*, *m115*, 133, 170, R13
St. George, South Carolina, R2
St. Helena Island, 104, *104–105*, *m104*, 116, R13
St. Helena Sound, *m2*
St. Matthews, South Carolina, R2
St. Patrick's Day, 14
Saluda County, R3, R13
Saluda River, *m2*, 188, R13
San Salvador Island, 102
Sand sculptures, 15
Sandhills Region, *m27*, 29, *29*, R14
Sanford, Mark, 281, R6
Santa Elena, 113, 114, 115, 117
Santa Maria (sailing ship), *102–103*, 108
Santee Dam, *m2*
Santee River, *m2*, 74, 91, 188, R14
Santee River Canal, 188
Sassafras Mountain, *m2*, 31, R14
Satellite photographs, 19, *19*
Savannah, Georgia, 170, R14
Savannah River, *m2*, 30, 66, 74, 90, 133, 135, 136, R14
Sayle, William, 122, *122*, R9
Scenes
  drawing, 123
  writing, 79
School(s)
  for African Americans, 212, 255
  civil rights in, 270, *270*, 271, 272, *272*
  colleges and universities, 234–235, *m234*, 237
  on plantations, 141
  ruling on separate but equal, 273
  segregation in, 239, 240, *240*, 270, *270*, 271, 272–273, *272*
  See also Education
Science and Technology
  Anderson automobiles, 246, *246*
  mapping from space, 19
  submarines, 208
  weirs, 92, *92*
  See also Inventions; Technology
Scottish Games and Highland Gathering (Charleston), 39
Sea Islands, 27, 190
Seal, of South Carolina, 13, 60
Secede, 201
Secession Convention, 201
Second Continental Congress, 169, 170
Secondary source, 43, *43*
Segregation, 239
  in hospitals, 270, 271
  in jobs, 241, 253, 266, 271, *271*
  in military, 252, 265, *265*
  in schools, 239, 240, *240*, 270, *270*, 271, 272–273, *272*
Self–sufficient people, 128
Senate Chamber, of State House, 61
Seneca, South Carolina, *m243*, R14
Separate but equal. See Segregation
Sequence, 116, 155, 184
Service industries, 284, *284*
Settlements, 104, 132–137, *132*, *137*, *m157*
  attacks by Native Americans, 105, 133, 134, *134*, 159, 165
  English, 3, 46, *46*, 118–123, *118–119*, *121*, *122*, *m123*, *m135*
  French, 110–112, *m111*, *112*, 117
  Spanish, 104–105, 110, 113, 114, 115, *115*, 116, 117, 133
  trade with Native Americans, 132, 133, *133*, 134, 157
Settlers, 104
Sharecropping, 213, *213*
Shellfish, *m269*
Shelters. See House(s)
Sheriff, 46, *46*
Sherman, General, 209, R9
Shipbuilding, 112, 252
Short stories, writing, 98, 138
Silversmiths, 191, *191*
Simkins, Modjeska, 271
Simmons, Monica, 304
Siouan language groups, 67, 75
"Sites of the Civil War" (Price), 153
Sit–ins, 274
Skills. See Chart and Graph Skills; Citizenship Skills; Critical Thinking Skills; Focus Skills; Map and Globe Skills; Reading Skills
Slave(s), 67, **104**, 122, *122*
  abolitionists and, 200, *200*, 201
  in cities, 194
  during Civil War, 204, 208
  craftworkers, 193
  education of, 194, 216
  end of slavery, 214
  houses of, 141, 194, *194*
  leaving U.S. after American Revolution, 173
  North vs. South on, 201
  on plantations, 118–119, 127, 128, 129, 141, 180, 190, 194, 198
  population of, 137, *203*
  registering, 147
  rights of, 194, 210
Slave badges, *194*
Slave markets, 129
Slave quarters, 194, *194*
Slave revolts, 137, 193
Slave states, 199
Slave trade, 129
Smalls, Robert, 239, *239*, R9
Smith, Alice Ravenel Huger, 197, *259*
Social class, 189–194
  enslaved African Americans, 194, *194*
  free African Americans, 193, *193*, 210
  lower class, 192, *192*
  middle class, 191, *191*
  planter class, 190, *190*
Society, 14
Soldiers' Relief Association, 207
Solution, 48
Songs, 4–5
Sons of Liberty, 162, 163, *163*
Sources
  primary. See Primary Sources
  secondary, 43, *43*
South
  in Civil War, **204**–209, *206*, *209*
  dependence on slaves in, 198
  disagreements with North, 201
  Great Migration from, 254–255, *254*, *255*
  industries in, 241, 242–247, *244–245*, *246*, *247*
  landform map of, *m63*
  way of life in, 189, 198
South Carolina, *m2–3*, *m226–227*
  in American Revolution, 166, 170, *m170*, 171, *171*
  in Civil War, 205, 206, 207, 209
  class system in, 189–194, *190*, *191*, *192*, *193*, *194*
  climate of, 74
  constitution of, 50, 178, 179, 211
  counties and county seats in, 46, *m146*
  employment in, 283
  first people in, 96–97, *96*, *97*
  flag of, 1, 37, *50*, *168*
  geography of, 8–9, *8–9*
  on a globe, 20
  government of, 13, *13*. See also State government
  governors, R4–R6
  Great Migration from, 254–255, *254*, *255*
  Great Seal of, 13, *60*
  growth of, 147, 156–159, *156–157*, 161
  heritage of. See Heritage
  history of, 10–11, *10*, *11*
  largest cities in, 25
  location of, 18, 21, 22–23, *m22*, *m23*
  military regiments of, 145, 206
  Native American place names in, 91, *m91*
  physical map of, *mA15*
  physical regions of, *m2–3*, 26–33, *26*, *m27*, *28*, *29*, *30*, *31*, *m290–m291*
  political map of, *mA14*
  population of, 1760–1880, 147
  rejoins the Union, 211
  as royal colony, 135
  secession from Union, 201
  settlements in. See Settlements
  slaves in. See Slave(s)
  southern ways in, 189
  state fair of, 292
  State House of, 2, 3, 13, 51, 52, 60–61, *60–61*, *m60*, 146, 179, *179*
  state song of, 4–5
  state symbols of, 3, 13
  statehood for, 177
  Supreme Court of, 51, 54, *54*, 57
  women's suffrage in, 257, *257*

*South Carolina* (Christian), 304
South Carolina Aquarium (Charleston), 291, *291, m291*
South Carolina Artisans Center (Walterboro), 291, *291, m291*
"South Carolina Colony, The" (Britton), 144
South Carolina Day, 4
South Carolina Heritage Fair, 233, 304
South Carolina Interstate and West Indian Exposition, 247
"South Carolina on My Mind" (state song), 4–5
South Carolina Peach Festival (Gaffney), *282*
South Carolina Railroad Company, 243
South Carolina 2nd Regiment, *145*
South Carolina Stamp Party, 162, *162*
South Pole, 20, *m20*, 21, *m21*, R14
Southeast, *m303*
Southern hemisphere, 20, *m20*
Soybeans, *m269*
Spain
   explorers sent from, 102–107, *102–103, 105, 106,* 110, 113, 114, 116, 117, 133, R7, R8
   Native Americans as allies of, 134
   settlements of, 104–105, 110, 113, 114, 115, *115,* 116, 117, 133
Spanish Florida, 114, *m114,* 133
Spartanburg, South Carolina, *m2, m243,* 252, R3, R14
Spartanburg County, R3
Speech(es)
   freedom of, 178
   giving, 115, 285
   writing, 34, 184
Spoleto Festival (Charleston), 15
*Spring Planting* (Green), *197*
Squash, 76, 84, 92
Stamp Act (1765), 162, *162*
Star Fort at Old Ninety Six, 154–155, *m154*
State capital. *See* Columbia, South Carolina
State fair, *292*
State government, 13, *13,* 50–55
   establishing, 176
   executive branch of, 50, *51, 55, 55*
   judicial branch of, 50, *51,* 53, *53*
   legislative branch of, 50, *51,* 52–53, *52, 57,* 237
   moved to Columbia, 146, 176, 179, *179*
   offices in, 56, *57*
   powers reserved for, 178

   taxes and, 53, *53,* 236
   women in, 257, *257*
State House (South Carolina), 2, 3, 13, *51,* 52, 60–61, *60–61, m60,* 146, 179, *179*
State parks, 9, 261, 290, *290, m290*
State song, 4–5
State symbols, 3
   animals, 3
   birds, 3
   flag, 37, *50,* 168
   flowers, 3
   Great Seal of South Carolina, 13, *60*
   palmetto tree, 3, *50, 50*
Statehood, for South Carolina, 177
States' rights, 199
Steam locomotives, 242–243, *243*
Stickball, 85, *85*
Stone Soup Storytelling Festival (Woodruff), 292
Stone tool, *97*
Stono River, 137
Stono Slave Uprising, 137
Stowers, Freddie, 252, *252,* R9
Stuart's Town, 132, 133
Submarine, *208*
Suburban towns, 267, *267*
Suffrage, 256
Suffrage movement, 256–257, *256, 257*
Sugar cane, 119
Sullivan's Island, R14
   Battle of, 146, 168, *168, m170*
Summarizing, 281, 298
Summerton, South Carolina, *272*
Sumter, Thomas, 171, *171,* 186, R9
Sumter County, R3
Sun Fun Festival (Myrtle Beach), *15*
Sunset, South Carolina, *m30,* R14
Supreme Court
   of South Carolina, 51, 54, *54, 57*
   of United States, 273
Swamp, 26, *26,* 28, *28,* 300–301, *300–301, m300*
*Swamp Fox, The* (DeSpain), 148–153
Symbols
   designing, 93
   flags, 37, *50,* 168
   on maps, 16, *m17,* 268, *m269*
   *See also* State symbols

## T

Table(s), 56
   analyzing, 75
   making, 195
   reading, 56–57, *57,* 59
Table Rock Mountain, 30–31, *30–31, m30,* R14

Table Rock Reservoir, *m30*
Table Rock State Park, 261
Tarleton, Banastre, 171, R9
Taxes, 53
   British Parliament and, 162, *162,* 165
   colonists' protests against, 162, *162,* 165
   on free African Americans, 193
   after Reconstruction, 236
   state, 53, *53,* 236
   on tea, 163, *163*
Tea
   as cash crop, 282
   taxes on, 163, *163*
Tea chest, *163*
Technology, 283
   cotton gin, 180, 181, *181,* 188
   cotton mills and, 283
   high–tech industries and, 283
   satellites, 19, *19*
   steam locomotives, 242–243, *243*
   submarines, *208*
   telephone, 246, 297
   *See also* Inventions; Science and Technology
Telephone, 246, 297
Textile(s), 130, *130,* 282
Textile mills, 198, 244–245, *244–245,* 283
Thinking skills. *See* Critical Thinking Skills
Thurmond, James Strom, 275, *275,* R5, R9
Tillman, Ben, 237, *237,* R5, R9
Time lines, 116
   reading, 116–117, **116–117**, 139
Tobacco, *m269*
Tools
   in agriculture, 180, *180,* 181, *181,* 188, 192, 213
   Native American, 77, 79, *97*
   stone, *97*
Tourism, 247, *247,* 284. *See also* Recreation
Town(s). *See* Cities; Communities
Townships, 136, *m136*
Trade, 79
   blockades and, 168
   among colonies, 119
   between England and colonies, 118, 119, 126, *126–127*
   imports and exports, 285
   among Native Americans, 79, *79,* 87, *m87*
   between Native Americans and settlers, 132, 133, *133,* 134, 157
   in slaves, 129
Trade center, 188, *188*
Trade-off, 286
Trading posts, 157
Traditions, 77, *77*
Trails. *See* Roads and trails

Trains, 188, *242–243,* 243
Traits. *See* Character traits
Transportation, 243
   by automobile, 246, *246,* 283
   by boats and ships. *See* Boats and ships
   by cart, *141*
   by railroad, 188, 242–243, *243, m243*
   as service industry, 284, *284*
   by wagon, 146, *m157,* 158, *158,* 161
"Transportation Yesterday and Today" (Ring), 233
Travel industry, 247, *247*
Trees
   Angel Oak, 6–7, *m6*
   in Congaree National Park, 300, *300–301*
   palmetto, 3, 50, *50,* 92, *92,* 168, 293
   as state symbol, 3, 50, *50*
Tribe, **75**. *See also* Native Americans; *individual tribes*
Trustworthiness, 166
Tubman, Harriet, 200, *200,* R9
Turning point, **172**
Tuskegee airmen, 265, *265*

## U

Underground Railroad, 200, *200*
Union, 204–209, *207, 209*
Union, South Carolina, 244
Union County, R3
Unit projects
   class magazine, 5, 64
   heritage fair, 233, 304
   honoring a hero, 153, 224
   making a museum, 71, 144
United Nations, 251
United States, *mA8–A13*
   birth of, 173
   Constitution of, 50, 177–178, *177, 178*
   divisions in, 198–201, *198, 200, 201*
   government of, 177–178, *177, 178*
   landform map of, *m32–33*
   overview map of, *mA8–A9*
   physical map of, *mA12–A13*
   political map of, *mA10–A11*
   population in 1800s, 198
   South Carolina secedes from, 201
United States Army, 251, 252, *252*
United States Marines, 252, *252*
United States Postal Service, 254
Universities and colleges, 234–235, *m234,* 237
Upcountry, *m2*
   after American Revolution, 176

## Urban areas

in American Revolution, 171, *171*, 172, *172*
canals in, 188
Great Snow Campaign in, 167
loyalists in, 165, 166, 167, 171, 172
representation in state government, 176, *177*, 179
winter in, 167, *167*

**Urban areas,** 241
**Utah,** 256

## V

**Vacation places,** 247, 288–293. *See also* Recreation; Tourism
**Venn diagrams,** 181
**Vesey, Denmark,** 193, R9
**Village(s)**
mill, 245
permanent, **91**
walls around, 76
**Village life**
of Catawba tribe, 76, *76*
of Cherokee tribe, 84, *84*, 85, *85*
of Cusabo tribe, 90–91, *91*
**Village mounds,** 85
**Virginia,** *209*
**Vocabulary skills,** 35, 59, 62, 99, 139, 142, 185, 219, 279, 299, 302
**Votes and voting,** 45, *45*, 46
African American rights and, 210, 211, *211*, 237, 238–239, 257, 274, 275, 276, *276*
laws on, 238–239, 257, 275
for members of British Parliament, 162
women's rights and, 256–257, *256*, *257*
**Voting Rights Act,** 275

## W

**Wadmalaw Island,** 282
**Wagons,** 146, *m157*, 158, *158*, 161
**Walhalla, South Carolina,** R3
**Walls,** around villages, 76
**Walterboro, South Carolina,** 291, *291*, *m291*, R2, R14
**War(s)**
American Revolution. *See* American Revolution
civil, **204**. *See also* Civil War
French and Indian, 159, *159*
Stono Slave Uprising, 137
World War I, 250, 251–253, *251*, *252*, *253*
World War II, 264–267, *264*, *265*, *266*
Yemassee, 134, *134*
**War Between the States.** *See* Civil War
**War bonds,** 253
**Washington, George,** *178*, R9
in American Revolution, 173, *173*
cup of, *217*
in French and Indian War, *159*
statue of, *60*
visit to Charleston, 220, *221*
**Washington, William,** 172, R9
**Water,** bodies of, 28, *28–29*. *See also* names of individual bodies of water
**"Water Dance" (Locker),** 144
**Wateree Lake,** *m2*
**Wateree River,** *m2*, R14
**Weather,** 74
**Weathers, Andrea,** 64
**Weirs, 92,** *92*
**West, Joseph,** 122, *122*
**West Indies,** 104, 105, 129, *130*, R12
**Western hemisphere,** *mA6–A7*, 21, *m21*
**Wheat,** *m269*

**"When a Storm Comes Up" (Fowler),** 64
**"Where Water Comes From" (Ahearn),** 5
**Whitney, Eli,** 180, 181, R9
**Wilkinson, Eliza Yonge,** 145
**Williams, Jack H.,** 264, *264*
**Williamsburg County,** R3
**Wilmon–Goggins, Juanita,** 277
**Wilson, Woodrow,** 250, *250*, 251, *251*, R9
**Winnsboro, South Carolina,** 157, *m157*, R2, R14
**Women**
as abolitionists, 200, *200*
African American, 239, 255, *255*, 257, 265, *265*, 271, *271*, 274, 277
in art, 197, *259*
civil rights of, 277, *277*
in Civil War, 207
education of, 190
in government, 257, *257*, 277, *277*
as inventors, 130, 131, *131*
jobs of, 253, *253*, 255, *255*, 265, *265*, 266, *266*, 271, *271*, 277, *277*
as leaders, 106, 257, *257*, 274, 277, *277*
in literature, 64, 144, 190, *190*, 304
in manufacturing, 253, 265, *265*
Native American, 76, 77, 78, 83, 84, *84*, 86, 106
preservation work of, 258
voting rights of, 256–257, *256*, *257*
in World War I, 253, *253*, 256
in World War II, 264, 265, *265*, 266, *266*
**Woodruff, South Carolina,** 292
**Woodward, Dr. Henry,** 122, *122*, R9

**Woodworkers,** 191
**Work.** *See* Jobs
**World**
physical map of, *mA4–A5*
political map of, *mA2–A3*
**World War I,** 250, 251–253, *251*, *252*, *253*
**World War II,** 264–267, *264*, *265*, *266*
**Writing activities**
advertisements, 247
articles, 131
biographies, 173
journal entries, 107, 184
letters, 58, 138, 218, 278, 298
news stories, 167, 267
newspaper headlines, 209
paragraphs, 34, 58, 298
persuasive writing, 58, 138
questions and answers, 98, 241
scenes, 79
short plays, 278
short stories, 98, 138
speeches, 34, 184
**Wylie, Lake,** *m2*
**Wyoming,** 256

## Y

**Yemassee tribe,** 133, 134, *134*
**Yemassee War,** 134, *134*
**York, South Carolina,** 158, R3
**York County,** R3
**Yorktown, Virginia,** *173*

## Z

**Zoos,** 290, *290*, *m290*

For permission to record copyrighted material, grateful acknowledgment is made to the following sources:

*Andrea Brown Literary Agency, on behalf of Margot Theis Raven:* From *Circle Unbroken: The Story of a Basket and Its People* by Margot Theis Raven. Copyright © 2004 by Margot Theis Raven.

*I. Wilson Baker Photography:* Cover photograph by Wilson Baker from *The Island Child: Or More About Weenie!!* by Monica Simmons. Photograph copyright © by I. Wilson Baker Photography.

*Denny Music, Inc.:* From "South Carolina on My Mind" by Hank Martin and Buzz Arledge. Lyrics © copyright 1979 by Denny Music, Inc.

*Dial Books for Young Readers, A Division of Penguin Young Readers Group, A Member of Penguin Group (USA) Inc., 345 Hudson St., New York, NY 10014:* From *The Great Ball Game: A Muskogee Story* by Joseph Bruchac, illustrated by Susan L. Roth. Text copyright © 1994 by Joseph Bruchac; illustrations copyright © 1994 by Susan L. Roth.

*Farrar, Straus & Giroux, LLC:* From *Circle Unbroken: The Story of a Basket and Its People* by Margot Theis Raven, illustrated by E. B. Lewis. Text copyright © 2004 by Margot Theis Raven; illustrations copyright © 2004 by E. B. Lewis.

*Harcourt, Inc.:* Cover illustration from *Water Dance* by Thomas Locker. Copyright © 1997 by Thomas Locker.

*Holiday House, Inc.:* Cover illustration by John & Alexandra Wallner from *A Picture Book of George Washington* by David A. Adler. Illustration copyright © 1989 by John C. and Alexandra Wallner.

*Henry Holt and Company, LLC:* Cover photograph by Richard Samuel Roberts from All *Around Town: The Photography of Richard Samuel Roberts* by Dinah Johnson. Photograph copyright © 1998 by the Estate of Richard Samuel Roberts.

*Legacy Publications:* Cover illustration by Bob Thames from *Hermy the Hermit Crab Goes Shopping* by Andrea Weathers. Illustration © by Bob Thames.

*The Rosen Publishing Group, Inc.:* Cover illustration from *Fort Sumter* by Charles W. Maynard. Copyright © 2002 by The Rosen Publishing Group, Inc.

*Sandlapper Publishing Co., Inc.:* Cover illustration from *Spunky Revolutionary War Heroine* by Idella Bodie. Copyright © 2000 by Idella Bodie.

*Sleeping Bear Press:* Cover illustration by Mary Whyte from *P is for Palmetto: A South Carolina Alphabet* by Carol Crane. Illustration copyright © 2002 by Mary Whyte.

## ILLUSTRATION CREDITS

Page 22-23, 28-29, Geoff McCormack; 74-75, Dennis Lyall, 77, Lois Wooley; 84, Patrick Faricy; 86, Dan Brown; 66-67, 90-91, 92, Luigi Galante; 102-103, Richard Schlecht; 121, Peter Siu; 126-127, 226-227, Roger Stewart; 133, George Gaadt; 146-147, Kevin Tweddell; 148, 149, 150, 151, 152, 153, Rick Farrell; 158, Scott Cameron; 163, Harcourt; 257, Nenad Jakesevic.

All maps by MAPQUEST.com.

## PHOTO CREDITS

Cover: Transparencies, Inc. (capitol dome); Ken Kinzie/Harcourt (flag detail); Transparencies, Inc. (waterfall); Picturesque (fishing boats); Bill Robertson/Transparencies, Inc. (mill)

**PAGE PLACEMENT KEY** (t)-top ( c)-center (b)-bottom (l)-left (c)-right (fg)-foreground (bg)-background.

## TITLE PAGE AND TABLE OF CONTENTS

ii © Hunter Clarkson; iv © Joseph Sohm; Chromosohm Inc./Corbis; v Courtesy of the Charlesfort/Santa Elena Project; vi © Hunter Clarkson; vii © David Rackley.

## UNIT 1

Opener: (fg) © Joseph Sohm; Chromosohm Inc./Corbis; (bg) © Charles Slate, photographer, with courtesy of Brookgreen Gardens, S. C.; (spread) © Charles Slate, photographer, with courtesy of Brookgreen Gardens, S. C.; 1 (r) © Joseph Sohm; Chromosohm Inc./Corbis; 2 (l) © Joseph Sohm/Visions of America, LLC; 2 (c) © Ariel Skelley/Corbis; 2 (r) © David Meunch/Corbis; 3 (tl) © Erwin Nielson/Visuals Unlimited; 3 (tc) © Raymond Gehman/Corbis; 3 (tr) © Photolibrary/IndexStock; 3 (cl) © Steve Maslowski/Visuals Unlimited; 3 (cc) © Royalty-Free/Corbis; 3 (cr) © Mike Booher/TRANSPARENCIES, INC.; 3 (bl) © www.kusunensemble.com; 3 (bc) © Bob Krist/Corbis; 3 (br) © Sam Holland; 4-5 © Artist Billie Harmon for Harcourt School Publishers 6-7 © Annie Griffiths Belt/Corbis; 8-9 © Jane G. Faircloth/TRANSPARENCIES, INC.; 9 (t) © J & D Richardson/photographersdirect.com; 9 (c) © Jane G. Faircloth/TRANSPARENCIES, INC.; 10 (t) © Topham/The Image Works; 10 (b) © Gibson Stock Photography; 11 (t & b) Courtesy of the South Carolina State Museum; 12 (t) © Bill Aron/PhotoEdit – All rights reserved; 12 (c) © Erv Schowengerdt; 12 (b) © Digital Vision Ltd/SuperStock; 13 (t) Joseph Sohm/Visions of America, LLC; 13 © One Mile Up/fotosearch.com; 14 (l) © Gale Harper/In-Sight Photography, Inc.; 14 (r) Bob Krist/Corbis; 15 (l) © Michael T. Sedam/Corbis; 15 (r) © Joe Viesti/Viesti Associates.; 16 (c) Barbara Rozavsky, Photographer; 18 © Wilson Baker; 19 © Getty Images; 20 © Ron Slenzak/Corbis; 26 © Ariel Skelley/Corbis; 28 QT Luong/terragalleria.com; 28 © Jane G. Faircloth/TRANSPARENCIES, INC.; 30 (t) © Harrison Shull Photography; 30-31 © Jeff Greenberg/PhotoEdit – All rights reserved; 36-37; © Ron Rocz Photography; 38 © Ariel Skelley/Corbis; 39 top © Andrzej Wisniewski/Alamy; 39 (b) Royalty-free Corbis; 40 © www.kusunensemble.com; 41 © Bob Krist/Corbis; 42 (t&b) Courtesy of Historical Center of York County; 44 Mikael Karlsson/911 Pictures; 45 (tl) © Sven Martson/The Image Works; 45 (tr) © Bonnie Kamin/PhotoEdit – All rights reserved; 45 (bl) © Tetra Images/Alamy; 45 (br) © AFP/Getty Images; 46 (b) Courtesy of Colleton County Sheriff's Office, Waterboro, SC; 46 (t) © Bob Krist/Corbis; 47 © Mark Richards/PhotoEdit – All rights reserved; 48 © Ken Karp/Harcourt; 49 © Robert Brenner/PhotoEdit – All rights reserved; 50 © Joseph Sohm; Chromosohm, Inc./Corbis; 51 (t) © Sam Holland; 51 (bl) © Dennis MacDonald/PhotoEdit – All rights reserved; 51 (br) © Sam Holland; 52 (b) © Sam Holland; 53 (t) © Eyewire Collection/PictureQuest; 53 (b) © Banana Stock/PictureQuest; 54 (t) © Jack Owen Photography; 54 (b) © John Neubauer/PhotoEdit – All rights reserved; 55 Courtesy of the Office of the Governor, State of South Carolina, www.scgovernor.com; 60-61 (bg) © Joseph Sohm/Visions of America, LLC/Workbookstock.com (l) © Joseph Sohm; Chromosohm, Inc./Corbis; 60 (l) © Joseph Sohm/Chromosohm, Inc./Corbis; 60 (r) © Sam Holland; 61 (tr) © Hunter L. Clarkson; 61 (b) © Sam Holland.

## UNIT 2

Opener: (fg) Courtesy of the Charlesfort/Santa Elena Project; (bg) © Rich Stevenson/TRANSPARENCIES, INC.; (spread) © Rich Stevenson/TRANSPARENCIES, INC.; 65 (r) Courtesy of the Charlesfort/Santa Elena Project; 66 Scott Cameron; 67 Bill Maughan; 68 Susan L. Roth; 72-73 © Craig Lovell/Corbis; 76 & 79 (t&b) © Catawba Cultural Preservation Project; 78 Luigi Galante; 82 © Ken Taylor/Wildlife Images; 83 © Ottmar Bierwagon/Spectrum Stock Inc./www.photographersdirect.com; 84 Gino D'Achille; 85 © Marilyn "Angel" Winn/Native Stock; 88 © Kevin Fleming/Corbis; 92 Bob Pardue/Photography/photographersdirect.com; 94 © Ed Bock/Corbis; 96 (t & b) © Darryl Miller/South Carolina Society of Archaeology; 97 (t) From poster *South Carolina Archaeology Month 2004*, South Carolina Society of Archaeology; 97 (cl) © Darryl Miller/South Carolina Society of Archaeology; 97 (cr) From poster *South Carolina Archaeology Month 2004*, South Carolina Society of Archaeology; 97 (b) © Darryl Miller/South Carolina Society of Archaeology; 100-101 © Joe Viesti/Viesti Associates; 104-105 © Gayle Harper/In-Sight Photography, Inc.; 105 © SSPL/The Image Works; 106 (t) Conquistador Historical Foundation, Inc., Hernando de Soto Historical Society, Inc., The Spanish Manor House, 910 Third Avenue West, Bradenton, FL, 34205; 106 (b) © The Granger Collection, New York; 108 © Bettmann/Corbis; 110 © Mary Evans Picture Library; 110-111 © Bob Krist/Corbis; 112 © The Granger Collection, New York; 113 (l & r) Courtesy of the Charlesfort/Santa Elena Project; 115 © James L. Amos/Corbis; 116 © The Granger Collection, New York; 117 (l) Bill Barley/Photri Microstock; 117 © Corbis; 118-119 (l) © Robert Llewellyn; 119 (t) © The Granger Collection, New York; 119 (rc) © The Bridgeman Art Library 119 (rb) Collection of McKissick Museum, University of South Carolina; © Philadelphia Museum of Art/Corbis; 122 Courtesy of the artist, Darby Erd; 123 © Stock Montage; 127 (t) © George Contorakes/Masterfile; www.masterfile.com; 128 (t) George Caadt; 128 (b) © John Neubauer; 129 Rice Mortar and pestle from South Carolina ca. 1875. Courtesy of the South Carolina State Museum; 130 (t) © The Granger Collection, New York; 130 (c) © Jacqui Jurst/Corbis; 130 (b) © National Trust Photographic Library/Stephen Robson/The Image Works; 132 © David G. Houser/Corbis; 134 © The Granger Collection, New York; 135 © Corbis; 136 Private Collection; photograph courtesy of Old Salem Inc.; 140-141 (l & t) Courtesy of Historic Brattonsville; 141 (2nd r) © Pressly Hall/TRANSPARENCIES, INC.; 141 (3rd r) Courtesy of Historic Brattonsville; 141 (br) © Pressly Hall/TRANSPARENCIES, INC.

## UNIT 3

Opener: (fg) © Hunter Clarkson; (bg) Second South Carolina Regiment; (spread) Second South Carolina Regiment; 145 (r) © Hunter Clarkson; 154-155 © Sam Holland; 156-157 & 159 © The Granger Collection, New York; 162 (t) Massachusetts Historical Society; 162 (b) © The Granger Collection, New York; 163 (b) Daughters of the American Revolutions Museum, Washington, DC; 165 (t) © Bettmann/Corbis; 165 (b) The Colonial Williamsburg Collection; 166 (t) © Bettmann/Corbis; 166 (b) © The Granger Collection, New York; 167 Toni and Jim Bible; 168 (l) *General William Moultrie, Jr.* (1730-1805) Rembrandt Peale, Oil on canvas, Gibbes Museum of Art/Carolina Art Association, 1976.015.0001; 168 (r) South Carolina Historical Society; 169 (tl)

Bettmann/Corbis; 169 (tr) © Joseph Sohm, Visions of America/Corbis; 169 (br) Independence National Historic Park Collection; 170 Courtesy of Terry and Debra Flowers; 171 (t) © The Granger Collection, New York; 171 (b) Courtesy of the Sumter County Museum; 172 & 173 © The Granger Collection, New York; 174 (l) © Richard T. Nowitz/Corbis; 174 (r) Jeff Greenberg/Visuals Unlimited; 176 © The Granger Collection, New York; 177 (l-r) © The Granger Collection, New York; Courtesy of the South Carolina State Museum; © National Portrait Gallery, Smithsonian Institution/Art Resource, New York; © The Granger Collection, New York; 178 © The Granger Collection, New York; 179 (t) © Mark Cunningham/Harcourt; 179 (b) © Corbis; 180 (t) © North Wind Picture Archives; 180 (b) © Bob Pardue Photography/photographersdirect.com; 181 Bettmann/Corbis; 186-187 © Bob Krist/Corbis; 188 A Grinevald *Congaree River at Columbia, South Carolina*, c. 1859 watercolor, colored crayons on paper Columbia Museum of Art, Museum purchase with funds donated by Mrs. Milton Safran as a memorial to her husband CMA 1975.41; 189 (t) © Joe Sohm/The Image Works; 189 (b) © Lance Nelson/Corbis; 190 & 191 (t) © Culver Pictures, NY; 191 (b) Hunter Clarkson; 192 (t) © Jane G. Faircloth/TRANSPARENCIES, INC.; 192 (b) © North Wind Picture Archives; 193 (t) © Smithsonian American Art Museum, Washington DC/Art Resource, NY; 193 (b) © Bob Pardue Photography/photographersdirect.com; 194 (t) © New York Historical Society, New York, USA/Bridgeman Art Library; 194 (b) Courtesy of the Charleston Museum; 195 Collection of McKissick Museum, University of South Carolina; 197 (t) Ready for the Harvest, from the series, A Carolina Rice Plantation of the Fifties, ca. 1935, Watercolor on paper, by Alice Ravenel Huger Smith, Gibbes Museum of Art, Carolina Art Association, 1937.09.16; 197 (b) *Spring Planting* 1988. Oil on Masonite by Jonathan Green. From the Collection of Shiegki Masui. Photograph by Tim Stamm; 198 © Bettmann/Corbis; 199 (t) © The Cocoran Gallery of Art/Corbis; 199 (b) © Bettmann/Corbis; 200 (t & b) and 201 © Bettmann/Corbis; 204-205 John Ross Key 1837-1920 *Bombardment of Fort Sumter, Siege of Charleston Harbor 1863* circa 1865 (oil on canvas 29 x 69 inches) Collection of the Greenville County Museum of Art, Museum purchase with funds donated by Suzanne Chochrane Austell; Dorothy Hipp Gunter; Buck and Minor Mickel; Dorothy P. Peace; John I Smith Charities; Ball Unimark Plastics; First Union National Bank of South Carolina; Michelin Tire Corporation; 1988 Museum Antiques Show, Elliott Davis & Co, CPAs; sponsor; 1989 Collectors' Group. 206 (t) © Tria Giovan/Corbis; 206 (b) Medford Historical Society Collection/Corbis; 207 (t) © The Granger Collection, New York; 207 (b) © Corbis; 209 © Getty Images; 209 © Tom Lovell/National Geographic Image Collection; 210-211 (b) Courtesy of South Caroliniana Library, University of South Carolina, Columbia (Photography Wearn cdv); 211 (t) & 212 (t) © The Granger Collection, New York; 212 (b) Courtesy of South Caroliniana Library, University of South Carolina, Columbia; 213 (l) © The Granger Collection, New York; 213 (r) Jackson County Historical Museum; 214 © Sam Holland; 216 (t) *Robert and Elizabeth Gilcrest* by George Cooke, Oil on canvas, Gibbes Museum of Art/Carolina Art Association, 1957.16; 216 (b) & 217 (all) Courtesy of the Charleston Museum, Charleston, S.C.; 220-221 (bg) © Bob Krist/Corbis; 221 (tl & tr) © Jane G. Faircloth/TRANSPARENCIES, INC.; 221 (bl) © David G. Houser/Corbis; 221 (br) © John Neubauer.

## UNIT 4

Opener: (fg) © David Rackley; (bg) © Bill Woodward; (spread) © Bill Woodward; 225 (r) © David Rackley; 234-235 Courtesy of Clemson University; 236 Architect of the Capitol; 237 (t) © Getty Images; 237 (b) & 238 (t) © The Granger Collection, New York; 238 (b) © Time & Life Pictures/Getty Images; 239 (t) © Corbis; 239 (b) © The Granger Collection, New York; 240, 241 © Corbis; 244 (t) © Corbis; 244 (b) –245 (b) Courtesy of South Caroliniana Library University of South Carolina, Columbia; 245 (t) Library of Congress Prints & Photographs Division, National Child Labor Committee Collection LC-DIG nclc-01488; 246 From a copy, courtesy of South Caroliniana Library University of South Carolina, Columbia; 247 (both) Courtesy of Special Collections/Samuel Hyde Collection/College of Charleston, S.C.; Courtesy of Historic Columbia Foundation; 251 (t) © The Granger Collection, New York; 251 (b) Florida State Archives; 252 (t) © Corbis 252 (bl) © Reuters/Corbis; 252 (br) © Bettmann/Corbis; 253 (both) © Swim Ink/Corbis; 254 (t) Jacob Lawrence *And the migrants kept coming* Panel 60 of THE GREAT MIGRATION series. Digital image © The Museum of Modern Art/Licensed by SCALA/Art Resource, NY; 254 (b) Erv Schowengerdt; 255 (l) Florida State Archives; 255 (r) © The Granger Collection, New York; 256 © Bettmann/Corbis; 257 (b) © Sam Holland; 258 © Eric Horan; 259 (l) *The Mill and Barn*, from the series, A Carolina Rice Plantation of the Fifties, ca 1935, Watercolor on paper, by Alice Ravenel Huger Smith, Gibbes Museum of Art, Carolina Art Association, 1937.09.21; 259 (c) © Condé Nast Archive/Corbis; 259 ® Photofest, NY; 260 (t) © Bettmann/Corbis; 261 (b) – 262 (b) © Bettmann/Corbis; 263 (t) South Carolina Library, University of South Carolina, Columbia 263 (b) Sunslope; 264 (l) © Bettmann/Corbis; 264 (r) Courtesy of the South Carolina State Museum; 265 (t) © AP Photo/USAF/Wide World Photos; 265 (b) © Bettmann/Corbis; 266 (l) © Corbis; 266 (r) Getty Images; 267 From *Spartanburg Portrait of the Good Life* by Scott Gould and Mark Olencki; 270 Courtesy of Cecil Williams Images; 271 (t) © Time & Life Pictures/Getty Images; 272 (t & b) Courtesy of Cecil Williams Images; 273 (t) Cecil Williams Images; 273 (b) www.cmohs.org Official Site for the Congressional Medal of Honor Society; 274 (t) © Bob Adelman, 1965/Magnum Photos; 274 (b) © AFP/Getty Images; 275 (t) © Martin Simon/Corbis; 275 (b) © AP/Wide World Photos; 276 © AP Photo/Susan Walsh/Wide World Photos; 277 Courtesy of Terry Dozier; 280-281 © Cynthia Blair Miller for Freedom Weekend Aloft, Greenville, SC; 282 Courtesy of the Town of Gaffney, SC; 283 © Lester Lefkowitz/Corbis; 284 (tl) © Catherine Wessel/Corbis; 284 (tr) © Annie Griffiths Belt/Corbis; 284 (bl) © Dave G. Houser/Corbis; 284 (br) © Bob Krist/Corbis; 285 © Andre Jenny/Painet, Inc.; 288-289 © Kate Philips/Studio K, Inc.; 289 (t) 289 (t) Courtesy of Family Kingdom, Myrtle Beach, S.C.; 290 (t) © Clay Bolt Nature Photography/photographersdirect.com; 290 (c) © Mark Cunningham/Harcourt; 290 (b) © Bruce Roberts; 291 (t) © Getty Images; 291(c) Courtesy Pickens County Museum of Art and History; 291 (b) © Mark Cunningham/Harcourt; 292 (t) © Eric Horan; 292 (b) Glen and Glenda, official mascots of Rock Hill SC's annual Come-See-Me Festival, a ten-day salute to Spring; 293 (t) Terri Tipton, photographer; 293 (b) Courtesy of Sea Grant Consortium Charleston, S. C.; 296-297 (all) © Mark Cunningham/Harcourt; 300 (bg) © David Muench/Corbis; 300 (l & r) Courtesy of the National Park Service; 301 (l & r 1st) Courtesy of the National Park Service; 301 (r 2nd) © Klaus Honal/Corbis; 301 (r 3rd) © W. Perry Conway/Corbis; 301(rb) © D. Robert Franz/Corbis